The W... Love

A NOVEL

DAVID H MARTIN

David H Martin has asserted his right under the Copyright, Designs and Patents Act 1988 to be identified as the author of this work.

This is a work of fiction. Names, characters, places and incidents either are the product of the author's imagination or are used fictitiously. Any resemblance to actual persons, living or dead, events or locales is entirely coincidental.

Copyright © 2022 David H Martin

All rights reserved.

ISBN: 9798367230284

A man that looks on glass,
On it may stay his eye;
Or if he pleaseth, through it pass,
And then the heaven espy.

George Herbert

CONTENTS

Chapter One	1
Chapter Two	12
Chapter Three	47
Chapter Four	81
Chapter Five	114
Chapter Six	141
Chapter Seven	178
Chapter Eight	216
Chapter Nine	240
Chapter Ten	288
Chapter Eleven	315
List of Music	352

CHAPTER ONE

The door of the prison cell slammed shut with a life-sapping metallic clang. The sound of its bolts shooting home told Simon he would have contact with no-one for the next twelve hours. Not that he minded. He had always been content with his own company. Indeed, he often spent more time absorbed in his own inner thought-world than in the world around him. But at least then he had been free to choose which of the two worlds he inhabited. Since commencing his prison sentence there was no choice. All decision-making had been stripped from him. He was subject to an unbending prison regime.

His day began at eight o'clock standing outside his cell and answering the morning rollcall.

"Copeland," barked an impassive prison officer.

"Sir," was the required answer.

The other inmates stood outside their cells answering their names as each was called.

"Zamoon."

"Yeah, man."

"The reply is 'Sir' unless you want a spell in P Block," rasped the officer conducting the rollcall.

"Sir," drawled the drug-pusher in his most sarcastic voice.

THE WAGES OF LOVE

Simon had never encountered the world of drugs before and the evil-looking Zamoon did not exactly make him want to strike up an acquaintance with the prison's drug baron; but Zamoon was always alert for prisoners whom he could interest in the illicit wares he somehow managed to obtain, even in prison.

"You want to live in this hellhole for ever?" he enquired when he encountered Simon in the recreation area. "I can get you out of here in a flash. All you need is one snort and you'll be transported to paradise. No more iron bars. No more brick walls. No more 'Yes, sir. No, sir'. Instead, you can float on the clouds, with beautiful women at your feet asking what they can do to please you. Believe me, man, once you've escaped this hellhole, you'll never want to come back. I can keep you supplied with weekly snorts for some of your prison wages. As soon as you get paid, pass the bucks to me and I'll drop off the stuff."

The offer was one Simon could easily reject. He had no need of hallucinatory drugs to escape his prison cell. He had something infinitely more effective that cost him nothing and had no adverse side-effects.

"Collier-Smith."

"Sir," answered the little prisoner further down the landing. Collier-Smith might be small in stature, but Simon soon learned he was by far the cleverest man on the block.

"What you in here for?" asked Simon when Collier-Smith challenged Simon to a game of table tennis in the recreation area one afternoon. "Being cleverer than my boss," was the laconic reply.

"How come?" enquired Simon.

THE WAGES OF LOVE

"My boss thought he was the cleverest man alive. He claimed he could smell a good deal a mile away. He bought and sold businesses like you and I might buy and sell second-hand cars. He bought businesses cheap, stripped them of their assets and resold them making a fortune in the process. He was full of his own clever wheeling and dealing! But when it came to financial accounts, he was as innocent as a new-born baby. He couldn't understand trial balances, nominative ledgers and double-entry accounting no matter how hard he tried. It was me who managed the money. He needed me. He couldn't function without me. And so I reckoned he should split the profits with me, fifty-fifty. That'd be fair. But no: he refused to give me more. He wanted me to manage his finances without getting anything in return. I found that demeaning. I've got brains. Why shouldn't I be properly rewarded?

"Well, I reasoned, if he didn't play fair with me why should I play fair with him? He never suspected a thing. And he never would, if he hadn't got mixed up in a dodgy deal that alerted the authorities to him.

"Of course, once the police intervened, all the books were seized. When the police accountants went through them they uncovered my alternative source of income. Two years for embezzlement I got. But I don't feel guilty. I didn't hurt anyone. I didn't murder or rape anyone. I simply helped readjust the financial imbalances of capitalism – and for that I have to serve time at Her Majesty's pleasure."

The table-tennis ball fell to the floor and Simon's insight into the fraudulent activities of others came to an end.

"Mullinger."

"Sir," answered the prisoner to the left of Simon's cell. Mullinger was a sexual deviant who took a perverse delight in little girls. He attempted to interest Simon in his perversion.

"Have you read *Lolita*?" he asked. "You should. It's a book about a nymphet – a girl between eleven and fourteen - and the hypnotic effect she has on a middle-aged man. That could be me, really. I adore nymphets. So innocent and pure. So trusting and amenable, if you know what I mean. I don't know why they lock people up simply for liking little girls. Edgar Allen Poe had a nymphet. He married a thirteen-year-old girl called Virginia. Not a very appropriate name, really, after Poe got his hands on her. I hear you like little girls."

"I do not," replied an affronted Simon. "The psychological harm inflicted on such girls is incalculable. You should be ashamed of yourself for abusing children." From then onwards Simon studiously avoided Mullinger, as did most of the other prisoners. But it was not just the prisoners on his landing that contributed to Simon's sense of alienation. The prison officers were also highly unpredictable. Some were moody. Prison Officer Steele appeared to suffer from recurring bipolar disorder.

"What a happy band of workers we have here this morning!" he exclaimed in his raucous voice as he entered the Electrical Components Disassembling Workshop and surveyed the prisoners half-heartedly working at the benches. "What we need is a jolly old singsong to get everyone working happily. Copeland: you're a musician. Get everyone singing."

"What do you want us to sing?" asked a hesitant Simon.
"How the hell should I know!" retorted PO Steele. "You're the music teacher. You choose the bloody music."
Simon surveyed the other inmates working at their benches. "Does everyone know *The Sun Has Got His Hat On*?" he enquired of his fellow inmates. He was met with scowls and pursed lips.
"Teach it to 'em," barked the belligerent PO Steele.
And so, with great foreboding, Simon began to sing:

> *The sun has got his hat on*
> *Hip, hip, hip, hurray.*
> *The sun has got his hat on*
> *And he's coming out to play.*
> *Now we'll all be happy,*
> *Hip, hip, hip, hurray*
> *The sun has got his hat on*
> *and he's coming out to play.*

The final lines were lost in a tumult of raucous ridicule and sarcasm directed at the unfortunate Simon.
"Is that the best you can do?" roared the incensed PO Steele. "No wonder they kicked you out of your teaching job if that's the rubbish you made your pupils sing?"
In an attempt to redeem the situation, Simon suggested, "Perhaps some of the other men might like to choose something for us to sing."
That was like waving a red flag at a bull. PO Steele thundered, "I'm the one who decides who does what here, not you. If I want your advice – which I don't – I'll ask for it. Now just get on, the lot of you, and undertake your work

in silence. And woe betide anyone who doesn't fulfil his daily work quota by the end of the morning."

In the days that followed, prisoners would sidle up to Simon and softly sing in his ear "The sun has got his hat on, hip, hip, hip hurray" before scurrying away in gales of laughter.

Prison life was raw, unpredictable and dehumanising. But at least Simon had his own cell. He much preferred that to sharing with someone else. He soon discovered that other prisoners did not share his love of music. That may not have been a problem for inmates to whom music was merely the background wallpaper of life; but for Simon, music was his lifeblood. It coursed through his veins and sang in his head. It invaded his consciousness and lifted him out of himself. Music was his lifeblood and had been ever since he was a child. Without it he would rather be dead. The prospect of sharing a cell with someone who objected to music would be a punishment greater than he could bear. Furthermore, he much preferred solitude and silence to the discordant sound of continuous pop music pumped out of transistor radios in the cells of other inmates.

There was not much silence to be found within the prison once each new day began. Metal gates slammed open and shut as prisoners were escorted to their place of work. Maniacal laughter and aggressive insults ricocheted amongst the more psychologically unstable inmates. Stern orders were barked by the impassive prison officers who were focused on maintaining a distance between them and those in their charge. Added to which, the distorted prison Tannoy system continually relayed instructions that boomed around the cavernous Victorian penal establishment.

Prison life was noisy, clamorous and dehumanising. It was not a place a sensitive composer would choose to inhabit. His arrival in prison eight months before had come as a cruel shock. He had been assured by his barrister he would, in all probability, receive a suspended sentence. Instead, the judge imposed a two-year custodial sentence. He remembered reeling from the shock of her verdict. He felt he had done nothing wrong and yet the full force of the law was being thrown at him. Why? Simply as a reward for love. But love cut no ice with the female judge. All she cared about was the letter of the law. According to the law, he deserved punishment. And so, handcuffed and dazed, he had been led from the court to a waiting prison van and ignominiously transported to one of Her Majesty's penal establishments. There had been no opportunity for goodbyes. He had been denied the opportunity of talking to the person the court cruelly described as "the victim." He had been treated like a sack of potatoes, bundled from one place to another, rather than a sensitive man with a soul. When he arrived at the prison, he was stripped of his identity and given a prison number. His property was listed and placed in a safe-locker to await the day of his release. He, along with the other new inmates, had been issued with three pairs of socks, three pairs of pants, two jogging bottoms and three tee shirts. He was told he could request other clothing from relatives should he wish; but, never being greatly concerned with clothes, he decided he would make do with the regulatory prison wear. That also got over

the problem of deciding who to ask for help. The number of those he could call upon outside the prison was decidedly limited; and he could not bear the thought of further rebuffs from those he once considered his friends. To all intents and purposes, he was cast adrift in an alien environment, amongst men with whom he would never normally associate, deprived of freedom, music and love.
"You'll commence your time here as an entry grade prisoner," announced the prison officer with two stripes on his shoulder epaulettes. "That means you start at the bottom with no privileges. If, during the course of the first fourteen days you demonstrate good behaviour, you'll move to the standard grade of the Incentives and Earned Privileges Scheme. You can then begin earning money for the tasks you undertake and for good behaviour. After three months, if your conduct has been deemed acceptable, you can apply for the Enhanced level which entitles you to further privileges."
The prison officer surveyed the small cohort of newly-arrived prisoners standing before him as if to assess which would be the troublemakers and which would be the amenable and compliant ones. He had recited the induction instructions and prison rules to innumerable cohorts of new arrivals and felt, over the years, he had developed a sixth sense that enabled him to distinguish the sheep from the goats. But whatever his verdict on Simon, he did not disclose it.
"Copeland: you're to have a single cell on the third landing. It will be better for you to be on your own in view of your offence. We don't want any harm coming to you."

Simon noticed the other men casting sideway glances at him, keen to discover the reason for his jail sentence. Simon was relieved to have his own cell. It distanced him from the cigarette-smoking inmates and the all-pervasive culture of drugs that existed within the prison. It meant he avoided arguments over which television channel to view or, indeed, whether or not to have the television on. It also meant he did not have to reveal the details of his former life to a complete stranger. There were some things he preferred to keep to himself.

Having a cell of his own gave him space to think and to dream. He had always been a dreamer. Even as a young child he preferred solitude to the company of others. For the first five years of his life he had no other company save that of his elderly parents. It was the penalty he paid for being the youngest of a family of six. His three elder brothers spent most of their life at boarding school and, even when they returned home for the holidays, they were largely uninterested in him. The age-gap between them was too great. To all intents and purposes, he was an only child. Consequently, he had learnt to entertain himself. And he became quite adept at doing so. He would retreat into a world populated by giants laid low by boys like himself; roaring lions whose mouths were snapped shut just as he was about to be eaten by them; and storm-tossed boats that miraculously weathered the severest storms and transported him safely to port and the cheers of those gathered on the quayside.

He smiled as he recalled his childhood fantasies. At the time they seemed so real. They had caused both fear and

exultation in his young heart. The stories were now
consigned to the rubbish-bin of childhood fantasy, but the
feelings they evoked were as real as they had ever been.
The prison psychologist claimed his problems stemmed
from his childhood. But that seemed unfair. His parents
may have been elderly and conservative in their ways, but
they always treated him kindly. There may have been a
yawning age chasm between him and his parents, but he
had no reason to doubt they had his best interests at heart,
even if he did not always appreciate it at the time.
"So much psychology seems to consist of apportioning
blame to other people in order to absolve personal
responsibility," he thought to himself. "Having a vicar as a
father should have given me a strong foundation for life.
He gave me a clear sense of right and wrong. The strong
Christian moral guidelines he taught and practised meant I
had no excuse for straying from the straight and narrow and
ending up in this prison cell."
An image of his father came into his mind. He remembered
how well-respected his father had been in the village where
they lived. Men would raise their hats when they
encountered him walking around the parish. Elderly ladies
would dismount from their bicycles and discuss flower
arrangements for the forthcoming Sunday church services.
Children in the village school would listen attentively as he
conducted the morning act of worship; and when he asked
them to close their eyes and put their hands together to join
him in prayer, they never thought to refuse. The Reverend
Copeland was a greatly respected man in the eyes of his
parishioners; and even those who did not subscribe to his

religious beliefs paid him the courtesy of keeping their divergent views to themselves. In Simon's childlike eyes, his father and God were synonymous. What his father said was sacrosanct. He noticed that even his mother invariably deferred to his father. When his father spoke, his mother would nod in agreement.

For most weeks of the year there were only the three of them living in the large rambling Victorian vicarage. Nothing disturbed the tranquillity of his life until, that is, Rosie appeared.

CHAPTER TWO

Simon could still vividly remember the first time he met Rosie. It was one of those long, hot summer days when life in the countryside seemed to come to a standstill and a deep sleep descended on all living creatures. The cows stood motionless under the ancient oak trees availing themselves of the precious shade offered by the overhanging branches. The village school stood empty and abandoned by pupils and teachers for the annual six-week summer holiday. No vehicle passed through the village and no adults were to be seen. Only he, it seemed, was out and about on that hot and sultry afternoon.

The heat of the day unconsciously drew him to water. Behind the village hall was a small stream. It was never more than a babbling brook even after the heavy winter rains. But its gentle tinkling sound always pleased Simon. The stream seemed to produce its own music. Many an hour he spent sitting on the grassy bank beside the stream listening to the play of the water on the half-submerged stones littering its pebble-bed. On such a soporific day as this, the tinkling stream acted as a magnet drawing him to its cool and musical waters. Here was a place to sit and dream the afternoon away.

Great was his surprise on nearing the stream to find someone else there. It was a small girl of about his own age. Rather than sitting on the bank and gazing into the flowing water, she had removed her shoes and socks, tucked her dress into her knickers and was standing in the middle of the stream allowing the crystal clear cold water to splash over her feet and ankles. For a moment Simon stood transfixed. Who was this strange girl? Where had she come from? And why was she standing all alone in the stream? He felt possessive about the stream. He had never found anyone else there before and he was unsure if he really wanted to share the stream with someone else. He hesitated, unsure what to do or say.

But he had no need to worry. The girl had no such inhibitions. She waved to him and called out, "Come on in! It's lovely!" It was not something he had ever done before. Streams were for sitting beside rather than venturing into. Nevertheless, the girl seemed to be enjoying herself in the middle of the stream and so Simon decided to join her. Unlacing his black toe-cap shoes and removing his grey woollen socks, he carefully padded into the water. It was deliciously cold.

"See, I told you it was lovely," smiled the girl. "But you have to watch out for tadpoles. They get between your toes if you're not careful and my granddad says they cause Athletes' Foot."

"What's Athletes' Foot?" he innocently enquired.

"It's what athletes get, and it hurts a lot."

"My bothers are athletes. They run in a lot of races at school. They're very fast," Simon proudly declared. "When I'm big, I'm going to run just like them."

"How many brothers have you got?" asked the girl.

"Three. But they're much older than me. I don't see them very often."

Simon looked more closely at the girl standing beside him with her dress tucked into her knickers. Her eyes were set widely apart. He noticed they were blue. Not the blue of the sky but the deep blue of the sea. Her short hair was light brown and ruffled. It seemed she was unconcerned with her appearance. His mother was always concerned about how he looked whenever he ventured into the world beyond the vicarage. He wondered what his mother would say now if she could see him without his shoes and socks, standing in the middle of the deliciously cool and fast-flowing stream. She would probably frown with disapproval. But the thought of his mother's frown rapidly vanished as he gazed into the radiant, smiling face of the girl.

"Do you come here often?" asked the girl in a somewhat pert voice.

"Only when I want to be alone and listen to the music of the stream," replied Simon abstractedly. "It's the best place I know to hear beautiful sounds. One day I will capture the sounds in music so you and everyone else will be able to hear them, even when you are far away from this stream."

"That's a lovely thing to do," replied the girl. Then, after a moment's thought, she asked, "Can I be in your music?"

Simon had never considered the possibility of people in music. In his world, the only people he really knew were his parents. He did not want them intruding into his inner world of imagined sounds and dreams. But this girl was different. Perhaps she could be captured and retained in the world of his imagination. She was certainly intriguing. She had appeared from nowhere and appeared to share his love of solitude.

"Could you describe the way the sun glints on the water?" asked the girl before adding "That's what I like most about this stream. I like the sound of the water and the way the sunlight dances on its surface."

"One day I will," asserted Simon with a certainty beyond his years.

The girl smiled. Then, taking his hand in hers, she proceeded to kick the fast-flowing water as a football-player might launch an energetic attack on the opponent's goal. She sent a spray of water high into the air. The cloud of water droplets seemed to hang in the air for a split second before falling in a shower that drenched both of them. It was so sudden and unexpected that Simon did not know how to react. Should he recoil in horror at getting his clothes wet and knowing the stern reprimand he would receive from his mother or should he relish the wanton abandonment of the strange girl he had so unexpectedly encountered and whose lack of restraint seemed exhilarating and exciting?

She was standing beside him whereas his mother was far away in the shadowy recesses of the vicarage. The abandonment of the girl won the day. He, too, kicked the cold water with even more force than her. He was, after all, a boy and boys were stronger and more courageous than girls. Before long, the two of them were soaked to the skin. But they were incredibly happy. The sound of their laughter and their shrieks of pleasure filled the hot summer afternoon with the sheer joy of being alive. Never had Simon experienced such free abandonment and delight. The two of them kicked and splashed until both were breathless. Then they clambered out of the stream and onto the bank to dry off in the hot afternoon sun.

As they lay side by side on the grassy bank, Simon realised he knew nothing about the girl lying beside him.

"What's your name?" he enquired.

"Rosie," she replied.

"Mine's Simon," he added, thinking it only polite to share his name with her as she had told him hers.

"How old are you?" he asked.

"Nine," she answered.

"I'm nine, too," he replied feeling rather pleased they were the same age.

"Where do you live?" he asked.

"Keeper's Cottage," replied Rosie, "on the edge of South Wood. My dad is the gamekeeper on the Chorley estate. He knows all the paths and tracks through the woods, and I'm learning them, too." Then, after a momentary pause she confided, "I know where there's a badgers' sett."

Simon's eyes opened wide in amazement. He had never seen a badger, let alone the place where badgers lived. And yet this girl, who had appeared from nowhere, seemed to know the district so much better than him.

"Would you like me to show you?" she asked. "We could meet here tomorrow and I could take you to the place. But you must promise not to tell anyone. It's a secret place. No-one knows about it. You have to promise not to tell anyone."

What boy could resist discovering a secret location unknown to others? His curiosity was aroused and the thought of spending the next day in the company of this unusual girl was strangely appealing. Without hesitation he nodded agreement

The two of them remained on the bank of the stream for the remainder of the afternoon as their clothes gradually dried in the heat of the afternoon sun. Their conversation was sparse. Their sense of friendship seemed to transcend the need for words. They were at ease in each other's company. Simon had made a new friend.

When he returned home, his mother was quick to notice his crumpled shirt and damp shorts but Simon was able to preserve the secret of his new friend by saying he had slipped and fallen into the stream behind the village hall whilst searching for tadpoles, and this had satisfied her curiosity.

At dinner that evening, his father enquired of his youngest son how he had occupied his day. Simon merely relayed his tadpole story whilst omitting any reference to his newfound friend.

The following day, when his father was safely ensconced in his study preparing his Sunday sermon and his mother was visiting a housebound parishioner with a basket of soft fruit harvested from the vicarage garden, Simon slipped unnoticed from the house and headed for the stream behind the village hall. The sun was already the undisputed ruler of the cloudless sky and the day promised to be as hot and soporific as the previous day had been.

Upon arriving at the stream Simon was disappointed not to find Rosie waiting for him. He had assumed she would be there to greet him. For a brief moment, a wave of sadness swept over him. Perhaps she would not appear. Perhaps he would never see her again. Perhaps the previous day was the sum of the happiness he would experience during the six weeks of the school summer holidays. He thrust his hands into the pockets of his shorts and stared despondently at the ground beneath his feet. He aimed a desultory kick at a stone on the bank of the stream, but this only served to remind him of the joyous water-kicking he had shared with Rosie the previous afternoon. His spirits sank still further.

He must have lingered beside the stream for half-an-hour before Rosie eventually appeared. She was breathless from running and it took her a minute or so to regain her composure before she could explain why she was late.

"I had to feed the chick pheasants before I could leave," panted the breathless Rosie. "My dad was up all night guarding against poachers and so I had to feed the chicks this morning. I wish they were all together in one place, but my dad won't do that. He insists on having the pens scattered throughout the woods."

Simon knew nothing about rearing pheasants, but he could tell from Rosie's agitated state it must be a demanding business.

"Anyway," continued Rosie, having by now regained her composure, "let's go to the badgers' sett."

She strode forward along the village street, with Simon by her side, towards the woods at the west end of the village. It was a long trek but eventually they left the scorching heat of the sun overhead and entered the dappled shade of the wood. Here all was deliciously still and cool. Nothing moved as they walked beneath the overarching trees and through the shoals of dead leaves underfoot. It was a place completely unknown to Simon. He had never ventured into the woods before and felt strangely vulnerable and unnerved. Rosie, however, exhibited no such misgivings. She appeared to know instinctively which path to take. Simon was glad of her presence. As they ventured deeper into the wood, the only sound was that of birds high above them in the trees.

"Listen," commanded Rosie as she abruptly came to a halt and held a finger to her lips. "Can you hear a woodpecker?" she whispered.

Simon strained his ears and, sure enough, not far away came the sound of a woodpecker drilling into the trunk of a tree with the rapidity of a machinegun discharging. The two of them stood transfixed to the spot as the bird continued its drilling for tree insects.

Without moving, Rosie confided to Simon, "There are two sorts of woodpecker in this wood: the green woodpecker and the black and white woodpecker. My father can tell the difference just by the sound they make when they are pecking, but I can't. I can tell a lot of birds though, by the songs they sing."

Simon's sense of admiration for his new friend grew by the minute. He had heard of a French composer who captured

birdsong in his music, but he had never been able to
distinguish the songs of the birds he heard. Now, here was
a girl who claimed she could do just that. She was just the
friend he wanted. He would learn from her and she could
help him become a great composer. Together they would
make music that captured the sights and sounds that were
all round them. He knew he had found a very special friend.
Eventually the two of them reached a small clearing in the
woods. To one side of the clearing was a steep bank littered
with mounds of freshly excavated earth and dark tunnels
disappearing into the bank
"This is the badgers' sett," whispered Rosie in a hushed,
awe-filled voice. "There is one boar, two sows and three
cubs at present. No one must know about them. If the
farmers discovered this sett they would come and kill the
badgers. We mustn't let that happen. Promise me you won't
tell anyone about this place."
Simon nodded solemnly.
The two of them stared intently at the bank, with its piles of
excavated spoil and its dark tunnels disappearing deep
underground.
"Will we see the badgers?" asked Simon in a whisper.
"Only if we keep very still," replied Rosie. "They normally
come out at night to go hunting for food but, sometimes,
on a hot summer's day like today, they come out to play."
Hunkering down, the two of them kept watch in the hope
and expectation the badgers would provide them with a
display of carnivora gambolling and high jinks. Their
patience was eventually rewarded. A rustling was heard and
then the black and white snout of a badger appeared at the

entrance of one of the underground tunnels. The badger sniffed the air and turned its head this way and that to see if the coast was clear. Then, suitably satisfied, it scampered out of its tunnel and into the grassy dell. It remained very still, as if listening to see if it was safe for the other members of the badger family to emerge into the bright sunlight. Only when it was satisfied did it emit a strange squeak that told the others all was well. Soon, a procession of other black and white striped badgers, of varying sizes and weights, lumbered into the forest glade and began gambolling and chasing each other with unrestrained freedom. It reminded Simon of his and Rosie's exploits in the stream the previous day. The family of badgers was as happy and carefree as he and Rosie had been. A smile stole over his face.

The two of them lay motionless, concealed by the bracken and other ground-covering, watching the family of badgers cavorting and enjoying their freedom. Not for them the rigours of a school timetable. Not for them the stern disapproving stares of adults. Not for them the need to earn a living or observe a moral code. They were free spirits and Simon felt an inexpressible bond with them.

Whether or not Simon's feelings spilt over into accidental physical movement, or whether there was some other movement that frightened them, but the family of badgers suddenly scurried back to their sett and disappeared underground. Their frolicking in the hot summer sun was at an end and they returned to the dark bowels of the earth until night-time when they would venture out once more, this time in search of food.

Simon turned to Rosie and whispered, "That was wonderful! Thank you."

Rosie registered no reaction. She had seen badgers cavorting on many occasions and it was not a new experience for her. But inwardly, she was pleased Simon had shared her secret and been moved by the antics of the woodland badgers.

"What shall we do tomorrow?" he asked.

"I could show you my favourite meadow," replied Rosie. "It's looking beautiful just now. There's also a mysterious cottage overlooking the meadow. I can show you that, too."

Simon's eyes opened wide with excitement. "I would like that," he replied.

After agreeing to meet by the ancient oak tree at the south end of the village the following day, they went their separate ways.

"Where have you been all morning?" asked his mother as Simon slunk into the vicarage somewhat belatedly for lunch.

He knew he could not tell his mother about the badgers' sett. He had promised Rosie solemnly to preserve their secret. Something also instinctively told him not to tell his mother about Rosie. He sensed she would not approve of his new friend. And so, he supplied a vague answer about exploring a nearby beauty-spot and losing track of time. His mother shook her head to register her incomprehension at her son's fondness for wandering off on his own. He was a strange boy, she thought. None of her other sons had behaved in this way. But then, they had each other for company. Perhaps it was a mistake for her and her husband to have had a fourth child so long after the other boys had grown-up. To all intents and purposes, Simon had been condemned to a solitary life. Sending him to a preparatory boarding school had provided him with other children of a similar age with whom to interact during term-time but this had further isolated him when he returned home for the school holidays. Her husband, however, did not share her concerns. He belonged to the old school. He believed boys should learn to stand on their own feet from an early age, play hard, work hard and develop the muscular form of Christianity he practised. This would enable them to surmount life's difficulties just as he had done. Perhaps he was correct, she mused, although Simon did not appear to fit the mould her husband envisaged. So much of Simon's time seemed spent daydreaming. She often caught him staring into infinity, lost in thought and oblivious of everything around him. What would become of him, she wondered?

The following morning, when his father was ensconced in his study preparing yet another sermon with which to upbraid his congregation, and his mother was attending to household chores, Simon slipped out of the vicarage and headed for the ancient oak tree that stood beside the road to the south of the village. The old oak tree had witnessed hundreds of years of human activity. It had provided a climbing challenge for energetic young boys and a secret meeting place for lovers' trysts. It held the memories and secrets of generations within its annular rings. Human life might be fleeting, but it had stood immovable and implacable as the generations came and went. As Simon stood beneath its spreading boughs, he gazed intently at the tree's wide girth and grey, crinkly bark and wished he could penetrate its secrets.

His musings were brought to an abrupt end by the sudden appearance of Rosie. As before, she was out of breath having run from her home to their pre-planned rendezvous.

"We've had a policeman at our house," panted Rosie in a state of high excitement and exhaustion. "My dad called him. He caught men trying to steal pheasants from the Estate last night. The men ran away when they saw my dad coming, but my dad thinks he knows who they are. He phoned the police and PC Jones called this morning and wanted to know everything about it. My dad told me to leave the room, but I overheard them talking from outside the door. The policeman called it poaching. My dad was very angry. He told the policeman he could lose his job if he there weren't enough pheasants for Lord Chorley's autumn shoot. The policeman said he would make enquiries and report back." Then, after a brief pause, Rosie asked, "Have you ever had a policeman at your house?"

Simon wrinkled his young brow and thought deeply before recalling the one and only occasion he could remember. "Yes," he said. "When someone broke into the offertory box in the church and stole the money from it. I remember my dad was very angry. He said it was an act of sacrilege."

"What's sacrilege?" asked Rosie.

"I don't know," replied Simon, "but it must be something very bad to make my father angry."

Having shared experiences of their encounters with the local constabulary, Rosie selected the footpath for them to walk. It led through three shady coppices before emerging into a large sloping meadow. The meadow faced south and basked in the full warmth of the midmorning sun. The meadow grass was peppered with a spectacular array of delicate wild flowers luxuriating in the warmth and stillness of the morning.

"This is my favourite meadow," declared Rosie. "There are so many different wild flowers growing here."

Crouching on her haunches, she gently held a pale pink flower between her fingers. "This is centaury," she declared, with all the assurance of a horticultural expert at Kew Gardens. "When the weather's fine, the flowers remain open in the morning until noon; but they close in damp weather or if the sky is overcast."

"That's a bit like me," answered Simon. "I'm always at my best when the sun's shining, but I sulk when it's overcast or wet."

Rosie gave Simon a sideways look. She had never seen him sulk; but then, she had only ever seen him on sunny days.

"Look at this," she instructed, as she carefully placed her small fingers around a pink meadow flower. "This is musk mallow. Can you smell it?"

Simon crouched down beside her and inhaled through his nostrils.

"The musk scent is much stronger at night," announced Rosie.

"How do you know that?" asked a surprised Simon.

"I once came here at ten o'clock on a summer's night searching for one of our puppies that had gone missing and I was overwhelmed by the smell of musk mallow."

"Do you often go out at night?" asked an astonished Simon.

"Not often. But when I do, I love discovering animals that sleep during the day and only come out at night. Perhaps, we could arrange to go on a night expedition together."

Simon's eyes opened wide in amazement. What a strange girl she was! She appeared to be more at home in the natural world than with her parents in their woodland cottage. Much as he would relish a nocturnal adventure with Rosie, he somehow thought his parents would not approve. Such a venture would have to be planned and executed without their knowledge and with extreme care.

From her crouching position, Rosie leaned backwards and collapsed onto her back amidst the springy grass. Simon followed her example. The two of them lay side by side looking at the blue dome of heaven overhead. The sun warmed them. All was well with the world. They were back in the Garden of Eden where all was pure and undefiled. If only the whole of life could be so wonderful!

Their revelry was broken when Rosie suddenly called out, "Look, over there. Can you see that beautiful Painted Lady?"

Simon quickly raised himself on his elbows and scanned the field for evidence of a woman wearing excessive make-up. "I can't see a lady," he declared. Rosie laughed before saying, "Not a woman, silly – a butterfly. Look, over there. That beautiful orange and black butterfly is called a Painted Lady."

"How do you know the names of butterflies and flowers?" asked Simon.

"I've learned them from my father," replied Rosie. "He knows the names of every tree, flower, animal, butterfly and insect. Does your father?"

Simon thought for a moment. He somehow doubted his father would have such an encyclopaedic knowledge of botany. His father read extensively, but his reading-matter tended to be theological or philosophical. Somehow he doubted his father would be able to put names to flowers and butterflies.

"Probably not," replied Simon. "But I would love you to teach me their names." Then, seeing a pale yellow butterfly fluttering within inches of them, he enquired, "What's that called?"

"A Brimstone," replied Rosie with absolute assurance.

"And that one?" asked Simon, pointing to a pale blue butterfly just a few feet away from them.

"That's a Holly Blue," Rosie instantly replied.

Simon's admiration for his new friend was boundless. She was a wonderful fount of knowledge. Simply being with her was a delight and pleasure. He wished they could lie side by side in the meadow all summer watching butterflies flit past them whilst the scent of wildflowers filled their nostrils.

But Rosie favoured more energetic pursuits. She could sit out-of-doors at any time observing nature all around her; she wanted to show Simon the ruined cottage.

It nestled at the edge of the wood that bordered the isolated meadow. It had presumably once been home to a forester or gamekeeper and his family but had long been abandoned and fallen into disrepair.

"Come and look at the ruined cottage," instructed Rosie.

The two of them rose to their feet and walked across the meadow until they came to the ruined building. The low fence that marked the boundary of its once productive vegetable garden was broken and partly missing. The garden itself was a tangle of brambles, nettles and weeds. The windows were unglazed and pale green paint peeled off the front door.

"This way," commanded Rosie, as she carefully picked her way through the undergrowth to the place where the kitchen door had once been. Now there was just a yawning aperture.

Stepping over the threshold of the cottage, Rosie led the way into its dark interior.

Simon could recognize an old kitchen sink, but nothing else remained to show it had once been a kitchen where meals were prepared. Stepping gingerly forward through the gloom, the two of them entered the living room. It had an old black-leaded cooking-range with provision for an open fire at its centre.

"Who lived here?" whispered Simon.

"I don't know," replied Rosie. "It's always been like this," she asserted as she recalled her previous visits to the old cottage. "But I like to think of a family sitting in this room, huddled together around the fire, with food cooking on the range and the sound of talking and laughter – a bit like the cottage where I live."

It would certainly be a cosy place in which to live, thought Simon, although he was not sure he would choose it in preference to the more commodious vicarage.

The two of them then stealthily crept up the rickety stairs to explore the bedrooms and the open landing that presumably served as a third bedroom if required. The upstairs rooms were devoid of all trace of previous occupation. Only the faded floral wallpaper witnessed to long-ago human habitation.

"Let's imagine we're the people living in this cottage," suggested Rosie with girlish glee. "You can be the father and I'll be the mother." Then without a moment's pause she called out, "Husband, we need more logs for the fire." Rapidly adjusting to his new acting role, Simon replied, "I've got some here, dear, all ready and seasoned. They should make a good blizzy."

"What's a blizzy?" asked Rosie, immediately stepping out of character.

"A good blaze, with leaping flames and a crackling sound," replied Simon. "I bet they had lots of blizzies in this hearth when there were people living here."

Rosie and Simon continued their playacting for a long time. Anyone observing them would have thought they had been married for fifty years. Eventually they tired of their game and Simon announced, "I prefer being out-of-doors." And so the two of them abandoned the ruined cottage and returned to the meadow in order to luxuriate once more in the heat of the midmorning sun.

"What shall we do tomorrow?" Simon asked. And then, before Rosie could reply, he asked, "Have you ever been inside a vault?"

"What's a vault?" asked Rosie.

"It's a place where dead people are buried," revealed Simon. "There are some in the churchyard and I know how to get into one of them."

Rosie's eyes opened in amazement.

"But isn't it scary – with dead people inside?"

"No," replied Simon. "They're in lead coffins. They can't get out. The kings of Egypt were buried in vaults with all their treasure. We could search to see if there's any treasure in the churchyard vault."

Rosie had introduced Simon to a whole new world of birdsong and forest animals but now it was his turn to introduce her to what lay beneath the ground in his father's churchyard.

The vault in question was one he had often wanted to explore, but a certain childhood fear, coupled with a desire to share the experience with someone else, had deterred him. With his new-found friend, he could venture underground. It would be like the men in the bible story who crawled up the tunnel into Jerusalem and gained the praise of the king for their skill and daring.

His mind was made up. He looked beseechingly at Rosie and then, to his great joy, she nodded her head in agreement. Ambling back through the wood, they arranged to meet the following morning at the rear of the village school.

When Simon's mother left the vicarage on her afternoon round of visits to the housebound and elderly, Simon stealthily scoured the vicarage cupboards for a battery-operated torch. He then crept into his father's study where he knew a key to the burial vault of the Chorley family was kept. Carefully removing the key from the drawer in which it resided, he carried it and the torch into the garden and hid both of them in a secret place of his own choosing in readiness for the following day's adventure.

That evening at dinner, his father asked him how he had spent his day. Simon knew his father believed that every minute of the day was a precious gift from God and should be used productively. His father would hardly approve of a day squandered in the meadows with an unknown girl. He repeated, therefore, the story he told his mother at lunchtime.

"What you need to do is some serious reading," replied his father. "When I was your age, I read all Sir Arthur Conan Doyle's books. Great adventure stories! Packed with thrills aplenty! How that man could write! I reckon my English vocabulary and literacy improved immeasurably as a result of reading his books. There's nothing like a good author to fire the imagination and help one transcend the mundane things of life."

Simon listened obediently as his father reiterated one of his favourite themes. Indeed, Simon often had the impression he was being used as a guinea-pig for a forthcoming sermon on which his father was working. Rising above the mundane things of the world was a theme that ran through nearly all his father's sermons. Perhaps it was this that had made Simon into something of a dreamer, always searching for what lay beyond the everyday things of life. But whereas his father satisfied his other-worldly yearnings by immersing himself in sacred and secular literature, Simon found words inadequate. It was music that excited and fired his imagination. Music, he had discovered, could stimulate his deepest feelings and express his most profound yearnings far better than words.

It was the music teacher at his prep school who first opened his eyes and ears to the beauties of music. He encouraged the young Copeland to take up the violin. It was not long before the music teacher realised that, besides being an adept learner, his young pupil also possessed a very rare gift – the gift of perfect pitch. Whereas most musicians use a tuning-fork or a note from another instrument to locate musical pitch, there were some, blessed by the gods, who needed no such external help but had a perfectly developed innate sense of pitch. Simon was a member of that special company. Once his music teacher realised this, Simon was encouraged to embark upon the piano as well as the violin. He was also quickly drafted into the school choir. Music became his life. Not only was he able to excel at playing and singing but he developed an ardent missionary zeal to listen to as much new music as possible. His tally of favourite composers grew by the month. Suddenly the world around him took on a new dimension. He discovered the beauties of nature could be captured by a symphony orchestra. The English composer Frederick Delius showed how this could be done. He discovered that the excitement and exultation of forward propulsion and unrestrained brio was capable of musical expression. Had not Elgar proved this in his marvellous *Introduction and Allegro for Strings*? The sheer zest for life had been magnificently captured by Mendelssohn in his *Italian Symphony*. This realisation opened an entirely new world to the youthful Simon, and he resolved to devote his life to emulating the great romantic composers and encapsulating the world around him in the music of eternity.

Simon doubted if his father would understand. Apart from choosing hymns for the Sunday church services, his father showed no interest in music. Even the hymns he selected were chosen for their theological content rather than their musicality. It was best, therefore, to merely nod his head in agreement to all his father said. He had discovered that was the best way to preserve the calm of the vicarage.

The following morning found Simon loitering behind the empty village school awaiting the arrival of Rosie. In his pocket he had the battery torch and the key to the Chorley family vault. Although there was no sign of Rosie, Simon was not unduly concerned. He surmised she was probably feeding the pheasant chicks again. But, as the minutes ticked away, doubts began to assail him. Perhaps Rosie was not so keen on venturing underground as he was. Perhaps girls were more timid than boys. Perhaps she would have chosen to spend the day elsewhere. But, just as his doubts were gaining the upper hand, she appeared around the corner of the school playground. Just as before, she was panting and out of breath. It was some time before she was able to offer an apology for her late arrival and explain that she had been made to undertake extra tasks around the home before she could leave.

Once she had regained her composure, the two of them headed for the churchyard. On their way they passed Mrs Fitzwilliam. Simon's father always referred to Mrs Fitzwilliam as "a pillar of the church". She was rarely to be

found far from the church building. She acted as the key-holder who opened the church every morning and locked it again every evening. She busied herself laundering the altar linen and ensuring the brass altar cross and candlesticks gleamed. She could always be relied upon to be in her accustomed pew whenever there was a church service. And because so much of her time was occupied at the church, she had developed a proprietorial ownership of the building. She held the vicar in the highest esteem. Simon disliked her. She was continually knocking on the vicarage door and intruding on family life and she treated Simon as if he was an embryonic minister of religion. Seeing Simon and Rosie walking towards her, she beamed an icy smile and asked, "And what, may I ask, are you two up to today?" Simon had no intention of telling her of their proposed plans and so he merely muttered incoherently about going for a walk whilst endeavouring to pass her with all possible speed.
"Who was that?" enquired Rosie once Mrs Fitzwilliam had passed.
"Just someone my father knows," replied Simon before quickly turning the conversation to their morning's adventure. "I've got the key to the vault, but we must be careful no one sees us. Adults don't like children having adventures. They always try and prevent them. If there are any adults in the churchyard when we enter, we'll pretend we're just reading inscriptions on headstones. No-one will mind us doing that."
But, when they passed through the lych-gate and into the churchyard, Simon was relieved to find it devoid of all

human beings. The two of them had the burial ground to themselves. The churchyard was not extensive, but it encircled all four sides of the ancient parish church. Some sections were older than others. It was to one of the older sections that Simon headed, closely followed by Rosie. There, close to the wall of the ancient church stood a table-top tomb. It was very old and in a poor state of repair.
"This is where the Chorleys are buried," declared Simon. "They have a special underground room to house their coffins. This table-top tomb hides a flight of stone steps leading down and under the church. If we slide the side panel to one side, you can see the steps."
So saying, Simon pushed against the panel in question and, sure enough, a gaping void appeared. Taking the torch from his pocket he shone its beam into the darkness. It revealed a flight of twelve stone steps leading down to a substantial wooden door.
Turning to Rosie, he asked, "Are you ready?"
Rosie nodded her agreement.
"I'll go first," declared Simon, thinking that, because he was a boy, it was his place to lead the way. So saying, he squeezed his small body through the gap in the side of the tomb and took a couple of steps into the darkness.
"It's fine in here. Nothing to worry about," he confidentially relayed to Rosie who was still standing outside in the bright summer sunlight. After a moment's hesitation, Rosie followed Simon's example and squeezed her small body through the gap and into the darkness of the vault. The two of them stood for a moment at the head of the stone steps to allow their eyes to adjust to the darkness.

Then they carefully descended the flight of steps to the stout wooden door at the bottom.

Reaching into his pocket for a second time, Simon produced the key he had previously removed from his father's study and inserted it into the lock. At first, he thought the lock would not yield, but, after exerting his full strength, the ancient mechanism creaked into action and the door before them no longer barred their way.

Simon cast a quick glance at Rosie's face. He saw excitement mingled with terror. Neither of them knew what they would discover on the other side of the door. Had he been alone, Simon might, at this point, have lost courage and turned back into the warmth and sunshine of the world above. But now was no time to show fear. He had a friend with him. Together they would explore the hidden secrets of the room behind the door.

Thus resolved, he pushed against the door. It creaked ominously as it eased open. There was a scurrying sound from within that caused both him and Rosie to freeze in fear; but Rosie, who was used such sounds in her woodland cottage, whispered, "It's probably only mice - or maybe a rat."

Simon felt he could cope with mice, but rats were another thing. He had heard somewhere that, if rats were cornered, they attacked whoever was between them and their means of escape. The thought of being attacked in an underground vault by an enormous and ferocious rat was not something that appealed to him. Rosie did not appear to share his fear. Perhaps this was because she was used to living amongst the wild creatures of the woods and they held no terror for her.

"Go on: open the door," she whispered.

Gently pushing against the old oak door, Simon inched it slowly open.

Shining his torch into the shadowy underground vault revealed stone shelving on either side. On the lower shelves were four large leaden coffins. They had once been the lead-lining of wooden coffins, but their wooden exteriors had long since rotted leaving just the sealed interiors. A pall of dust covered the final resting place of those entombed within.

Simon and Rosie stood in the doorway of the low-roofed underground vault surveying the contents. Simon felt Rosie's hand seeking his in the darkness. He was glad to take it. Not only did it reassure him that she was standing beside him in this macabre mausoleum, but also that she turned to him for reassurance and comfort. It made Simon feel strong and manly. No one had ever turned to him before for comfort. Rosie somehow gave him confidence. With her standing by his side, he felt sure he could do great things. A warm glow passed over him as he gripped her hand more tightly.

As the beam of Simon's torch scoured the shadows of the vault it alighted upon something on the floor that reflected its light. Stooping to see what it was, Simon discovered a brass plate. On it was inscribed AUGUSTUS LINDLEY, THIRD EARL OF CHORLEY 1772-1840. BLESSED ARE THE DEAD THAT DIE IN THE LORD.

Simon read the inscription aloud.

"That must be one of Lord Chorley's relatives," declared Rosie. "I know they've lived in the big house for a long time. Fancy having your very own underground house to live in when you die!"
"Yes," replied Simon. "And I guess the two upper stone shelves are waiting for the present Lord Chorley and his family when they die."
"I don't think I'd want to be buried down here," declared Rosie. "There's no sunlight. It's impossible to hear the song of the birds or know whether it's spring, autumn, summer or winter. I want to be buried under the sweet-smelling grass, with wildflowers dancing on my grave, where the warm rain of summer and the cold snow of winter can fall upon me. This is more like a prison. I don't like it."
"But just think," replied Simon, "we've explored a secret underground chamber that few others know about. We've been where few other people have ventured. We're fearless explorers, you and I."
Rosie smiled at Simon's boyish eagerness. She was pleased she had helped him realise a secret dream. But she had seen enough of the dark underground chamber and was keen to leave. Simon gave one last sweep of the vault with his torch before the two of them shuffled out through the low doorway onto the flight of steps. Having re-locked the stout oaken door, the two of them ascended the steps and, after a quick glance through the tomb's open side-panel to ensure no one was in the churchyard, the two of them returned to the welcome warmth and brightness of the summer's day.

"What shall we do now?" asked Simon, once the two of them had adjusted to the blinding brilliance of the summer's day.

"Would you like to see a secret pond where there are giant toads?" asked Rosie.

Simon's eyes widened at this suggestion and without hesitation he agreed to Rosie's proposition.

Just as they were leaving the churchyard, they encountered the busybody Mrs Fitzwilliam once again.

"Ah, Master Simon! We seem destined to continually meet each other. And who is this young lady with you?"

Simon had no desire to share his new friend's name with the interfering busybody and so he replied, "Just a friend of mine," and attempted to edge past the stocky matron before she could ask any further intrusive questions.

"I've no doubt she's a friend of yours. But such a pretty girl must have a name." And then, turning to Rosie she asked, "What's your name, dear?"

Poor Rosie felt trapped. She sensed that Simon did not want her to reveal her identity, but she had been brought up to behave politely towards adults. Refusing to answer an adult's question was not an option; and so, reluctantly she replied, "Rosie."

"Rosie? What a delightful name!" exclaimed the inquisitive Mrs Fitzwilliam. But before she could interrogate her further, Simon pulled on Rosie's arm and yanked her away from the person his father considered a pillar of the church - but whom Simon considered an interfering old busybody.

"I wish we hadn't met her," declared Simon, as they scurried down the village street in the direction of the woods. "I don't like her, although my dad thinks she's wonderful."

The two of them hurried onwards until they reached the seclusion of the woods. Once again, Rosie appeared perfectly at ease as they plunged into the dappled shadows and the forest of trees that prevented the summer sunshine penetrating this unfrequented corner of the parish. She led the way confidently along narrow, twisting paths and never hesitated when they came to a fork in the path. Simon's admiration for Rosie was boundless. In his eyes she was both a wild tree-nymph and a free spirit with an unerring sense of direction and a purposefulness that excited and intrigued him.

Deeper and deeper they plunged into the wood. By now Simon had lost all sense of direction. Without sight of the sun, it was impossible to tell the direction in which they were heading. He realised he was completely dependent upon Rosie. Without her he would be utterly lost. He edged closer to her. He even sensed an aura of safety and protection radiating from her small body. In her presence he felt perfectly safe.

After many twists and turns, the two of them eventually reached a clearing where overhanging branches gently caressed the still waters of a dark pond. Not a ripple could be seen on the surface of this mysterious, secret pool. Its surface resembled a black mirror reflecting no light and concealing whatever might lurk below its surface.

Rosie slackened her pace and gingerly edged around the near-most edge of the pool seeking the most advantageous vantage point from which to observe toads. Simon followed silently behind. Although both trod carefully and stealthily, their movements disturbed one of the pool's inhabitants and a loud plop followed by ripples in the pond, informed them that one toad at least had registered their presence and was taking evasive action. They kept their eyes focused on the spot in the pool from which the ripples emanated and, before long, their silent observation was rewarded when two bulbous eyes appeared above the waterline. The hooded, unblinking eyes scanned the wooded banks of the pool to see if the danger had passed before disappearing again beneath the surface only to reappear a moment or so later nearer the bank. Simon and Rosie watched transfixed as the toad finally hauled itself onto the bank and emitted a piercing croak as if to say, "I've done it!"

In reality, the toad's croak was to inform its partner of his whereabouts so the two of them could be reunited and discuss whatever it is that adult toads discuss whenever they come together in a knot. The sound of the toads' croaking filled the air and produced smiles on the faces of both Rosie and Simon. Simon immediately imagined how a bassoon might capture the sound of the toads and recreate this wonderful secluded woodland dell in all its beauty and mysteriousness. High sustained violin chords would be needed to capture the stillness of the scene, with distant horn calls to create a yearning for something that was transient and soon to disappear. If only he could capture this scene and preserve it for ever!

He glanced at Rosie and noticed that she was smiling at him. She had seen the faraway expression on his face and guessed he was enraptured by the secret woodland scene.

Simon smiled back somewhat bashfully. How wonderful it was to have a new friend who seemed to understand him! Never had he met anyone quite like Rosie. Since meeting her, he felt as if his whole life had been enriched and enlarged in some strange way. She excited him. He felt she understood him. He did not feel the need to put into words what he was thinking as they sat together on the banks of the woodland pool,. It was as if communication was possible without the use of words. An innate empathy existed between them. This was something he had not experienced before. In his eyes, Rosie was special. He was glad she was his friend.

Returning home, Simon bade farewell to Rosie at the edge of the wood and walked on towards the vicarage in a thoughtful frame of mind.

That evening at dinner his father repeated his oft-asked question, "And what have you been up to today young man?"

Simon explained that he had been exploring South Wood and had discovered the breeding place of toads. He did not mention he had done so in the company of Rosie. His father gave him a searching glance before adding,

"Mrs Fitzwilliam tells me that she saw you with a young girl this morning. Is that correct?"

Simon's thoughts towards Mrs Fitzwilliam were anything but Christian. Why had the interfering old busybody told his father about his friend? Now he would have to share Rosie with his parents. Something deep within him warned him that his parents might not approve.

"Yes, father. It was a girl I met the other day when I walked down to the stream."

"Mrs Fitzwilliam informs me her name is Rosie," continued his father. "The only Rosie in the parish that she knows is Rosie Evans from Keeper's Cottage in South Wood. Is this the girl with whom you were seen?"

Simon averted his eyes before replying.

"Yes, father. She's a very interesting person. She knows a tremendous amount about birdsong and animals and trees and wildflowers. She's teaching me their names and has promised to show me where eels hatch their elvers."

"I don't think that would be a good idea," replied Simon's father with all the gravitas he usually reserved for sermons dealing with original sin or moral transgressions.

"This Rosie whom you have befriended is the daughter of the Chorley gamekeeper. He and I do not see eye to eye. In fact, I have to say his views and his demeanour leave a lot to be desired. He has publicly accused me of preaching antiquated twaddle. He has no regard for the laws of God, the rites of the church or the sanctity of the priesthood. He is, I regret to say, a thoroughly irreligious man. It would, therefore, be entirely inappropriate for you to continue consorting with his daughter. I must ask you to terminate your acquaintanceship with this young girl."

Whilst his father delivered this sermon at the dinner table, Simon's mother quietly nodded her head in agreement. Simon could see he would gain no support from her. But he was unwilling to meekly accept his father's orders.

"Rosie is not like that!" he exclaimed. "She's gentle and sensitive. She would never say anything bad about anyone or anything. She's a good person."

And then, with adeptness far in excess of his years, he continued, "You say the world is God's creation and that He made everything in it. Well, Rosie loves God's creation. She loves nature in all its beauty. She must, therefore, love God just as much as you do."

Stiffening his back, and with a deep intake of breath like some Old Testament prophet about to pronounce doom on the city of Babylon, the Reverend Copeland declaimed, "Pantheism is an abhorrent heresy. It has led countless millions of individuals to forfeit their immortal souls by failing to differentiate between the Creator and His creation. One cannot worship plants or trees or hills or landscapes. They are merely God's handiwork. It is the Creator one should seek – through prayer and worship and study. These are the things the Chorley gamekeeper holds in contempt. No doubt he has conveyed his contempt for all things spiritual to his young daughter. That is why you are no longer to consort with her. I want to hear no more on this matter. You are to desist from having anything more to do with this young lady. Is that understood?"

Simon was slayed. He felt as if the overwhelming happiness of the past few days had suddenly and cruelly been snatched from him. He could see his father would brook no argument. The Vicar of Chorley had spoken.

But that was not all.

"Mrs Fitzwilliam tells me that you and that girl were seen in the churchyard earlier today. She thought it strange that the two of you were heading towards the church and so she took the precaution of following you. She tells me – and I must say I find this very difficult to believe – that you insinuated yourself into the Chorley burial vault. Upon searching my study, I find the key to the vault missing. Well, young man, what have you got to say for yourself?"

Simon hung his head in abject shame. His daring adventure had been observed by the pestilential, prying Mrs Fitzwilliam. He knew there was nothing he could say that would pacify his father and so he remained silent.

After what seemed like an unconscionable time, the silence was broken by Simon's father delivering his *coup de grace*: "This is what comes from consorting with the daughter of an atheist. No doubt she led you astray, just as Eve led Adam astray in the Garden of Eden. It's just as I thought. She has exerted a bad influence upon you which merely underlines what I have already said: you are to have no further dealings with her."

There was no way Simon could allow Rosie to assume the blame for their underground adventure that morning and so he countered by saying,

"No father, you're wrong. It wasn't Rosie's idea to explore the underground vault. It was mine. Indeed, I don't think she really enjoyed it. She much prefers being above ground in the sunlight listening to the birds and watching animals playing. I'm the one to blame."

With a further straightening of his back, the Revd Copeland terminated the conversation with a magisterial, "Kindly leave the table and go to your room. Tomorrow you will read Sir Arthur Conan Doyle's *Memories and Adventures* and, before dinner tomorrow evening, I will test you on the first ten chapters. From now on, your time will be occupied in useful pursuits rather than in idleness and mixing with bad company."

With downcast eyes and a leaden heart, Simon pushed his chair back and left the dinner table. He knew his father was wrong about Rosie, but he dared not oppose him. The Revd Copeland's word was law in the parish and a young boy like him could never succeed in going against his father's wishes. His father had dealt him a cruel blow, but he could see no escape.

And what of Rosie? What would she think when he failed to materialize the following morning? Would she feel abandoned and betrayed? Would she regard him as fickle and inconsistent? Would she be hurt by his absence? Or would she shrug off his disappearance and find new friends with whom to spend her time?

He never saw Rosie again. She was certainly not to be found sitting in the pews of the parish church on Sunday, which was the only opportunity Simon had of meeting other people. This was hardly surprising given her father's strong anti-religious views. But Simon often found himself thinking about Rosie. She was the best friend he ever had. She understood him. He enjoyed her company, her carefree abandonment, her free spirit and her sheer joy of living. Where would he ever find the like of her again?

CHAPTER THREE

When Simon awoke, the early morning sun was struggling to gain access to his cell through the high, barred window. The sunlight created a strange pattern on the wall opposite. It resembled the misshapen portcullis of a medieval castle. His accommodation was not medieval but, in many respects, it did not differ greatly from that of ancient times. Over the years, the brick walls of his cell had been given innumerable coats of glossy cream paint that merely served to accentuate the mortar courses between each row of bricks. The heavy metal door, that was the only means of entry and exit, had also been given the multi-layered, cream, gloss-paint treatment.
He was now six months into his sentence and his life had slipped into the unerring routine of prison life.
The silhouetted portcullis moved imperceptibly down the opposite wall of his cell until it rested on the door as the sun inched higher above the outer prison walls. It appeared to Simon as a portent, emphasising the fact he was doubly incarcerated – deprived of physical freedom and imprisoned within the thoughts of his mind.
Apart from the single bed on which he lay, there was just a stainless-steel toilet pan and sink in the far corner of the cell

and a rickety wooden table with an equally rickety plain wooden chair. The sparse furnishings did not bother him. He had never hankered after possessions. Provided he had clothes to wear and a well-tuned piano on which to play, he was content.

A smile spread over his pale face as he thought of the prison officers' reaction if he asked for a piano in his cell. "What do you think this is, Copeland? The bleeding Birmingham Conservatoire? Perhaps you'd like a church organ installed as well. There's enough noise on this wing as it is. The last thing we want is some would-be concert pianist serenading us at all hours of the day and night. If you want to play a musical instrument, why not take up the tissue-paper and comb? The Bronco toilet paper has got outstanding musical qualities if you blow hard enough."

The other prisoners on the wing would also have strong views on the subject, and would make them known in no uncertain terms. They appeared unconcerned at the raucous sounds of Caribbean rappers, grunge artists and punk-rockers emanating from the radio in the association area, but if ever classical music was heard on the wing, it was greeted with howls of abuse and ridicule. When the other inmates learned of Simon's musical background much of their intolerant behaviour was used as a way to needle him. He learnt to keep his head down and do nothing to provoke the other men on the wing. His days at private school had taught him to survive bullies, sadists, the aggressive and the downright perverted. He had always sought the company of those of a gentler disposition, who were more given to introspection than physical aggression.

He knew that a piano in his cell was not a possibility and so the rickety old table had to serve that purpose. The edge of the table was his keyboard. Here he could imagine the black and white keys spread out below his fingers and could, with his gift of perfect pitch, conjure music out of the ether. Chopin preludes and Debussy arabesques filled the twelve solitary hours he spent each day in his cell.

He smiled again as he recounted the pleasure derived from the sounds that populated his imagination. He felt genuine sorrow for the other men on the wing for whom music was a closed book. They would never experience the life-enhancing beauty and exaltation that music conveyed: how it spoke to the deepest yearnings of the human soul and how it was capable of lifting earthbound creatures to the very gates of heaven. To go through life without experiencing such ecstasy and enrichment was failing to live life to the full, he thought.

"Rise and shine!" shouted the stentorian voice of the prison officer outside his cell as the bolts of his cell-door shot open and he was able to escape from his twelve-hour incarceration and make his way to the communal washing facility.

The communal washrooms were just like those at his public school. The strongest and most aggressive individuals elbowed others aside as they took possession of a washbasin and then, not content with their physical conquest, ridiculed the physique or timidity of other would-be washers. Getting washed was an ordeal, but not nearly as daunting as using the communal showers. Here, out of sight of prison officers, any amount of degradation might occur.

Those prisoners liberally endowed with masculine accoutrements, took this to mean they could humiliate and abuse those less well endowed. Big-boned black prisoners were best avoided. Many of them had muscular bodies that would easily qualify them for the Mr Universe competition. They were not to be messed with. Indeed, Simon went studiously out of his way to avoid all contact with them. Many were serving time for grievous bodily harm, assault, wounding with intent, rape, knife crime and other violent offences. It was best to acknowledge their physical superiority and do nothing to antagonize them.

This was not always easy. There was never any way of knowing what might suddenly annoy them. Sometimes it was simply being in the wrong place at the wrong time that led to an explosion of unexpected anger.

"What you think you doin' man, staring at me like that?"

"I wasn't staring at you."

"You call me a liar, man? I say you was staring at me. And I don't like it. I don't like it one little bit. Aint y' seen a face like this before? Aint y' seen a fist like this? It could smash your little face into pieces. How d' like that, man? Your pretty little face smashed into a thousand little fragments."

There was no arguing with this sort. The best thing was to beat a hasty retreat. But even that had its perils.

"You turning your back on me? Didn't y' mummy tell you it was rude to turn y' back on someone when they is talking to you? Where's y' manners pretty boy?"

There was no way of placating those who were angry and resentful and looking for a whipping boy on whom to vent their spleen. The torrent of abuse and ridicule had simply to be endured, hoping that something would distract the bully and cause him to direct his anger elsewhere.

Prison life was intimidating and, often, the prison officers merely averted their eyes to what was happening on the wing. They seemed to think the inmates had only themselves to blame for their predicament, and that the treatment they received from other prisoners was part of their punishment.

Having survived his morning ablutions in the communal washroom, Simon was frogmarched back to his cell to eat his breakfast. He had collected it the previous day, along with his evening meal, from the prison cafeteria. Here he had been given a plastic partitioned plate and had then slowly passed down the line collecting a packet of cereal, a carton of UHT milk, a carton of orange juice, two slices of white bread and a dab of butter and jam. As he stood in the line, the prisoner behind him asked,

"Why do you choose such bloody difficult stuff for us to sing?"

A smile spread over Simon's face.

"It's not difficult once you've mastered the rhythm. You'll enjoy it before long."

"Depends what you mean by "before long". I reckon I'll be out on licence before I ever get any enjoyment from the stuff you inflict on us!"

"The greater the challenge," returned Simon, "the greater the sense of achievement. I tell you you'll enjoy it before long."

The unhappy singer was one of Simon's latest recruits to the prison choir. Dylan professed to be tone-deaf and

without a musical bone in his body; but, coming from Wales, Simon maintained such a thing was impossible. He told Dylan, Wales was the land of song and that he must claim his birth-right or never again be able to hold his head high amongst his fellow countrymen. The appeal to Dylan's nationalistic pride worked miracles and persuaded him to give the prison choir a trial. It soon became evident that, although he could not read music, and had only a sketchy understanding of pitch and rhythm, he was blessed with a very pleasant baritone voice. Simon encouraged the reluctant Welshman to persevere and now, some two months after joining the prison choir, Dylan was beginning to enjoy making music with the other likeminded inmates, even if he feigned the opposite. He also valued the extra couple of hours out of his cell that the weekly choir practice afforded.
"Why can't we just sing *While shepherds watched their flocks by night?*"
Simon smiled again. He knew Dylan was winding him up.
"There'd be no sense of achievement or satisfaction singing a turgid, well-worn old Christmas carol when there's so much better music waiting to be discovered," asserted Simon. "Trust me. It's going to be fine."
So saying, the two of them made their way back to their respective cells to eat their meals.
Swabbing down floors and sweeping corridors was mundane and tedious, but it passed the time and kept Simon out of the way of some of the rougher elements working in the machine shop or the electrical component disassembling shop. It also gave him time to think.

There was a lot of time for thinking in prison. His thoughts sometimes turned to the past and the events that led to his two-year jail sentence. These thoughts were bitter-sweet. He smiled inwardly as he recalled the good times, only to have the smile wiped away as he recalled the jealousy, rancour and hostility that had been heaped upon him by those nearest and dearest to him.

At other times, he concentrated his thoughts on prison life and devised strategies for surviving it. Anyone who thought prison life was a safe refuge from the anxieties and pressures of the outside world had clearly never been detained at Her Majesty's pleasure. Prison life may have removed anxiety about the necessities of life – food, clothing, warmth and shelter – but it forced him to live cheek by jowl with some of the most unsavoury people he had ever encountered.

In one sense, prison life was similar to life in a monastic community. Those who lived in monastic communities had their basic human needs provided but, unlike prison, the members of a monastic community were bound together by shared beliefs and a common purpose. They were united in heart and mind. Not so in Her Majesty's Prisons. In prison, the inmates railed against the injustices of life. They sought scapegoats to blame for their predicament. They appeared to derive a sadistic pleasure persecuting those weaker than themselves. And they had their own perverted code of justice. It was perfectly acceptable to have swindled or embezzled funds; tricked people out of their life savings; or worked internet scams that robbed banks, businesses and individuals of thousands of pounds. It was perfectly acceptable to have murdered adults, and traded in drugs, no matter what misery that caused to the lives of others. It was perfectly acceptable to have purveyed pornography or acted as a pimp, provided children were not involved. But those who were serving time for crimes that involved children were shown no mercy. They were the lowest of the low in the eyes of the other prisoners. They deserved no pity, no mercy and no understanding. And so prisoners took it upon themselves to punish those who had harmed children. Such unfortunate victims often had to seek protection by requesting segregation. This deprived them of free association and condemned them to endless solitary hours in their cells.

Simon spent some of his time thinking about the future and what he would do when his sentence ended and he was released back into the world. Would he be able to pick up the threads of his former life or would he have to make a fresh start? Would he be able to return to where he previously lived, or would he have to move to a different part of the country? Would he be allowed access to the ones he loved, or would there be restrictions placed upon his movements and whom he saw? He knew he would never be able to teach again.

Prison afforded a great deal of time for thinking.

He also discovered there was a great deal of time that could be used profitably honing skills and increasing knowledge. The prison education department offered courses in various subjects and, although most of these courses were designed for those who had somehow slipped through the state educational system and were defective in Basic English and

Maths, there were opportunities to undertake study at a higher level.

Having been to university, Simon already possessed a degree; but he was keen to continue his studies and, if possible, work for a Doctorate of Music. He broached the subject with the Head of Prison Education. She was a no-nonsense spinster.

"Why should Her Majesty's Prison Service pay for you to follow your pet interest when there are so many more deserving cases needing help?" she barked in her manly voice. "This is a prison, not an all-fees-paid outpost of the Open University."

Simon sensed she had somehow achieved her current position without having been to university herself. She was suspicious of graduates. She believed prison was a place of punishment rather than rehabilitation. Furthermore, she was completely unmusical. She had no interest in music whatsoever. She could see no useful purpose in turning out musical prisoners. It was a complete waste of the taxpayer's money.

"Teaching these creatures to read and write is useful. It means they've no excuse for not completing their Income Tax Returns. It means they can read prohibition notices, newspaper articles and warnings on medicines. It will make them useful members of society. But what possible use is a doctorate in music? If I want a doctor, I want one who can make me well: someone who can diagnose an illness and prescribe the correct medication. I want someone who can return me to health so I can become a useful member of society once more. Those are the doctors this country needs: not Doctors of Music."

Simon would dearly have liked to reason with her that music was as beneficial to good health as all the pills and potions prescribed by doctors. He would have loved to expound his belief that most of the world's woes stemmed from an inability to relate properly to the world around and the marvellous way music facilitated this process. He would have loved to explain to her how human beings consist of body, mind and spirit and that music ministered to the mind and the spirit just as drugs ministered to the body. But he knew all such reasoning was futile. She was a woman without love and no one devoid of love could ever appreciate the beauties of music. A different approach was required.

"It need not cost the Prison Service anything," replied Simon. "I have funds available to cover the registration and tuition fees. And it would be a more productive use of my time than playing ping-pong or sitting in front of a television. I would be grateful if you would forward my request to the Prison Governor for his consideration."

A scowl passed over the amazon's face. She realised she was being leapfrogged and did not like it. But then she did not like Simon. She regarded his crime as heinous. If she had her way, he would be locked in a subterranean cell and the key thrown away. People like him did not deserve the educational facilities provided by the prison service. He was abusing the prison facilities for his own personal advancement. And what was more galling, she knew the Prison Governor would accede to his request. In her eyes, the Prison Governor was weak and bent over backwards to make prison life bearable for the more educated inmates. She also knew that Simon had ingratiated himself with the Governor by undertaking the training of a choir for the annual Prison Christmas Carol Service. Such toady, sycophantism disgusted her.

"If the Governor is persuaded to let you follow your esoteric purpose, there will be no visiting professors allowed here. You will have to work entirely from written material and video links. And don't think you can have unrestricted access to our video links. The prison video system is designed for the use of the law courts. They take priority."

A more unhelpful Director of Prison Education it would have been harder to find; but Simon had learned that, when one is detained at Her Majesty's pleasure, one can expect no favours and few encouragements. He returned to his cell moderately hopeful his request would receive sympathetic consideration from the Governor.

The remainder of his day was devoted to preparing music for the evening choir practice.

In his school teaching days, he possessed unfettered access to photocopiers and computers programmed with the latest musical notation software. He had been able to produce vocal parts, notation files and multiple copies of music at the touch of a button. But in prison, music was still at the paper and ink stage. He had managed to obtain a copy of *Carols for Choirs,* but one book was of little practical use with a choir of sixteen men. Consequently, he had to laboriously copy the vocal lines of each of the carols the choir was to sing at the forthcoming Carol Service. It was a slow and painstaking business.

As he sat hunched over his rickety table, he imagined he was a medieval monk poring over an illuminated manuscript. Each stroke of his pen caused the music to advance along the stave and sound in his head. This was how the likes of Monteverdi and Palestrina composed their music, he thought; and so, who was he to complain at the slow progress he was making? He took a certain pride in belonging to a long line of musicians, stretching back to the Middle Ages, who heard beautiful sounds in their heads and then assiduously committed them to manuscript paper so others might share their pleasure.

The carol on which he was working was by one of Dylan's fellow countrymen. It was a setting of a medieval carol by the Welsh composer William Mathias.

> *"Nowell nowell, nowell nowell."*
> *"Who is there that singeth so: nowell nowell?"*

> *"I am here, Sir Christémas."*
> *"Welcome, my Lord Sir Christémas!"*
> *Welcome to all, both more and less!*
> *Come near, nowell!"*

> *"Dieu vous garde, beaux sieurs, tidings I you bring:*
> *A maid hath born a child full young,*
> *Which causeth you to sing*
> *Nowell nowell, nowell nowell.*

THE WAGES OF LOVE

"Christ is now born of a pure maid,
In an ox-stall he is laid;
Wherefore sing we all at a brayde:
Nowell nowell, nowell nowell.

"Buvez bien par toute la compagnie.
Make good cheer and be right merry,
And sing with us now joyfully:
Nowell nowell, nowell nowell!

Not perhaps the colloquial speech of the prison inmates, admitted Simon, but the music was exciting and culminated in a thrilling fortissimo shout of "Nowell". If that did not raise the prison roof and send pulses racing, then nothing would. The rhythm was irregular but once the members of the choir had mastered it, he felt sure there would be no problems. Perhaps the greatest problem was the accompaniment. It was a bravado piece for the organ. Simon needed to rehearse it on the chapel piano - but there were few opportunities to do so. Perhaps he could persuade the prison chaplain to allow him twenty-minutes on the chapel piano at the conclusion of the Sunday morning service. The chaplain was an amenable man.

When Simon first arrived at the prison, he purposely avoided the chaplain. Seeing the chaplain in his clerical collar walking around the prison in a black suit rekindled too many memories of his father for him to want to meet him. The chaplain, however, was charged with greeting all new arrivals and making his availability known to them.

"Ah Simon," beamed the ruddy-faced chaplain at their first meeting in the Reception Centre. "I see this is your first experience of prison life. You won't find it easy, but, approached in a positive frame of mind, it's tolerable. The thing to do is to play to your strengths. So, tell me: what are your strengths?"

Simon suddenly felt drained of all vitality. What were his strengths? He felt as if he had none whatsoever. He had once been a successful schoolteacher, but all desire to teach had long since evaporated. He could no sooner stand in front of a class and teach musical cadences, major and minor scales, harmonics, Italian dynamic markings and syncopation than fly. All desire to teach had disappeared. And what was left? What possible good was he to anyone? He sat slumped in his chair unable to answer the chaplain's most basic question.

But it soon became apparent that the chaplain did not really need an answer. He had undertaken some background research of his own.

"I understand you were a music teacher?" he revealed, more as a statement of fact than a question.

Simon meekly nodded his head.

"Splendid!" enthused the chaplain. "Just what we need: someone to accompany the hymn-singing on Sundays."

This was the last thing Simon wanted to do. He had been required to accompany hymn-singing at school assemblies but, apart from that, he had kept a healthy distance between himself and all things associated with the church. Any religious faith he may once have possessed had long since been discarded. Accompanying religious statements of belief was not what he wanted, and so he remained mute in the chaplain's presence.

It was only later, when Simon came to experience the weekly, grinding prison regime, that he realised attending worship in the prison chapel on Sundays was infinitely preferable to being locked in his cell for the whole day. Not surprisingly, most of the other prisoners opted for the hour of Sunday worship in the company of other prisoners rather than solitary confinement in their cells.

Prison hymn-singing was a turgid experience. The ever-enthusiastic chaplain believed that hymn-singing constituted an important part of an act of worship and so, even though there was no one to accompany the singing, he bravely played recorded instrumental hymn accompaniments to which the prisoners could sing. Or not, depending on their inclination and religious temperament. Most refused to sing. They stood with their mouths resolutely shut as if daring the chaplain, or the handful of prison officers present, to make them sing. The chaplain's response was to increase the volume of the amplified accompaniment so as to make it impossible to tell whether or not anyone was singing. Consequently, Sunday hymn-singing consisted of listening to the same hymn-tune played over and over again (depending on how many verses there were to a hymn) by a computer-generated machine. To anyone remotely musical, it was the equivalent of purgatory.

Simon endured it for six months before he snapped and, approaching the chaplain, offered to play the chapel piano for the Sunday morning act of worship. He realised this was a risky thing to do because it would immediately bring him to the notice of other prisoners. Some might admire his skill on the keyboard, but the majority would see him as a toady, seeking to ingratiate himself with the prison staff. They would then seize every opportunity of making life difficult for him. But, for Simon's part, it offered a chance to play a real piano and turn hymn-singing into a gratifying musical experience rather than a mechanical travesty of what real music should be. The chaplain clearly appreciated the change of musical accompaniment and was surprised by the prisoners' greater participation in hymn-singing.

Simon had honed his accompaniment technique at innumerable school assemblies. He knew that playing loudly was not the best way to encourage reluctant singers and so he varied the dynamics between verses, employing crescendos when the melody line soared upwards, followed by sudden diminuendos when a hushed effect was most telling. He managed to inject musicality into the often-threadbare hymn-tunes. Even prisoners who exhibited undisguised contempt for all forms of religion were forced to acknowledge that Copeland had skill when it came to accompanying hymns. And those of a more sensitive disposition actually congratulated him on his piano-playing. The chaplain derived great satisfaction from the change that came about since recorded musical accompaniments had been replaced by live piano accompaniments. He noted a marked improvement in the ambience of the Sunday worship. This prompted him to float the idea of a prison choir.

At first, Simon was sceptical. He could not imagine prisoners volunteering to sing in a choir. They would be taunted unmercifully by the more brutish inmates. They would have to endure barbed comments, scoffing and other more extreme forms of abuse. Simon had quickly learnt that many of the inmates had sadistic tendencies. They appeared to take delight inflicting pain and suffering on other inmates. They were always on the look-out for any sign of weakness in one of the other prisoners that could be exploited and used to inflict pain or distress. This was often achieved surreptitiously. A cup of hot tea would inexplicably be knocked from the hand of the sacrificial victim scalding him badly in the process. A man would slip in the showers and emerge with a broken hand or a bruised face. A cigarette burn would mysteriously appear on the body of someone who did not smoke. These and other sadistic punishments were meted out on those who had done nothing to antagonize their fellow inmates but had simply been singled out for punishment because of some perceived weakness or abnormality. Singing in a chapel choir would inevitably single someone out as a goody-two-shoes, a holy joe or a sycophantic scab and elicit a punishment that went with such a label. There was no way any of the prisoners on Simon's wing would ever agree to sing in a prison choir.

But the chaplain was more optimistic. He may have taken ordination vows from spiritual and religious convictions, but his years in the prison service had taught him a certain worldly cunning. He knew that the secret of success was not to appeal to the meek of the earth but to the strong. "Have you ever heard Winston sing?" he enquired of Simon. He referred to a West Indian prisoner who resembled the biblical Samson. "When I was undertaking my rounds on E Wing, I heard the most amazing sound coming from one of the cells. It was someone singing a Negro spiritual. I don't think I've ever before heard such a rich sonorous bass voice. It immediately reminded me of Paul Robeson - you know, the great black American singer. It was Winston singing to himself in his cell. I congratulated him on his magnificent bass voice and, although he attempted to make light of it, claiming it was white slave-traders who had made him and his countrymen sing that way, I could tell he was proud of his ability to sing. Now, if we could persuade him to join a prison choir, no one is going to rag him – not if they want to avoid broken bones, that is."

Simon had to smile at the chaplain's worldly wiles. The chaplain clearly saw Winston as a stalking horse who could lead others to join the choir. But Simon was still not convinced it was something he wanted to do.

With that sixth sense the other-worldly often possess, the chaplain realised Simon was undecided and so delivered his *coup de grace*.

"You could have complete freedom to choose the music," he declared. "You know much more about music than I do, and I suspect you're familiar with a wide range of Christmas music. I would leave the selection of the music entirely to you. It could be your Christmas Carol Service."

It was a tempting prospect. Simon knew a wide range of Christmas music - from medieval plainsong to contemporary pieces - but he was still not certain he was the person to train and lead a prison choir.

"Have a think about it," concluded the chaplain with another of his wide smiles. And that was how the matter was left.

Sometime later, when Simon was sitting in the association area, he was surprised to see the massive outline of Winston towering above him.

"I hear you wants me to sing in your choir," stated the West Indian, staring intently at Simon with fierce, coal-black eyes. "Just you get this, man: I aint gonna sing any of them soppy songs about little donkeys or little drummer-boys. If I'm gonna sing in your choir, I want to sing real music. Get it?"

Simon meekly nodded his head. The existence of this first choir recruit took him completely by surprise. But Winston was clearly not a man with whom to trifle, and so Simon sought to turn the situation to his advantage.

"That's great news. I'm only interested in real music. I can promise you some great pieces to sing. The only trouble is we need some more singers."

"That's no problem, man," retorted the big friendly giant. "I know half a dozen others who can sing. I'll have a word with them. They'll sing if I tell them."

Simon smiled another furtive smile. Never before had he known a choir formed on the basis of fear. Those whom Winston designated singers had no alternative but to join the choir – if they wanted to avoid a nasty accident, that was.

And so it was that the first rehearsal of the Prison Choir took place in the chapel immediately after association on the last Tuesday in October. Eight inmates clustered around the chapel piano to practise some musical warming-up exercises.

Simon wanted to hear each of the men sing to gauge the quality and range of their voices. He wanted to know if there were any tenor voices or if he was limited to baritone and bass voices. However, he did not want to put the men on the spot by subjecting them to an audition, and so he got all of them singing ascending and descending scales together using numbers.

One, two, one.
One, two, three, two, one.
One, two, three, four, three, two, one.
One, two, three, four, five, four, three, two, one.
One, two, three, four, five, six, five, four, three, two, one.
One, two, three, four, five, six, seven, six, five, four, three, two, one.
One, two, three, four, five, six, seven, eight, seven, six, five, four, three, two, one.

Smiles and some shaking of heads accompanied this exercise in musical notation and mental dexterity. But Simon sensed the men enjoyed the challenge and it enabled him to differentiate the voices in his embryonic choir. During his school teaching days, he always strove to stretch pupils to the limit of their ability. Not for him the easy option. He wanted pupils to strive for ever greater advancement. He discovered it was only from concerted effort that higher standards were achieved and personal satisfaction gained. The motley crew assembled around the prison piano may not have been top-flight achievers, but, nevertheless, he believed they should be stretched to see what they could achieve.

Some of the men rather sheepishly admitted to having sung in church choirs when they were kids, but none of them had ever sung in four-part harmony. It would be a challenge to teach them to do this and get them to hold their part against the sound of the others. But they had time on their side – and few other distractions. It was not as if choir practice had to compete with a night out with mates at the pub, or a stroll in the park with a girlfriend, or a visit to the local cinema. The prison choristers had nowhere else to go. They either attended choir practice or were confined to their cells. Not surprisingly, they opted for choir practice. The number of singers soon grew as other prisoners opted for an hour or so around the piano rather than entombed in solitary confinement.

All of this meant Simon had to provide multiple copies of words and music for the men in his choir. It was a tedious task, but it passed the hours and, when he was absorbed in music, all other concerns disappeared. Music had always been his solace: a private world into which he could retreat whenever the pressures of life became unbearable. It was his inner world where emotions were transformed into things of beauty; memories captured in an aura of sound; and the restlessness that had dogged him all his life translated into passionate yearning.

He wondered if any of his fledgling choir members would ever experience such feelings or whether the hardships and cruelties of the life they had suffered had robbed them of all sensitivity and the appreciation of the beauties of music. It was difficult to know. His knowledge of his singers was still at an early stage. There was a lot of bridge-building to do before they trusted him enough to share their innermost thoughts and feelings. Men in prison found it wiser to keep thoughts and feelings to themselves if they wanted to avoid ridicule, taunting or unwanted attention from the more sadistic members of the prison population.

As he transcribed notes onto paper for each of his eighteen choristers, he heard their voices singing in his head. There was Winston, with his sonorous bass voice; and his fellow Caribbean countrymen for whom music was such an integral part of life. They possessed a great sense of rhythm plus a natural exuberance that found its true expression in song. It would be a challenge disciplining their innate musicality and teaching them the art of listening to others and singing as a group rather than as unrestrained and uninhibited individuals.

Then there was Sarsung, the effeminate Indonesian, who was the butt of so many cruel barbs. He was a sensitive man who had suffered greatly at the hands of others but refused to be bowed or defeated. The prison choir was the silken ladder by which he climbed out of his personal abyss and misery and experienced beauty and hope. He had a light, lyrical tenor voice that was ably suited to singing the melody lines of the carols they were learning.

Justin and Cooper were a couple of confidence tricksters who had defrauded innumerable businessmen, but had no qualms whatsoever about their conduct. The rich were there to be robbed, as far as they were concerned, and they used their natural wiles and cunning to relieve others of their wealth.

"We're the Robin Hoods of today," they cheekily boasted. "We rob the rich to pay the poor. And, as the two of us are poor, that means we rob the rich to pay us. Society should be grateful for men like us righting the wrongs of a corrupt capitalist system. Politicians talk about the redistribution of wealth, but it's left to Jus and me to put it into practice. The rich are greedy. They don't need excessive wealth. They could easily share it round and we'd all be better off. But no; they squirrel it away and hope no one is going to find it. Selfish, I call it. I told the chaplain as much, and he agreed with me. He said, 'Give to him that asketh of thee, for it is more blessed to give than to receive'. So there you have it. Straight from the horses' mouth! I like that chaplain fella, which is why I agreed to sing in his choir. We revolutionaries have got to stick together, I say."

Duncan was a different kettle of fish altogether. He was morose and moody. Simon was never sure whether he really enjoyed singing in the choir or whether he saw the choir as the least of all possible evils. He was taciturn and, although he had a certain musicality, he never appeared to enjoy singing. He kept himself to himself and never offered a comment or gave expression to his feelings. He was a cold fish.

Dylan had a very pleasing light baritone voice. His only singing experience, prior to joining the prison choir, was as a member of the crowd at Cardiff Arms Park thundering out *Land of my fathers* to spur the home side to victory in the Six Nations Championship. Something of the joy and emotion of that experience had prompted him to volunteer for the prison choir. Singing in four-part harmony was proving more difficult than thundering out *Land of my fathers*, but, despite protestations to the contrary, he was enjoying making music with the other men at the weekly choir practice.

Choir practices were highly volatile. The members did not take kindly to instruction.

"Why you making us sing this line over and over again, man, when there's so many more lines we ain't sung yet? We's never going to get to de end at this rate."

"Shut it man! You's the reason we have to sing it over and over again. If you concentrated on doing what Mr Copeland tells ya we could all move on. Ain't that right, Mr Copeland?"

"Well, it is better to get things right before moving on to new material," placated Simon.

"Course it is, man."

"Is you saying I'm singing it wrong? Just you watch it, man. No one makes false accusations about me and lives."

With such outbursts, choir practices were highly volatile affairs. But such moments were offset by occasions when the men achieved a rare unanimity of sound that transformed them from a group of social rejects into an otherworldly choir of angels storming the portals of heaven. It was moments like this that brought a smile to their faces and won warm praise from Simon.

"You're really listening to one another," enthused Simon, "You're not singing as eighteen different people but as one vocal entity."

"That's right, man. We're a choir of angels singing in a pit of demons. My mamma would be real proud of me right now."

"What? Proud that you're doing time for murder?"

"I'm not talking about that! I'm a-talking about this singing. My mamma loved her hymn-singing. She may not have had much of a voice, but, man, had she got a pair of lungs! She could holler louder than anyone else in church."

Simon smiled at this rare insight into Winston's family life, but he knew he must not let Winston get carried away.

"There's a time to sing loudly and there's a time to sing softly. Good musicians know when one is right and the other is wrong. I still think we're climaxing too early in the final verse. Let's try it once again and see if we can gradually increase the volume to make it more exciting. Keep your greatest volume in reserve for the final 'Nowell'."

Once choir practice was over and the other prisoners prepared to disperse, Simon tidied up the music, closed the piano lid, and straightened the chairs at the front of the chapel under the watchful eye of the prison officers. Once he had completed the tidying-up, a prison officer led him back to his cell.

"Just let me give you a bit of advice," said the prison officer. "If I was you, I'd watch my backside. Some of the inmates here seem to have taken a dislike to you. They think you're sucking up to the screws and trying to get into the Governor's good books with all this choir stuff. If I was you, I'd be very careful. We don't want any accidents now, do we?"

And with that, he jangled his keys and motioned for Simon to enter his cell for the night.

This unexpected encounter with the prison officer rather unnerved Simon. He knew he had to be on the alert at all times and do all in his power not to draw attention to himself, but he thought that now he was working with a group of fellow prisoners, many of whom were capable of acting as his guardian angels, he had nothing to fear from the more perverted and twisted element within the prison. Not so, it would seem. His prominence as the chapel pianist on Sundays, coupled with the formation of the prison choir, had clearly brought him to the attention of either the envious or the downright psychotic. It was not a pleasant thought.

As the door of his cell clanged shut, he sat on the edge of his bed and put his head in his hands. Why was he being tortured yet more for the mistakes he had made? Being deprived of his liberty and locked away from concert halls, choirs and recorded music was one thing. But to be forced to live with men who, it seemed, should be in psychiatric institutions rather than prison, was taking punishment to an entirely different level. Why should he be made to live in fear? Why should he have to second-guess the actions of others? Why should he have to ensure he was always within sight of a prison officer? Why should anxiety be added to his loss of liberty?

When the judge sentenced him to two years imprisonment, he knew it would be a difficult time. He was a sensitive soul. He appreciated the higher things of life. He read poetry. He liked to see the Royal Ballet Company perform in Birmingham. He loved to commit to manuscript paper the music that welled-up inside him like a bubbling fountain. He knew he would miss of all these. But he had been unprepared for the social isolation he experienced within the prison walls.

It was true there were many hundreds of other inmates living within the cramped confines of the antiquated prison buildings; but none of them were his friends. Furthermore, none of them was ever likely to be a friend. They did not share his interests, his sensitivity or his passions. He had been cast adrift in an alien land with no one to love and no one to love him.

Simon had always craved love. His mother belonged to a generation that did not make a show of affection. She certainly cared for him and ensured he never went hungry or thirsty or lacking clothing or shelter; but she never showered him with love. An arm around his shoulder was the nearest she ever came to giving him a hug. A kiss on the forehead was the nearest she ever came to an outward demonstration of love. A soft word of encouragement was the nearest she ever came to an expression of affection. His mother had always appeared to live in the shadow of his father. He was the dominant parent and his mother seemed quite content for that to be so.

He remembered his mother always being occupied in good works. She saw her role in life as one who visited the sick and the elderly. This was Christian love in action, she maintained. It may have been the disinterested love of the Good Samaritan on the road from Jerusalem to Jericho, but it always struck Simon as a very impersonal and emotionally cold form of love. He yearned for the love Tristan had for Isolde; the love that Abelard showered upon Heloise; and the love that caused Romeo and Juliet to die rather than be parted. That was the love that moved mountains. That was the love that spoke to the heart. That was the love that caused men to attempt the impossible and perish in the attempt if need be.

Simon experienced love principally through music. Composers had miraculously captured and recreated the all-consuming power of love in some of their most beautiful music. He remembered, as a young boy, stumbling upon a recording of Tchaikovsky's *Fantasy Overture Romeo and Juliet*: the excitement of the Capulets and Montagues' feud dissolving into the soaring lyrical theme of the two lovers. It was a moment of revelation for him. Although he had never experienced such an emotion in his own life, he knew instantly what it must be like. His heart soared with the music and ached with the pathos of the final bars as the music dissolved into tragedy and resignation. In a way, the music mirrored the course of his life: supreme exaltation leading to despair and tragedy.

He once tried to explain to his mother how music encapsulated his deepest emotions, but his mother appeared strangely obtuse. Music meant little to her and she could not understand her son's obsession with it. Music was all very well for hymn-singing, and she could appreciate its function for dancing, but apart from that, music held little interest for her.

His mother was still mobile even though she was now well into her eighties. The one visit she made to the prison to see her errant son had not been a success. She entered the Prison Visitors Room with a straight back and a no-nonsense look on her face. She was wearing her preferred tweed suit and would have had a handbag hanging from her wrist had it not been removed by the prison authorities before she was allowed access to the jail. She gave Simon a tight-lipped smile as she took her seat at the other side of a plain wooden table that separated her from her son.

"You're looking pale," she declared with hardly a trace of emotion in her voice. "I expect it's through being indoors all the time."

"I am allowed recreation time out-of-doors for a short period each day," replied Simon, "although I can't pretend it compares with the outdoor experiences I had when I was a child living in the country."

Then, sensing his mother was unsure how to continue, Simon took the initiative and asked, "How are you managing on your own?"

Simon's father, who was ten-years older than his mother, had died the previous year. His parents had been married sixty-years. His father had continued as a parish priest until the age of seventy when compulsory retirement meant he had to vacate the spacious vicarage in which they had lived for the majority of their life and move to a small bungalow provided by the Church of England Pensions Board. His father found it difficult making the adjustment from being the person at the centre of parish life to a seeming nobody living in a retirement bungalow. His discontent spilled over into his marriage making things very difficult for his wife.

She did her best to encourage her husband and sought opportunities for him to visit elderly people living alone in the district. But, now that he was no longer the vicar of a parish, the elderly did not welcome his visits. Indeed, he got the distinct impression he was a *persona non grata* in many of the homes he visited.

He may well have had himself to blame for this. He believed pastoral visits should have a definite spiritual purpose. And so, he was never reticent about enquiring into the prayer life of those he visited, or the strength or otherwise of their "commitment to the Lord Jesus". He also felt it incumbent to read the scriptures to those whom he visited, irrespective of whether they wanted this or not. Whilst he was vicar of a parish, his parishioners endured this spiritual tutelage, but now he had no official position within the Church, and they were no longer beholden to him for burial space in his churchyard or a church funeral service when they died, they saw no reason to suffer his oppressive religious visits. Doors that his wife carefully opened for him were soon closed and the former vicar of Chorley found himself unwanted and unwelcome. This induced a form of depression simmering on righteous anger. His long-suffering wife had to bear the brunt of his great unhappiness.

She bore up well under the strain; but now that her husband had passed to his heavenly reward, she was free to follow her own interests without constantly having to think about him.

"I keep very active and, fortunately, I enjoy excellent health," she declared. "I recently took over as Treasurer of the local branch of the Mothers' Union." She revealed this information without the slightest trace of irony or, indeed, of pleasure. "It's always so difficult to find anyone willing to take on such jobs. I managed the housekeeping budget satisfactorily and, because I am a clergy widow, I suppose they thought I was trustworthy. Anyway, it's not too arduous, and I'm sure I'll be able to cope."

Simon had hoped his mother would share some of her inner feelings following the death of her husband, but, once again, she kept her emotions under strict control, preferring to talk about mundane matters rather than emotions and her mental state. It had always been thus, mused Simon.

"Fortunately," continued his mother, "they do not know I have a son in jail. If they did, I'm sure they wouldn't be nearly so trusting."

"I'm sorry, mother," replied Simon. "I know I've brought disgrace upon you and the family. It was the last thing I wanted to do."

"Then you should have been more responsible and not flouted God's laws in the brazen way you did," she countered. "You cannot claim ignorance. You were brought up in a respectable home. Your father and I taught you the difference between right and wrong from an early age. We deliberately shielded you from anyone who might lead you astray. I cannot think of anything more we could have done to keep you on the straight and narrow. But you turned your back on us and completely disregarded the moral laws by which we lived. You trampled on the fifth commandment by dishonouring your father and mother. You have brought disgrace upon the whole family. The only

mercy is that your father is no longer alive to witness the humiliation. I don't know how he would have coped."
This impassioned speech was the nearest his mother come to revealing the thoughts and emotions that lay beneath her resolute outward appearance. She had vented her pent-up anger over her youngest son's behaviour, and it had drained her of all vitality. She rose from her seat and prepared to leave. But Simon could not let her leave thinking he had deliberately set out to humiliate and shame his parents.
"No, wait a moment," pleaded Simon, as his mother hovered between standing and sitting. "You must listen to me. You and father had a solid marriage that saw you through many difficult times. It cannot have been easy raising four boys on just a clergy stipend. But you did, and I will always have the greatest admiration for what you achieved. I never sought to belittle your parenting or show ingratitude for all you did for me. But what worked for you does not necessarily work today. Women nowadays want a life of their own. They want to meet other people outside their normal social circle. They want to experience different lifestyles and discover what is right for them. They want excitement in their lives. They want to see the world and broaden their horizons. The old ways no longer work."
His mother's back stiffened. Simon could tell she did not approve of the changes that had come about in society during her lifetime, and he knew she would be incapable of accepting what he next had to say.
"You see, mother," he continued, "women today want to experience life in all its fullness. They're not content with being dutiful wives, cooking meals for their husband,

cleaning the house, washing and ironing the linen, purchasing groceries and rearing a large brood of children. They want something more, something greater. They sense there is more to life than this. They want to experience love in all its richness and splendour."

His mother snorted. "What they want to experience is fornication, adultery and other sins that are totally repugnant to God and all right-thinking people. And you played along with this. I need hardly remind you that 'The wages of sin is death'."

If Simon was to make any headway with his mother, he knew he had to use a different tack; and so he played the religious card.

"But haven't you always maintained that God is a God of love? If God loves us and wants us to love one another, surely that cannot be contrary to his will? What you see around you today is merely God's love overflowing in the lives of others. That cannot be bad, can it?"

"There is love and there is lust," retorted his mother, with her icy blue eyes boring deep into Simon's soul. "It needs a strong moral compass to distinguish between the two. Alas, your generation seems incapable of doing so; hence all the pain and misery in the world. You wouldn't be here in prison if you'd observed the laws of God. They were not given to restrict our freedom and prevent us experiencing the fullness of God's love: they were given so we might know His love in all its purity and fullness."

Simon knew there was an unbridgeable chasm between him and his mother. To his mother, the love of God consisted of acting as a doormat over which others might walk, performing charitable deeds and observing a strict set of moral laws. To him, the love of God was an unquenchable river flowing through his veins and lifting him above the mundane and superficial things of life. God's love was the spiritual power he experienced that bore him aloft and enabled him to see the world in an entirely new way. God's love was a force for good that transformed relationships and ennobled life. But he knew his mother would never understand this. Clearly, she had not experienced love in this way and it was useless trying to convince her.

"I can see you haven't learned the error of your ways," replied his mother. "Perhaps two years in this place will dampen your ardour and help you see where you went wrong. It is never too late to repent."

Simon sighed deeply. Secretly he hoped nothing would ever dampen his ardour. He had been created a loving child of God and he hoped he would remain one for the remainder of his life – sharing love freely with those who thought similarly.

"Well, I can't stop here all afternoon," continued his mother as she rose from her seat. "Are you expecting any other visitors?"

Simon shook his head. He had received no visitors whatsoever since arriving at the prison. He had been quietly jettisoned by his friends, colleagues and associates. No one had extended the hand of friendship, a listening ear or an understanding shoulder on which to cry. He had received no visitors since commencing his custodial sentence. No one had visited him – not even his wife.

CHAPTER FOUR

It was just before Christmas that Sandra came to Simon's attention. Like all school music teachers, he was required to organise an annual Christmas Carol Service. He carefully put together a programme of bible readings and carols for the service. The orchestra was to play the pastoral overture from Corelli's *Christmas Oratorio*; the school choir would sing five carols from around the world, plus a specially-composed carol of his own; and the congregation would let rip with *Hark the herald angels sing* and *O come all ye faithful*. But something else was needed, he thought, to bring the service to a fitting climax. It was then he thought of including a solo item in the service.

He had discovered a girl in the Upper Sixth who had a lovely soprano voice. She sang in the school choir, but Simon was sure she was capable of singing on her own; and so, he approached her with the suggestion she sang Adolphe Adam's *O Holy Night* as a solo. After the customary modesty common to girls of her age, she eventually agreed and she and Simon stayed behind after school to rehearse the piece. She had a remarkably pure soprano voice. Her intonation was perfect and she imbued the words of the Christmas song with a warmth and depth far beyond her years. Simon was captivated. He had always been deeply susceptible to the female singing voice and here he encountered it in all its purity and beauty. Together, the two of them perfected the integration of the rippling piano accompaniment with the song's slow, sustained, vocal line. It seemed to Simon as if two souls were blending into one in an ecstasy of otherworldly bliss. And when the piece soared to the high sustained A at its conclusion, it seemed to him as if the very doors of heaven were flung open and the full radiance of heaven flooded the two of them with ethereal splendour.

It was with tears in his eyes that Simon looked at Sandra and muttered, "Thank you. That was absolutely beautiful." She could tell he was deeply moved by the music and bestowed a shy, beatific smile upon him. It was a smile he never forgot.

The Carol Service went well. The Headmaster heaped praise upon Simon, telling him it was by far the most accomplished carol service he could remember.

"I've had many parents comment on the high musical standard you've achieved since you joined the staff. Your efforts will not go unnoticed by the governors, I feel sure. Music has always been one of this school's strengths and I'm sure that if you continue to work hard at it you'll raise the bar even higher. Well done, Copeland!"

With a hearty shake of Simon's hand, the Headmaster disappeared to bestow congratulations on others who had contributed to the success of the evening. Simon, for his part, wanted to congratulate his star performer. But tracking her down proved quite a challenge.

"Has anyone seen Sandra?" he enquired of the members of the orchestra as they folded away their music-stands and shuffled discarded sheets of music.

"I saw her heading for the cloakrooms," replied one of the more forthcoming pupils. Simon went in search of her. He found her alone in the cloakrooms applying a school scarf around her neck whilst wrestling with a music case.

"Ah, found you!" exclaimed Simon. "I just wanted to congratulate you on your magnificent performance. I always knew you'd sing it well but, you know, sometimes nerves get in the way, and the final result is not as good as it might be. But not in your case! You sang like a seasoned professional without a trace of nerves. Were you nervous at all?"

The seventeen-year-old pupil gave Simon a shy smile. "Just a bit," she admitted, "during the long introduction before I came in; but once I started singing, I forgot about everything else and simply concentrated on the music."

"I said you sang like a professional," continued Simon looking at the young girl under the utilitarian lighting of the cloakrooms and noting her long, shoulder-length black hair falling over her shoulders. "But I didn't really mean that. Professional singers are often note-perfect and carry off a performance with aplomb, but they don't have the qualities your voice possesses. You have such a pure, clean sound. It has an untarnished innocence that is your very own."

Sandra blushed and cast her eyes downwards. There was something about her modesty that fascinated Simon. Here was someone with a natural musical gift but no pretensions. She gave herself no airs or graces.

"Have you ever heard Dame Kiri Te Kanawa sing?" he enquired.

Sandra shook her head. She had never even heard of the New Zealand soprano.

"She has many of the vocal qualities you possess," he continued. "She came from very humble origins but is now an international star. She proves what's possible with determination and sensitive coaching. She's singing at the Symphony Hall on Wednesday next week. If I can get tickets, would you like to come with me to listen to her?"

This proposition came completely out of the blue and Sandra was unsure how to reply. She was unsure how her friends would react if they knew she was going to a concert – albeit, a classical music concert – with the school's music teacher. Would they be jealous, or would they taunt her unmercifully? And what would her parents think? They were divorced. Her father lived in Cyprus and served in the British Army whilst her mother had remarried and was living in the USA with her new husband. Originally, Sandra was to travel to Cyprus to spend Christmas with her father, but the plans had changed, and she had now to remain in the UK with her aunt. It was not a particularly alluring prospect. A night out with the young music teacher might relieve the boredom of the approaching Christmas holidays. And so, after just a moment's hesitation, she gave a shy nod of assent.

"If you give me your phone number," continued Simon, "I'll let you know if I'm successful obtaining tickets. We can then make the necessary arrangements to get to Symphony Hall."

With a wide smile and a wave of his hand he was off, leaving a somewhat bemused Sandra to button up her coat and return to the unwelcoming aunt's home in some perplexity.

Over the next few days there was an exchange of telephone numbers and Simon was able to inform Sandra he had successfully obtained tickets for the Kiri Te Kanawa concert.

He arranged to pick her up in his somewhat battered old sports car at six o'clock the following Monday evening. Rather than collect her from her aunt's house, he suggested a rendezvous outside the central railway station. There were always plenty of people coming and going at the train station and so it would be unlikely that anyone would pay much attention to a man collecting a young girl there.

Sandra, for her part, merely informed her aunt she was going on a school visit to Symphony Hall. She did not regard this as a lie. She was going on a visit to the concert hall arranged by her school music teacher. The fact that she was the only pupil was something she decided to conceal from her aunt. There was no point in provoking an unnecessary confrontation.

She spent much of the afternoon before the concert agonising over what she should wear. Did those who go to classical concerts dress up for the occasion? Should she aim for something elegant or should she wear something similar to what she would wear to a party? Should she strive to make herself look older than her seventeen years or should she simply revel in her youthfulness? Should she wear make-up, or would her music teacher expect to see the same natural face he saw every day at school?

And what would Mr Copeland be wearing? She knew his first name was Simon, but she had never used it. Teachers were always known by their surname and addressed accordingly. Should she continue to call him Mr Copeland even though they were not at school? It was uncharted territory for her, and she was unsure how she should act. Perhaps the best thing was to avoid using his name altogether.

After much deliberation, she eventually chose to wear one of her more conservative dresses. She reasoned it would not draw attention to her and yet was not frumpy or dowdy. She opted for the very lightest use of make-up simply to accentuate her large brown eyes and give her cheekbones a healthy hue. Suitably attired, she bade farewell to her aunt (who appeared unconcerned about where she was going or what she was doing) and walked the short distance to the railway station to await the arrival of her transport.

Since school term had finished for the Christmas holidays, Simon had time on his hands. He intended to return to the vicarage at Chorley for a family Christmas gathering, but he was in no hurry to do so. The thought of two weeks holed up in a country vicarage did not excite him. And so, he delayed his return for as long as possible.

He tried to busy himself setting the words of a Thomas Hardy poem to music. Once he had immersed himself in music, all other thoughts disappeared and time itself ceased to exist. But, on this occasion, he found he was unable to concentrate on his music. He felt restless. And his thoughts continually returned to Sandra and the visit to the concert hall that evening.

One of his colleagues, who taught science at the school, had remarked, "That girl has an amazing voice, don't you think?"

"She has the purest, most ethereal voice I think I've ever heard," replied Simon. "She has the ability to elevate music to an entirely new level."

"Steady on, old man," re-joined his colleague. "I said she had an amazing voice. You make her sound like a siren luring men to their destruction. If she has that effect on you, you'd better watch out. Remember she's a pupil and you're a member of staff. Don't get blown away by a pretty girl's voice or you might live to regret it."

Simon dismissed those words as the ignorant reaction of someone who did not understand the elevating power of music. To liken Sandra to an enchantress was patently absurd. She displayed no devious feminine wiles. In Simon's eyes, she was as pure and innocent as a new-born babe. Nevertheless, the cautionary words of the science teacher told him he must be circumspect in his dealings with his star singer; and this was partly why he chose to collect Sandra from outside the railway station where they could be anonymous amidst the hustle and bustle of arriving and departing passengers. Also, he did not want to meet Sandra's parents or any other members of her family. His sense of self-preservation informed him it was best to keep the visit to the concert hall a secret from others.

Sandra was waiting for him as he pulled up outside the railway station at a little after six o'clock.

"Sorry to keep you waiting," he smiled as he reached over to open the passenger's door of his two-seater car. "I got immersed in a piece of music I'm composing and didn't realise how the time had flown."

This was untrue. Time had dragged intolerably all afternoon and musical inspiration had been in short supply as he waited for evening to arrive and the planned visit to Symphony Hall.

Sandra smiled a wan smile. Did she know he was not telling the truth?

"That's OK," she replied, "I haven't been waiting long."

"I do hope you're going to enjoy tonight's concert," continued Simon. "It's a pretty mixed bag of musical goodies; but I think you'll appreciate Kiri Te Kanawa. She's singing Richard Strauss' *Four Last Songs*. Do you know them?"

It was a facile question. What seventeen-year-old girl was likely to know the work a German composer penned at the very end of his life? His question had the effect of making her painfully aware of the gulf that separated them. He had been to university and acquired a wide knowledge of music, whereas she was merely a schoolgirl struggling with 'A' levels in the hope of gaining entry to a university. She was seventeen and he was twenty-four. And yet he clearly liked her. She could tell that.

"*The Four Last Songs* were Strauss' last outpouring for the soprano voice," continued Simon. "He loved the soprano voice more than any other. Indeed, he married a soprano – Friedelane Pauline - and most of his songs were written with her in mind. He poured his love for Pauline into the

songs; and, although by the time he composed *The Four Last Songs*, she was far too old to sing them, they're really his valedictory farewell to her, to love and to the world."
Sandra smiled another of her wan smiles, uncertain how to reply. Her music teacher certainly did not waste himself on small talk. She found his intensity both unnerving and yet strangely compelling. But she kept her hands clasped on her lap and allowed him to continue talking as they sped on their way to Symphony Hall.
"Dame Kiri Te Kanava must have sung these songs scores of times but, whenever I've heard her, she always manages to bring something new to them. She has this unique ability to lift the words and the notes off the paper and imbue them with an almost mystical feeling. I shall be interested to see if you, a fellow soprano, sense this."
Then, realising he had monopolized the conversation since they met, he asked, "And what have you been up to since last Friday when school ended?"
"Not a great deal," was her honest answer. "I was supposed to be flying to Cyprus to spend Christmas with my father; but there's been a change of plan and he has to work elsewhere. My mother and her new husband have gone away together and so I'll be spending Christmas with my aunt in this country."
"Oh, that's hard luck!" exclaimed Simon. "Are you expected to mope around with your aunt until the start of the new term?"
"It looks that way," replied a somewhat resigned Sandra.

Simon made a mental note to see if there was anything he could do to rectify this situation. Meanwhile, they continued on their way to Symphony Hall.

After parking the car in a vast underground labyrinth of concrete, the two of them entered the milling concourse of the concert hall and found their seats in the Circle. Sandra removed her coat and draped it over the back of her seat. Simon had no coat, having braved the December weather wearing merely his jacket and trousers.

Sandra was relieved to discover there was no recognized dress code for classical music concerts and that her modest emerald-green dress looked perfectly acceptable amongst the other concert-goers.

Simon noted the dress she was wearing and the way it flattered her nubile body. It fitted perfectly at the bust, accentuating her youthful figure. It clung loosely to her body before passing over her slender hips with barely a glance. The dress terminated just above her knees and revealed a pair of beautifully-shaped legs. He was about to make a favourable comment about her dress but thought better of it. Any personal comments about her appearance might cause her embarrassment and make her think he had an ulterior motive in inviting her to the concert. And so he kept quiet.

The concert began with one of Mozart's later symphonies. Although Mozart was regarded as a god by most musicians, Simon could take him or leave him. There was no denying Mozart's skill and inventiveness but, compared with later composers, his music lacked full-blooded emotion. It was the music of the aristocratic court – all surface charm and wit but without passion or guts.

"Well, what did you make of that?" Simon asked turning to the young girl sitting beside him at the conclusion of the piece.

"It was hummable and bright," replied Sandra, "but it didn't make me want to leap out of my seat and start singing or dancing."

"That's a good thing," laughed Simon. "I'm not sure the other members of the audience would have appreciated it if you had done either of those things."

She laughed in return, revealing a set of perfectly white teeth.

"Perhaps Mozart wanted to demonstrate what a clever young man he was rather than get his audience jumping up and down in their seats," continued Simon. "I've always had ambivalent feelings about him. His cleverness often gets in the way of any genuine feeling or emotion, I think. Anyway, the next work in the concert is very different. I do hope you'll like it."

Just at that moment their conversation was interrupted by an explosion of enthusiastic applause as the conductor ushered Dame Kiri Te Kanawa onto the stage of the concert hall. The members of the greatly enlarged orchestra stood to greet the renowned soprano, who floated across the stage wearing an ankle-length, shimmering scarlet dress, before taking her position beside the conductor's podium. After acknowledging the applause of the concertgoers with a gracious bow and a warm smile, she focussed her attention on the task before her.

Simon glanced at Sandra and the two of them exchanged smiles.

A hush fell over the auditorium as the opening bars of the orchestral introduction to Strauss' *Four Last Songs* crept over the expectant listeners. When Dame Kiri entered, her voice sounded like another instrument weaving its way into the rich tapestry of sound that Strauss had created from his musical imagination. The delicate, mercurial sound of Dame Kiri's vocal line soared and ebbed like a never-ending river flowing effortlessly towards some distant ocean in which all human desires and longings were submerged in heavenly oblivion.

Sandra stole a sideways glance at her music teacher as the music surged and ebbed. She saw that he was completely absorbed in its sound-world. It was as if Dame Kiri held him in the palm of her hand and he was a piece of pliable clay that she moulded with each musical phrase, lifting him from the commonplace to the heights of heaven.

Although she did not know the music, and the German words were lost on her, Sandra was acutely aware of the skill of the soloist. She appreciated the importance of correct breathing to enable musical phrases to float on the air rather than seem snatched and grasped in an uncomfortable manner. She noticed how Dame Kiri held herself in reserve so she could end her phrases with an additional lift, thus increasing the dramatic effect. But, most of all, she marvelled at Dame Kiri's vocal range – from deep low ebony notes that throbbed with passion to ethereal silvery high notes that sparkled like diamonds glinting in the sun.

"If only I could possess such a voice," she thought to herself. But then she remembered that her music teacher had told her she had a voice very similar to Dame Kiri's and that "with determination and some skilful coaching" she would be able to sing just like the New Zealand superstar. Banishing such thoughts, she concentrated on the music as it moved remorselessly towards its conclusion.

In the last of the four songs, Strauss bade farewell to the world. The music grew in intensity as the bitter-sweet thought of death crept over the work. The pain of bidding farewell to the world and all that was beautiful was heart-wrenching. Simon was completely immersed in the music. As the emotional intensity of the music increased, he was overwhelmed by its power and, without realising it, he unconsciously gripped the armrest of his seat to steady himself and remain anchored. The armrest was all that separated him from Sandra.

Although her emotional reaction to the music was nowhere near as extreme as Simon's, she was holding the armrests on either side of her seat. This meant that when Simon suddenly clasped his hand on the dividing armrest, he inadvertently clasped his hand over hers. It was an electrifying moment for both of them. It was as if a high-voltage electric current passed between them, sending shockwaves that penetrated to the very core of their being. Somehow the music's passion had spilled over into their own lives. For one split second, they were welded together in an ecstasy of otherworldly bliss. It was a feeling that neither of them had experienced before and, for a moment, neither knew how to react. Neither dared look into the other's eyes. They both sat, with hands fused together, in a traumatic trance, staring ahead at the diminutive figure of Dame Kiri far below them, who was now acknowledging the applause of the concertgoers. Simon was torn between letting go of the small hand he gripped in his left hand to join in the tumultuous applause and wanting the handclasp to last for ever. Sandra shared his internal dilemma and waited to see what he would do.

When it would have been unconscionable to withhold applause any longer, Simon reluctantly let go of the small hand on the armrest and politely applauded. By so doing, he allowed Sandra to add her applause and appreciation for the smiling soloist.

As the applause eventually died away, Simon felt it necessary to apologize to his pupil for his physical expression of emotion at the conclusion of the work.

"I'm sorry about that," he stuttered. "I do tend to get carried away when I'm listening to beautiful music and I'm often unaware what I'm doing."

Sandra smiled a knowing smile and said, "I understand. The music was very beautiful. It must be very easy to be carried away by such intense sounds."

Simon blinked in amazement. Had she found the music intense? Did music have this effect upon her? Was she, perhaps, a kindred spirit?

He gazed with a new intensity at the young girl sitting beside him. She was certainly very beautiful. Her long, glossy black hair cascaded over her shoulders onto her emerald dress and encircled her innocent face in an aura of loveliness. Her deep brown eyes sparkled with youthful

enthusiasm; and yet her manner was reserved and a little shy. She smiled at Simon before adding, "Thank you so much for introducing me to such a beautiful piece of music and enabling me to hear Dame Kiri sing so brilliantly."
Returning to earth, Simon said, "I'm glad you enjoyed the experience. As I said before, I think your voice is very similar to hers. I would very much like to help you work on your voice so that - who knows? – one day you can appear on the concert platform of the Symphony Hall to tumultuous applause."
Sandra smiled again before adding, "That's very kind of you."
Then, sensing the conversation was in danger of becoming embarrassing Simon suggested they adjourned to the bar for interval refreshments.
The second half of the concert consisted of just one work: *Tchaikovsky's Fourth Symphony* with its sinister, fatalist, brass motto-theme that caused Simon to wonder if the finger of fate was pointing at him – with untold consequences in its wake.
The evening ended with Simon driving a somewhat subdued Sandra back to her aunt's house. When they arrived outside the house, he would dearly have liked to give his concert-going companion a farewell kiss to show how much he had enjoyed her company, but he knew that such a thing was out of order; and so he merely wished her goodnight and promised to make contact with her again before long.
Sleep eluded him that night. He replayed the events of the evening over and over in his mind. Did Sandra like him as

much as he liked her? Was it wise to nurture a relationship with one of his students? Should he devise new ways of meeting and being with Sandra or should he maintain a strict teacher-pupil relationship with the girl in the Upper Sixth? Was his teaching career more important than his personal happiness? Were there other, more mature, women out there in the world with whom he could form a deep, emotional relationship or had he found his soulmate in Sandra? These questions went ceaselessly around in his head before he eventually drifted into a light sleep.

When he awoke the next morning, the first thought that came into his head was of Sandra having to spend a loveless Christmas in the company of an aunt whilst he spent an equally tedious Christmas in the company of his parents. There must be some way, he reasoned, that the two of them could be together over the Christmas period and turn their unhappiness into joy. But, try as he might, he could think of no way to bring it about. Sandra was under the guardianship of her aunt, and there was no way her aunt would allow her to spend Christmas with an unknown man who was six years senior to her niece. And so, Simon had to bow to the inevitable and admit defeat.

This did not mean, however, he could have no contact with Sandra over the Christmas holidays. He had her phone number and he resolved to contact her at least once every day, ostensibly to cheer her up, but also to add excitement to his own life.

The clandestine phone messages tended to be somewhat stilted and awkward, with Simon doing most of the talking; and it did not escape his notice that it was always he who phoned Sandra and never vice versa. But, the daily phone calls helped the Christmas holidays pass more quickly than might otherwise have been the case and before long a new school term would commence when he and his star student could be in close proximity once more.

*

There was a school tradition of mounting a musical production just before Easter; and so, as soon as the spring term commenced, Simon collaborated with the Head of the English Department, on a production of *Trial by Jury* by Gilbert and Sullivan.

The Head of English was a middle-aged man named Eric Shaw. He had general oversight of the production with Simon acting as the musical director, training the singers and ensuring the musical content was of a proficient standard. The two men worked well together.

"I've toyed with the idea of bringing the work up to date and setting it in a present-day courtroom," the Head of English enthused. "But the trouble is 'Breach of Promise' is no longer a civil offence and the whole thrust of the piece would collapse without it. I think we have no alternative but to keep the work as a Victorian period-piece," declared Eric at their first meeting.

"In that case," replied Simon, "the emphasis will have to be on verisimilitude and creating an authentic Victorian atmosphere. The music is very Victorian and so there should be no difficulty achieving that. The important thing is to get the correct people playing the right parts."

"Have you got anyone in mind for the main characters?" enquired Eric.

"Yes. I've discovered a girl with a marvellous soprano voice who would be superb as Angelina."

"Is that the girl who sang the solo at the Christmas Carol Service?"

"Yes. Her name is Sandra Durrant and she's in the Upper Sixth. I think she would make a superb Angelina."

"Right. Well, that's one part filled. What about the Judge and the Plaintiff?"

The meeting went on to identify pupils best suited to fill the other roles before proceeding to a rehearsal schedule and identifying members of staff who might take responsibility for costumes, makeup, scenery and lighting. After an hour or so, a framework had been established for the end-of-term production and Simon was free to find Sandra and acquaint her with her next challenge.

His opportunity came at the end of the school day when he passed Sandra in the corridor just as the classrooms were disgorging their students.

"Ah Sandra," hailed Simon. "Just the person I wanted to see. Have you got a minute?"

Sandra nodded and smiled. As she did so, her raven black hair fell over her shoulders like molten silk. Simon thought he had never seen such pure beauty before.

"Come up to the music room." His words were neither an order nor a request but more an invitation to accompany him to his own workspace.

"Have a seat," he smiled as they entered the music room. "Now tell me, how are things going at present? We don't seem to have had a chance to speak since the beginning of the new term. How did you survive Christmas with your aunt?"

A wry smile spread across Sandra's face.

"It wasn't the best Christmas I've ever had," replied Sandra with downcast eyes, "but I did appreciate your phone calls. They cheered me no end."

"Good," replied Simon. "My Christmas was pretty miserable too. Talking to you helped me no end. Now, let's get down to business. I have some exciting news. You have a big break coming your way. There should be a fanfare of trumpets at this point but, alas, I've forgotten to organize the trumpeters."

Sandra smiled at his forced humour.

"Following your brilliant performance at the School Christmas Carol Service, you have landed the main part in the forthcoming school production of *Trial by Jury*," announced Simon. "Needless to say, I extolled your singing ability to Mr Shaw and he's agreed that you should play the part of Angelina. I've no doubt you'll be superb. I can see you now, standing there in the courtroom, attired in full bridal trousseau, and captivating the heart, not just of the wicked judge, but of every other member of the audience – me included."

Sandra stared incredulously at Simon throughout his impassioned speech. He clearly believed in her ability to sing the leading female role and, whatever misgivings she might have concerning the amount of extra time and work required for the production, she knew she could not disappoint him. He was like a little boy offering her a

present purchased with his scant pocket-money. It would be churlish to refuse.
She smiled another of her shy smiles that turned Simon's legs to jelly.
"So does that mean you'll do it?" asked Simon eagerly.
"Well, I don't know the role or even the operetta for that matter; but if you think I can do it, I'll give it a try."
"Splendid," beamed an ecstatic Simon. "You'll be magnificent. And don't worry about not knowing the work. I will personally teach it to you. You've nothing to fear. Rehearsals start on Monday."
And so saying, the tête-a-tête in the music room came to its conclusion.
The following Monday Sandra and the other principals clustered around the piano in the music room working through their parts, with Mr Copeland at the piano. Note-bashing was not a part of the job that Simon enjoyed. But the drudgery of endlessly repeating phrases in order to get them correct was alleviated by Sandra's presence in the room. Whenever he despaired of the Counsel for the Plaintiff ever getting his notes right, or the Judge keeping in time, Sandra's understanding smile lifted his spirits and brought a smile to his face. These smiles did not go unnoticed.
"Mr Copeland seems to be sweet on you," observed Lizzie Pearson, who was playing one of the bridesmaids. "I've noticed him watching you. You want to be careful. You know what some of these old men are like."
Sandra was tempted to spring to Simon's defence. He was certainly not an old man and any suggestion that his interest

in her was in any way perverted angered her; but she
thought twice about replying, thinking her protestations
might be regarded as proof of deeper feelings. And so she
merely shrugged her shoulders and acted as if she was
unconcerned.

Rehearsals continued throughout the ensuing weeks.
Sometimes they took place around the piano in the music
room, when the emphasis was on getting the vocal lines
correct, and at other times they were on the school stage,
when the emphasis was on movement and choreography.
The comic nature of the work resulted in great hilarity and
high spirits and everyone appeared to enjoy the rehearsals -
none more so than Simon.

Whenever Angelina held centre-stage and sang, Simon was
transported to another world. Her pure, clean, silvery voice
thrilled him to his core. She had taken to her part
effortlessly and Simon relished the times they spent
together at the piano perfecting her vocal line.

As the date of the performance approached, Simon
suggested to Sandra that they undertook some work on the
conclusion of the operetta.

"As you know, the piece ends with a great vocal ensemble
involving all the principals and chorus. Mr Shaw is keen to
have the principals at the front of the stage for this; and so
the Judge, who has been sitting on a raised dais at the back
of the stage, will come down to the front, take you by the
hand, twirl you around before catching you in his arms and
kissing you, just as the final curtain falls. Are you up for
that?"

Sandra laughed, revealing her perfectly aligned white teeth.

"It sounds like the ideal conclusion," she replied in a playful voice.

"Right then," said Simon. "Are you willing to practise it - with me playing the part of the Judge?"

Sandra nodded. Simon noticed that her nod was more eager than previously.

Launching into the piano accompaniment to the final chorus, the two of them sang together until they approached the final pages. Then Simon broke off from accompanying their singing and moved round behind Sandra. Approaching her from behind, he seized her hand in his, spun her around and embraced her in a long, passionate kiss. All singing ceased. The two were fused together in an explosion of love and desire. Simon could feel Sandra's nubile breasts pressing against his chest. Her lips were soft and sweet. Her long flowing hair enfolded the two of them in a sea of ecstasy. She made no attempt to free herself from his passionate embrace. She gave herself unreservedly to him and melted in his arms. Two souls had become one. It was to be the defining moment in their lives.

Simon wanted the moment to last for ever. He was loath to release his hold on the object of his love. But when they did eventually draw back and look into each other's eyes, Simon knew from the smile on Sandra's face, that a bond of unbreakable love had been created between them.

He also knew he had done wrong. He had taken advantage of one of the students in his care. He had broken the law on which the educational system of the country was based. Nevertheless, he had experienced the most thrilling moment of his life and he knew he was willing to risk everything for the sake of Sandra.

The two of them looked into each other's eyes. Not a word was spoken until Simon eventually stammered, "I'm sorry: I shouldn't have done that."

Sandra shook her head. "Don't say that. It was beautiful. Thank you for making me so happy."

Simon smiled at her innocent expression of love. She was indeed beautiful. She was also gentle and unassuming. She had a rare inner calm that, coupled with her outstanding musical ability, made her the soulmate Simon had always sought.

"I think, for our own safety, we ought not to mention this to anyone," declared Simon. "It might prove difficult if it was discovered that a teacher and a student were in love with each other. It will be better if we keep this a secret."

Sandra nodded assent as the two of them, reluctantly, brought the rehearsal to its conclusion. But from thenceforth, nothing could ever be the same again.

Trial by Jury was duly performed at the end of the spring term before a capacity audience of parents and pupils. It received outstanding praise, with the headmaster once again congratulating Simon on the quality of the music and, in particular, the singing ability of the principal soprano. However, there were two parents missing from the audience: Sandra's parents. Her father remained in Cyprus and her mother in America with her new husband. Neither showed the slightest inclination to return to England to see their daughter perform the leading role in the stage production.

Shortly after the show, as Simon was walking along the corridor leading to the science labs, he encountered Will Turner, the science teacher.

"Well done, Copeland," lauded the scientist. "Another great musical success to your credit! – and with the beautiful Sandra Durrant in the leading role. A pity her school work isn't as good as her singing. I've noticed a marked deterioration in her academic work this term. Her singing seems to be leading her astray. If she doesn't pull her socks up, she won't get the grades she needs to go to university – and that would be a great pity. Music is all very well, but it won't provide her with a job. She needs to concentrate on her academic work if she's to leave this school with the qualifications she needs. Perhaps you could have a word with her. She seems to listen to you."

Simon was somewhat taken aback by this broadside. He had not realised his developing relationship with Sandra had caused her to neglect her schoolwork. He looked for an opportunity when the two of them could meet and talk. Now that the school production was over, it was difficult to arrange trysts.

However, the End of Term Assembly was looming and the Head was keen to make it a memorable occasion with pupils reading poems, a dramatic retelling of the biblical Passion narrative and some musical items. To this end, Simon approached Sandra and asked if she would be willing to sing *I know that my Redeemer liveth* from Handel's *Messiah*. Without a moment's hesitation she agreed. This provided just the cover the two of them needed to meet together in the music room to rehearse the aria.

Making music with Sandra was the nearest Simon came to heavenly bliss. He moulded the musical accompaniment to mirror Sandra's exquisite, silvery, vocal line. The two fused together in a synergy that was otherworldly. For Simon, it was a foretaste of heaven.

At the end of their rehearsal, Simon clasped Sandra in his arms and hugged her with all the passion and ecstasy the music had released in him. She responded with joy and the two of them sealed their music-making with a long passionate kiss.

It was only after their musical lovemaking had subsided that Simon raised the subject of Sandra's schoolwork.

"Your science teacher, Mr Turner, has been talking to me," stated Simon with a pained look on his face. "He tells me that your school work has deteriorated this term and there's a real possibility you won't achieve the grades you need to go to university."

Sandra averted her look from Simon and gazed out of the music room window with a faraway look on her face.

"I've decided I don't want to go to university," she announced. "It would mean leaving you, and I don't want to do that. I want to be wherever you are."

Simon did not know whether to view this as the greatest accolade he had ever received or whether to throw up his hands in horror at diverting a young person from a university education and robbing her of her life's chances. A pained look spread over his face.

He answered, "If you throw away the chance of going to university you'll never get it again. I would dearly love you

to remain here so we can be together; but I don't want you later to resent your lost chances and blame that on me."
"I'll never do that," retorted Sandra with a conviction far in excess of her years. "What's a university education?" she continued: "Simply three more years of academic work ending with a piece of paper saying I know something about a certain area of study. I want more from life than that. I want to experience the things that really matter: beauty, love and passion - all the things that music provides. You've opened my eyes to these things and I want to share the remainder of my life with you so that we can experience them together."
Simon had no answer to her passionate outburst. He shared the same feelings as she did. It would be hypocritical of him to argue otherwise. He grasped her hands in his and said, "If that's what you've decided, I'll support you all the way."
Their rehearsal in the music room came to an end and the subsequent rendition of Handel's famous soprano aria from *Messiah* had a passion and a spiritual ecstasy that Simon had never before experienced. Simon viewed Sandra's expression of faith in the resurrection as a reflection of her faith in him. Two souls were fused together and there was no turning back.
During the Easter holidays, Sandra celebrated her eighteen birthday. "Celebrated" may have been too strong a word to describe the sedate birthday cake and bottle of champagne her aunt provided to mark her niece's coming-of-age; but Simon more than made up for the deficiency by taking Sandra first to an upmarket restaurant for a sumptuous

meal and then to the *Hippodrome Theatre* for a performance by Welsh Opera of Wagner's *Tristan and Isolde*.

The two of them sat holding hands in the darkened auditorium without fear of being observed. As the music surged and swelled, so Simon and Sandra were carried forward on a wave of sensual love. The agony and angst of the two lovers on stage resonated in their own hearts. Love never came without difficulties and troubles; but love also had the capacity to surmount difficulties and troubles and achieve a state of blessedness that only a few select souls could experience.

Simon would dearly have liked to take Sandra back to his flat at the conclusion of the opera, so the erotic lovemaking they had witnessed on stage could continue there, but prudence told him that, although Sandra was now an adult, she was still a student at his school and, as there were only nine weeks to the end of the school year, it was wiser to maintain a correct pupil-teacher relationship, lest in succumbing to the passion of the moment he forfeited all future happiness. He explained his feelings to Sandra as they drove home from the theatre in his old battered sports car. She smiled and nodded her understanding. She was prepared to wait.

The final term at school seemed interminable for both of them. Sandra sat her A-levels without enthusiasm and with little attempt to succeed. Simon contained his frustration at having to live apart from Sandra and, to all intents and purposes, behave towards her at school as if she was merely another of the students he taught. It was not an easy time for either of them. But, eventually, the term came to its conclusion. Sandra was free to leave and await her A-level results and Simon had six weeks' holiday stretching before him. The two of them were freed from the shackles of school and able to go their own way.

That way had been carefully planned.

Without informing her aunt or either of her parents, Sandra had resolved to marry Simon at the first possible opportunity. Simon urged caution, but Sandra's mind was made up. She had experienced enough of her parents' unconcern and the oppressive tutelage of her aunt. She was determined to break free and begin a new life with the man she loved.

Simon wondered if he should inform his parents of his impending marriage, but thought better of it. His parents would want to interrogate Sandra about her religious beliefs and would insist on a church wedding – neither of which Simon wanted. And so, without any formal engagement, the two of them approached the local Registry Office and set a date, two weeks hence, for their forthcoming marriage. It was to be a ceremony without guests. Indeed, no one was to know about it until after they were married.

Simon gave Sandra money with which to purchase a modest wedding dress and his flat served as the logistical centre for planning their nuptials and concealing all evidence of it from others.

Their marriage duly took place in an office with just the registrar and two witnesses drawn from a back office in attendance. It was a formality. But it provided Simon and Sandra with a Marriage Certificate that enabled them, henceforth, to be Mr and Mrs Copeland: to live together, for better for worse, for richer for poorer, in sickness and in health, to love and to cherish, till death did them part. They emerged from the Registry Office with wedding rings on their fingers and faces wreathed in smiles. Simon held his young bride in his arms and kissed her with all the love that flowed from his heart. She was his Isolde. Together they would face the world and embark upon life's journey as husband and wife.

But first, they had to break the news of their marriage to their families.

Sandra's aunt was horrified when the couple arrived on her doorstep and announced their new married status. The aunt had never met Simon, and the thought of her young niece, who had been committed to her care by her sister, marrying an unknown stranger, filled her with horror. How would she ever be able to explain to her sister what had happened? She would be held personally responsible for failing to adequately supervise her niece. It was the sort of calamity that one only read about in novels. She was distraught.

"Aunt, you have nothing to blame yourself for," answered Sandra. "You looked after me until I became an adult. Now I'm old enough to make my own decisions and lead my own life. I have thought long and hard about this, and am convinced it's the right thing to do. I love Simon and he loves me. We are going to make a wonderfully happy married couple. Now just sit down and let me make you a cup of tea."

Simon could not fail to marvel at the way his new wife coped with the delicate situation. But he was not given the luxury of admiring his wife's interpersonal skills for long because Sandra's aunt immediately turned her attention on him.

"And how did you, young man, come to meet my niece?" she rasped in a none-too-friendly tone.

"We met through our shared love of music," replied Simon. "Sandra has the most beautiful soprano voice. I'm sure there's a great future awaiting her if she decides to take up music as a profession."

"I hope she can do better than that!" retorted the aunt. "How are you going to maintain this marriage whilst she's away at university?"

"Sandra is not going to university," Simon calmly replied. "She's decided university is not for her and is remaining here with me."

Her aunt wrung her hands in despair. "Just as I thought!" she exclaimed. "She's throwing her life away simply to live with a man who looks much older than her and no doubt seduced her with blandishments and flattery. I can see this all ending in tears."

Simon shrugged his shoulders and smiled as he said, "I'm only six years older than Sandra. That's not a great age difference these days. Perhaps I will bring some maturity to our relationship whilst Sandra will bring youthful enthusiasm and fun. But the thing that unites us is our great love of music. We plan to make music together for the remainder of our lives. That can only result in joy and pleasure rather than the tears you prophesy."

"I just don't know what I'm going to tell Sandra's parents. They'll be mortified," sobbed the aunt.

Simon refrained from remarking that Sandra's parents had shown little interest in their daughter's welfare to date and, even if they were initially angry, their feelings would rapidly subside and they would continue their lives much as they had done before.

Just then, Sandra re-entered the room carrying a tray of tea. She fussed over her aunt before asking if she could use the telephone to inform her parents of her new married status. Her aunt was only too relieved to let Sandra perform the task. It was one she had dreaded undertaking. And so, once the tea had been served, Sandra disappeared to make her international telephone calls. She was missing from the room for a considerable period, during which time Simon sought to maintain a somewhat stilted conversation with Sandra's aunt.

When Sandra reappeared, she had a wide smile on her face. "I don't think they really believed me," she beamed. "They kept telling me to stop being silly. But I persevered and told them all about you, Simon, and how happy I am to be your wife. Aunt, I think you'll be hearing from my parents before long. Do, please, tell them how happy I am and that they have nothing whatsoever to worry about. Now, Simon, come and help me collect my belongings from my room. I don't have many things, and I've already packed the clothes I'm taking on honeymoon. Come on: let's get this done as quickly as possible."

With that, the two of them disappeared upstairs to retrieve Sandra's personal belongings.

Having bidden farewell to the dazed and perplexed aunt, Simon and Sandra returned to Simon's flat, grabbed all that was necessary for their honeymoon, and pointed the old sports car in the direction of the Lake District.

Simon had booked a holiday cottage for two at Buttermere. This was to be their secret honeymoon destination where they could be together without interference or disturbance. They located the small, stone cottage with no difficulty and, once they had unloaded the car, they collapsed into each other's arms in the small bedroom. Their passion knew no bounds. They were head-over-heels in love and revelled in simply being together. Simon wanted to consummate their marriage there and then, but Sandra was surprisingly mature in her attitude.

"I think it would be better if we waited until this evening," she whispered. "I don't want it to be a rushed affair. I want it to be beautiful. I want it to be something I remember for the rest of my life. I want it to be very special."

And with that she gently extricated herself from Simon's embrace and began unpacking her suitcase. They then walked hand in hand along the track leading from the cottage. The sun was slowly sinking in the west and bathing the idyllic landscape in a warm golden hue. They exchanged very few words but simply luxuriated in the tranquillity and beauty of the landscape. Nature mirrored the joy that was in their hearts.

Returning to their cottage, they prepared an evening meal together. Simon found it strange sharing common household chores with someone else; but it was an experience he relished. His years of isolation were at an end. From henceforth he had a companion with whom to share his life – a beautiful, gentle, soulful companion with hidden depths he had yet to discover and swathes of mystery he had yet to fathom.

Once they had eaten their evening meal and cleared away the debris, they fell into each other's arms once more. Sandra then led her new husband to the bedroom and allowed him to gently undress her. As each article of clothing fell from her body, Simon was overwhelmed by her beauty and his love for his new wife. She removed his clothing. The two of them sank onto the bed in a passionate outpouring of love.

"Please be gentle," whispered Sandra. "I'm a virgin."

Simon expected nothing else, and, with all the skill and delicacy at his command, he gently eased himself into his recumbent wife. He noticed her wince, but no sound escaped her lips. She clung tightly to him. The physical manifestation of their love encapsulated the spiritual union of their souls. They were no longer two but one.

"Those whom God hath joined together, let no man put asunder" were words that echoed down the years from the many church marriage services Simon had attended. He and Sandra were now one, never to be parted.

CHAPTER FIVE

Simon never really expected his wife to visit him in prison. The love they once shared had somehow turned to dust. He shook his head in pained disbelief. "Where did I go wrong?" he asked himself; but no answer came.

The memories of the good times they shared together were a great source of solace to him during the long hours he spent alone. He often thought about her and wondered what had become of her. Had she banished him from her life altogether and embarked upon a new direction, or did she still recall the good times they spent together and regret their parting? He had no way of knowing. The letters he wrote to her went unanswered. To all intents and purposes they lived in different universes. He had no knowledge of her life whilst she, surely, could not imagine what life was like for him in prison.

It was at times such as this that unimaginable sorrow overwhelmed him. He sat in his cell, with his head in his hands, struggling to make sense of all that had befallen him. Life had seemed so promising. He had a job that gave him satisfaction. He had married a beautiful girl with unbelievable musical ability. He relished music and the world of creative imagination it unlocked. He experienced the wonder and pleasure of conjuring music out of the ether and committing it to paper so others could share his pleasure. His life had been so full of promise and potential and, yet, somehow, it had all gone wrong.

He knew he would never again be able to teach music – well, not in a school anyway. His teaching colleagues had shunned him. His family had disowned him. Those he loved had turned on him. He felt alone and wretched. At times such as this he became very depressed. Darkness and despair crowded in upon him like snarling demons braying for his soul. His life had lost its purpose. He was adrift on a limitless ocean, with no way of knowing if he would ever reach land and safety. Thoughts of suicide sometimes invaded his mind. Perhaps he would be better dead? He was unloved. Without love life was not worth living. He would not be missed. If he ended it all, people might say kind things about him at his funeral, but within next to no time he would be forgotten. Those who had known him would continue their everyday lives and the memory of him would disappear. His life would have no meaning or value. He was in the depths of despair. The words of an old psalm echoed in his head.

> *Out of the deep have I called unto thee, O Lord:*
> *Lord hear my voice.*

The words reminded him that what he was experiencing was not unique. Others had endured the same desolation and despair. He recalled the creative genius of Oscar Wilde condemned to years in a prison cell because of his love for another and yet, from that experience, emerged works like

De Profundis and *The Ballad of Reading Gaol*. Thinking of others similarly afflicted helped sustain him in his blackest moments. If Wilde had been able to survive two years' hard labour in Reading Gaol, surely he could survive his time in prison. He had been sentenced to two years' imprisonment, but he knew he qualified for automatic release at the end of a year. One year was not long to endure his present confinement.

Metaphorically shaking himself, he knew he must adopt a more positive attitude towards prison life. He might as well use his time productively if he was to spend a year incarcerated within the walls of a penal establishment. His involvement in chapel services and the subsequent formation of a chapel choir had come to the notice of the Prison Governor. When Simon presented his application to pursue an Open University Doctor of Music degree, the Governor readily agreed. He approved of inmates bettering themselves and leaving prison better qualified than when they entered it. It showed that his prison was forward-thinking and actively engaged in rehabilitation. It concerned him not one iota that a Doctorate in Music was a largely impractical qualification. It would look good on the quarterly returns he submitted to the Ministry of Justice; and so he summoned Simon to his office.

The Prison Governor was an ex-military man in his late fifties. He was bald and the dome of his head reflected the light of the fluorescent tube above it. He had a bluff manner of speech.

"Ah, Copeland," he began as Simon was led into his office and made to stand before his desk. "I see you want to pursue a course of study in… what is it? … ah yes, music. Surely you have some sort of qualification in that already, don't you?"

"Yes, sir," replied Simon. "I have a Bachelor of Music degree; but I've always wanted to go further and, in particular, undertake musical research into the Czech composer Zelenka."

"Never heard of him," retorted the Governor, "but then my musical tastes are more Gilbert and Sullivan."

"I think you'll find," replied Simon, "that Sir Arthur Sullivan was no stranger to Zelenka's unusual suspended cadences. Zelenka was quite an innovator. I'd find it fascinating to pursue the lines of musical development that stemmed from his fertile musical mind."

"Is there a book in it?" enquired the Governor, anchoring a conversation that was rapidly in danger of going over his head into something quantifiable.

"A Doctorate requires a substantial written thesis that may well be of interest to a musical publisher if it was thought there was commercial potential."

"And what if no one wants to publish your work? Will it bring any benefit to you?"

"I think so," replied Simon with some caution. "I hope to return to some form of musical employment on my release, and the more qualifications I have, the greater my chances of securing employment."

"But not in a school, I hope you realise."

"Indeed. My school teaching days are over. But there are other musical opportunities in the community and I'd like to put my skills to good use."

"Well, you've certainly improved the musical landscape here. The chaplain tells me chapel services have improved appreciably since you began accompanying the hymn-singing. Well done."

Then, after a moment's pause for reflection, the Prison Governor barked, "I'm minded to grant your request - although the Prison Director of Education is none too keen. You'll have to tread carefully so as not to antagonize her. Have you anything to say?"

"No, sir. And thank you. I'm extremely grateful for your support."

"That will be all. You may go."

And with that the interview terminated.

Simon left the Governor's office with a spring in his step. The prison officer, who accompanied Simon to the Governor's office and was tasked with seeing him returned to his cell, raised his eyebrows and asked, "Who's this Zelenka fella? Would I know any of his music?"

"Probably not," replied Simon. "He's not very well known in this country; but from a musical standpoint, he was a great musical innovator particularly in harmony and counterpoint."

"What the bloody hell is counterpoint?" asked the accompanying officer.

"It's when a composer places melodies in layers on top of each other. There's quite an art to it because the melodies have to harmonise in a vertical way as they move forward horizontally."

"What's the point of that? I like a good tune I can whistle or sing. You can only sing one bloody tune at a time."

"Quite so," replied Simon, "and a great deal of good music consists of just a good tune with some sort of accompaniment supporting it. But if you want to stretch your mind, there are so many more ways of making music, and they can be even more rewarding to listen to."

"A proper little clever clogs aren't you?" retorted the prison officer, thinking his appreciation of music had somehow been belittled by Simon's explanation of counterpoint. "Well, at least I can go home in the evening and listen to the Rolling Stones, with a pizza in one hand and a bottle of beer in the other. That's what I call a rewarding musical experience. A lot of good your counterpoint will do you banged up here! Have you got your Holy Joe choristers singing counterpoint yet? I bet they'd love that. Just remember: this is a house of correction, not the bloody Birmingham Conservatoire. Don't think you're going to skive off work with this music malarkey. You're here to serve time, not bloody enjoy yourself at the taxpayer's expense."

And with that he pushed Simon into his cell and slammed the door shut.

Sinking onto his bed, Simon reflected on the vast chasm that existed between the things that interested and moved him and the things that interested and occupied the lives of others. It was like living in an alien world where no one spoke the same language as him, or thought like him, or felt like him. He had been cast adrift in an alien environment. His task was to survive.

A day or so later, he was taken from his floor-cleaning duties and led to the Education Wing to report to the

Director of Prison Education. This formidable woman was no friend of Simon's. He remembered their last bruising encounter. She was clearly a force with which to reckon and he braced himself for what lay ahead.

"Copeland," snapped the armour-plated amazon as she rose from behind her desk to reveal the finely-tailored Jaeger tweed suit she was wearing. "I see you've inveigled yourself into the Governor's good books and he's minded to let you follow a course of study in … music." This last word was uttered with complete disgust. "Never, in all my years as Director of Education, have I known an offender wish to study music. Engineering? Yes. That can lead to a well-paid job in the manufacturing and service industries. A foreign language? Yes. That can open doors into multinational companies. Physics and chemistry? Yes. They can lead to numerous job opportunities. But music? No. A complete waste of time, in my opinion! Music is there to be performed and heard, not analysed and dissected. People who play instruments and sing can earn a living. But what earthly good is studying some eighteenth-century, obscure, European composer whose music is rarely, if ever, heard?" Simon remained silent during this tirade, but he derived a certain satisfaction from the fact that the Director of Education had bothered to research Zelenka. He waited for her to straighten her well-cut jacket and proceed.

"We have, of course, had offenders in the past who wished to follow courses of study with the Open University, and so the machinery is in place to facilitate this. We have never, however, had an offender who wished to undertake musical scholarship."

A great intake of breath sounded in her nostrils
"I have been in contact with the relevant department at the Open University," she continued, "and the OU Registrar has requested you submit an application form clearly detailing your area of study. The OU will then assess its suitability and, if it is satisfied it meets its criteria, it will assign a tutor to you. You will, therefore, complete this application form and return it to me within twenty-four hours."
So saying, she terminated the interview and left Simon to exit her office clutching the form he was required to complete.
Although he had received no encouragement from the person tasked with promoting education within the prison, he felt he was making progress and an interesting voyage of musical discovery lay ahead.
"Why you looking so satisfied with yourself?" hissed an ominous voice from over his shoulder as he re-entered E Wing on his way back to his cell.
Glancing around, he saw the menacing face of one of the other prisoners. It was a prisoner with whom he had had no previous contact. Neither was it someone to whom he felt naturally drawn. The downturned mouth and scarred face of the man at his side, witnessed to a life of brawls, punches and knife wounds. It was the face of someone without pity or mercy.
"Been sucking up to Holy Joe again, have ya? So you can tinkle the old ivories? Well, you'd better look out. We don't like sods like you here. That pretty little face of yours could

look very different after some broken bottle work. You'd better watch out, pretty boy, if you value your life."
Simon held his peace during this menacing encounter. As far as he was aware, he had done nothing to antagonize this prisoner and it seemed, from what was said, his only failing was a willingness to accompany hymns for the chaplain at the Sunday morning act of worship.

He found himself in a dilemma. Should he inform the chaplain of the threat made against him and seek the chaplain's advice? Or should he simply resign as pianist at the Sunday morning service without any explanation, in the hope this would divert attention away from him? He knew that the second option was unlikely to work. The chaplain was sure to quiz him over his decision. And, if he resigned as pianist for the Sunday services, he would also have to withdraw from the Christmas Carol Service. He had expended a great deal of time and effort on his ragtag-and-bobtail choir. There was no way of knowing how the choir members would react if he suddenly resigned. Something told him they would not be very pleased. The aggression he might receive from them could be even worse than the threats of the brute who waylaid him in the corridor. Conversely, he was unsure if talking to the chaplain would help or hinder his cause. The chaplain had certainly exhibited worldly cunning in the formation of the Christmas choir, and so, perhaps, beneath his somewhat otherworldly exterior, there might lurk a sharp mind that would know how best to deal with the situation. It was a difficult dilemma. Simon was unsure how to proceed.

The decision, however, was taken out of his hands when he next encountered the chaplain.

"Ah Simon," beamed the chaplain with his customary smile. "Do come in. I want to have a word with you."

So saying, he pulled out a chair and invited Simon to sit on it.

"It's come to my attention," continued the chaplain, "that some people in this place are attempting to make difficulties for you."

Simon's eyebrows rose as he wondered how on earth the chaplain knew of his altercation with the brute on E Wing.

"Alas, envy is one of the seven deadly sins, and there are inmates here who have succumbed to its temptation. The fact that you are a competent musician, and able to play the piano with distinction, causes waves of envy to well up in the hearts of those who are not so gifted. It's an emotion as old as time itself. Was not Cain filled with envy at his brother's success? And, as we both know, his envy led him into even greater evil: nothing less than murder. Now, the last thing Her Majesty's Prison Service wants is murder on its premises."

Simon felt his mouth go dry. Was the chaplain saying there was a plot to murder him? This was worse than anything he had previously imagined.

"And so I had a word with the envious element within the prison population and alerted them to my cognisance of their intentions," continued the chaplain. "I reminded them of the withdrawal of privileges that would follow any precipitous action on their part. And, if that was not enough, I even held before them the likelihood of a transfer

to Her Majesty's Prison at Princetown. I must say, the thought of serving the remainder of their sentence on Dartmoor did not greatly seem to appeal to them."
Simon sat speechless in the presence of the prison's undercover mover and shaker. "I'm sorry your musical ministry has brought trouble upon you," continued the chaplain, "but I don't think you'll have any further inconvenience. In my experience, once something has been brought into the open it loses much of its malignancy. Just let me know if anything else untoward occurs."
And with that he handed Simon a list of hymns for the forthcoming Sunday service, shook his hand, and ushered him to the door.
Simon's respect for the little man of God grew enormously. He might not look very prepossessing, but he certainly had his finger on the pulse of prison life and he was not afraid to use his position to exert influence and ensure peace and goodwill existed within his workplace.
That evening's choir practice went surprisingly well. The moans and groans over William Matthias' unusual rhythms and syncopation, and the choir members' deliberate mispronunciation of the French and Latin lyrics, merely masked their growing feeling of confidence that they were making good progress with *Sir Christemas*. This gave Simon confidence to introduce a new carol. It was one he had composed himself.
Ever since he was a young boy, Simon had relished committing the sounds he heard in his head onto paper. He sought to capture his inner sound-world so he could relive each experience and share each moment of beauty or

excitement with others. Composing music was a safety-valve that allowed him to express his deepest emotions in a safe and ordered way. The notes on the paper may just have been black dots and dashes to other people, but for him they were brim-full of memories, suffused emotions and eternal yearnings. Other people might find fulfilment and beauty in art, or literature or scientific research; but, for him, authentic existence was only to be found in music. Music spoke to his heart. It had the power to move him to tears and lift him to the very portals of heaven. It was the language he understood best. It carried him above the mundane concerns of life and heightened his experiences and aspirations. He could not imagine life without music. As a boy, he often debated within himself the contrasting claims of sight and sound. If he had to lose either his sight or his hearing, which would he choose? It was an agonizing dilemma.

He relished the beautiful world and had no wish to never again see the sun rise, or look down from a high hill on the coloured counties spread far below him, or look into the sparkling eyes of a loved one, or watch the unfolding seasons resplendent in their vibrant seasonal colours. He held all of these dear. The gift of sight enabled him to appreciate them. But the gift of hearing was even more precious to him. He could not imagine living in a silent world, where it was impossible to hear the sound of the sea breaking on the seashore, the call of the birds, the excited laughter of children, and, most of all, the beautiful music others had created which brought solace and pleasure when all else failed. He knew that to lose his hearing would be the hardest cross for him to bear. And yet, he knew that other musical composers had suffered in that way. Beethoven began going deaf at the age of 28 and by the age of 46 he was composing music he would never hear. It existed only in his head and that propelled him to continue composition. Vaughan Williams went deaf in old age, but this did not prevent him experimenting with all kinds of new sounds and different and unusual combinations of instruments. Smetana, Zelenka's fellow countryman, had a hearing impediment in later life, and yet he used this to stunning effect in his String Quartet *From My Life* where the first violin holds a sustained, harmonic E replicating the continuous sound inside his head preceding his eventual deafness.

The battle the youthful Simon enacted between sight and hearing was difficult to resolve, but, if push came to shove, he knew he would forfeit sight in order to retain hearing. It was within the aural world of music that he was most fully alive. His present incarceration meant he was denied the delights of the concert hall and opera house, and even recorded music was in short supply; but he could at least continue to make music in his head.

He used the small allowance he earned in prison to purchase music manuscript paper. Most of the other inmates used their allowance to purchase cigarettes or drugs (if they could obtain them without being detected). His purchase of manuscript paper resulted in predictable ribald comments from other inmates and prison officers.

"Hoping to get onto *Top of the Pops* with your latest little number, are you?"

"What's it going be then? Jailhouse Rock?"
"Don't be stupid! He's goin' to write a heavy-metal symphony. It's goin' be called All Banged Up."
"Well, I hope he don't expect us to listen to it. It's bad enough having to endure his bleeding hymn tunes."
Simon was able to absorb all these barbs. The important thing, as far as he was concerned, was that he had manuscript paper on which to commit his innermost thoughts and yearnings. The lack of a piano or some other musical instrument did not concern him greatly because he was able to hear the sound of the music he composed in his head. Sitting in the solitary silence of his cell every evening, he conjured up an imaginary sound world that was all his own. Melodies flowed through his mind with accompanying chords pulling his music into never-ending new and strange harmonic regions.
Simon had taken the words of one of the carols in *The Oxford Carols for Choirs* and composed his own musical setting of them. By now, he knew the sound of each of the choir members' voices and so, as he worked on his composition, he heard the sound of their singing in his mind's ear. He smiled as he sent the descant melody soaring to a high G, knowing exactly how it would sound when sung by the Indonesian Sarsung. The underlying punchy accompaniment, consisting of short, staccato, jabbing chords, were ideally suited for the voices of Winston and his Caribbean compatriots. His new Christmas carol would be his prisoners' carol, capturing the pain of captivity with the hope of better things to come offered to the world by the babe in the manger.

Having completed the carol to his satisfaction, he spent numerous evenings carefully copying it so that all sixteen members of the prison choir could have their own copy. Now came the moment of truth. Would they take kindly to his new composition or would they treat it with disdain?
"What's this, man?" demanded Winston when Simon handed out copies of the new carol to the men gathered around the chapel piano. "You didn't tell us we was going to have to sing new stuff you has written."
"I like to surprise you," replied Simon. "I've written this especially for all of you. We will be performing a world premiere at this year's Carol Service. You might all become famous. Remember, all carols have to begin their life somewhere. *Silent Night* was written by an Austrian schoolmaster for a remote Alpine church that didn't even have a properly functioning organ – and his carol went all round the world."
"Yeah, man. But his carol had a tune. Has this carol got a tune or is it another of them airy-fairy pieces?"
Simon feigned a pained look. "Winston, you disappoint me. When have you ever known me make you sing airy-fairy pieces? We only sing good music in this choir."
"Well, man, I hope this is good, otherwise your guts is goin' be plastered all over them walls."
Simon smiled before adding, "I bet Beethoven never had to endure threats like that when he rehearsed *Missa Solemnis* with his choir."
But Simon was not unduly perturbed. He had learnt that such banter was part of prison life. No one wanted to appear weak or subservient to anyone else and so

expressions of physical violence were everyday forms of speech.

"If you just follow the music, I'll play through the piece to give you an idea of what it sounds like."

Without more ado, Simon played the carol on the piano in its entirety. It was the first time he had physically heard it. Prior to that moment, it existed entirely in his creative imagination. Now he was able to share it with others.

The men clustering around the piano listened in silence as Simon's fingers moved over the piano keys and the music of the carol filled the cavernous expanse of the chapel. Stealing furtive glances at the pianist, they could see Simon was totally immersed in the music. It was as though he was possessed by some other-worldly force that flowed through his fingers and resulted in magical beauty and harmony.

There was a long pause at the end of the play-through. For a moment no one spoke. Then the silence was broken by Justin: "Fucking beautiful!" he exclaimed. "How do you do it? I wish I could make sounds like that out of nowhere. I could make a bloody fortune."

"You don't need to write music," added Cooper to his compatriot in crime. "We could make a fortune passing this stuff off as our own. What ya say, Simon boy? Jus and me'll act as your managers. We'll make sure the stuff brings home the bacon. With the three of us working together, we can't lose!"

The jocularity masked the fact that the men clustered around the chapel piano were visibly moved by Simon's composition and were keen to begin learning their parts. The practice ended with a general feeling of satisfaction.

The disparate members of the choir were slowly forming into a unified and disciplined ensemble. And, what was more, they were enjoying their weekly hour of music-making with Simon around the chapel piano. Things were looking up.

Things were also looking promising regarding Simon's enrolment application for his Doctorate of Music postgraduate course of study with the Open University. Having completed the application form, he returned it to the Director of Education within the specified twenty-four hours she had stipulated.

She took it from him and cast her eye over its contents. "It seems to me that people are made doctors of this, that and the other for knowing more and more about less and less. Before we know it, we'll be having Doctors of Music who have conducted extensive studies into *Baa baa black sheep* or some other childish nursery rhyme. They might know every possible thing there is to know about the nursery rhyme, but what possible use is that to anyone else?"

Simon tried hard to conceal a smile. He knew that postgraduate research was often highly specialised and of little utilitarian value either to the national economy or the sum total of humankind's happiness; but there was value and worth in all knowledge and research. The insights that one person discovered enlarged the understanding of others, which in turn might lead to even greater advances. But it was no good attempting to persuade the prison's Director of Education of this and so he held his peace.

"And this Zelenka person," continued the female dragon-slayer. "The fact that his music is rarely, if ever, heard surely shows he was a mediocre composer. If he'd been any good, we would be listening to his music today, just as we listen to Mozart or Beethoven or Bach."

"Well, as a matter of fact," interjected Simon, convinced at this point that he was on safer ground when talking about music rather than the philosophy of education, "Bach held Zelenka in very high regard and the two of them corresponded. It was just the vagaries of fate, and the fact that Bach had a large family that was able to promote his music in the years following his death, and Zelenka died unmarried and childless, that contributed to the subsequent differing fortunes of the two composers."

"I find that hard to believe," rasped the unmarried Director of Education. "Good will always out. If this Zelenka had written good music it would be performed today. The fact that it isn't proves he was second-rate and that you're wasting your time researching his life and music. If it was up to me, I wouldn't countenance such a waste of the prison's resources and facilities. But it seems I've been overruled. I will forward your application and await the outcome. I cannot say I'm filled with any great confidence the Open University will view things my way. It seems to have a very distorted approach to education. It distributes degrees and doctorates like confetti. Anyone can get one these days. They're hardly worth the paper on which they're written."

And so saying, the Director of Prison Education, who had not been to university herself and so did not possess a degree let alone a doctorate, waved Simon out of her office. As Simon was led back to his cell on E Wing, the thought crossed his mind that he was probably better qualified to be the prison's Director of Education than the present incumbent. But would he want her job? Probably not. For one thing there was a complete absence of female students to educate, and it was always female students whom he found most interesting.

"Been talking to Holy Joe about me, have you, pretty boy?" sneered a menacing voice behind him as he crossed the association area. "Don't think he can save ya. You just got yourself into a whole lot of extra trouble, loser." And with that, the scarred and ugly face of Simon's *bête noire* slid back into the recesses of the wing leaving Simon to walk to his cell with a deepening sense of foreboding. It was a chilling reminder that life in prison was very unpredictable. There was never any way of knowing when the next attack was coming or what form it might take. Vigilance and nervous anticipation were required at all times: none more so than at mealtimes.

Prisoners were fed in the canteen on a staggered rotation basis. The prisoners on each wing were called in turn by prison officers to form a line at the cafeteria counter and collect their food. The food was served by fellow inmates – usually those nearing the end of their sentence - which were thought likely to behave responsibly rather than forfeit their impending freedom. These servers operated their own perverted code of justice. They either favoured certain prisoners if they liked or feared them, or else penalised those whom they disliked or considered fair sport for ribaldry. On some occasions, Simon received a decent meal, whilst on other occasions, custard, intended for his pudding was "accidentally" ladled over his vegetables. Sometimes portions were generous, whilst at other times they were miniscule. It was pot luck, depending on the mood and inclination of the server.

But it was not just at the serving counter that petty feuds and preferences were enacted. The very process of moving from the cells to the canteen and back again was fraught with danger. A leg might suddenly shoot into the aisle causing an unsuspecting passing inmate to trip over it sending his food flying in all directions. Or, someone walking back to their cell with his plate of food and a mug of scalding tea, might unexpectedly be elbowed by someone walking in the opposite direction, causing him to spill them either over himself – which was considered richly deserved – or over other prisoners, who then went ballistic, threatening all kinds of hideous consequences to the unfortunate person whose food or tea it was.

Metal cutlery was not permitted in the prison, but the plastic substitutes could cause considerable injury if thrust with enough force into a fellow inmate. All of which made prison mealtimes a period when extra vigilance was required.

Simon always breathed a sigh of relief when he had collected his food and safely returned to his cell to eat it. The hour of association at the end of each day before lock-up at 6.00.pm was also a time to be on one's guard. Simon usually sought out a member of his choir with whom to consort because he felt safe and conversation was possible with them.

"How are you finding the new music, Duncan?" enquired Simon, as he took his place next to the taciturn and morose man who rarely revealed any emotions.

"Could be a damn sight easier," came the laconic reply.

"All new music is difficult at first," replied Simon. "Some of the mainstay works in the orchestral repertoire were deemed too difficult when they first appeared. Shostakovich's *Fourth Symphony* was rubbished by the players when they tackled it for the first time, but now it's the bread and butter of all symphony orchestras."

"Good job we don't have a prison orchestra then," returned the dour loner as he flicked the pages of the magazine he was reading, "or else you'd be making the players learn that."

"You sound as if you don't like music," declared Simon, "and yet you never miss a choir practice."

Simon's statement was followed by a long pause as Duncan considered his reply. The pause was masked by the rapid turning of the magazine's pages. When he eventually spoke, he turned his head sideways to place Simon clearly in his line of vision, before replying, "My mother was a singer. She used to sing in concerts. She had a good voice. Of course, I was never interested in her singing. Boys ain't interested in singing. There are other things to do when you're a young lad. But now she's dead, I often think of her. Singing made her happy. She forgot her troubles when she was singing. So, if singing made her happy, I thought I'd give it a try. My voice is nothing like hers, but, when I sing in your choir, I imagine her looking down on me and smiling. It helps me."

A silence descended. It was the longest utterance Simon had ever heard from the lips of Duncan. He sensed that he had opened his soul for a brief moment and given him a glimpse into his world. He had no idea why Duncan was in prison – and he had learned it was best never to enquire of prisoners the reason for their confinement – but somewhere along the way, he sensed Duncan had strayed from the straight and narrow symbolized by his mother and he was now looking back to her for help and guidance.

"Do you remember any of the pieces your mother used to sing?" asked Simon in an attempt to encourage his choir-member to share more of his inner thoughts.

"She once sang a very sad piece about a woman crying over the death of her lover: *What is life if thou art dead?*"

"Ah!" sighed Simon, "Orfeo's Lament from *Orpheus and Eurydice* by Gluck: a very beautiful and heart-wrenching piece! It perfectly captures the grief of losing a loved one. It was written for a low voice – a mezzo-soprano - and so your mother must have had a low, powerful voice."

"It was incredibly powerful. When she was singing she was in another world. I could tell by the look in her eyes that nothing else mattered to her except the words and the notes she was singing."

Simon whispered from the depths of his being: "Music is extremely powerful. That's why it must always be performed well."

"That doesn't mean it has to be bloody difficult," replied Duncan, bringing the conversation back to earth with a vengeance.

Simon smiled. "You're perfectly correct. Good music can be very simple and effective. Perhaps we should include some easier pieces in our carol service. I'll have a think about it."

And so saying the two men ended their conversation and returned to their respective cells for the night.

When the members of the prison choir next met for their weekly rehearsal in the prison chapel, Simon suggested the inclusion of some carols from other countries. Turning to Winston, the burly West Indian, he asked, "What do you sing in Jamaica at Christmas, Winston?"

"Man, we sing songs that go back to the plantations when we had to slave and die for you white men. We sing and we clap for the birth of Jesus."

And without further ado he began singing and clapping

> *Mary had a baby, yes, Lord,*
> *Mary had a baby, yes, my Lord,*
> *Mary had a baby, yes Lord,*
> *The people keep a-comin' an' the train done gone.*

The other West Indians immediately took up the refrain and joined in with rhythmic clapping and swaying bodies. Then, to Simon's utter amazement, they broke into rich three-part harmony that filled the chapel with a sound both joyous and passionate.

> *What did she name him? Yes, Lord,*
> *What did she name him? Yes, my Lord,*
> *What did she name him? Yes Lord,*

The people keep a-comin' an' the train done gone.

She named him Jesus, yes, Lord.
She named him Jesus, yes, my Lord.
She named him Jesus, yes Lord.
The people keep a-comin' an' the train done gone.

Named him King Jesus (Yes, Lord)
Named him King Jesus (Yes, My Lord)
Named him King Jesus (Yes, Lord)
The people keep a-comin' an' the train done gone.

The other men clustered around the piano listened in wonder. None of them had heard such unrestrained and uninhibited singing before. It was like a summer breeze from a tropical island dispelling the gloom of a cold winter's night.

"That was superb!" exclaimed Simon as the *acapella* performance came to a close. "I never knew you could sing in close harmony like that! We must include that carol in the carol service. It will ignite the whole event and bring a smile to everyone's face."

"Yeah, but what does it mean?" Dylan asked. "All that stuff about the people keep a-comin' an' the train done gone?"

"Man, you just ain't got no brains," retorted Winston. "Didn't they teach you at Sunday School about the glory train? Unless you climb aboard, you ain't going get to the Promised Land. Jesus says 'Get aboard while there's time'. Ain't that right, Simon?"

Simon was taken completely aback by this theological question addressed to him. His father would have had no hesitation answering with a weighty discourse on redemption and the need for repentance; but Simon had long ceased to have any interest in theological matters. His interest was with music. Composers set religious texts to music, but it was the music that interested him and not the theology behind the words. And so Winston's direct question completely disarmed him. He lamely answered, "I suppose that's what the carol is saying; but, let's leave the theology to the chaplain and concentrate on the music." Once choir practice had ended and Simon was back in his cell for the long night shut-down, he mused on Winston's question. Why had the West Indian assumed he would agree with his religious viewpoint? Why had Winston turned to him to settle a question of belief? Surely the fact he was teaching them Christmas carols didn't automatically make him a committed, card-carrying Christian? But, more worryingly, why had he felt so inadequate when the question was put to him? Did he still possess a faith or had the events leading to his imprisonment destroyed any belief he once had? These were unsettling questions and he was unsure of his answer.

He decided to banish all such troublesome thoughts and sit at his rickety table, which doubled as his silent piano, and shadow-play Schumann's *Scenes from Childhood*: a reminder of when life was less complicated and innocence abounded. He found sleep difficult that night. The events of the choir practice continued to haunt him. Why had he never thought of asking the members of the choir what they would like

included in the carol service? Some of them were clearly very musical, even if they didn't realise it. Perhaps the service should contain carols from other countries around the world. He must make enquiries and see what resulted.
The following morning, as he queued to use the ablutions block, he found himself standing next to Sarsung, the Indonesian with the amazing high tenor voice.
"I've been thinking," said Simon, without revealing he had lain awake for most of the night thinking about the music for the carol service, "that we ought to include some carols from around the world." Then, addressing Sarsung directly, he asked, "What do you sing in your country at Christmas?"
Sarsung thought for a moment to consider his reply. Then, with a wide smile on his face, he said, "I tell you the best Christmas carol we sing. It's my favourite. It's the most beautiful carol you've ever heard. It is called *Malam Kudus*. It is indeed beautiful."
Simon had never heard of the piece, but he could tell by the smile on Sarsung's face that it created a profound effect upon him. He made a mental note of its name and, when he next met the chaplain to receive the forthcoming Sunday hymn numbers, he made a request.
"I wonder if it's possible to obtain a copy of an Indonesian Christmas carol that Sarsung has recommended to me. It's called *Malam Kudus*. I thought it might be good to include carols from around the world in order to reflect the wide range of ethnicities we have here."
"What a splendid idea!" beamed the chaplain. "I'll see what I can do."

A week later, when Simon met the chaplain again, the man of God flourished sheets of music in his hand. "It took some finding," he announced, "but I eventually tracked down the piece you wanted. I hope you can make good use of it."

Simon took the sheet music from the chaplain and nonchalantly cast his eye over it. His heart almost stopped beating. He froze. For a split second he could not believe his eyes. The music had Indonesian words, but the music was music he knew only too well: *O Holy Night* by Adolphe Adam.

"Is something wrong?" enquired the chaplain, with a concerned look on his face. "Is it the correct piece you wanted?"

Simon nodded. But his mind was not on the chaplain. His mind was back in the school classroom with his star pupil, Sandra. The sound of her clear, pure soprano voice flooded his consciousness with emotions too complex to absorb. He managed to mutter a few hurried words of thanks to the chaplain before retreating, as quickly as possible, to the privacy of his cell to come to terms with this unexpected bolt from the blue.

CHAPTER SIX

The week Simon and Sandra spent at the cottage in Buttermere was the best week of Simon's life. He came to realise his former life had been only half a life. He had lived for himself, but now he had someone else with whom to share his passions, his love and his interests. He revelled in sharing with Sandra the mundane tasks that previously, out of necessity, he had undertaken alone. Preparing meals, washing-up, laundering clothes, ironing and such like became a pleasure. He had someone with whom to share them. Sandra's ready smile and laughter filled him with joy. He could hardly believe his good fortune in having found such a soulmate.

The two of them spent hours walking hand in hand across the Lakeland fells. Each new vista produced evermore radiant smiles and sighs of pleasure from deep within. They were in love. Life was beautiful. The future opened its arms to them and they had every intention of walking confidently into it, hand in hand, seizing every opportunity of happiness it afforded.

Back in their cottage, they sat with their arms around each other listening to music on the radio. Some music Sandra recognised, but Simon appeared to know every piece that was played.

"This is Wagner, again. And listen! It's the prelude to *Tristan and Isolde:* the opera we saw at the *Hippodrome* at Easter!"

He had a never-ending fund of stories to tell of composers, disastrous first performances, fateful commissions and other musical stories. Sandra smiled at his boyish enthusiasm for music. He may have been six years older than her, but in many ways he was just a schoolboy with his likes and dislikes, his passions and his energy, his simplicity and his appealing naivety. She gave him a sudden hug.

"What was that for?" enquired Simon in mock surprise.

"It was to tell you, I love you."

And with that, the two of them rolled onto the floor as the music of Wagner urged them to ever greater heights of passion and pleasure.

The week at Buttermere came to an end all too soon and the two lovers had to wave goodbye to the cottage that had been their first married home and drive back to Simon's flat which was to be their permanent married residence.

Sandra set to work with a will to turn Simon's somewhat disorganized bachelor flat into a home for a married man and his wife. She brought order and a woman's touch to the home; but there was no disguising the fact the flat was small. It would have to do for the time being until they had charted a new direction in life.

Simon's main possession was an upright piano. He would sit at it and teach Sandra music he considered ideal for her beautiful voice. Her musical repertoire increased day by day and each new piece was accompanied with laughter and smiles. They shared a common love of music and music would be the glue that bound them together.

Towards the end of the school holidays, the 'A' level results were published. Sandra appeared unconcerned that she achieved less-than-good results.

"Why do I want A-levels when I have you?" she coquettishly smiled at Simon.

"That's all very well," replied Simon, "but have you thought what you're going to do if you're not going to university?"

"I'll find an office job that pays well, so I can pay my way and we can save money to buy a home of our own."

"But won't you find office work dreadfully boring?" he asked.

"It'll be a means to an end. It will keep me occupied whilst you're at school; and all the time I'll keep my eyes open for something that I really want to do."

"OK, if you're happy with that. But I do wish you would do something with that lovely voice of yours! That's your real talent."

Sandra smiled. "I suspect there aren't many singing positions going, especially for someone who hasn't been to Music College. But I'll keep my eyes open and, who knows what might happen?"

Sandra obtained work in the office of a local insurance broker. The work was humdrum, and the other girls in the office polite rather than overtly friendly; but the job kept her occupied and the money she earned contributed to the household budget.

Simon returned to school after the summer holidays with some apprehension. He was unsure how his teaching colleagues would react when they learned of his marriage. It was Deidre Wilson, the Girls' PE teacher, who was the first to comment.

"What's that ring on your finger?" she asked in shocked surprise. "Don't tell me you're married!"

Simon smiled and shyly nodded his head. "Yes," he replied. "I got married during the summer holidays."

"And who's the lucky girl?" enquired the eager Miss Wilson.

"Sandra," replied Simon, "Sandra Durrant that was."

"What!" exclaimed the PE teacher: "The girl in the Upper Sixth?"

"That's right. The girl who *was* in the Upper Sixth," he replied, placing emphasis very firmly on the word "was". "Music brought us both together. Our love of music has clearly spilled over into our personal lives and so we've tied the knot and are stepping out into the world to make music together."

"Well, this is a surprise!" exclaimed Miss Wilson, before realising that her shock at learning of the new liaison had prevented her offering congratulations. "I hope you'll be very happy together," she added, almost as an afterthought. Then, in some confusion, she nodded rapidly and hastily scuttled away, using a games lesson as her excuse for her rapid departure.

Simon was unsure what to make of her reaction. He had expected a few raised eyebrows when fellow members of staff learned of his marriage to Sandra, but he was unsure if Deidre Wilson's reaction presaged trouble or simply genuine surprise. It was not long before he found out. Miss Wilson was clearly very adept at communicating news around the staff room. Before the first day of the new term was over, every member of staff knew of the music teacher's marriage to the former Sixth Former.

"I now see why Sandra Durrant's work suffered so much last term," rasped the Head of Science when he encountered Simon in the corridor at the end of the school day. "I think you should be ashamed of yourself. You've ruined a young girl's chances of going to university and achieving success in her life."

"Hey, steady on!" retorted Simon. "I did all I could to persuade her to work hard for her A-levels, but she'd made up her mind university was not what she wanted. It doesn't suit everyone. She has other talents she wishes to develop, and I intend giving her all the help and support she needs to do so."

"I'm amazed her parents allowed her to marry at such a young age!" replied the Head of Science. "If she was my daughter I would have had something to say about it. No eighteen-year-old girl can possibly know her own mind. And if an older man comes along and sweeps her off her feet, she doesn't stand a chance. I think you've got a lot to answer for." And so saying, he stormed off along the corridor leaving Simon decidedly shaken.

Not all members of staff were so condemnatory. The younger ones exchanged winks and knowing smiles when they encountered Simon around the school premises.
"Done all right for yourself, Copeland, I hear," was a typical reaction.
"I rather fancied her myself," was another comment. "But I suppose I didn't stand a chance against you, lucky bugger."
Mr Shaw, the Head of English, took a more considered line. "I noticed Miss Durrant exercised a powerful influence over you when we were working on *Trial by Jury*, but, I must say, I never thought that within the space of a few weeks, the bride on stage would become a bride in reality. Working on stage can often result in sudden love matches. I've seen it happen before. I just hope you're suited to each other and that you can strut and fret on the world's stage with confidence in the years ahead. I don't expect it will be easy, but if you can maintain the love you currently have for each other, there's no saying what can happen."
Other members of staff refrained from either congratulating Simon on his marriage or criticising him for marrying a girl from the Sixth Form. But Simon viewed their indifference as disapproval. It would seem he had crossed the Rubicon that separated teachers from pupils and his colleagues were unhappy about it.
The day ended ominously when Simon received a message that the Headteacher wished to see him.
Making his way to the Head's office, Simon knocked tentatively on the door. His knock was answered from within by a command to enter. The Head was seated at his desk at the far end of his office. He made no attempt to

stand but simply motioned Simon to a chair positioned on the other side of his desk. The Head's face displayed no emotion. He merely looked at his music teacher with unblinking eyes and said, "I understand you are now a married man."

Simon smiled.

"I suppose congratulations are in order," continued the Head. "However, I'm told your new wife is Sandra Durrant, a pupil in last year's Upper Sixth. Is that correct?"

Simon could sense that trouble was looming and he gulped before quietly replying, "That is so."

"In that case," replied the Head, "congratulations are certainly not in order. Whatever can you have been thinking, marrying one of our Sixth Formers? Don't you know that all intimate relations between teachers and pupils are strictly prohibited? You've brought shame on yourself and on the school."

Simon had no intention of meekly absorbing the Head's anger and, before the Head could say anything more, he interjected.

"I have done nothing wrong. My conduct towards Miss Durrant, during her time at this school, was entirely right and proper. She is now no longer a pupil at this school. She is eighteen years of age and an adult. She's free to do as she pleases and she freely chose to marry me. There's no law to prevent that."

The Head inched forwards across his desk so that the distance between him and Simon diminished.

"In my experience, Copeland, marriage is always preceded by courtship. Do you mean to tell me there was no courtship taking place whilst she was a pupil at this school? I find that very hard to believe."

"It depends what you mean by courtship," replied Simon. "Sandra and I collaborated together on musical events at the school, but nothing untoward occurred I can assure you."

"Then why did you have to marry at the first possible opportunity? Is she in the family way?"

Simon was incensed. "I tell you there were no sexual relations between us before our marriage. I know the law and I ensured we remained on the right side of it. Our marriage may seem unusual to you, but I can assure you, I've acted with integrity at all times. You have nothing to fear on that account."

"It's not what I fear," retorted the Head. "What are parents going to think when they learn that a pupil, placed in *loco parentis* at this school, has been abducted by a teacher and is now his wife within days of leaving the school? What are they going to say? How will they feel about the welfare of the daughters they have in the Sixth Form? You have severely damaged this school's reputation by your precipitate actions."

Stung by this broadside, Simon retaliated. "No parent has anything to fear on my account. My marriage to Sandra is the result of a shared love of music. We could have formed a secret liaison and lived together without you or anyone else knowing. But we chose the open and honest way. We wanted a proper, legal union in which each of us made lifelong vows to the other. We've been perfectly open and straightforward. I'm not responsible for what others may say behind our backs; but, to all intents and purposes, we are a legally married couple with all the privileges and responsibilities that go with marriage. Rather than damage the school, my new-found happiness can only improve my teaching and spur me to even greater achievements."

The Head glared at his errant music teacher. "I beg to differ," he snapped. "Indeed, I think your position at this school is untenable and my advice to you is to start looking for another job as soon as possible."

"Are you sacking me?" asked a confused and bewildered Simon.

"I would if I could," retorted the Head, "and I will, rest assured, if any evidence of improper behaviour on your part comes to light during the time Sandra Durrant was a pupil at this school. You've forfeited my confidence, and I think it would be in your own best interests to look for an appointment elsewhere."

"I think that's exactly what I will do," replied Simon seething with anger. "I've devoted myself to this school and worked tirelessly to advance the standard of music here; but, if I'm no longer wanted, I'll go elsewhere."

The Head nodded vigorously and motioned with a wave of his hand for Simon to leave.

It was a very dejected and sullen music teacher that returned to the matrimonial home at the end of the day. Sandra had already returned from her job. She greeted Simon with one of her radiant smiles.

"How did the first day at school go?" she eagerly enquired. Then, seeing Simon's downcast countenance, her expression changed to one of anxious concern. "What's the matter?" she asked, "What's wrong?" Then, throwing her arms around his neck, she hugged him as a mother might hug a tearful child. "Tell me about it," she whispered. Holding back the anger welling up within him, Simon told her of his interview with the Head.

"The beast!" exclaimed Sandra. "I never did like him. He was only ever concerned with outward appearances. What would the governors think? What would parents say? What would the local community think? He was never interested in his pupils as individuals. We were just pawns he could manipulate to advance the reputation of his school and allow him to bask in its glory."

Despite his anger, Simon smiled at his new wife's outburst. She might be only eighteen-years-of-age, but she was perceptive and imbued with insight in excess of her years. He hugged her to himself before saying, "You're the best thing that ever happened to me. Together we'll overcome our troubles. With you by my side, I feel I can achieve anything."

The remainder of the evening was spent quietly preparing an evening meal and then musing over the future.

"It may well be best if I do look for another job," declared Simon. "It will mean we can make a fresh start where we're not known. We'll be Mr and Mrs Copeland and no one will be able to rake up our past. Perhaps it would be best if we moved somewhere new. After all, we're embarking on a new chapter in our lives, and a new home, with new friends, and new opportunities to make music, will all be for the better."

"I would like that," whispered Sandra. "Let's do it."

And so, from that moment onwards, Simon scoured the pages of *The Times Educational Supplement* searching for music teacher vacancies. He found the atmosphere at his current school debilitating. Not only did his teaching colleagues treat him distantly but he often heard gaggles of pupils giggling uncontrollably as he walked past them. It seemed they knew of his marriage to the former Sixth Former and put their own gloss on it. He realised his position at the school was untenable and so he redoubled his efforts to find a new position.

His chance came when he replied to an advertisement at a fee-paying private school seeking to appoint a Head of Music. He was duly called for interview and, on the basis of the musical productions he had mounted, the special services he had organized, his leadership of the school choir and orchestra, his degree in music and his compositional skills, he was offered the post. The salary was greatly in excess of what he had been earning and the future looked rosy. It meant he and Sandra would have to move to a different part of the country, but they viewed that as an exciting new adventure.

With his greatly increased salary, coupled with Sandra's modest earnings and the help of a mortgage, they were able to purchase a small semi-detached house near his new school. The weeks ticked down to Christmas and the end of Term. Simon bade farewell to his old school without any feelings of regret or nostalgia and he and his wife moved into their new home just in time to celebrate their first Christmas together.

Two days before Christmas, there was a rat-a-tat-tat on the front door. Sandra answered the knock and was amazed to find her mother, accompanied by her mother's second husband, standing on the doorstep.

"Oh my darling," gushed her mother as she threw her arms around Sandra's neck. "Oh, my poor, poor little girl! How I feel for you! You poor, poor thing!"

Sandra stood rooted to the spot as she indignantly replied, "I'm not a poor thing. I'm perfectly well and extremely happy."

"But how could you do such a thing?" gushed her mother. "How could you go off like that and get married without even letting your dear mother know? You don't know the agonies I've been through. I said to Leroy – oh, by the way, let me introduce Leroy to you." So saying, she spun around and beckoned to the tall black man of African descent standing in the doorway to enter the room. "This is my husband, Leroy. Leroy: this is my dearest, most precious daughter Sandra."

Sandra extended her right hand to the black man out of politeness, but no smiles were exchanged.

"Why did you do such a thing?" Sandra's mother demanded. "Getting married is a major step in anyone's life and I should have been there to support you. A mother always wants to be at her daughter's wedding, and I've been denied that opportunity. I'll never get over it. I feel I've been robbed of my darling daughter."

Sandra patiently endured her mother's gushing tirade. She had endured it all her life. She knew the words meant nothing. Her mother was someone who thought only of herself. Any concern she expressed towards Sandra was palpably false. Her mother had experienced no remorse when she abandoned her daughter to the care of a sister so she could disappear to the United States with her new husband. She had never displayed any maternal love towards her daughter, and so her present outburst of emotion was as false as it was cloying.

Sandra calmly replied, "Our wedding was a very quiet and simple affair. We purposely didn't want a fuss. We simply wanted to embark upon a new chapter in our lives without the difficulties split-families can cause."

As Sandra spoke, Simon silently entered the room from the kitchen where he had been overhearing the conversation.

"Simon," beamed Sandra, "let me introduce my mother and her husband, Leroy."

"So this is the young man who stole my daughter!" shrieked Sandra's mother. "You brute! I should have known it would be someone much older than her. Didn't I say, Leroy, my darling daughter must have fallen prey to an older man and been incapable of resisting his wiles?"

"Mother!" exclaimed a shocked Sandra. "Please control yourself! This is my husband you're addressing. He didn't seduce me, as you imply. He's only six years older than me, which is nothing by today's standards." Then, as an afterthought, she added, "How much older are you than Leroy?"

"That's none of your concern, young lady," snapped her mother. "Leroy and I were made for each other. Isn't that true, sweetie?"

Leroy gave his wife a wan smile.

"Well," continued Sandra, "Simon and I were made for each other, and I have no doubt we will be blissfully happy together."

"How can you be when you're so young? You know nothing of life. It will all end in tears, mark my words."

"Just as your life and my father's ended in tears?" interjected Sandra.

"How cruel and ungrateful you are! No one knows what I went through with your father! He appeared loving and tender on the outside, but inwardly he was unbending and controlling. He forbade me to shop for new clothes! Just imagine that – forbidding a woman to buy new clothes! I cannot live without decent clothes. Beautiful clothes bring me to life. They inject passion into my soul. Isn't that so, Leroy?"

Leroy frowned; but before he could reply, Sandra's mother was in full flow once more.

"By withdrawing my monthly clothing allowance, your father effectively condemned me to walking around naked. I have never felt so wretched in all my life! I was robbed of my identity. I was unable to look other people in the eye when I met them wearing the same outfit as when I last saw them. You cannot know the shame and degradation I experienced. And yet your father was completely impervious to my pleas. He refused to reinstate my personal allowance. He was the meanest, most miserly man I've ever known."

Then, turning her head to Leroy, she purred, "Not a bit like you, dear."

Leroy smiled another of his wan smiles. He was either a man of few words or the ability to speak had been driven from him by his wife's incessant monologues.

"You never know what a man is like until you're married to him," declared Sandra's mother. "It wasn't until I was married to your father that I discovered the sort of man he really was. I doubt if you have been married long enough to discover the true character of your husband; but I wouldn't be surprised if he's just as controlling as your father. All men are the same."

Then, glancing at Leroy out of the corner of her eye, she quickly added, "Except you, darling. You're not like other men. You know how to treat a woman."

Then, turning to face Sandra, she said, "You're far too young to be married. That man over there will hold you in slavery. You'll be putty in his hands. Your life is ruined - and all because you didn't talk to me before you rushed into this disastrous marriage. I could have warned you of the dire consequences!"

Sandra had endured her mother's tirade for so long, but now she felt the need to reassert herself.

"How could I talk to you when you'd abandoned me and gone off to the States with your new husband? When have I ever been able to talk to you? You've never listened to me. You've always been caught up in your own little world. You've never been interested in me. Simon listens to me. He understands me. We think alike. We are very much in love."

Ignoring Sandra's credo, her mother returned to the fray unabated. "I cannot think what my sister was doing, allowing you to consort with this man. I entrusted you to her care and she's sorely betrayed my trust. I instructed her to keep a watchful eye on your movements. I know what young girls are like. But she failed in the sacred trust I placed in her. She either closed her eyes to what was going on or else actively connived in it. I wouldn't put that past her. She always was a devious individual, even as a child. But now she's an adult, I thought I could trust her. I would never have placed you in her care if I thought this would happen!"

Sandra's sense of justice meant she could not permit her aunt to shoulder responsibility for the events that had unfolded and so she calmly replied, "My aunt knew nothing of my friendship with Simon. She bears no responsibility for the events that have unfolded. If anyone is to blame it is probably you. You abandoned me. You never really wanted me. I was a nuisance. I got in the way of your socialising and flirting. You couldn't wait to push me onto your sister so you could jet off to the States. You starved me of love. Is it any wonder that now I have found love in Simon I should want to be with him for ever? He's able to give me the love you so selfishly withheld."

"You ungrateful child!" retorted Sandra's mother. "No one will ever know the sacrifices I made for you. But I have not come here to be insulted. You are clearly deaf to a mother's entreaties. You've made your bed and now you must lie on it."

And with that, she spun around and stormed out of the house, with Leroy meekly following behind like an obedient lapdog.

"Wow! What was all that about?" asked Simon as he crossed the room to his young wife.

"It was another of my mother's histrionic exhibitions. She loves to be the centre of attention. Sometimes I think she wants the entire world to revolve around her. She resents the fact she was unable to attend a big wedding, dressed in all her finery, rather than any concern for my well-being. She's always been like that."

Then seeing the pained look on Simon's face, she smiled and said, "But don't worry. I'll never be like her. All that nonsense about girls growing more and more like their mothers as they get older will not be true in my case. If you ever see the slightest trace of my mother in me you're to tell me instantly so I can stamp it out." So saying, she threw her arms around Simon's neck and gave him a long passionate kiss on his lips.

*

Some months after his marriage, Simon summoned the courage to write to his parents informing them of his new married state. He knew they would be displeased. He knew his father would have wanted a church wedding and his mother would be hurt that neither of them had even been invited to the nuptials. But, nevertheless, he had to inform them and await their reply.

He received a muted response. They congratulated him on his marriage but he sensed the underlying sadness and anger that lay behind their civilized reply. They ended their letter by inviting Simon and his new wife to spend a couple of days with them at Christmas. When Simon shared this invitation with Sandra, he was surprised at her response.

"Yes. Let's go. I would like to meet your parents," she said. "I think you'll find them very judgemental and emotionally cold; but, if you're up for a challenge, then I'll tell them we'll arrive on Christmas Eve and leave on Boxing Day." And so it was that on Christmas Eve, the two of them drove to the sleepy country village where the Revd Copeland ministered to his rural flock. They drew up outside the large Victorian vicarage.

They were met in the hallway of the vicarage by the grey-headed vicar and his plainly-dressed wife. Handshakes and smiles were exchanged and Mrs Copeland senior took control of the domestic arrangements, showing her new daughter-in-law the modest facilities the vicarage possessed, whilst Simon's father shepherded his youngest son into his study, closing the door behind them.

"I must say your marriage came as a great shock to your mother and me. Your poor mother was very distraught. Of course, we always hoped you would get married and that you would be married in the parish church, as your older brothers did. But to learn you had married in a Registry Office, and with none of the family present, came as a great shock."

"I am sorry, father, for any pain I've caused you and mother; but, when you know you've found your soulmate for life, not a minute can be wasted. We were unwilling to live in sin and so we went for a quick wedding."

Simon hoped this reference to the avoidance of sin would be well-received by his father. His father always had a lot to say on the subject and the fact that his son had married rather than co-habited won the vicar's approval.

"Well, I hope you have indeed found your soulmate for life just as your mother and I found each other all those years ago. Marriage is an unbreakable bond. It is indissoluble. I sincerely hope you've found your true helpmeet for life."
His sermon completed, he turned the conversation to Sandra. "Now, tell me about your wife."
"I think," replied Simon, "she should tell you about herself. She's quite capable of doing so."
"In that case, let's move to the sitting room, where we can all enjoy a glass of sherry before dinner," uttered the vicar with an accepting wave of his arm.
Sandra excelled as a guest at the vicarage. She helped Mrs Copeland with the cooking and domestic chores and used all her feminine charms to humour the vicar. When the question of religion arose – as it always did when the Revd Copeland was present – Sandra recounted her performance of *I know that my Redeemer liveth*. "The words and the music," she said, "are so perfectly aligned. I do not know how anyone can doubt the resurrection when listening to such a beautiful outpouring of faith and trust."
It may not have been the doctrinal reasoning the Revd Copeland favoured, but his heart warmed towards his new daughter-in-law. He might be able to make something of her, he thought.
The couple attended church on Christmas morning and enjoyed standing side by side singing the well-known Christmas carols. Numerous smiling, sideway glances were exchanged between the two of them. The other people in the congregation were left in no doubt that the vicar's youngest son was very much in love with his new wife.

After a hearty Christmas dinner, in which Sandra played a full part in both the preparation and the cooking, the family of four relaxed in the vicarage sitting room. When Simon mentioned that his wife had a remarkable soprano voice, the Revd Copeland insisted she gave an impromptu performance. And so, with Simon accompanying on the piano, Sandra sang the long, languorous soprano solo that opens Part Two of *L'Enfance du Christ* by Berlioz. It was the Virgin singing a lullaby to her new-born son cradled in her arms. The music possessed great tenderness and Sandra made the long, languorous lines float on the air with delicate tenderness, as the two older people sat transfixed by the beauty of her voice and the appropriateness of the music for Christmas Day.

By the time Simon and Sandra left the vicarage on Boxing Day, they had successfully repaired any broken fences that previously existed between Simon and his parents. Sandra had been welcomed into the Copeland family and the future looked promising.

Although Simon had a job waiting for him at the beginning of January, Sandra had to resort to the Job Centre to find a clerical job that would provide her with something to do each day whilst Simon was teaching. She found a job in the office of a small engineering company. The other employees were friendly and many were of a similar age to her. She quickly made friends with a girl in her mid-twenties named Lizzie. She discovered that both she and Lizzie shared a common love of music. Lizzie and her husband, Rex, were members of the local choral society and Lizzie encouraged Sandra to join.

"Simon: how would you feel about joining a choir?" asked Sandra when Simon returned from a day's teaching at his new school. He smiled, before adding "That depends on the choir. I spend most of my life encouraging other people to sing; but I suppose there's something to be said for being on the other side, as it were, and allowing someone to encourage me. The musical director would have to be good! I couldn't endure a third-rate choirmaster."

"No one could ever be as good as you," replied Sandra with a mischievous twinkle in her eye. "But are you willing to give it a try? There's a girl in the office who sings with her husband in the local choral society and she's keen that I join."

After only a moment's thought, Simon agreed. Anything that would enable his wife to integrate into the new community would be beneficial, he thought. It would also enable her to make use of her beautiful singing voice.

"OK," he replied, "Let's give it a try."

The following Tuesday, the two of them presented themselves at the weekly rehearsal of the choral society. Simon was welcomed with open arms. The choir was very short of tenors and glad to welcome any man with a tenor voice – especially if he was musically proficient. Sandra took her place amongst the phalanx of sopranos and both she and her husband enjoyed a pleasant evening's music-making with like-minded people.

At the conclusion of the rehearsal, Sandra introduced her husband to Lizzie, who in turn introduced her husband, Rex, to both of them.

"Singing always makes me thirsty," declared the avuncular Rex, "and so we're off to the *Cardinal's Hat* for a beer. Would you care to join us?"

Simon and Sandra gladly assented and the four of them repaired to the local hostelry for post-rehearsal drinks.

"Sandra tells me you're a music teacher, Simon," said Lizzie.

"That's right," admitted Simon, before adding he was new to his present job and was still finding his feet.

"Your wife has a fabulous soprano voice," added Lizzie. "The two of you must be a very musical couple."

"It was our love of music that brought us together," declared Sandra, "Simon is too modest to tell you, but he's also a composer, and he has the gift of perfect pitch. He's composed music for school concerts and, I think, if he could choose to be anything at all, it would be a composer."

Simon blushed modestly before adding, "I also greatly enjoy performing and listening to music."

"Does that mean you'll continue with the choral society?" asked Rex. "We need all the men we can get, especially if we're to sing *Belshazzar's Feast* next year, which is what our musical director has got his sights on." Then, realizing he had focussed exclusively on Simon, he hastily added, "And we need some good sopranos as well to cope with those horrendous top A's. I don't know what Walton was thinking about when he wrote that piece."

Simon and Sandra smiled as they warmed to Rex and Lizzie. They were kindred spirits and they sensed that making music together would bring them great pleasure.

The weekly choral rehearsals, followed by an hour or so in *The Cardinal's Hat,* spilled over into invitations to each other's homes for meals.

"What a lovely home you have!" exclaimed Lizzie when she entered Simon and Sandra's modest, semi-detached house for the first time.

Simon smiled and said, "That's all down to Sandra. You should have seen my flat when I was a bachelor!"

"Simon is being too hard on himself," replied Sandra. "His flat was our first married home and all it required was a little tidying. It served us well until we moved here."

"How long have you been married?" Rex enquired.

"Nearly eight months," replied Sandra with genuine pride in her voice.

"Is it that long?" asked Simon. "It seems like only yesterday we were performing the nuptials." Then, before his guests could probe any deeper into their past lives, Simon said, "Shall we pass through into the dining room and make a start on Sandra's wonderful cuisine? Not only can she sing but she can also cook. She never ceases to amaze me with her hidden talents."

Their friendship grew and Simon derived much satisfaction from seeing his wife's friendship with Lizzie blossoming. Meanwhile, at school, Simon worked hard with his pupils. It was a co-educational school with approximately five hundred students. He headed a music department that consisted of him and one other teacher– a somewhat mousey, unmarried female named Miss Clutterbuck. Simon knew she would not survive a term in a state school, but, within the private sector, she was shielded from the more demanding pupils and pursued her rather esoteric interests in Baroque and Renaissance music - even though these interests were not shared by the vast majority of her pupils. As Head of Music, Simon had responsibility for the school's musical curriculum, training the school choir and orchestra, accompanying hymn-singing at the collective acts of worship, organizing concerts, producing an annual musical stage production, timetabling peripatetic freelance instrumental instructors, planning school concert visits and supporting Miss Clutterbuck when things got out of hand in her classroom. All of which meant he was kept extremely busy.

When Rex suggested the formation of a singing quartet, consisting of himself, his wife, Sandra and Simon, to perform at a forthcoming social event in the local church hall, Simon was not keen.

"What sort of music do you want to perform?" enquired an unenthusiastic Simon.

"Light stuff," replied Rex. "You know: Gilbert and Sullivan; perhaps a few parodies of some well-known pieces; some close-harmony barbershop pieces; and perhaps something that you've written."

Rex knew exactly which buttons to press to achieve his objective.

"Oh do let's give it a go!" exclaimed Sandra with girlish glee. "It would be a bit of fun; and you need some fun to counteract all the hard work you do at school. All work and no play makes Simon a dull boy."

And so, under pressure from his wife, Simon agreed to the formation of the singing quartet. There was no denying rehearsals were fun. Simon soon entered into the spirit of the group and arranged some very clever parodies of well-known musical pieces for the four of them to sing. Rex had a sonorous bass voice and Lizzie was happy to sing alto. Turning to Sandra, Lizzie had said, "You have a much better soprano voice than me. I think you should sing the top line and I'll sing the alto line."

Simon then took up Rex's invitation to contribute a piece of his own. Taking the words of a wistful Irish poem, he set them to music. In his mind's imagination he could hear the four distinct voices of the quartet and, almost without realising, he shaped the music to suit each individual voice. He reserved his very best musical inspiration for the melody line that Sandra would sing. He lovingly clothed the words of the poem with her beautiful, sweet, clear, thrilling voice sounding in his head. The other three singers supported the melody with harmonies that were as beautiful as they were novel. Sandra declared the end result a musical gem. Rex and Lizzie were visibly moved after the first run-through. Turning to Simon, Rex declared, "You have a rare and wonderful talent, Simon. And Sandra has the voice of an angel. That piece could have been written especially with the four of us in mind."

"It was," laughed Simon. "I heard each of your voices in my head. All I had to do was put the sounds down on paper."

Rex shook his head in disbelief. "I don't believe it. Sheer genius! You're wasted as a school teacher. You should be Master of the Queen's Music."

And on that jocular note, the first rehearsal of Simon's Irish song came to an end.

It was a very happy Mr and Mrs Copeland that returned home after the evening's music-making. Sandra threw her arms around Simon's neck and declared, "I'm married to a genius. Soon the whole world will know it. I've always known you're special. From the very first moment I met you, I knew you were no ordinary teacher. You are all that I ever wanted and I love you dearly."

They kissed before climbing the stairs to the matrimonial bedroom and expressing their love in a very physical way. Sandra was no longer the former Sixth Former he had married. She was now a mature young woman - and Simon was passionately in love with her.

The church social at which the Singing Quartet made its debut, was a Cheese and Wine Party. The great and the good of the district were invited to the event in order to raise funds for a replacement church roof. The church hall was thronged with guests – none of which Simon and Sandra knew. The evening followed a predictable course, during which the volume of conversation in the hall rose ever louder and louder as over a hundred people laughed and shouted at each other whilst balancing glasses of wine in one hand and cocktail-sticks bearing cubes of cheese and pineapple, in the other hand.

Two thirds of the way through the evening, the vicar mounted the stage to give a speech. He was a middle-aged man much given to public speaking. The thought of addressing the assembled gathering did not faze him in the slightest.

"Ladies and gentleman," he beamed from the front of the stage. "What a pleasure it is to welcome you all here this evening to our Cheese and Wine Soiree in aid of the Church Roof Restoration Appeal. All of us who are fortunate to have a home of our own, with a roof over our heads, will know that every so often we have to carry out repairs to our roofs. Sometimes it's a missing tile, sometimes it's a re-pointing job, sometimes it's a blocked gutter and so on. If you're anything like me, and have an aversion to heights and working off ladders, we are willing to dig our hands into our pockets and pay someone to put it right. Well, that's just what we've got to do at St Agatha's. The only trouble is, the church roof is about twenty times the size of most house roofs; and it's not just a few tiles that are missing, or a bit of pointing that's needed. No. It's the whole roof that has to be replaced. The old copper nails holding the tiles are all perishing and so…."

The vicar's fundraising spiel continued unabated. He may not have been in his pulpit but he was still six-feet above interruption as far as his captive audience was concerned. After ten minutes or so, he eventually reached his summing-up.

"And so I hope you will all complete one of the pledge cards on the tables around the hall and hand them to me at the end of the evening. I will be standing by the exit to receive your kind offers of help. Now, to sugar the pill, so to speak, we have some original entertainment for your delectation. Here, to entertain us is the Bourneland Quartet: Sandra and Simon Copeland and Elizabeth and Rex Osbourne."

With an enthusiastic clapping of his hands, the vicar left the stage and the recently formed Bourneland Quartet moved forward to make its first public appearance. Commencing with some humorous pieces from Gilbert and Sullivan operettas, followed by items from light opera and some satirical parodies of well-known classical pieces, the concert moved to the item Simon had composed specially for the occasion.

A silence fell upon the hall. Perhaps it was because Simon's piece was lyrical and serious after the high-jinks and tomfoolery of the earlier pieces; but a discernible hush descended as everyone in the building listened intently to Sandra's pure soprano voice soaring heavenwards above the accompaniment of dissolving chords and heart-wrenching harmonies supplied by the three other members of the Quartet. Sandra held the hundred or so people present in the palm of her hand. All eyes were on her as the aching melody of the song transfixed her listeners. It was a moment of sheer ecstasy in an otherwise tedious evening. As the last notes faded into silence, the audience remained silent. No one wanted to break the spell and clap. But, once the applause did start it was thunderous. The members of the Quartet acknowledged the prolonged applause with numerous bows and smiles before reverting to a final patriotic piece with which to end their performance.

As the four of them walked off stage to the room at the back of the hall that served as The Green Room, they were approached by one of the guests. He was a man in his forties with a full head of greying hair and steel-blue eyes. Ignoring Simon, Lizzie and Rex he made a beeline for Sandra.

"That was absolutely marvellous!" he enthused. "You have the most remarkable voice I think I've ever heard! The sheer range and texture of your voice makes it outstanding. You have a great future awaiting you as a singer. Here: let me give you my card. My name is David Spelman of BCS Studios. Would you let me have a tape of your singing so I can let other people hear it? There'll be no shortage of interest in a voice like yours, I can tell you. Will you do that?"

All this while, Simon was edging nearer to Sandra to ensure he overheard what the man was saying. When Mr Spelman finished speaking, Simon interjected, "I'm Sandra's husband," he announced. "What music does BSC Studios record?"

"We do all genres," replied Mr Spelman, "except classical." Simon raised his eyebrows before asking, "Would you say the piece my wife sang this evening was classical?"

"Good Lord no!" exclaimed the studio executive. "It was contemporary. It was somewhere between romantic soul and experimental. But it suited her voice perfectly."

Simon nodded his head before turning to his wife and saying, "I think we could supply Mr Spelman with a tape, don't you?"

That night there was a great deal of excitement in the Copeland household. The performance by the Quartet was quickly forgotten as Simon and Sandra discussed the possibilities that lay in the future.

"I'm glad it's not just me that thinks you've got a superb singing voice," whispered Simon into his wife's ear as they lay side by side in bed that night. "This could be your big break. But I hope you're not tempted to squander your voice on rubbish. So much popular music is trash. You can do better than that. Your voice demands good music. Promise me you'll only sing good music."

Sandra turned her head on the pillow and looked into Simon's pleading eyes.

"I will always be guided by you," she whispered. "Then I know I'll never go wrong."

After a loving embrace, they went to sleep in each other's arms, not knowing what the future held in store for them. The following day, Simon transcribed the accompaniment of his new song into a computer-generated orchestral arrangement so Sandra could make a recording using it. The final result pleased both of them and so a copy was duly despatched to Mr Spelman at BCS Studios. There then followed an anxious wait. Simon and Sandra began to wonder if they had been victims of a perverted prank. But, just when life had resumed its normal pattern and all thoughts of a possible recording contract had disappeared, a phone call from David Spelman reignited their hopes and dreams.

The voice at the other end of the line barked, "Hi, Simon. It's Spelman here. Thank you for the tape. I've passed it around and, just as I thought, there's a lot of interest in doing something with Sandra's voice. We would like her to come to the studios and talk contracts. It might be best if she had a manager with her to ensure she gets a good deal. If she doesn't already have a manager, there's a very good agency company I can recommend if you want to take down the details."

And so arrangements were made for Sandra and Simon to visit BCS Studios with a manager, if she had one.
When Simon told Sandra of the plans she retorted, "I don't need a manager. You can be my manager. You'll know what's best for me."
Simon smiled at his wife's blind faith in him before adding, "I'll watch over you like a hawk and ensure no one exploits you; but I really don't know anything about the commercial recording business and I think it might be good to have someone else on our side when we visit BSC's offices."
Sandra agreed, and so they approached the singers' and songwriter's agency recommended by Mr Spelman. When the agency learned that Sandra had been approached by BSC Studios, it was very willing to allocate one of its agents, Mr Charles Ferris, on a commission basis, to act as Sandra's manager and accompany her to the meeting at BSC's offices the following week. As luck had it, the meeting was scheduled during the school Easter holidays, and so Simon was able to accompany his wife and Mr Ferris to the interview.
BSC Studios occupied a sizeable building. It owned a number of recording companies trading under different names that were all part of its empire. Seated around the table in the boardroom with David Spelman were two other men: a man who was introduced as Head of Finance and the other as the Contracts Manager. They sat on one side of the table whilst Simon, Sandra and Charles Ferris occupied the other side.
"Right. Now let's get down to business," declared Mr Spelman as soon as the introductions were completed.

"We'd very much like to offer you, Sandra, an initial one-year recording contract, during which we would require you to record an album containing a minimum of fifteen songs."

The conversation then moved to financial arrangements and here Mr Ferris came into his own citing other singers' terms and haggling with the BSC representatives over money, royalties, franchising, publicity and such like – things about which Simon and Sandra knew nothing. Simon was more concerned with the integrity of the music Sandra would sing and insisted she had the final say over the music she recorded.

"We'll take her views into account, of course," replied Mr Spelman, "but, at the end of the day, this is a commercial proposition and we have to retain the right to decide what's most commercially viable."

"But she must have a right of veto," asserted Simon. "My wife has a wonderful voice and I'm not willing to let her prostitute it for quick material gain. Whatever she sings must be of high musical value."

There was some whispering amongst the studio executives before Mr Spelman came up with a compromise. "Alright, Sandra can have the final say over what she sings provided she produces fifteen tracks that are acceptable to us."

This proved acceptable to all parties, handshakes were exchanged and lawyers were instructed to draw up contracts.

As they travelled home, Simon and Sandra reflected on the new direction their life was taking.

"Whoever would have thought that within a year of our marriage you'd have a recording contract?" remarked Simon in amazement.

"And all because of that song you wrote," replied a radiant Sandra.

"My song and your wonderful voice: it's an unbeatable combination," beamed Simon. "We must just hope the general public likes our joint collaboration." And then, remembering what Mr Spelman had said when he first heard Sandra sing, he asked, "Do you remember what Spelman said about our song when I asked him if it was classical music: 'Good Lord, no!' he exclaimed. 'It was contemporary. It was somewhere between romantic soul and experimental.' The poor man obviously thinks classical music is simply music from the past. He doesn't realise the classical tradition is very much alive and kicking and continues today in contemporary music."

During the weeks that followed, as Simon and Sandra waited for the legal paperwork to arrive, their thoughts were never far from the challenges that lay ahead. Although Simon continued his relentless pursuit of musical excellence amongst the pupils at school, and Sandra dealt with the mundane paperwork of the small engineering company for whom she worked, her future singing career was never far from their thoughts. Then, one day, Sandra surprised her husband by handing him a sheet of paper covered in her handwriting. "Read this, Simon," she said, "and tell me what you think of it. Do you think these words could form the basis of a song?" Simon scanned the page of poetry before him. It was a love poem. He smiled as he absorbed its beautiful phrases and skilful rhyme scheme. The metre of the poem was irregular but he knew it was capable of a musical setting. He looked at his wife anxiously awaiting his verdict. "It's beautiful," he replied. "I never knew you could write like this!"

Sandra smiled another of her heart-warming smiles. "I pictured you as I wrote the words, just to tell you how much I love you."

"You're a remarkable woman!" exclaimed Simon, "and I'm the luckiest man in the world to be married to you. I'll mull over the words and wait for musical inspiration to come. Somehow, I don't think I'll have long to wait."

And so it proved. Within two days, Simon had set Sandra's words to a beautiful melody with a ravishing accompaniment. That evening, the two of them gathered around the piano and rehearsed the song, fine-tuning it as they went.

"I think we have the first of the fifteen items we need for your album," smiled Simon to his wife. "Let's hope we can come up with fourteen more that are equally good!"

Over the next few months, the two of them collaborated on a series of new songs. They ranged from passionate love songs to cheeky teasing songs; from slow outpourings of the heart to chirpy satires on school life; from wistful, nostalgic yearnings to affirmative declaratory pronouncements. The lyrics were written by Sandra. Sometimes they followed discussion with Simon, and sometimes they stemmed from ideas Simon suggested. But it was Sandra who put words to paper and proved adept at producing rhyme schemes that were good and often innovative. Simon relished the challenge of setting his wife's words to music. All the while, he had Sandra's singing voice firmly in his head, so that every song he wrote was purposely shaped with her in mind.

"At this rate I'll soon be another Schubert," declared Simon, as he put the finishing touches to their fifteenth song. "He composed over six hundred songs before he died at the age of thirty-one. I'm twenty-four which means I have seven years in which to catch up with him."

"Did he have a wife who wrote the words for his songs?" asked Sandra coyly.

"He wasn't as lucky as me," replied Simon. "He never married. Most of his songs were settings of words by the German poet Goethe; although he also cast his net far and wide and set other words that caught his fancy. He was an amazing dynamo of musical inspiration and industry. Six hundred songs before he was thirty-one!"

"Fortunately, Mr Spelman only wants fifteen," stated Sandra. "I don't want my husband in an early grave by the age of thirty-one!"

Simon smiled before adding, "I think we should work on a few more songs so we can present Mr Spelman with, say, twenty, and then he can choose which of the twenty he wants to use. That way, he'll feel in command and it might make for an easier relationship between us."

"Quite the little Machiavelli," replied Sandra with arched eyebrows. "Your influence might rub off on me – so beware!"

Within three months the two of them had assembled a portfolio of twenty songs, ranging widely in content and musical style. They were proud of their collaboration and took delight in lovingly committing them onto a tape for onward transmission to Mr Spelman.

A further month passed before they received a considered response from the music mogul.

"Hi Simon. It's Spelman here. We've listened to Sandra's songs and we like them very much. Of course, we can't do them with just a piano accompaniment and so we'd like to commission you to undertake orchestral arrangements. You seem to have a good musical ear and we feel sure you'll be the best person to work on the songs. Aim for variety. Don't make them all sound the same. Give them some individuality. The songs are good and Sandra has the voice of an angel, but they'll be even better with good arrangements. Let me have something when you're ready."

When Simon relayed Spelman's conversation to Sandra, the two of them were ecstatic.

"He likes our songs," said Simon. "He likes your voice. And now he wants me to orchestrate the songs. We're becoming quite a miniature musical business! I'll have great fun with the orchestration. And, with the full resources of a major recording company footing the bill, I'll not spare myself."

So saying, Simon set to work with a will, employing the full resources of a symphony orchestra, electronic instruments and chamber ensembles to accompany their twenty songs. Life then moved very rapidly for the husband and wife song-writing duo. The two of them spent a week at the recording studios during the school summer holidays, recording, editing, revising and polishing the fifteen songs that were to appear on Sandra's debut album. There then followed a day at the photographer's studio when Sandra was photographed in various poses, under different lighting, wearing a wide variety of clothes provided by the studio's marketing division. Innumerable meetings about publicity, promotional appearances, interviews and such like were held and Sandra was coached by the studio's public relations department in what to say and what not to say. Everything was in order for the release of Sandra's first album entitled *Journey into Love* on 15 November of that year. The date was chosen purposely by the recording company to capture the lucrative Christmas market. Sandra was not looking forward to telling her boss at the engineering company about her new career; but he was remarkably sanguine about it.

"I wish you every success," he generously said, "But, if things don't work out, there will always be a job for you here."

And with that Sandra bade farewell to Lizzie and her other work colleagues and embarked upon a new adventure as a professional singer.

CHAPTER SEVEN

Simon looked back at the launch of Sandra's singing career as the high-watermark of their marriage. Sandra had achieved national recognition. His judgement of her singing voice had been vindicated. The future was brimming with promise and he and Sandra were as happy as sand-boys. *Journey Into Love* was well-received by the popular music press with many critics extolling the exciting new voice that appeared on the album. After a sluggish start, sales of the album began to increase as radio stations broadcast more and more tracks from the album. Sandra made a number of appearances at musical events and was interviewed by some of the national newspapers.
"Tell us about yourself, Sandra.
"Do y' come from a musical family?
"When did y' start singing?
"Do y' write all your own material?
"Who's y' favourite artist?
"Who's y' boyfriend?
"When y' going on tour?"
The questions came thick and fast.

Despite her youth, Sandra remained remarkably calm and gave reasoned and sensible replies to each and every question. However, she had to do so without the support of Simon. His teaching commitments prevented him accompanying her to London for interviews and publicity engagements and he became increasingly anxious for his young wife.

The recording studio, meanwhile, was keen to promote its new star and increase sales of the album. It proposed a three-week regional tour in the post-Christmas period when Sandra, along with a couple of other groups the recording studio had under contract, would give concerts in various parts of the country. Simon could not accompany his wife because of his teaching commitments and was none-too-happy about her being on her own for three weeks.

"Is there no way you can avoid doing this?" he asked his wife in a pleading voice.

"Let's ask Mr Ferris," replied Sandra, "He'll know if I'm obliged to undertake a promotional tour or if I can decline. I don't really want to be separated from you for three weeks, living in hotel rooms, and mixing with people I don't know, but I may have no choice."

Charles Ferris, her agent, informed Sandra she was under no contractual obligation to undertake promotional tours. "However," he said. "If you want to further your singing career you need exposure. The more the general public see and hear you singing, the more your reputation will grow and the greater the sale of your recordings. I would strongly advise you to use this opportunity to further your career."

And so, with a heavy heart, Simon agreed to Sandra undertaking a three-week national tour organized by BCS Studios. It was a tearful parting. He felt as if he was casting his young wife adrift on a dangerous sea populated by theatrical sharks, rapacious men and an army of show-business people with dubious morals and even less integrity. But at least BCS Studios provided a chaperone to accompany Sandra for the duration of the tour. Simon trusted his young wife implicitly: it was the other members of the music industry he was less sure about.

The tears flowed as Sandra bade farewell to Simon and embarked upon her promotional tour. She and Simon arranged to speak to each other every day by phone and Simon undertook to travel to wherever Sandra's Saturday night concert venue was on each of the three weeks of the tour so he could see her performing on stage and then spend the night with her before returning home in readiness for school the next day.

On the first Saturday of the tour, Simon undertook the long drive to Glasgow where Sandra was performing at the *Glasgow Hydro*. He arrived midway through the afternoon and the two of them quickly found a café where they could be together and she could tell Simon everything that had happened during the previous week.

"The first concert in Cardiff was the most frightening," admitted Sandra. "When I peeped at the audience from backstage, my legs turned to jelly. I'd never seen so many people – all of whom had paid good money – waiting to hear me sing. I remembered you saying a performer's nerves can often ruin a performance, especially in the case of singers who depend on good breath control. And so, I undertook the breathing exercises you taught me – and they worked. It helped also that the blinding stage-lighting made it seem as if I was singing into an empty void. Once I began singing, all other thoughts disappeared and I sang as if it was just me and you in the room. The applause at the end of each song took me completely by surprise. It made me realise I wasn't alone but singing to over a thousand people."

Then, with a shy smile, she confessed, "It's a great feeling to hear sustained and prolonged applause. It gave me a warm glow inside. It told me people liked me. They liked my singing. They liked our music."

Simon returned the smile as he clasped his wife's hands in his.

"I can't wait to hear you perform tonight," he replied. "I just know you're going to be sensational."

And in his eyes, she was.

That evening, he sat at the back of stalls watching his diminutive wife walk across the stage to a central position as the sound of the backing track, that he had written and orchestrated, filled the auditorium. Then Sandra's voice entered with her pure silky sound floating on the air. She enunciated the words of her songs perfectly. She moulded each phrase with the skill of a performer twice her age. She carefully controlled her volume, always holding in reserve her most fervent singing for the climax of each number. She may have been only nineteen-years-of-age but she was professional to the core. Simon felt waves of pride wash over him as he listened to her ravishing performance. This was his wife. This was the girl to whom he was married. This was the singer he discovered. This was someone of whom the world would have to take note.

When the young people sitting either side of him broke into enthusiastic applause, he wanted to say to them, "That's my wife you're applauding! Isn't she wonderful?"

Simon's euphoria, however, didn't encompass the whole concert. He found the supporting acts trivial and musically worthless. Indeed, he felt inwardly angry that his wife was being made to perform alongside such second-rate musicians. In his eyes, the lack of talent in the supporting acts rubbed off on his wife and diminished her performance. Sandra deserved better, he thought.

After the concert, Simon collected Sandra from the Stage Door and the two of them went back to the hotel where Sandra was staying.

"Where's your chaperone?" asked Simon as they drove to the hotel.

"Oh, she isn't really a chaperone. She's just a production assistant from the Studios dealing with administration," revealed Sandra. "I suppose she would help me if I asked. But she certainly doesn't shadow me and protect me from over-zealous fans."

"Have you had many of those to deal with?" asked Simon.

"One or two," admitted Sandra. "I've found it best to leave the theatre by the back entrance, rather than use the Stage Door and risk confronting such people."

Simon frowned. It added to his concern for his wife's welfare.

Simon's overnight visit to Glasgow came to an end all-too-quickly and he was forced to bid an emotional farewell to his wife and return home to his teaching duties whilst Sandra continued her run at the *Glasgow Hydro*.
Sandra received good reviews at each of the venues where she performed. The public clearly liked her and sales of *Journey into Love* soared, much to the delight of David Spelman and the management of BCS Studios.
When Sandra returned home at the end of her three-week national tour it was with a feeling of great personal satisfaction. She had proved she was capable of negotiating the tricky world of the music industry; she had received warm and rapturous reactions from the audiences to whom she sang; and she had advanced her career considerably.
Simon was not so satisfied.
He had missed his wife terribly during her three-week absence. His weekend journeys to the far-flung corners of the British Isles had left him tired and irritable. And he felt frustrated that his wife's precious singing talent was being squandered amongst third-rate, poor-quality performers. This was not how he envisaged her singing career progressing.
Then there was the money.
Sandra's contract with BCS Studios guaranteed her a lump sum plus royalties based on the sale of *Journey into Love*. It seemed like a good arrangement at the time; but, once her agent deducted his commission and the recording studios extracted fees for copyrighting, promotional expenses and such like, the money Sandra eventually received was

nowhere near what she and Simon had anticipated. This further fuelled Simon's unhappiness.

Matters came to a head when BCS Studios approached Sandra about an extension to her contract. The company wanted her to commit exclusively to them for an additional five-year period.

"Why should we let them cream off all the profits?" asked an indignant Simon. "We do all the work. We write the songs. I arrange them. You sing them. We don't need BCS Studios. We could easily hire an independent studio to record our numbers, and then we could market the recordings ourselves. That way, we would be in complete control and be much better off financially. The Beatles did that when they established their *Apple* label. Why don't we do the same?"

Sandra was somewhat more cautious. "Let's ask Mr Ferris for his advice," she suggested.

Mr Ferris was less than enthusiastic. "Running a recording company is no easy matter," he stated. "It needs someone at the helm who knows what they're doing. Neither of you has the time or the expertise to do it, and so you would have to employ someone to act on your behalf. They would want a cut of the profits. You would merely be exchanging one management company for another."

"But at least the new company would be under our control," countered Simon. "We would have full managerial oversight of our music and how best to present it."

"It's a risky strategy," replied Mr Ferris, "as the Beatles discovered to their cost."

"Nevertheless," countered Simon, "I want to do it." And then, looking into his wife's worried eyes, he said, "It will be for the best in the long run. Just you wait and see."
So came into being *Angelina Music Limited* – a company exclusively devoted to the music of Simon and Sandra Copeland – with a name derived from Sandra's first public performance on stage in *Trial by Jury*.
"I like the name Angelina", declared Simon. "It suits you perfectly: you have the voice of an angel."
But Simon was being less than honest when he advanced the idea of owning their exclusive recording company. Besides acting as a platform to advance his wife's singing career, Simon also wanted a platform from which to promote his own music. Nothing gave him greater pleasure than composing. Music was the language by which he communicated. Making music was his reason for living; but he lacked an opportunity to publicise his compositional pieces. Getting new music performed and published was notoriously difficult. So, he reasoned that, if he and Sandra owned their own recording company, he would be able to advance his own career as a serious musical composer alongside Sandra's career as a popular singer.
Following the success of their first collaboration, Sandra embarked upon a new set of lyrics for Simon to set to music. The two of them bandied ideas backwards and forwards as they searched for subject-matter for their new songs.
"Did you hear about that man in Ayrshire who has just married the girl he fell in love with fifty years ago?"

"Why did he wait so long?" asked an incredulous Sandra.
"He thought she didn't love him and so he went away and pined for the next fifty years."
"That's so sad," sighed Sandra. "What a wasted life!"
"But when they met again, fifty years later," continued Simon, "he told her of the love he'd always had for her, and now they're married."
"There must be a song in that," declared Sandra. "I'll see what I can do".
And indeed, the result was a song about unrequited love spanning a lifetime before finding its final consummation. Sandra's portfolio of new songs grew, with Simon adopting ever more adventurous music for Sandra to sing. If he was required to compose songs, he vowed they would, at least, be musically stimulating songs utilising all the musical tools at his disposal.
Before the year was over, Simon and Sandra had assembled fifteen additional original musical items for inclusion on a new album. Using the funds from the sale of the first album, they financed the recording and production of the second under the *Angelina Music Company* label. Rather than employ someone to manage the company, Simon undertook the task himself.
It was to prove his undoing.
Every spare moment away from the school classroom was devoted to marketing, distributing and promoting the new album.
"Sir: is Sandra Copeland really your wife, sir?" asked an excited boy in Year Eight.

Simon gave a wry smile before acknowledging the marital connection.

"Cor, sir, she's got a super voice!"

"She has indeed," replied the very proud Head of Music.

"I particularly liked her first album *Journey into Love*. There were some great songs on it," raved Sandra's youngest fan. "But I'm not so keen on her latest album. The music gets in the way of her singing," declared the Year Eight music critic.

Simon was taken aback. "What do you mean by that?" he asked. "How can music get in the way of singing?"

"I dunno, sir, but it does."

It was a somewhat dejected Head of Music that struggled with the remainder of that day's lessons. Did his music detract from Sandra's lovely voice? Was his desire to stamp his musical originality on her songs actually proving detrimental? Had the music critic of Year Eight spoken the wisdom of babes and sucklings?

Whether this was so or not, there was no denying reviews of their new album were more muted than for the first. They were polite rather than ecstatic. Likewise, sales spluttered and stalled with none of the enthusiasm that had greeted Sandra's first album.

All of this spurred Simon to even greater feats of industry. Every spare minute he had was channelled into promoting the new album. But the stress of achieving commercial success, plus the heavy school workload he carried, began to take its toll. He grew tired, and, as he grew tired he became irritable. He snapped at Sandra and vented his frustration and unhappiness on her.

This was a side of her husband she had never seen before. Simon had always been the tower of strength, the steadying force, the rock on which she depended. A change had come over him and it was not a change she liked.

Matters took another lurch for the worst with the unexpected appearance of Sandra's father. As far as Simon knew, Major Durrant was stationed in Cyprus with the British Army and was likely to remain there for a considerable time on a long tour of duty. It came as a shock, therefore, to open the front door and find the erect figure of her father standing on the threshold.

"You must be Simon Copeland," declared the erect and well-built man on the doorstep. His skin was sunburnt from living in Cyprus and his unblinking eyes were deep brown and penetrating. Simon knew instantly who he was. He had exactly the same eyes as Sandra. Indeed, he had many of Sandra's facial characteristics.

Remembering the awkward scene when Sandra's mother unexpectedly arrived, Simon swallowed with apprehension at the unannounced visit of her father. Did the father's presence presage another ugly scene, he wondered? But Major Durrant was more in control of his emotions than Sandra's mother. He extended his right hand to Simon as he announced, "I'm Frazer Durrant, Sandra's father."

"This is an unexpected surprise," replied Simon, as he adjusted his mind to deal with whatever was coming. After shaking the outstretched hand he asked, "Won't you come inside?"

THE WAGES OF LOVE

The major strode into Simon and Sandra's home with his ramrod back and head held erect and waited to be invited to take a seat.
"Do please take a seat and I'll tell Sandra you're here. I'm sure she'll be delighted to see you after such a long time apart."
As Simon left the room to find his wife, he regretted his parting words to his father-in-law. He should not have mentioned the length of their separation. It sounded as if he was being critical of his father-in-law for abandoning his daughter for so long.
Finding his wife in the garden, he broke the news to her.
"We have an unexpected visitor in the sitting room," he revealed. "Who do you think it could be?"
Sandra shrugged her slender shoulders before replying, "I've really no idea."
"Well, brace yourself for a shock," continued Simon. "It's none other than your father."
A look of astonishment swept over Sandra's face, followed by an ear-to-ear smile. Without another word, she ran into the house and into the outstretched arms of her father. The two hugged each other and Simon was left in no doubt of the love that existed between them.
When they had adjusted their bodies to normal social conversation, Sandra introduced her husband to her father.
"Daddy, this is Simon, my husband. He's a great composer. He's written the music to all the songs I've performed. He's a genius and one day he'll be as famous as Edward Elgar or Benjamin Britten."
The major gave Simon a long hard stare before adding,

"Yes. I could hardly believe my eyes when I read about your meteoric rise to fame in the musical world. And this young man is the force behind it, I gather. I found it difficult to believe what I read when I received your letter telling me you had married this young man. It appeared very precipitative. I know young people today live different lives to my generation, but I just hope you've made a wise decision."

"Oh daddy, I have!" exclaimed Sandra. "Without Simon I would never have been noticed as a singer. He spotted my voice and the two of us form the perfect musical partnership. I write the lyrics and Simon sets them to music. It would seem we're a winning combination."

"I trust so," replied the not-so-convinced Major Durrant. "But there's more to marriage than just music."

Simon, who had held his peace as his wife and her father renewed their estranged relationship, felt he could no longer remain silent.

"Indeed," agreed Simon. "But music has the ability to speak to the very deepest passions and emotions within the human breast. It's the spiritual language that communicates at a very deep level. Two people who are able to share this invisible bond are bound to each other more strongly than by the marriage bond itself."

Major Durrant raised his eyebrows, "Maybe. Or maybe that's simply a way of pulling the wool over your eyes to conceal the absence of more enduring ties." Then, after a moment's reflection, the major continued, "Speaking as someone who made a mess of his marriage, I know how important it is to share common values and beliefs. I hope that your youthful marriage has something more substantial than ephemeral music on which to build."

"We were drawn to each other by a common love of music," replied a frowning Simon. "So long as the music continues to flow through our lives it will act as the glue that binds us together."

"Well, it has certainly brought you fame and fortune. But that has its dangers too, especially in a couple so young. I hope you're getting good financial advice. It's one thing to make money, but it can just as easily be lost," stated the practical, down-to-earth army major.

"We haven't made much money so far," replied Sandra, "because we've ploughed the profits from the first album into forming our own recording company. It will give us greater artistic control over the music we write and record. It was Simon's idea and he's working very hard to make it a success."

"Well, just make sure you keep an eye on where the pennies are going," Major Durrant advised his daughter. "My big mistake was to take my eye off the ball when your mother went on her never-ending shopping sprees. Before I knew it, we were head over heels in debt. And debt is not something that's easy to manage. It placed great strains on our marriage and resulted in our eventual breakup. Make sure your husband doesn't squander what you've earned."

Simon was stung by this comment, particularly as *Angelina Music Limited* was not performing very well and he felt personally responsible for the downturn in their finances. He would dearly have liked to quit his teaching job and devote himself entirely to their recording company. This, he thought, would also allow him more free time for musical composition. But, the Copeland finances were too precarious for him to abandon the good salaried post he had at his school, and so he had to juggle two demanding roles simultaneously. *Angelina Music Limited* was suffering as a result.

Looking straight into Simon's eyes, Sandra's father declared, "I wouldn't tolerate my daughter being exploited. I'm relying on you, young man, to safeguard her interests and ensure she gets the full rewards to which she is entitled. The entertainment business is a sordid industry. I didn't rear my daughter so she could be exploited."

Simon could not help thinking that Sandra's father's present concern for the welfare of his daughter was in marked contrast to what had gone before. He had been quite willing to abandon Sandra to the care of his former wife's sister whilst he disappeared to distant parts. He had no qualms about abandoning his daughter at Christmas time and leaving her isolated with her aunt whilst he enjoyed the bonhomie of the officers' mess and the convivial company of likeminded colleagues. Simon could not escape the conclusion that his father-in-law's unexpected appearance was a result of the new-found fame Sandra had achieved and the financial benefits that followed. The soldier had more than a fatherly interest in his little girl, thought Simon. He sniffed money and wanted to ensure it remained in the Durrant family.

Rising from his seat and refusing all offers of refreshment, the major embraced his daughter with a final fatherly hug before adding, "Remember what I've told you." And then, with a slightly dismissive glance at Simon, he assured his daughter, "Remember, I'm always there for you whenever you need me."

With a dismissive handshake to Simon, he strode out of the house.

"Wow!" exclaimed Simon when he and Sandra were alone together again. "What did you make of that? I don't think your father warmed to me, do you?"

"He doesn't know you as well as I do," replied a consolatory Sandra. "I guess all fathers are protective of their daughters. He probably thinks you snatched me away from him without a by-your-leave. He cares for me, even if he has a strange way of showing it. I sometimes think I'm much more like my father than my mother."

"That's a relief!" replied Simon. "I don't think I could cope if you were like your mother."

And with that, the two of them burst into laughter and hugged each other. All seemed well again.

But the seeds of doubt had been sown. From that moment onwards, Sandra began to take a more active interest in the financial aspects of her singing career. And Simon became more anxious about the financial health of *Angelina Music Limited*.

Although the second album Sandra and Simon released was nowhere near as successful as the first, Simon decided they must work on a third album – if only to repair the poor finances of their recording company. And so, the following year was devoted to writing, refining, re-writing, arranging, reworking and fine-tuning another fifteen songs for inclusion on Sandra's third album.

Whereas other songwriters hit on a winning formula and repeated it endlessly, Simon's innate musicality would not let him do this. He wanted to stretch himself and produce innovative and original compositions that would add something to the musical tradition stretching back to Hildegard of Bingen, Bach, Handel, Mozart and Schubert. But the more he stretched himself, the more he stretched the tolerance of his listeners. He might well be happy producing new and original harmonies and unusual vocal lines, but his listeners, who were the great record-buying public, might not be quite so keen on such innovations. A gulf was developing between Simon's artistic aspirations and the record-buying public's likes and dislikes.

Sandra was the first to recognize the dichotomy.

"Darling," she purred in her most seductive voice, "I know you're the most wonderful composer who has ever lived, but don't you think you're asking too much of our audience in the music you're writing now? Don't you think it would be better to keep to what we know sells?"

"Oh, please, don't ask me to write rubbish," cried a pained Simon. "If I have to write endless songs, at least let me write ones that are musically satisfying! I long to work on something other than songs! Even though Schubert wrote over six hundred, he also wrote nine symphonies and innumerable chamber pieces. I feel constrained and hemmed-in by having to turn out endless five-minute songs. I want to write great music. I know I can, and yet I'm trapped on a never-ending treadmill of popular songs. The only way I can survive is by making the songs innovative and original. Take that away from me and I will be musically dead."

"Darling," replied Sandra, "You know I would never make you do anything that offended your artistic temperament; but, do remember, I have a musical career as well. At the moment it's in danger of stalling because we're not giving the public what it wants. Sometimes you have to trim your sails to the prevailing wind if you want to make progress. I love singing your compositions; but if the public doesn't like them, I'll have no opportunity to sing. Singing is as important to me as composing is to you. Somehow we've got to find a balance."

Simon knew his wife was correct but the search for common ground proved elusive. The fifteen songs that eventually appeared on Sandra's third album were a compromise between Simon's constrained musicality and Sandra's need for popular material to reignite her career. Alas, the end result proved unsuccessful.

The national press music critics slated the new album and bewailed the fact that a new and aspiring young voice had been given less-than-good and perverse material to sing. The critics continued to praise Sandra's voice but damned the album with "a great talent still searching for the right music" and "a voice that promised so much wasted on second-rate material."

Simon was mortified when he read the reviews. Then he was angry. How dare the popular press damn his music as second-rate! The stuff they extolled every day was the second-rate stuff. His music had originality and musical creativity. He stood in the proud tradition of the great masters of lieder and song. His music was infinitely better than the rubbish they trumpeted week after week in their philistine publications. What did they know about good music? Their tastes were as plebeian as most of their readers. How dare they rubbish his music!

His anger spilled over into home life. He could see that Sandra was downcast and disheartened by the mauling her new album received at the hands of the critics. Although she did not blame Simon for the poor reception of their album, he sensed an unspoken resentment on her part. He, in turn, became morose and irritable. Their previously happy existence underwent a gradual deterioration as the joy disappeared from their relationship and the sheer necessity of getting on with life took over.

With the downturn in sales of their recorded albums came a downturn in their finances. The money made from Sandra's initial commercial success had been ploughed into the formation of *Angelina Music Limited*. As sales dried up so did the finances of their recording company. Before another year had passed they had to put their company into voluntary liquidation.

With their income-stream dried up, Sandra had to return to full-time salaried employment. Her former employer at the engineering works was pleased to welcome her back, and Lizzie Osbourne, who was now only working part-time on account of having a new-born child, was delighted to have Sandra as a work colleague once again. There was initially much chatter in the office about Sandra's singing career. The other employees wanted to know the background tittle-tattle of the music industry; but, this soon subsided as colleagues sensed that Sandra carried a sense of failure and, by talking about her singing career, they were merely reopening old wounds and preventing her from moving on with her life.

Simon struggled with his teaching career. He was just as busy as ever running the school's music department, but his heart was not in the job. His dream of using his very own recording company to produce and market his musical compositions lay in ruins. The will to compose deserted him. He went through the mechanics of being Head of Music whilst nursing a great sadness and hurt.

Sandra, with the intuitive insight of the fairer sex, knew all was not well with their marriage. The music that had once been its glue was rapidly disappearing. She and her husband had become more distant towards each other. They no longer had a common purpose and the future looked uninviting.

Sandra was the first to broach a subject on which she and Simon had rarely spoken.

"Simon," she whispered, as the two of them sat on the sofa one evening reading, "Don't you think it's time we started a family?"

Simon raised his eyes from his book with a startled look on his face. It was a subject he had barely considered.

"Start a family?" he uttered, more in disbelief than as a question.

"Yes," replied Sandra. "We've been married now for five years and I think it's time we started a family. It's the ideal time. We no longer have other commitments to take into consideration. Our lives are settled and we're just the right age to become parents."

"Well," replied Simon. "I hadn't really given the subject much thought. I suppose I always wanted children; but it will completely change our way of life. I've noticed that children have a way of taking over: little dictators that have to be obeyed. Do you really think you're ready for such an undertaking?"

"I think it would be good for us," declared Sandra. "Having a child will draw us closer together. We'll have a new reason for living and life will have laughter and joy once more. I feel ready for such a step. Do you?"

Simon laughed. "Well, if that's what you want, who am I to stand in the way?" And from that moment onwards the two of them set their sights on welcoming a new arrival into the Copeland household.

The new direction in which their lives were heading certainly brought about a change in their moods. Simon went about his teaching with more of a spring in his step. No longer did he see the pupils in his classes as the anonymous offspring of others but as archetypes of the son or daughter he would soon have. Miss Clutterbuck noticed the change in his demeanour and remarked, in her timorous way, "You seem much happier these days. Is there a reason for this?"

"Not particularly," replied Simon, not wanting to share his procreational lovemaking with the dyed-in-wool spinster. "It must be the onset of spring that has put a spring into my step."

"Spring always has that effect on me," declared the mousey Miss Clutterbuck, even though Simon had never seen any evidence of it in his music colleague. "I can understand why the sixteenth-century madrigalists wanted to sing "Fa-la-la-la-la-la-la-la-la" every spring."

With the bit firmly between her tiny teeth, Miss Clutterbuck launched into an impassioned spiel about one of her favourite composers. "I always think Vivaldi captured the spirit of spring perfectly in his *Four Seasons*. I can hear the flowing creeks, the singing birds (of different species, each specifically characterized), a shepherd and his barking dog, buzzing flies, storms, drunken dancers, and hunting parties whenever I listen to the music. Wasn't he clever to depict the goatherd sleeping whilst his barking dog is heard in the viola section? Sheer genius! The festive sound of rustic bagpipes to which the nymphs and shepherds lightly dance never ceases to delight me."

Simon looked at his colleague more in pity than scorn. She, alas, was destined to remain unmarried for ever. She would never experience the joys of lovemaking or parenthood. She would never cradle a new-born baby in her arms or experience the joy of being addressed as mummy. She was destined to pass through this world alone and unloved. Music was her only consolation. She could appreciate the creativity of others even though she was incapable of it herself. She was a dried-up specimen of womanhood unable to fulfil her maternal purpose in life. Simon felt pity for her.

Conversations between Simon and Sandra concentrated more and more on the expected newcomer to the Copeland household. Practical matters, such as where to locate the nursery, the equipment they would need, modified work patterns and such like tended to replace conversations about music.

But as the months slowly stretched into years, and still no baby Copeland was conceived, both Sandra and Simon became more and more anxious. They thought conception would simply be a matter of course; but when Sandra's monthly periods arrived with unerring regularity, they realised that conceiving a baby was not as straightforward as they envisaged.

Once again, a pall of sadness and disappointment descended upon them. Each wondered if they were to blame for their inability to conceive. Irrational feelings of guilt took hold and these were accentuated because neither of them felt able to share their feelings with the other. Eventually they summoned courage and made an appointment to visit their doctor. The doctor listened sympathetically to their predicament and, after giving some banal advice about relaxing more whenever they made love and not thinking about conception but simply enjoying each other's bodies, he arranged for tests to be carried out. Each had blood samples taken. Sandra underwent an ultrasound scan and Simon had to provide a specimen of semen so his sperm count could be evaluated.

When they returned to their doctor, they learned that the tests had confirmed that everything seemed to be in order, except Simon had a somewhat low sperm-count for a man of his age. As this was not a bar to conception, their doctor agreed to refer them to a specialist IVF Clinic. In the meantime he again encouraged them not to think of making a baby but simply enjoy each other's bodies whenever they made love.

It was all very well for their GP to advise relaxed copulation and the banishment of thoughts about babies, but, in reality, it proved impossible to follow his advice. Their infertility cast an oppressive shadow over their love-making and, indeed, over the whole of their lives.

There was an inordinate waiting period before they were actually summoned to the IVF Clinic for an initial consultation.

They were seen by Dr Guttaccini who, judging by his swarthy skin and pronounced accent, they assumed was Italian.

"Now tell me," smiled Dr Guttaccini, "how long have you been trying to make a baby?"

"For over two years," replied Simon thinking it was incumbent on him to speak for them both.

"Two years?" repeated the doctor with his black, perfectly etched eyebrows rising to meet his luxurious black curly hairline. "Why, that's nothing in the great scheme of things. Some of the couples I see have been trying for ten years or more. But we'll see what we can do. First, we'll double-check the hormones in Mrs Copeland's blood. Then we'll carry out another ultrasound scan and an X-ray to make sure there are no blockages preventing conception. And you, Mr Copeland: we will need another specimen of your semen to check it is as it should be. After this, I will see you again. Now, do you have any questions you wish to ask me?"

"Yes," answered Simon before the doctor could terminate the consultation and usher them from his room in double-quick time. "What does the treatment entail?"

"Ah yes," replied the doctor, as if this was something that had inadvertently slipped his mind. "The treatment is in six phases. First, we will suppress Mrs Copeland's natural menstrual cycle. Then we will boost her supply of eggs by the use of medication. Thirdly, we will monitor the maturing eggs to ensure all is as it should be. Fourthly, we will collect the eggs from Mrs Copeland's ovaries. But don't be alarmed. This is a straightforward procedure using a needle inserted into the ovaries through the vagina. We will, of course, sedate you for this, Mrs Copeland. Fifthly, we will fertilize the eggs with your sperm, Mr Copeland, in the laboratory. This will take six days. And then finally, we will transfer the embryos into Mrs Copeland's womb using a catheter. This is very straightforward and will require no sedation." Having finished his medical textbook lesson in *in virto fertilization* he beamed at Simon and Sandra before adding, "So now you know."

Simon, however, wanted more information.

"How long will we have to wait before we know whether or not the treatment has been successful?" he anxiously enquired.

"Approximately two weeks after the procedure has been completed, Mrs Copeland will be offered a pregnancy test and then we will know whether it is good news or not so good. In the meantime, do continue making love. Who knows, you may be successful and no longer need my help."

And with that he smiled an even wider smile than before as he rose from his chair to escort his patients from his consulting room.

The clinical atmosphere of the IVF Clinic did nothing to restore Simon and Sandra's emotional equilibrium. They felt they were guinea-pigs in a laboratory undergoing procedures to advance medical research. And the counselling that the IVF Clinic provided did nothing to restore their confidence. No matter how much counselling they were given, they found the whole experience dehumanising. Simon thought producing a baby should be a joyous and natural thing, the result of passionate lovemaking such as Wagner depicted in the erotic prelude to *Tristan and Isolde*, but instead it was being turned into a cold, clinical business in which sperm was surgically taken from him and inserted into an unconscious, inert Sandra. This was hardly the erotic love that drove a desperate Isolde over the raging seas to fall into the arms of her beloved Tristan.

Human love had been transformed into a clinical procedure devoid of all emotion. Both Simon and Sandra felt shamed and devalued by the process.

After another long anxious wait, the two of them were again called to the IVF Clinic for the start of the treatment. Sandra was shown how to inject herself in order to suppress her natural menstrual cycle. She put a brave face on it; but to Simon, she appeared like a drug-junkie giving herself a fix in the hope of achieving an out-of-the-body experience. This continued for two weeks before she discarded the first course of injections and moved to the second that was designed to boost her supply of eggs. After an additional ten days of this, her arm was beginning to resemble a pincushion.

"Oh darling," wailed Simon, "I can't bear to see you putting yourself through all of this!"

"It will be worth it in the end," replied Sandra with a serenity based on her belief that a healthy baby would result.

"I hope so," answered Simon, even though he shared none of Sandra's certainty.

Simon supplied a sample of his semen for testing. Once again, he was found to have a low sperm-count which might account for their inability to conceive.

Numerous follow-up visits to the Clinic followed for ultrasound scans before Dr Guttaccini was ready to collect eggs from Sandra's ovaries.

"You will not know a thing about this," the doctor reassured Sandra, "because you will be sedated. And do not worry. I have performed this procedure multiple times and know exactly what to do."

Simon provided another specimen of his sperm so the fertilization process could be undertaken in the laboratory. Simon bewailed the fact that the joy of procreation had been reduced to a test-tube scientific experiment in a sterile laboratory.

Whilst the laboratory technicians were engaged in their work, Sandra had to suffer the indignity of a pessary inserted into her vagina to prepare the lining of her womb for the fertilized embryo.

The two of them returned to the clinic for the final stage in the process: the transfer of two embryos into Sandra's womb.

There then followed an anxious two-week wait to see if the process had been successful. They tended not to speak about it, but the subject was never far from either of their minds. Simon could tell that Sandra was desperate to have a child. The maternal impulses within her had been activated and now she could think of nothing else. He feared that if they failed to produce a child, the consequences would be serious.

He recalled his childhood memories of women in the bible who failed to conceive: Sarah, the wife of Abraham; Rebekah, Isaac's wife; Rachael, one of Jacob's wives; Hannah the wife of Elkanah. How was it, he wondered, they all eventually conceived? And why were they described as barren? Was it always the woman's fault that no child was conceived or was that just the thinking of a male-dominated society? Life was certainly not easy for people in the past; but somehow they had triumphed over adversity. He hoped the same would be true for Sandra and him.

After two weeks, Sandra underwent a pregnancy test. Alas, she had failed to conceive despite all the work of the medical people at the IVF clinic.

Great was the gloom that descended upon the marital home. Both Simon and Sandra made valiant efforts to break through the gloom, but all attempts at humour or distraction were ultimately futile.

The IVF Clinic advised a delay before repeating the treatment. And so another year passed before Simon and

Sandra presented themselves again at the Clinic for the next course of IVF treatment.

The result was exactly the same.

They waited yet another year before repeating the process a third time. Once again it was unsuccessful. They had exhausted their three attempts at IVF provided by the National Health Service, and still they had no child. Despite the exorbitant cost of private treatment, they sank their meagre savings into one final course of private IVF treatment. Not only did they find this physically and emotionally draining but Sandra also experienced continual hot flushes and headaches. They were slowly being destroyed by their quest for a baby.

When they realised all avenues were closed to them, they reluctantly resigned themselves to being a childless couple. Their lives continued along much the same lines as before, but now there was a deeper, more unsettling undercurrent. Outwardly everything may have seemed as before but internally both Simon and Sandra were deeply unhappy. They attempted to mask their unhappiness by re-joining the local choral society and socialising with Rex and Lizzie. This was not as easy as before. Rex and Lizzie now had two small children of their own and their social life revolved around their children.

Singing in the local choral society was the highlight of Sandra's week. It was her only opportunity to use her voice and recreate the sounds that had once drawn forth the enthusiastic applause of hundreds. It was her personal safety-valve that allowed her to forget her troubles and lose herself in beautiful music. Simon was aware of the positive effects singing had on Sandra and so he willingly accompanied her to the weekly practices, even though he was often tired after teaching students all day at school. He soldiered on with the choral society for six additional years until he eventually reached breaking-point. Simon had always said he would sing in the choral society provided the music was of a high order. Usually it was. The musical director worked through the great choral masterpieces of the past – Verdi's *Requiem*, Elgar's *Music Makers*, Walton's *Belshazzar's Feast* , Mendelssohn's *Elijah* and such like – and all was well. But the breaking-point came when it was announced the next work they were going to tackle was Andrew Lloyd Webber's *Requiem* written in 1985. Simon groaned. Of all the great choral masterpieces he and the other hundred members of the choral society could sing, they were being asked to sing an undigested potpourri of musical styles by the showbiz composer of *Cats* and *Evita*. Simon could hardly believe his ears. When the work first appeared it had been slated by the music critics. They described it as "Carl Orff without his pile-driving impetus" and "a mere shadow of Puccini." The eclectic mix of musical styles resulted in tunes that were short-breathed and broken-backed commonplace clichés. Simon could not bear the thought of devoting weeks of his after-school free-time rehearsing such small beer.

"I couldn't believe my ears!" exclaimed Simon when he re-joined Sandra, Rex and Lizzie at the end of the rehearsal. "Who in their right mind would waste time singing such third-rate drivel?"

Rex laughed at Simon's indignation. "Steady on, old man," he replied, "It might not be as bad as you think."

"It's a hundred times worse!" declared Simon.

"But it has a well-known name attached to it," continued Rex, refusing to be browbeaten by Simon's emotional outburst. "People will pay good money to see and listen to a Lloyd Webber piece. It should guarantee us a good source of revenue."

"I've no intention of prostituting my musical values simply to swell the society's finances," stated Simon.

"We sometimes have to take the rough with the smooth," declared Lizzie, attempting to act as a peacemaker and calm Simon's anger. "There have been innumerable works I've not enjoyed, but we just have to give it our best, knowing that something better is probably just around the corner."

"Anything would be better than Webber's pirated confection. The only reason it ever saw the light of day was because he had unlimited money to throw at it. I cannot believe that Lorin Maazel and Plácido Domingo threw their artistic integrity out of the window to perform the piece. Money certainly talks."

Simon's last comment came from deep within his subconscious, whether he realised it or not. He was denied the opportunity of having his music performed because he lacked the money to fund performances, still less recordings. He begrudged Lloyd Webber his success and his envy coloured his musical judgement.

When he and Sandra were home, Sandra said, "That was a deplorable display of bad temper before Lizzie and Rex. I hardly knew which way to look. I know you have very firm views about good and bad music, but I think you should learn to be more accommodating."

"I'm sorry if I embarrassed you," replied Simon with hardly a hint of remorse in his voice. "It's because of the high regard I have for music that I cannot bear to see it trivialised and demeaned. It physically hurts me. I just cannot sing the Lloyd Webber piece. It would pain me to do so."

"In that case," declared Sandra, "I will have to attend rehearsals on my own. I want to learn the work and form my own opinion of it."

"Fine, if that's what you want to do," replied Simon.

And so, from that point onwards, Sandra bade farewell to Simon every Tuesday evening and attended choral society rehearsals alone. She did, of course, have Lizzie as a companion and the two of them were thrown together much closer as a result of Simon's absence. They often met together after work, with Sandra accompanying Lizzie on her walk to the childminder to collect Lizzie's two children. But whenever Sandra saw Lizzie with her two children it only increased the heartache deep within her. After such encounters she would often shut herself away and weep. Simon did his best to console his wife and assure her that his love for her was not dependent on having children. He reassured her of his love but somehow his words and gestures failed to reignite the love they once had for each other. They were growing apart.

The lovemaking, that had always been such an integral part of their marriage, began to diminish. Neither felt the desire they once had to demonstrate love in a physical way. Rather than drift to sleep in each other's arms, as they had done at the commencement of their marriage, they slept with their backs to each other.

The smiles that had once been the *lingua franca* of their marriage disappeared and were replaced by unsmiling faces and downturned mouths. The joy had departed from their lives and both were unhappy.

Simon no longer experienced the urge to compose. The springs of creativity within him had dried up. He went through the motions of living and working, but without any enthusiasm. Sandra, moreover, found her life aimless. When she looked back and reflected on her success as a singer, the performances she had given, the crowds that clapped euphorically at the end of each number, the far-flung places she had visited, the reporters who interviewed her, the lyrics she composed and the feelings of excitement and exultation she experienced, she was plunged into the depths of despair. Her married life, that had started so full of promise, had led her to working as an office clerk for an insignificant engineering company. It seemed as if that was all she had to look forward to – and she resented it.

Her resentment was increasingly directed at Simon. He was the one who had snatched her away from the university place that was awaiting her. He was the one responsible for stalling her singing career by his stubborn refusal to listen to wiser advice and his pig-headedness in founding his own disastrous recording company. He was the one who squandered the money they made from their initial success. He was now the one unable to father a child and help her become the mother she so desperately wanted to be.

They bickered. Simon spent more and more time at school filling his life with extra-curriculum activities, organizing a school music festival, forming a chamber choir and such like. These were things over and above the call of duty; but they occupied his time and prevented him dwelling on his unhappiness at home. Sandra had no such extra-curricular activities to fill her spare time and so, when she came home to an empty house, she would mope and resort to watching television to while away the hours.

Matters came to a head one fateful Friday evening when Simon announced he was going with a group of pupils for a musical weekend in Buckinghamshire.

"You never told me about this," Sandra snapped angrily.

"It must have slipped my mind," replied Simon with no great sincerity.

"What am I supposed to do while you're away enjoying yourself?" retorted Sandra.

"It's not exactly a case of enjoying myself," retaliated Simon with feigned pain in his voice. "You should try taking a bunch of kids on a residential weekend! You'd soon discover it's no picnic, I can tell you."

"You've never taken pupils on weekend events before," returned Sandra. "Why are you doing it now?"

The real reason Simon was doing so was to escape the suffocating atmosphere of home. He felt he needed to get away and share the company of others, rather than vegetate at home with a sullen and uncommunicative wife. But he could not say this, and so he replied, "It will advance my career. The Head is particularly keen on extra-curricular activities. It looks good in the school prospectus. And it may help me move up a couple of points on the pay incremental scale. You never know."

"So what am I supposed to do this weekend whilst you're away?" Sandra demanded angrily.

Simon was gradually losing his composure in the face of Sandra's continual hostile questioning. Why did he have to tell her what to do whilst he was away? She was a grown woman. She was quite capable of deciding for herself how to spend her leisure time. She may once have been a young schoolgirl, who needed his help with decision-making, but they had now been married for nineteen-years and she could surely decide for herself how best to use her time.

"Well?" demanded Sandra, staring defiantly at her husband. "What am I supposed to do whilst you're away enjoying yourself?"

Simon finally lost his composure and retorted angrily, "Why is it I always have to tell you what to do? You're a mature woman. You should be capable of organising your own life. The trouble with you is you have no interests. Apart from the engineering company and household tasks, you have no other interests in life."

Stung by this broadside, Sandra quickly retaliated.

"My great interest was singing. But you ruined that for me. I had a tremendous career in front of me but, thanks to you, it now lies in ruins. You used me to further your own ends. You weren't really interested in my singing career. All you wanted was for people to hear your music and say what a wonderful composer you were. You made me sing the music you wanted people to hear, not what was popular and would give me success. I was just a pawn in your plan to be a great composer."

"You don't know what you're talking about," retorted Simon. "The music I wrote for you was infinitely better than the rubbish the music industry was turning out by the bucketful. It was original. It was skilful. It was filled with creativity. It wasn't my fault the Great British Public refused to accept it. It's always been the same. Great music has always been rubbished on its first appearance. Stravinsky's *Rite of Spring* was booed and catcalled at its first performance because it was original, and different, and demanding. But now look at it! It's a staple of the orchestral repertoire."

"How is it then," demanded Sandra, "that a decade has passed since you presented your original, skilful and creative music to the general public and still it's gone unnoticed? Your music was a disaster, but you're too full of yourself to admit it. You may well continue churning out musical compositions, and living in hope that one day they might be successful; but what of me? My opportunity of becoming a professional singer has gone for ever. I'm an empty shell washed up on the seashore and left to remain there for ever whilst you go off for the weekend with a bunch of young people having a good time and forgetting all about me."

Ignoring the having-a-good-time barb Simon replied, "If you want to recommence your professional singing career, you should do something about it, rather than sit at home snapping at me at every opportunity."

"How can I?" screamed Sandra, with tears running down her cheeks. "You prevented me going to university or

Music College. Because of you, I've no musical qualifications. There are no openings for me in the world of professional music. I'm a non-entity."

The emotional temperature in the room soared as Simon launched a counter-attack.

"I never prevented you from going to university or Music College. It was your decision. You were unhappy. You were unloved by your parents. You were cast adrift with that ghastly aunt with whom you were living. You saw me as the perfect means of escape from your unhappiness. You threw yourself at me knowing full-well I'd be unable to resist your charms. Don't blame me for the direction your life has taken. You've only yourself to blame."

"How dare you accuse me of throwing myself at you!" screamed Sandra. "I was a seventeen-year-old girl whom you seduced. I was innocent and powerless in the face of your advances. But I believed in you! I thought you'd guide and support me through the years ahead. And what did you do? You squandered the money I earned. You wasted it on a madcap dream of owning your own recording company. All that I achieved disappeared. Now I have nothing. My sole source of income is the wages I get from a boring and soul-destroying job at an engineering company. I'm thirty-seven with no career, no savings and no baby."

"I suppose I'm to blame for there being no baby?" shouted Simon angrily. "You may as well blame me for everything! I'm clearly the one who's in the wrong! Why didn't you demand a sperm-count from me before we married, to ensure I could father children?"

THE WAGES OF LOVE

The shouting match reached its climax with Simon sounding the death-knell to their nineteen-year marriage. "I wish I'd never married you!" he screamed before storming out of the house to seek refuge in one of the local pubs. That night, Sandra slept in the spare room.

The following morning Simon packed an overnight bag and left for the residential musical weekend in Buckinghamshire. Not a word was spoken between the two of them. The iron had entered their souls and the future was bleak.

When Simon returned on Sunday evening from his weekend away, he found the house empty. Lying on the kitchen work-surface was a note in Sandra's handwriting. It said, "I am leaving. I can no longer live with you. I need a new start. Sandra."

CHAPTER EIGHT

Simon sat on his narrow regulation-sized prison bed with his head in his hands sobbing. The tears rolled down his cheeks like rivulets trickling down a glass windowpane on a wet afternoon in November. But the claustrophobic walls of his cell were oblivious to his pain. They had witnessed more than a century of unhappiness. Simon was just another pathetic individual incarcerated within their walls who was overflowing with remorse for past misdeeds. "Where did I go wrong?" Simon continually repeated to himself as he sat crouched and crumbled on his prison bed. "Did I really take advantage of a young girl and use her for my own ends? Perhaps I wrongly believed she was exactly like me: someone seeking love to give meaning to her life. Perhaps I overlooked the age difference between us and assumed she was more mature than was actually the case. Perhaps I was beguiled by her wonderful singing and blind to all rational considerations. Perhaps… perhaps… perhaps."
Simon shook his head. "It's no use saying perhaps all the time," he reasoned. "What's happened has happened and

there's no way of changing it. But I do wish I'd spotted the disaster coming. If only I'd been alert to her unhappiness, I could have done something to alleviate it. I overlooked her feelings because I was fixated on my own future. I wanted to become a recognized composer and I channelled all my energies into that. I was selfish. I wanted what was best for me and, once Sandra's singing career failed to progress, I effectively wrote her off as no longer able to further my ambitions. I treated her dreadfully."

With this realisation came another uncontrollable outburst of weeping.

"I ruined her life," sobbed Simon. "I took her best years and used them for my own ends. She will never regain those years. Their loss will act as an eternal reproach for her childlike trust and faith in me."

Echoing down the years, he heard words he had not heard since he was forced to attend church on Sundays: "If anyone causes one of these little ones to stumble, it would be better for him to have a millstone tied around his neck and be cast into the depths of the sea." A shiver ran down his spine. He had been the stumbling block that caused Sandra to fall from innocence into the mire of unhappiness. In seeking his own happiness and fulfilment, he had trampled on a young, impressionable girl and destroyed her life in the process. It was a thought that was too painful to contemplate.

Neither did he know what to make of her silence. He had heard nothing from her, or about her, since he was sent to prison. "What was she doing now?" he wondered. "Had she found someone else with whom to share her life? Where

was she living, and, most important of all, had she found some way to use her beautiful singing voice?"
Hearing her pure, limpid soprano voice sounding in his head caused his tears to cease and be replaced by a shy smile. "She did have the most marvellous voice," he said to himself. "It was the voice of an angel. She was able to use it to exquisite effect. Her soaring top A's thrilled me to the core. She had a rare gift and, even if she was young, she knew how to use her gift. She had sophistication well in advance of her years. That's what people forget. They think I cradle-snatched a young schoolgirl, but I didn't. She was musically as mature as me. We were equals. The first album we recorded showed we were equals. Her wonderful singing and my original music was a marriage made in heaven."
Then, realising the truth of this assertion, he shouted, "I didn't take advantage of her! We were equals. We formed the perfect partnership. We were made for each other."
Just then, the peephole on his cell door slid open and a voice enquired, "You alright in there?"
Simon hung his head in sorrow before muttering, "I'm fine."
The peephole snapped shut and Simon was left alone with his thoughts once more.
"What would have happened," he asked himself, "if Sandra had conceived and had a baby? Would things have turned out differently?"
The more he thought about this, the more unsure he became. "It might have bought us a bit of time," he mused. "Sandra would have had a new focus on which to lavish her love; but, ultimately, I don't think it would have been the

answer. It would have been a diversion rather than a solution. We both needed to find personal fulfilment. We both needed to fulfil our innate potential and rise to the heights of which we were capable. Rather than help, a baby might have added to our troubles, pushing us further apart and adding more pressure on our unfulfilled lives. Perhaps it was best we didn't have children."

Then, with a shake of his head, Simon admitted, "At least there are no children to endure the shame of having a prison-lag for a father." And with that thought, he lay on his bed and slowly drifted to sleep.

The next morning, prison routine took control once again. He successfully negotiated the shoving and jostling of the ablutions' block and returned to his cell for the morning inspection before commencing work swabbing floors and cleaning handrails. Midway through the morning he received an order to go to the Education Block and report to the Director of Education.

He was received with the customary coldness by the gorgon who ruled the prison's educational facility. The battle-clad dragon launched into a tirade without any perfunctory introduction.

"The Open University has decided to facilitate your desire to study for a Doctorate in Music - although why that should be is beyond me – and wishes to discuss with you the nature of your thesis and the area of research you will undertake. I have made arrangements for you to speak to a Professor Lawson, via video-link, at three o'clock this afternoon. You are to present yourself in the video-room promptly. I will be in attendance to ensure whatever plans

are made are in accordance with prison regulations." And with that she dismissed the prisoner as if she waving away an offending odour that had suddenly reached her nostrils. Simon was escorted back to his cleaning work on E Wing by an impassive prison officer.
"I don't think she likes you," observed the officer.
Simon smiled. "I gained that impression, too."
"Mind you, I don't think she likes any men."
And with that Simon resumed his floor cleaning duties as he ruminated on the ways of the fairer sex. Had the Director of Education been crossed in love? Was this the reason she hated men? Or had she always been emotionally frigid and distant as a result of a repressive childhood? Whatever the reason, Simon was sure someone, somewhere, was responsible for making her the person she was. It was a sobering thought; and he was not slow to make a connection with Sandra. He worried that he had soured her and made her into someone who would always be suspicious of men? Would she erect a protective shield around herself to ward off any further emotional hurt? It was a chilling thought, and one he quickly sought to dispel. Sandra was completely different from the Prison Educational Officer. Sandra had music in her soul whereas the dragon in the Education Department had none. Banishing his uncomfortable thoughts, he continued with his prison work until three o'clock in the afternoon.
At three o'clock he was escorted to the video-link suite where the Director of Education was awaiting him. She looked testily at her wristwatch, but refrained from comment.

"Come this way," she instructed as she led Simon to a desk on which a monitor and camera was located. "Sit here. Time is at a premium. You must be concise so we can get this over as quickly as possible."

Just then, the screen sprang to life and the face of an elderly, grey-bearded man appeared. He seemed to be short-sighted and stared intently into his camera.

"This is Professor Lawson," he announced in a stammering voice. "Am I addressing Mr Simon Copeland?"

"Yes, sir," replied Simon from his seat in front of the monitor.

"Ah good!" replied the professor. "We have successfully established contact. I'm delighted you want to pursue research into the Czech composer Zelenka. A much neglected composer, in my estimation, but an extremely innovative one none-the-less. I have read your application and see you wish to undertake research into the formative influences that moulded Zelenka, with an analysis of his harmonic and contrapuntal technique and the effect these had on subsequent musical developments. Is that correct?"

"Yes, sir," replied Simon. He was certainly being concise and he hoped the Director of Education approved.

"Now," continued the professor, "I suggest you begin by reading Janice B Stockigt's *Jan Dismas Zelenka – A Bohemian musician at the court of Dresden* published by the Oxford University Press in 2000. This is an excellent introduction to the basic musical material, and then Jaroslav *Smolka's Jan Dismas Zelenka, Prague: Akademie múzických umění v Praze, ISBN 80-7331-075-9* published in 2006. This is a somewhat harder book to access but is essential for your research. Will you be able to obtain these books given your …um… circumstances?"

Simon turned to the Director of Education for an answer. She stiffened her back before stating, "We have neither of those books in the prison library. They will have to be outsourced. And that will entail cost." Then, under the unremitting myopic gaze of the OU professor, she conceded, "But we will endeavour to locate them."

"Excellent," beamed the professor before adding, "Once you have read those two books, Mr Copeland, we will undertake another long-distance tutorial and discuss the framework for your research. Is there anything you wish to ask me?"

"I'm sure there will be innumerable questions once I've read the two books but, for the time being, I have no questions." Simon hoped his concision would be well-received by the Director of Education.

"In that case, I wish you a very good afternoon," concluded the professor as the screen went blank and Simon and the Director of Education were left alone in the room.

"I can see this course of study is going to involve the prison service in incalculable cost," snorted the woman entrusted with the educational development of offenders, "and will involve me in a considerable amount of additional work. I'm sure these recommended books are not to be found on the shelves of *W.H. Smith* and the County Library Service is unlikely to have them in its collection. If I'm not careful, I will be scouring the entire country for such obscure publications. You must think I've nothing better to do than attend to your esoteric interests. Don't expect instant results. I will let you know if and when I am successful." Simon was dismissed and able to move to the association area for an hour's recreation with the other inmates on his wing.

"Where have you been?" asked Dylan as Simon slumped onto a chair beside the table-tennis table.

"Put through the mangle by the Director of Education," replied a resigned Simon. "She hates me."

"She hates all men," replied Dylan. "She told me I had the handwriting of a five-year-old child. Bloody cheek! I couldn't even write when I was five. I've never had any difficulty reading my writing. Neither does the bookie when I hand him my betting slips. I may not have fancy handwriting; but who the hell needs fancy writing these days? The trouble with her is she can only see the negatives. She can't see the bigger picture. She concentrates all her energies on numeracy and literacy while the world passes her by. She's like a dried-up shell washed up on the seashore."

Simon froze. That was exactly the simile Sandra used to describe herself on the night they parted: a dried-up shell washed up on the seashore. Was the Director of Education a presage of what Sandra would become? Once again, the thought unsettled him. He would never forgive himself if he'd turned his wife into a replica of the Prison Director of Education.

"You all right, Simon?" asked an anxious Dylan as he saw the colour drain from Simon's face.

"Yes," replied Simon. "I'll be alright as soon as I've banished all memory of that gorgon from my mind. I think I'll go and lie down in my cage, if you don't mind, so I'm ready for choir practice tonight."

And so saying, he retired to the comparative privacy of his cell to quieten his conscience.

Choir practice that evening saw the usual sixteen choristers gathered around the chapel piano to continue work on *Sir Christemus*, the carol Simon had written, the West Indian *Mary had a baby* and a couple of other carols from around the world. But Simon did not rehearse Sarsung's *Malam Kudus*. He could not bear the thought of reliving the memories associated with the piece.

"How come we're rehearsing the black men's carol but not mine?" queried Sarsung, with a pained look on his face. "My carol is much more beautiful."

"Don't you come that with us, sonny Jim," retorted Winston. "*Mary had a baby* was sung by my mamma. She had a big, big heart: double the size of your piddling heart. She sang from the heart and I won't have a word said against her. Get it?"

"I've got nothing against your carol, big man. I just say mine is more beautiful. How come we're not rehearsing it, Mr Choirmaster?"

Throughout this banter Simon was trying to think of an excuse for postponing work on *Malam Kudus*. When Sarsung eventually put the question directly to him, Simon was ready with an answer: "Because I've yet to arrange the backing parts to support the melody. Hopefully it will be done in time for next week's rehearsal."

"Well don't leave it too long, man," countered Winston. "Christmas is coming fast, real fast, and we don't want to be under-rehearsed."

Simon smiled. Winston was transforming into a real professional who was clearly focussed on the performance and the need to acquit himself with honour.

"Don't worry," smiled Simon, "We've still got three weeks left. Now, let's have another attempt at my little number. I'm still not happy with those chords on page two. They need to go like this."

And then, without any accompaniment, he sang each of the parts in turn. The others listened in silent awe. Their musical director was able to pitch notes perfectly without any instrumental help.

"How come you can sing like that, man?" demanded Winston when Simon finished: "without any help from the piano?"

"It's all down to practice, Winston. If you keep practising you'll be able to do the same."

Winston shook his head in disbelief before adding, "You got a big talent, man."

At the conclusion of choir practice, as the other prisoners were being escorted back to their respective wings and Simon was gathering up the music, the chaplain appeared.

"Ah Simon," he said with his customary smile. "How are things going?"

"The music is coming along well," replied Simon "and should be okay in time for the Carol Service."

"I wasn't thinking about the music," replied the chaplain. "I was thinking more about you. I thought you looked a little downcast."

Simon was unsure he wanted to share his unhappiness over the breakdown of his marriage with the prison chaplain and so he replied, "I'm fine."

The chaplain gave him a long, hard stare. He clearly knew things were not fine with Simon but he was powerless to pry. Instead, he recalled his experiences with other dejected prisoners over the years.

"I sometimes think," he continued, "that Christmas is the hardest time of the year for those in prison. We are separated from our loved ones just when families traditionally come together. Memories of past Christmases return to haunt us and exacerbate feelings of loneliness and unworthiness. You must tell me, Simon, if you're experiencing such feelings. I'm here to help."

The chaplain paused without taking his eyes off Simon. He was giving Simon an opportunity to share his unhappiness, if he wished. He could see from Simon's face that all was not well, but, unless Simon was willing to share his pain, there was little he could do to help.

When the pause was in danger of becoming embarrassing, the chaplain concluded by saying, "Remember, I'm always available if you want someone to talk to." And with a quick inflection of his eyebrows he said, "Let me accompany you back to the Wing."

Once Simon was ensconced in his cell for the night, he ruminated on the chaplain's words. Did his face advertise his inner feelings? Were his feelings of guilt and shame over the breakdown of his marriage clear for all to see? Would it help to share the aching void in his heart? And should he share his pain with the chaplain? He knew practically nothing about the man – whether he was happily married or a confirmed bachelor. Had he ever experienced the surge of uncontrollable youthful passion or was he a celibate in stoic control of his bodily appetites? There was no way of knowing.

Simon sat at the table that doubled as his silent piano, and soulfully played *The Death of Ase* from the *Peer Gynt Suite* by Grieg. The slow moving minor chords perfectly captured his feelings over the death of his marriage. Happiness had been replaced by sorrow; youthful ambition by dejection and despair. It was a very sad prison choirmaster who drifted into sleep that night.

The following day was one Simon never wanted repeated. At midday, he joined the queue at the prison canteen to collect his lunch tray. He suddenly felt a painful jab in his ribcage that caused him to lurch forward into the inmate in front of him.

"What the bleeding hell!" exclaimed the prisoner into whom Simon had catapulted and, by so doing, sent the man's food spilling far and wide. The inmate swung round and punched Simon in the face causing him to fall backwards into the arms of the man behind.

"I don't want the fuckin' bastard," shouted the prisoner behind him. "Have him yourself." And so saying, he forcibly propelled the reeling Simon forwards so he crashed a second time into the prisoner he had just antagonized.

"Fucking hell!" screamed the incensed inmate who had now lost all his lunch. "Come back for more?" And with that he aimed another punch this time at Simon's midriff. The other inmates, sensing a fight was breaking out, began thumping their fists on the cafeteria counter and shouting obscenities, the purpose of which was difficult to fathom. The commotion alerted the prison staff to impending trouble and, within a minute, three burly prison officers pushed themselves into the melee at the serving counter and extracted the three inmates who were responsible for the disturbance. One of the three was Simon. All three were marched off to the Senior Prison Officer for interrogation. The Senior Prison Officer was a no-nonsense officer. He was in his mid-fifties and had spent his entire working life in the Prison Service. He knew how to deal with schizophrenics, drug abusers, bullies, sexual deviants, blasphemers, pugilists, loudmouths, and those he considered animals rather than human beings. He brooked no disturbance to prison routine. Troublemakers were anathema to him. He did not tolerate them and he knew exactly how to deal with them.

"What's the meaning of this disturbance?" he barked. Simon noticed the SPO's bald head glistening with minute beads of perspiration. He was clearly in a sweat over something prior to the unwelcome arrival of the three prisoners standing before him. As none of the three prisoners answered, one of the escorting officers supplied the details.

"Disturbance in the canteen, sir. Food thrown on the floor. Fighting. Prisoners Corbett, Lancing and Copeland."

The SPO glared at the three men who had interrupted the task on which he had been engaged.

"I will not tolerate such behaviour in this establishment. The three of you will spend three days in solitary confinement. Perhaps that'll teach you to behave in future." And with a curt nod of his head to the prison officers, he dismissed the trio of miscreants without any attempt to ascertain blame or innocence. To him, all were equally guilty of disturbing the smooth running of Her Majesty's Prison and needed to be taught a lesson.

The three prisoners-under-escort were led to the Segregation Unit where each was locked in a bare cell having just a fixed iron bed and a plastic mattress. The walls of the cell were glazed tiles and the floor was untreated concrete. There was a French-style hole in the ground that acted as a combined lavatory and shower outlet. The cell was clearly designed to facilitate hosing-down if the occupant's behaviour proved bestial. There was a very small window set high in one wall allowing light to enter the cell but affording no view of the world outside.

Simon sank onto the mattress nursing his aching jaw. He had failed to anticipate the punch aimed at him and had taken the full force of it on his right jaw. His solar plexus also ached from the second blow he received. He felt dreadful. He had eaten no lunch and felt faint.

The injustice of his position was not lost on him. He had done nothing wrong and yet was being punished in exactly the same way as the other two who had used him as a punch-ball to bat backwards and forwards. He now had seventy-two hours of solitary confinement with which to contend.

Occasionally, the peephole in the door of his cell opened and an officer shot a glance inside to ensure Simon was still alive; and, in the evening, a tray of food was delivered to him. But, apart from that, Simon was left in solitary isolation: until, that is, the chaplain appeared.

"Ah Simon," the chaplain began in his customary manner, "May I join you on the side of your bed? You've clearly fallen on hard times. It happens to the best of us. A brawl in the canteen, I understand?"

Simon nodded wistfully.

"It never occurred to me you were a pugilist," remarked the chaplain with a wry smile on his face. "Indeed, I always regarded you as a rather gentle spirit. I suspect, therefore, that this brawl was not of your making." He ended his suspicion with an upward inflection of his voice as if awaiting a response.

"No," sighed Simon, "It most certainly was not. Indeed, I'm unsure exactly what happened. One minute I was queuing for my lunch and the next I was being batted backwards and forwards like a shuttlecock between Corbett and Lancing. I don't know what I've done to antagonise them, but they've clearly got it in for me."

The chaplain gave an understanding nod of his head. "There are, alas, some here who have a very perverted view of life. They take it upon themselves to mete out punishment on those they consider sinners. But, in assuming the role of God, they lack His omniscience and fall into all kinds of errors. I will seek to enlighten them but, alas, there are some who have been so badly scarred by the traumas they've endured, that they're incapable of differentiating right from wrong or good from bad. That means we have to be very understanding and ready to forgive those who trespass against us."

"I don't hold a grudge against them," replied Simon. "I just wish they'd leave me alone."

"A very understandable wish," replied the chaplain. "It might help to remember Our Blessed Lord and the unjustified pains and torments meted out to him when he had done no wrong. If he was able to bear such injustices it gives hope for us, I feel sure."

Simon did not reply. The last thing he wanted was to engage in a theological discussion with the chaplain.

"I understand you have to spend seventy-two hours in the Segregation Unit," continued the chaplain. "That's a long time to be on your own with just your thoughts for company." He cast a sideways glance at Simon to see if there was a response, but none came. And so he continued, "Especially if one's thoughts are not happy ones."

Simon sensed the chaplain was prompting him to share the pain in his heart but something prevented him from responding. Instead, he replied, "I'll be alright. I'm used to being on my own. Most of my childhood was spent in solitude. I'll be alright."

The chaplain nodded sagely before rising from his perch on the side of the bed and preparing to leave.

"My job description," he announced, "stipulates I undertake a daily visit of all prisoners in solitary confinement. You'll see me again tomorrow. And remember, if you wish to share any concerns with me I will deal with them in the strictest confidence."

And so saying, he summoned the guard and exited the cell leaving Simon to ruminate on what had been said.

The chaplain was true to his word (and Job Description) and visited Simon on each of the three days he was incarcerated in the Segregation Unit. But Simon held his peace and told the chaplain nothing about his marriage and its disastrous failure.

Prison life then resumed its former routine with Simon being extra vigilant to avoid all contact with Corbett and Lancing whenever he visited the canteen. He was aware of the hostile looks they shot in his direction but he always turned his head and continued as though he had not noticed them.

Fortunately for the fledging prison choir, Simon's incarceration in the Segregation Unit did not coincide with the weekly Tuesday evening choir practice and so no valuable rehearsal time was lost. However, he bore a large bruise on his right jawbone that was quickly noticed by the men who gathered around the chapel piano for the weekly singing practice.

"What you been doin', man?" asked Cyril, one of the blacker-than-black Caribbean members of the group. "That's a real pearler you've got there, man."

"It's nothing," replied Simon wanting to pass over the subject and get on with the choir practice.

"We all knows how you got that bruise," declared Stanley, another of the Caribbean songsters. "But don't you worry Mr Choirmaster. We'll get even for you. Just wait and see."

A chorus of assent went up from the other members of the choir.

Simon was deeply moved by the choir members' loyalty and support but, whether because of the words of the chaplain or because of his own sense that violence only leads to more violence, he replied, "It's good of you to have my welfare at heart; but I'd rather there was no retaliation. What has happened has happened, and I would like to draw a line under the whole business."

"Man, you is just as innocent as a new-born babe; but you have music running through your fingers and for that we forgives you."

Simon smiled, nodded his head in gratitude, and pressed onwards with *Sir Christemus* that was coming along in leaps and bounds. Indeed, all the pieces planned for the Christmas Carol Service were shaping up nicely and the sounds that filled the chapel were both exciting and heart-warming. The members of Simon's motley band of singers were revealing previously hidden musical depths and the music they created filled them with pride and satisfaction. Music was working its magic and bringing wholeness to broken lives. Simon even felt able to tackle *Malam Kudus*, the Indonesian version of *O Holy Night*. Once Sarsung began singing the melody line, Simon realised his tenor voice differed so greatly from Sandra's liquid soprano voice that comparisons were impossible. Rather than resurrect past memories for Simon, Sarsung's rendition of the piece, with the sustained harmonies supplied by the other members of the group, meant it became an entirely different piece. In a sense, it was cathartic. It banished memories from the past and enabled him to concentrate on the present and the task in hand: to produce a musically first-rate Christmas Carol Service for the inmates and staff of Her Majesty's Prison.

Life continued along well-oiled prison lines for the next couple of days and memories of the altercation in the prison canteen began to fade.

Ten days before Christmas, Simon received an order to make his way to the Education Wing and report to the Director of Education. Presenting himself to her in her office he received her usual no-nonsense brusque greeting: "At great trouble, and no little expense, I have successfully located the two books specified by the Open University. I hope there will be no further requests for obscure and difficult-to-obtain books. You will sign this form and, by so doing, you accept full responsibility for the safe return of these books. Should you fail to do so you will meet the full cost of replacements from your allowance. Is that clear?" Simon nodded his head in acknowledgement and duly signed the gorgon's form.

"When you've read them and formulated your scheme of work, I will arrange for you to have another video-tutorial with Professor Lawson, although why I should be doing this I have no idea."

And, with a curt wave of her arm, she dismissed Simon. He made his way back to his cell accompanied by a prison officer, to pour over the two tomes. He quickly became immersed in the world of Zelenka and the early eighteenth-century in which he lived and composed the majority of his music. In his imagination, he heard the musical examples in the book leap off the page and sound in his head. It was music to delight and challenge, and he revelled in it.

Perhaps it was his preoccupation with Zelenka that caused him to lower his guard and become less vigilant about his own personal safety; or maybe the former events in the canteen had faded from his memory to be replaced by his preoccupation with the forthcoming Carol Service; but he was totally unprepared for the next attack when it came. Communal showering was an integral part of each day's routine. Her Majesty's Prisons believed that cleanliness was second only to punishment. Every inmate had therefore to shower once a day. The shower block was where prisoners came into close naked contact with each other and was a place where sarcasm, ridicule and humiliation abounded. Furthermore, because of the way the communal shower block was designed, it was impossible for the prison officer in charge to keep an eye on all that was taking place. There was one part of the communal shower that was hidden from even the most watchful prison officer.

It was in just this area that Simon found himself cornered by his *bêtes noires*, Corbett and Lancing, plus a third prisoner who was unknown to him. The three men crowded in on him thus effectively isolating Simon from the other prisoners in the shower.

"The little paedo," growled Lancing through his yellow teeth. "The pretty boy who likes the girlies."

Simon froze. The three men clustering around him were all much bigger than him and physically stronger. He knew he had no way of defending himself against such a trio and so he pinned his hopes on other inmates alerting the prison officers to his plight.

"Twisted and depraved," contributed Corbett. "I wonder what goes on in your dirty little mind?" And so saying, he suddenly jerked up his right leg and kneed Simon in the groin. Simon howled in pain and doubled up in consequence. Immediately, the other two assailants piled in with blows and more knee jerks. Simon reeled under the onslaught.

"That's for all kids you've buggered up," shouted Lancing, as he rained down another punch.

"That's for having such a dirty little perverted mind," shouted Corbett as he brought his knee into contact with Simon's chin.

"And this one's for Vicky," screamed the unknown third man as he aimed a tremendous punch at Simon's reeling head. "For all you fuckin' did to her."

It was the knockout blow that sent Simon crumpling onto the wet floor. There he lay inert – a lifeless, unconscious, naked wreck.

Simon had no recollection of what happened after that. When he eventually regained consciousness, he was in a bed in the prison hospital. His head throbbed. His lower lip was cut. His eyes were swollen and partially closed. His ribcage felt as if a road-roller had passed over it. He felt battered and dejected. Never before had he felt so physically bruised and broken. This was his *hodie horribilis*.

Not only did his body cry out in pain but his soul echoed the cry. How had his life plunged to such depths? He had never knowingly hurt anyone or deliberately harmed others and yet he was now being punished unmercifully. He had been made to live with psychopaths and creatures that were more animal than human. These were not people with whom he normally associated. He was a human being imbued with spirit and aspirations. He sought the higher things of life – the things that were above, as he recalled one of the biblical writers putting it. He was not a man of violence. He sought to rise above all that was sordid and bestial and delight only in the nobler things of life. He was an artist; a man imbued with sensitivity; a person who wanted to live and love in peace. But now he was in hell. As his mind wrestled with the injustice of his life, he gradually became aware he was not alone. A person had silently arrived at his bedside and was gazing down upon him. It was the chaplain.

Seeing recognition dawn on Simon's face, the chaplain very gently enquired, "How are you feeling, Simon?"

"Dreadful," came the cold reply.

"Too bad!" whispered the chaplain. "I'm sorry it should have come to this. I hold myself partly to blame. I should not have put you in the firing line. I should have foreseen that, by asking you to lead the music in the chapel, I was drawing attention to you and setting you up as a target for attack. I hope you'll forgive me."

Simon closed his eyes and muttered, "I thought it was you who was supposed to offer forgiveness to others and not vice versa."

"We are all miserable sinners, no matter what our position in life," replied the chaplain. "We are human and we all make mistakes. There's nothing unusual about that. But we have to learn from the mistakes we make so as not to make them again."

Then, after a long pause, Simon replied, "I'm not even sure I made a mistake when I married Sandra. I married her because I loved her. And she loved me. I feel sure of that. But somehow things went wrong, and now I'm here – broken and bruised and inwardly screaming in pain. It all seems so terribly unfair. I'm being repaid cruelly for loving a beautiful and talented girl."

The chaplain listened quietly as Simon shared the burden that had weighed on his heart ever since he entered the prison.

"She no longer loves me," whispered Simon. "Indeed, she hates me. And I know I'm to blame."

"Don't be too hard on yourself," consoled the chaplain. "You're experiencing the death of a loving relationship; but after death comes resurrection. You will rise above your present unhappiness and misfortune and, given your great talents, emerge a stronger and better man. I must not tire you. You must rest and regain your strength. We can talk again tomorrow."

After giving Simon God's blessing, the chaplain glided away leaving Simon to ruminate on what had been said. He wished he possessed the chaplain's sanguine faith. He knew the chaplain was a good man, doing a difficult job in a hostile environment, and his heart warmed to him.

For a while, Simon dwelt on the similarities and differences between his father, who was a priest, and the prison chaplain. It appeared to him that both possessed a strong faith that guided their thoughts, words and actions; but his father's faith was more a religious duty that was undertaken without much enjoyment; whereas, the prison chaplain's faith appeared to be much more relaxed and non-judgemental. He had no doubt which of the two he preferred.

His reflections on those in holy orders were rudely interrupted when the attack in the shower block invaded his mind once more. He winced as he recalled the trio of malefactors gathering around him. He could smell their breath as they closed in upon him. He saw the evil leer on their faces as they launched their assault. But, most of all, he recalled their words. They thought he was a paedophile, which he was not. They thought he abused little girls, which he did not. Then he recalled the words of the unknown assailant who landed the final cruel blow: "This one's for Vicky". How did he know about Vicky?

CHAPTER NINE

Simon found life without Sandra bleak. He returned to an empty house after each day's teaching. He went through the motions of preparing a meal for himself, but his heart was not in it and often he did not bother, making do instead with a pizza or fish and chips that he collected on his way home. The house was strangely silent.

He made various attempts to contact Sandra. He phoned her repeatedly but received no answer. He left recorded voice-mail messages that went unanswered. He sent text messages but received no reply. To all intents and purposes Sandra had completely disappeared from his life.

He learned from Lizzie that Sandra had initially stayed with her and her husband for a week whilst she searched for alternative accommodation. When she found somewhere of her own, she declined to tell Rex and Lizzie where it was for fear they would tell Simon. She wanted to sever all ties with him and live an independent life, she told them.

"I'm sorry, Simon," said Lizzie, with real regret in her voice. "You were such a lovely couple and we had such fun together... and now it's come to this. I don't want to

interfere, but is there no way you and Sandra could sort out your differences? Perhaps some relationship counselling would help?"
"I'm willing to do anything to get her back," declared Simon. "But she won't even talk to me. How can counselling help if she won't even talk?"
Lizzie nodded her head sagely. Sandra had been adamant that she never wanted to see or hear from Simon again. Nevertheless, Lizzie asked Simon, "Can I tell her you're willing to go for counselling if she's willing?"
"Of course," Simon instantly retorted. "And tell her I still love her. I will do whatever she wants if only we can be together again."
And with that the two of them parted.
But no response from Sandra was forthcoming. The wall of silence that separated them remained impenetrable. With each day that passed, Simon knew his marriage was over. Sandra had no desire to reignite the love they once shared. She had firmly closed the door on that chapter of her life and wanted to move on. She had no intention of responding to Simon's entreaties.
All of which left Simon in limbo. He went through the motions of getting up in the morning, travelling to school, teaching harmony and counterpoint, inverted progressions and modulations, major and minor scales, instruments of the orchestra and so forth, but without any of his former enthusiasm. He returned to an empty house in the evening and busied himself with his latest composition. But life had no joy for him.

The days passed. He kept occupied. His zombie-like manner was noticed by his work colleagues and remarked upon in the school staffroom. Even the mousey Miss Clutterbuck commented upon it.

"I hope you don't mind me saying, Mr Copeland, but you look very down in the dumps these days. Is everything alright?"

Clearly everything was not alright, but Simon was loath to tell the middle-aged spinster about his marital problems. Yet, he knew it would only be a matter of time before news of his wife's departure seeped out and all would know of it. And so, he decided to unburden himself to his music colleague.

"I regret to say Sandra and I have split up," he revealed. "Things have not been going well for some time and now we've decided to go our separate ways."

"Oh I am so sorry," replied the timorous Miss Clutterbuck. "I thought it must be a personal problem you were experiencing. I know how heart-wrenching it can be to lose a loved-one. Of course, I've never experienced losing a spouse, but I have experienced losing Tabitha my beautiful Burmese cat. She was my constant companion for over thirteen years. We went through thick and thin together. I felt she understood me. I used to share my anxieties and fears with her, and she always seemed to understand. She would look into my eyes with calm reassurance. I knew I had someone who understood me. And then she died. The pain of losing her was unbearable. I felt bereft. And so I know exactly how you must be feeling at present, Mr Copeland."

Simon did not know whether to laugh or cry. His deep emotional bond with Sandra was nothing like Miss Clutterbuck's affection for her cat, and it was ludicrous to draw such a parallel. And yet, he realised that the absence of love and affection was the same whether it was between human beings or humans and their pets.

"Thank you for being so understanding," he replied to his diffident colleague.

Having unburdened herself of her most painful experience, Miss Clutterbuck was in no mood to cease.

"I'm sure you've found," she continued, "that in such circumstances, music can be an endless source of consolation. I don't know what I would have done when I lost Tabitha had it not been for the gift of music. I allowed the Great Masters to lift me out of my sorrow and transport me to the heavenly realms where there is no more sorrow or crying but life everlasting. I listened endlessly to Franz Liszt's *Consolations*. Such beautiful piano pieces! I even played them myself, in my own fumbling way, and derived enormous strength from them. I suspect you have pieces you turn to at moments such as this?"

Simon smiled and nodded, whilst thinking he would never again be able to listen to Liszt's *Six Consolations* because of their association with the deceased Tabitha.

"Strangely enough, I tend to gravitate to Bruckner," he said. "Although I don't have his unshakable faith, I derive strength from the way his music rises above the petty concerns and cares of the world and scales the very heights of spiritual experience. I gain great strength from the slow movement of his unfinished *Ninth Symphony* where he seems to be hammering on the very doors of heaven in an attempt to get in. His music helps me see life in a new perspective. And, just at the moment, that's what I most need."

"Bruckner's music, alas, is far too heavy for me," replied the self-deprecating Miss Clutterbuck. "But, no matter: whether it's medieval polyphony or romantic impressionism, music has the great ability to take us out of ourselves and release us from our cares and worries."

Simon was in perfect agreement with Miss Clutterbuck's latter point. He marvelled how he and his teaching colleague could be so different in character and personality and yet be united by a common love of music. Music really did transcend all barriers. But rather than continue reflections that were rapidly in danger of entering the esoteric realms of philosophy, Simon brought the conversation down to earth by turning to practical matters.

"What about this year's School Production?" he announced in a business-like tone. "Have you had any thoughts about a suitable work?"

Miss Clutterbuck blinked at the sudden change of direction in their conversation and racked her brains to think of a suitable suggestion.

"I suppose we could do another Gilbert and Sullivan," she stammered in a half-hearted manner. "I know we've often done G&S in the past, but it is well within the capabilities of our students and I'm sure the parents always enjoy the actual performances."

Simon was not so sure.

"Gilbert and Sullivan is a bit old hat," he replied. "Why don't we try something new? Why not tackle a new work?

I've got plenty of time on my hands at present and I could have a go at writing something especially for the talent we possess. It could be purposely written for each of the students playing the principal roles; and I could ensure the orchestral parts were well within the capability of the school orchestra. What do you think?"

Miss Clutterbuck was nothing if not loyal. She knew her Head of Department secretly longed to be a successful composer and she also knew about his early success writing music for his wife to sing, and so she gave him a motherly smile and replied, "I think that would be a splendid idea. Do you have a subject in mind?"

"I thought I might take *The Diary of a Nobody* by George and Weedon Grossmith as the subject-matter and ask Mrs Crawford, the Head of English, if she would provide a libretto."

"Splendid!" cried Miss Clutterbuck, clapping her little hands together in an excited expression of delight. "I can't wait to hear the result."

Simon then took his proposal to the Headteacher to gain his endorsement.

Charles Finlay, the Head of the fee-paying private school, was very different from the Headteacher of Simon's former school. Mr Finlay was quietly-spoken and studious. He appeared more at home in the school library than in the hurly-burly of school life; but his studiousness appealed to parents who wanted their children to have a civilized educational experience far removed from what they considered the state educational jungle. Many of the parents lived and worked overseas, and felt confident placing their

children in the safe and reliable hands of Mr Finlay and his staff of teachers and boarding-house parents.
Mr Finlay rose from behind his desk as Simon entered his office.
"Good morning, Simon," he beamed.
He had heard of Simon's marital difficulties and wanted to do all he possibly could to alleviate any unhappiness Simon might be experiencing; but his concern did not extend to enquiring into his staff's personal lives. It was not an area he liked entering. He was perfectly at home in academia, but broken relationships and raw emotions were things he wished to avoid, if at all possible. Consequently, he steered the conversation immediately to the purpose of Simon's visit.
"So what is it you want?" he enquired with a quizzical look on his egg-shaped face.
Simon explained his plans for the next School Production and immediately received a glowing endorsement from the Head.
"I've always considered *The Diary of a Nobody* one of the funniest books ever written," he confessed. "Charles Pooter's pomposity and sense of his own importance, punctuated by his continual gaffes and social humiliations, makes it one of the enduring classics of comedy," he declared. "I've read it many times. Even though it's dated, the humour still rings true. I will be fascinated to see how you and Mrs Crawford turn it into a musical. It will be a real feather in the school's cap: the world premiere of a new musical. I wish you well. Keep me informed how things are

going." And with that, the interview was amicably concluded to the satisfaction of both men.

Eileen Crawford, the Head of English, proved amenable to Simon's suggestion and set to work writing a libretto for him to set to music. She may not have been a budding T.S. Eliot or even a second-rate John Betjeman, but she knew enough about literature to produce a workmanlike piece that incorporated varying metrical rhyme schemes, comic dialogue and opportunities for dramatic characterisation. Once she had finished the libretto and secured Simon's approval, Simon was keen to start work on the music. However, before he began, he needed to know who would be singing the main parts so as to be cognisant of their vocal range. Also, he wanted to listen to their singing voices so that when he was composing he could hear them in his head. With this in mind, he publicised the forthcoming production and invited students to audition for the various parts.

There was a good response, and, by a process of elimination, the main parts were cast as follows:

Mr Charles Pooter (a London office clerk)
> Henry Longbridge

Mrs Carrie Pooter (his wife)
> Susannah Stock-Holmes

William Lupin (their son)
> Toby Hickinson

Mr Gowing (their neighbour)
> Rajeem Hindlafarim

Mr Cummings (an enthusiastic bicyclist)
> William Rhys-Jones

Sarah (their maid)
>   Rita Chang

Daisy Mutlar (Lupin's first fiancée)
>   Victoria Burrows

Mr Murray Posh (who marries Daisy)
>   Christopher Keville-Davis

Mr Hardfur Huttle (an over-opinionated American)
>   Rory Sinclair

Lille Girl (Murray's sister and Lupin's second fiancée)
>   Ophelia Cunningham

In addition to the principals, there would be a Chorus for *The Mayor of London's Ball for the Representatives of Trade and Commerce* and a semi-chorus for *The Holloway Comedians* performing troupe.

It was a demanding line-up requiring a great deal of music, but Simon relished the challenge.

As he set Eileen Crawford's words to music, he heard each of the principals' voices in his head: the gravelly baritone voice of Henry Longbridge singing the main male role; the limpid soprano voice of Susannah Stock-Holmes in the leading female role; the clearly-articulated voice of Toby Hickinson playing the irascible Lupin; the reedy-voice of Rita Chan, playing the long-suffering maid; and the powerful mezzo-soprano voice of Victoria Burrows playing the loose and fancy-free Daisy Mutlar.

He smiled to himself as he magicked melodies out of the air for each of them to sing. The more he worked on the score, the more each of the students became living characters in his mind. They were no longer students wearing school uniforms, sitting in serried rows, listening to him explaining compositional technique. They were characters straight from the pages of *The Diary of a Nobody*. He breathed life into them. He accentuated their personalities. He revelled in their individuality and exalted them to the pantheon of theatrical actors and singers.

Working on *Meet the Pooters* was the perfect antidote for his loneliness. Every available spare minute was filled with creative activity. His evenings were spent hunched over his writing-table, either scribbling ideas onto manuscript paper or transferring ideas into a music-notation programme on his computer. Whole weekends were devoted to nothing else except the forward progress of *Meet the Pooters*. Page after page was filled with musical notation. Each burst of creative activity culminated in Simon sitting at the piano and playing through what he had written. He saw and heard what he had created and it was good: it was very good. Christmas came and went.

Simon remained at home working on his score throughout the Christmas holidays. He did not mind spending Christmas alone. It was preferable to spending it with his parents and enduring their disapproving looks and pointed comments. Miss Clutterbuck, bless her, invited him to share Christmas Day with her in her solitary apartment; but Simon politely declined. He preferred to compose rather than make polite conversation with the piteous spinster. Provided he filled his time with creative activity, he knew he would be fine.

By the beginning of the spring term, Simon had completed the score. It had been a mammoth undertaking, but he was proud of his achievement and keen to commence rehearsals.

He soon got to know the students playing the leading roles as he taught them their parts and explained how he wanted each part sung. He discovered aspects of their lives about which he had been previously unaware. He learned that Henry Longbridge came from a split family. He had spent Christmas with his mother and New Year with his father. He gave the impression of being perfectly at ease with this, but Simon sensed a festering, underlying anger behind the cool facade. He was clearly hurt by his parents' separation. Susannah Stock-Holmes also came from a split family. She had spent Christmas with step-brothers and step-sisters, which she neither liked nor who liked her. Again, Simon sensed unhappiness.

Rajeem Hindlafarim, Rita Chan and Victoria Burrows had spent Christmas in the school boarding house because their parents were overseas. They had shared Christmas Day with the house-parents but otherwise the two-week Christmas holiday had been incredibly boring for them.

So many unhappy young people, thought Simon.

Working on *Meet the Pooters* had the effect of lifting the spirits of all concerned. Any Christmas sadness was soon replaced by high spirits as the cast became more and more confident of their roles and the music became more and more part of their lives. As Simon walked around the school, gaggles of students would suddenly burst into a phrase from the show to let him know they were enjoying it. The six male principals developed a strong sense of camaraderie and were often found in each other's company.

The four female principals made Mr Copeland the focus of their attention. Their feelings towards him were a combination of awe at his compositional skills and pleasure at the way he was willing to spend time helping them with their parts.

The four girls were in Year 11 and were at that stage in life when they were changing from giggling schoolgirls into nubile young women. They were also at the stage of casting their eyes around for attractive men on whom to fantasize. Their daily close contact with Simon made it inevitable he would become the focus of their adolescent attentions. After rehearsals, the four girls huddled together in the boarding house and discussed Simon's qualities and attributes.

"I saw him secretly looking at you yesterday at the end of the rehearsal," declared a somewhat envious Susannah to the diminutive Rita Chang. "I think he likes Chinese girls."

"Don't be so silly," retorted the girl from Hong Kong. "We all know its Vicky he really likes."

"Why me?" exclaimed the startled Victoria. "I've done nothing to lead him on – yet, that is." All four girls immediately burst into laughter.

"I wonder what sort of girls he really likes?" mused Ophelia. "Do you think they have to be musical or just sexy?"

"He probably likes them both ways," Victoria replied slyly. This provoked yet more laughter.

"I noticed he was wearing a wedding ring last year, but this year it's missing," observed Ophelia. "Do you think he's divorced?"

"We'll have to find out," declared Susannah, with a determined look in her eye.

"Do you think he'd tell us if we asked?" enquired the innocent Rita.

"Probably not," replied Victoria. "But there are other ways of finding out."

"How do you mean?" asked Rita.

"Well, by getting to know him better, so that he lets his guard slip," replied Victoria. "Men can be manipulated to get whatever you want from them," she declared with the assurance of a woman twice her age and greatly experienced in the wiles of seduction. "Remember Miss Waite's RE lesson about Samson and Delilah? And I don't mean how embarrassed she got when we asked her what 'putting him to sleep on her lap' meant."

At this, the four girls burst into uncontrollable laughter. When they calmed down, Victoria continued, "I bet I could discover Mr Copeland's past love life."

The other girls looked at Victoria with a combination of disbelief and awe.

"How could you do that?" enquired the innocent Rita.

"By using my glorious body and good looks," purred the promiscuous Victoria.

"You wouldn't dare!" declared Susannah.

"Oh yes I would," retorted Victoria. "I need something to brighten my life at present. It would be a challenge. But I'm up for it. However, not a word about it to anyone, do you hear? If I'm to do this, I've got to do it secretly."

The other three girls pledged silence and waited expectantly to see how Victoria's plans materialised.

Simon was completely unaware of the scheme that was being hatched and proceeded full steam ahead with rehearsals. Every day after school he rehearsed the music with the members of the cast. Eileen Crawford directed the movement on stage whilst Simon accompanied on the piano, halting proceedings whenever he thought the singers were departing from his score or struggling with their parts. This gave Victoria an idea. She deliberately made mistakes so Simon had to concentrate on her.

"I'm sorry Mr Copeland," apologised the abject and doe-eyed Victoria. "I just don't seem able to get this right."

"Don't worry," Simon instinctively replied. "Stop behind when the others have gone and I'll go through your part with you. We'll soon get it right."

Victoria's three friends exchanged knowing glances with each other. Vicky had engineered a one-on-one session with the Head of Music. Could this be the beginning of her seduction strategy, they wondered?

At the end of the rehearsal, as the other members of the cast drifted away, Simon called Victoria to the piano where he was seated.

"I don't understand why you went adrift just now," he smiled. "I thought you'd mastered your part admirably. But, don't worry: we can easily do some more work on it, provided you don't have to dash off anywhere."

"Oh no," replied the sixteen-year-old with a winning smile. "I've got all the time in the world."

Simon looked at her more intently. She had a very pretty face. It was framed by long chestnut hair that cascaded onto her shoulders in a carefree manner. When she smiled she revealed a perfect set of white teeth that would have done justice to a toothpaste advertisement. He noted her eyes were deep brown – very similar to those of his estranged wife.

"Right," declared Simon, coming out of his momentary trance and getting down to business. "Let's pick it up from Cue Letter M."

For the next half-hour or so, Simon and Victoria Burrows worked on the part of Daisy Mutlar, the brash and vapid gold-digger who ensnared the innocent Lupin Pooter for her selfish ends. Simon had written the part especially for Vicky's husky mezzo-soprano voice. He wanted her to sound seductive and Vicky was very willing to oblige. Their rehearsal was punctuated by sudden eruptions of laughter as the two of them relished Daisy's audacious wiles. Vicky threw herself into the characterisation and imbued Daisy with sly coquettishness and purring vowels.

"I knew you'd do this well," declared a delighted Simon. "I had your voice firmly in mind when I wrote this music for you. The part is tailor-made for you, and you do it superbly. I can't imagine what went wrong at today's rehearsal. It seems to me you've now got the music well in hand."

Vicky gave Simon one of her most loving smiles. Simon thought he had rarely seen such a beautiful smile.

"It is so much easier to sing when you're accompanying me," added Vicky. "It would be so much easier if I could accompany myself on the piano, but I stopped having piano lessons when I was thirteen. I wish I'd continued."

"It's never too late to start again," replied Simon.

"Yes," declared Victoria with a look of determination on her young face. "I think I would like to." Then she delivered her *coup de grace*. "Would you be willing to give me lessons?"

Simon looked at the young girl standing beside him. He did not undertake private piano tuition. He was too preoccupied with his job as Head of Music. Furthermore, he preferred to use his free-time working on musical compositions. Teaching the piano was a laborious and soul-destroying occupation. Elgar discovered that when he was forced to undertake violin teaching before he became famous. And yet the girl standing beside him was certainly very personable. He knew he would enjoy her company. A little female company would not come amiss now he was without a wife. He looked into Vicky's deep brown mysterious eyes and saw both excitement and ruin lurking there. Part of him knew he should decline. The other part of him knew he was powerless to do so. What was the harm of sharing half-an-hour a week at the piano with a beautiful young girl? It would be a teacher-pupil relationship. Provided he kept it that way, all would be well. And so, after a moment's hesitation, he replied, "OK. Let's give it a try and see how you get on."

As he uttered those words, the brass Fate-motif from Tchaikovsky's *Fourth Symphony* sounded in his ears, as it had done all those years before when he accompanied Sandra to Symphony Hall.

It was arranged that Vicky would have her first piano lesson with Simon after school on Friday afternoon.

Vicky's three friends could not contain their excitement when they learnt of the arrangement.

"I always said he secretly fancied you," declared the somewhat envious Susannah.

Vicky arched her eyebrows and smiled a sly seductive smile.

"Did he seem keen to take you on as a piano student?" asked the inquisitive Rita.

"He thought about it for a few seconds," replied Vicky, "but all men are the same. They can't resist a beautiful girl."

This provoked shrieks of laughter from the other three girls.

"You're so vain," declared Ophelia.

"How do you know he fancies you?" asked Susannah. "It might just mean he wants to keep you on a short rein until the production is over. Once he's had his moment of glory, and everyone has said what a marvellous composer he is, he'll drop all of us like a ton of bricks and move on to his next project."

"That just shows how little you know about men," retorted Vicky, speaking as one who had run the gamut of men all her life. "Once a man begins fantasying about a girl, he can't just switch off. The more he sees me the more he'll want me – just you wait and see."

"You're so devious," declared Rita. "No man stands a chance with you around."

Vicky smiled a self-satisfied smile. The other girls clearly thought she was worldly-wise and sophisticated beyond her years. And this pleased her. The love she had been denied by her parents she would find elsewhere. Mr Copeland happened to be the person closest to hand. He was good-looking and moderately young. She still did not know the details of his personal life, but she suspected he was unattached. She felt quietly confident she could mould him in the way she wanted. She might even let him take her virginity.

"So when's your first piano lesson?" enquired the curious Rita.

"Friday afternoon, at the end of the school day, in the music room," replied Vicky.

"Not a very romantic location for seduction," observed the envious Susannah. "Are you planning to have if off on top of the grand piano?"

At this, Rita and Ophelia burst into laughter.

"Don't be so silly," replied Vicky. "I said I was going to find out about his love-life and whether or not he was married. That was all. Everything else is just a means to an end."

"But what if he wants to find out about you and how far you're willing to go?" asked a leering Susannah. "You might have to give something in return."

Vicky arched her eyebrows once more before responding: "He may be a lot older than me, but I intend to be the one in control."

Rehearsals for *Meet the Pooters* continued throughout the week. Eventually Friday arrived. Simon had been so preoccupied with the musical production and his teaching commitments that he had hardly given a thought to the first piano lesson he promised Victoria Burrows from Year 11. But as his Friday afternoon teaching commitments drew to their end, he realised he had an extra half-hour of work awaiting him. Perhaps, he thought, he had been unwise agreeing to this extra task. The weekend beckoned and he wished he could close the music room door and go home, even though it would be to an empty house.

Nevertheless, once Vicky arrived, his spirits lifted. Her smiling, vivacious character banished all doubts about the arrangement and he welcomed her into the room.

He greeted her with "Hi there, Vicky". Vicky was not slow to notice he addressed her by the name her friends used and not by the more formal Victoria he had used before.

"How are you feeling at the end of another gruelling school week?" enquired Simon in a jocular vein.

"I'm fine," replied a radiant Vicky, "and really looking forward to playing the piano again."

Simon noted she had removed her school tie and opened the top buttons of her shirt to create a more casual appearance for her extra-curricular music lesson.

"Excellent," declared Simon. "I remember you told me you'd previously undertaken piano lessons. What Grade did you reach?"

"Only Grade Three, I'm afraid. It was when my parents split up. I had to move away from the town where we were living and had piano lessons, to go and live with my mother elsewhere. In the upheaval, I failed to find another teacher and my piano playing came to an abrupt end."

Simon gazed tenderly at the girl standing before him. Who could know the trauma she had endured and the disruption it had caused in her young life? He surmised it was not just piano tuition that went by the board when the family disintegrated. Her whole life must have been shattered into

a thousand shards. His heart went out to her. He felt he wanted to enfold her in his arms and reassure her that life was not always hard and cruel. But that would hardly be the way to begin an inaugural piano lesson and so he quickly banished the thought and concentrated on the task in hand.
"Grade Three, you say. Can you remember any of the pieces you played then?"
"Oh yes," responded Vicky with enthusiasm. "I remember *Für Elise* by Beethoven."
"Do you think you could play it now without the music?" asked Simon.
"I'm willing to try," replied Vicky.
And so saying, she removed her school blazer and made her way to the baby grand piano in the corner of the music room. Sitting at the keyboard in her shirtsleeves, and with a shy smile in Simon's direction, she began playing the opening bars of Beethoven's bagatelle. All went well until she came to the tricky demi-semi-quaver passage on page three. Wrong notes proliferated and eventually she came to a halt.
"I'm sorry," she pleaded in obvious distress. "I seem to have lost it."
"Don't worry," replied Simon, fearing she might dissolve into tears at any moment. "It's a tricky passage and many a proficient pianist has come to grief over it. Up until that point, your playing was magnificent. You've not forgotten what you learnt all those years ago. Well done!"
Vicky gave her music teacher a wan smile. She could tell he liked her. He praised her playing even though she knew it was far from magnificent.

"Now," declared Simon, "Let's see if we can find some new suitable music for you to work on. I've got a pile of piano music in the music stockroom. Come on through and we'll see if there's anything you fancy."

So saying, he led the way into the adjoining stockroom. The stockroom was little more than a windowless corridor with wooden shelving occupying the entire length of the left-hand wall. There was just enough room for one person to pass along its length.

Simon led the way with Vicky following behind. At the far end of the stockroom, Simon reached up and obtained a pile of piano music from one of the shelves.

"What have we got here?" asked Simon to no one in particular. Placing the pile of music on the lowest shelf, he began to leaf through it with Vicky standing close beside him. He felt her body pressing against his as she leaned over to look. He struggled to concentrate on the task in hand.

"What about this?" he asked, as he produced the music of Beethoven's *Moonlight Sonata*. "Do you know it?"

Vicky lent over to have an even closer look and, in so doing, pressed even harder against Simon's body.

Knowing he had to keep talking in order to divert his attention from her body, he said, "I think the opening movement is well within your capabilities. It's marked *Adagio sostenuto* which means it proceeds at a slow, steady pace with the low octaves in the left hand giving gravitas to the music. There are no demi-semi-quavers in this piece to catch you out," he added, with a smile into her inclined face that was just a few inches from his. He felt his temperature rising. If he was not careful he knew he would commit a major indiscretion in the secrecy of the stockroom. With a sudden straightening of his back he said, in a business-like voice, "Let's go and give it a try." Vicky also straightened her back but made no attempt to leave the stockroom. This meant Simon had to squeeze past her in the room's narrow confines. As he did so, his body brushed against her breasts. He experienced new waves of electrical excitement thrilling through his body.

Emerging from the stockroom, he took a deep breath and resolved to control his baser instincts. He led the way to the piano, placed the music on the music stand, and invited Vicky to take her seat at the keyboard.

"The piece is in C# Minor which means it has four sharps – F, C, G and D. You have to imagine you're standing on the shore of a lake at night. The moon is low in the sky and moonlight is flecking the ripples on the surface of the water. All is still and calm. The music perfectly captures the serenity and peace of the scene. You'll see the right hand consists of a continuous stream of slow arpeggios. If you play those, I'll supply the octaves in the bass. That way, you'll only have to concentrate on one hand. Are you ready?"

And so, the two of them embarked upon a duet, with Vicky sitting at the music-stool and Simon leaning over her and supplying the bass line. As he did so, his eye caught her open shirt. It revealed her cleavage. He closed his eyes and tried to concentrate on Beethoven's slow moving bass line; but it was no good. His mind was in turmoil. He felt himself torn in all directions. He was no longer the professional music teacher but a rudderless male battling with deep primeval urges. Perhaps it was not surprising that he lost his place and made a pig's ear of the bass line. Vicky ceased playing and looked at him with a pitying smile. Simon stammered, "I'm sorry. I wasn't concentrating," and then, in an attempt to redeem the situation, he attempted humour. "I've got the easiest part and I got it wrong, whereas you've a more demanding part and you play it brilliantly. Perhaps you ought to be the one teaching me." Vicky laughed before coyly adding, "What could I possibly teach you?"

It was a flirtatious invitation to move beyond music and explore her other attributes - and it was not lost on Simon. But her very forwardness caused Simon to draw back. He realised she was leading him on and he needed to take evasive action.

"I think we'll call it a day," he announced as calmly as possible. "You take the music away with you and practise in readiness for your lesson next Friday."

"I'll do that," she quietly replied as she rose from the piano stool, put on her blazer and walked to the door, giving Simon one last lingering look over her shoulder as she left. As soon as she returned to the boarding-house, Susannah, Rita and Ophelia surrounded her and demanded to know how she had got on. Vicky smiled a sultry smile. "He can't resist me," she declared. "He's gone weak at the knees and he's like putty in my hands."

The collective eyes of the other girls widened to their maximum extent.

"Did he touch you?"

"Did he put his arms around you?"

"Did he kiss you?"

Vicky maintained a superior pose before answering: "I'm not going to tell you. It's better if you don't know. This is my special relationship and I intend to keep it to myself. It's no use trying to get information out of me. From now on, my lips are sealed. My relationship with Mr Copeland is private and will remain so."

Despite the protests of the other girls, and their unremitting attempts to extract information from Vicky, she maintained her silence. The other three girls eventually lost interest and ceased to interrogate her.

Meanwhile Simon's mind was in turmoil. He had been left in no doubt that the sixteen-year-old Vicky was lovesick for him and would give herself unreservedly to him if he allowed it. But he knew her advances were a trap. If he succumbed to her alluring charms he would be lost. He knew his life was empty and he craved the love of a woman; but a sixteen-year-old student, for whom he was acting *in loco parentis*, could not be the object of his yearnings. He knew he must resist the temptation embodied by Vicky. Simon worked every waking hour of the next week simply to keep occupied and his mind off the seductive Vicky. At each day's rehearsal of *Meet the Pooters* he treated Vicky in exactly the same way as all other members of the cast. He showed no favouritism towards her and criticised her shortcomings in the same way he did with the other students. Susannah, Rita and Ophelia were convinced Mr Copeland had "gone off" Vicky and delighted in gossiping about it when Vicky was not present.

THE WAGES OF LOVE

Simon was both half-dreading and half-anticipating his late Friday afternoon encounter with his sole piano pupil. He planned to stand at the opposite end of the baby grand piano to Vicky as she played the music she had been practising that week. But, when her playing went awry, he had to leave his place of safety and move around the piano to stand behind her, and, before long, he was leaning over her shoulder, with her luxurious chestnut hair brushing his face, only millimetres away from her inviting lips.

She looked into his eyes and he was lost. Their lips met and a long, lingering, passionate kiss brought music-making to a halt.

When Simon finally extricated himself from Vicky's embrace he stammered, "I really shouldn't have done that." "Why not?" asked Vicky in a voice that encompassed surprise and not a little hurt. "If you love someone, you have to show it." Then, before Simon had a chance to answer she declared, "I love you." He had not heard those words addressed to him for years. They caused his moral resistance to crumble. All rational judgement was banished. Here was a beautiful girl who loved him. He needed loving. He had been cruelly denied the love of his wife and his life was empty and shrivelled. He was going through the motions of living, but there was an aching void at the centre of his life. He knew he had to fill that void if he was ever going to experience life's joy and delight again. Here, before him, was a most beautiful girl, who was offering to give his life meaning once more. She loved him with the pure, unsullied love of an innocent adolescent girl. She offered him an escape from his present desolation and unhappiness.

THE WAGES OF LOVE

It was unexpected and not of his doing. He had chanced upon this beautiful girl and she was offering him salvation. He would be foolish to cast it aside. Second chances did not come often in life, but, whoever controlled his destiny had now given him a second chance. He could return the love she had for him. His maturity could complement her youthful innocence. Both would blossom as a result. Bending close to her again, he whispered, "I love you – with all my being." Their arms went around each other and they reprised their previous extended kiss.

When they eventually untangled their arms and drew apart, Simon became very practical. "We mustn't say a word about this to anyone. A teacher should not have a relationship with a student. It's dynamite and could destroy both of us. We must observe great care. There must be no hint of any special relationship between us. You must not whisper a word of this to your friends or we'll both be destroyed. If you really love me you must promise not to say a word about this to anyone."

Vicky smiled. She knew he was fatally enmeshed in the net she had cast over him. She had him in her power. She could use him as she wished and she relished the sense of power she possessed. "Of course I'll keep it a secret," she purred. "I don't want either of us to get hurt."

"Good," said Simon as a wave of relief swept over him. "We'll have to keep up the pretence that there is nothing going on between us for the remainder of the term. We have the school production in ten days' time and then it's the end of term. We can spend time together during the Easter holidays, if that's what you want."

"I can't wait," enthused the pensive Vicky.

"I'm afraid you'll have to," responded the practical Simon. "But it's not long to wait. The time will soon pass and then we can be together."

The following days were occupied with the final rehearsals and the three evening performances of *Meet the Pooters*. The cast rose to the challenge magnificently. The performances went without a hitch and everyone was full of praise for the composer and Head of Music.

"Splendid!" declared the studious little Headteacher at the conclusion of the first night's performance. "I thought you captured the character of Charles Pooter and his irascible son Lupin to perfection. I shall never again be able to read *The Diary of a Nobody* without hearing your music sounding in my ears. I don't know how you did it, but it was first-class. And didn't all the principals do well? I thought Victoria Burrows was superb as the avaricious and flirty Daisy Mutlar. That girl will go far, I think."

Simon smiled and nodded in agreement. Little did the Head know how far she would go.

Miss Clutterbuck was also fulsome in her praise of the production. "Oh Mr Copeland!" she enthused. "What a triumph! I've been speaking to some of the parents and they've all been singing your praises. They said that, since you joined the staff, the standard of music-making in this school has soared. I don't know whether I should be pleased by that as I was partly responsible for the previous music-making; but nothing should detract from your skill as both a composer and musical director. You obtained the very best from each of the cast members. You seem to know how to stimulate and fire them. A rare gift! It will be a difficult act to follow when we come to plan next year's production. I was thinking that perhaps we should tackle something entirely different, so as not to invite odious comparisons. I wondered if you'd ever considered Henry Purcell's *The Fairy-Queen*? A truly delightful work, and very rarely performed these days. We could stage a twenty-first century revival. What do you think?"

Simon could think of nothing more unsuitable for a school production. No self-respecting student would want to prance around the stage dressed as a fairy singing falsetto. But rather than dash Miss Clutterbuck's dreams, he simply replied, "I'll think about it."

In fact, the only thing he really wanted to think about was the forthcoming three-week Easter holiday and the opportunity it presented to share time with Vicky.

It was a tricky situation that required great tact. Vicky was in the care of her boarding house-parents. Nothing must be done to alert them to the situation. And yet, they kept a watchful eye on all the girls in their care and were sure to enquire into Vicky's movements during the Easter holidays. Simon resolved to speak personally with the house-parents and inform them of the piano lessons he was giving Vicky. He asked them if it would be alright for Vicky to continue with her lessons during the Easter holidays. It would mean visiting his house on the three Friday afternoons of the holidays. Vicky's house-parents were in full agreement with this arrangement; indeed, they were rather glad another member of staff was sharing the student care that devolved onerously on them during school holidays. It was thus

arranged that Vicky would make her way to Simon's house on Friday afternoons for her piano lessons.
Simon waited anxiously for Vicky's first appearance. He paced restlessly backwards and forwards in a state of high agitation. He was unsure how things would progress and how he should behave. It came, therefore, as a great relief when the front doorbell sounded and he saw Vicky standing on the doorstep with a wide smile on her face.
"You've come," exclaimed Simon with a mixture of wonder and relief.
"Didn't you think I would?" asked Vicky, with an arched rising of her perfectly shaped eyebrows.
"I wasn't sure what to think," replied a nervous Simon. Then, realising it was up to him to continue the conversation, he asked, "What do you want to do?"
He could see she was carrying the piano music he had given her, but he was unsure if that was because she wanted a piano lesson or merely as a cover for something else.
"I want to go to bed with you and make love," she replied without a moment's hesitation.
"Are you sure about that?" questioned Simon.
"I've never been surer of anything in my life," she said.
"In that case …" commenced Simon; but he never completed his sentence. Instead, he took her hand and led her up the stairs to his bedroom. It was the bedroom he and Sandra occupied for nineteen years. Closing the door behind them, he took the eager Vicky in his arms and the two of them became locked in a passionate embrace. As they did so, they stumblingly unbuttoned each other's

clothing until they were both naked. Then, collapsing onto the bed, they indulged in unrestrained carnality.

Simon brought nineteen years' sexual experience to their lovemaking. He knew exactly how to rouse Vicky and keep her on the very pinnacle of sexual delight. And even though Vicky was a complete novice, she was a fast learner. By the end of an hour, they had both experienced the unbridled delights of lovemaking before collapsing with post-coital exhaustion.

Turning to Simon, Vicky whispered, "That was wonderful. When can we do it again?"

Simon laughed and said, "I would love to do it every day with you; but that's not possible. We must limit ourselves to Friday afternoons for the time being. It's too dangerous to try anything else. But don't worry. I'll think of some way we can be together for much longer. Leave it to me."

Then, realising the time, he instantly sat up in bed and said, "Quick! We must get dressed. Your one-hour piano lesson is over and you have to return to the boarding house without delay."

Vicky was in no hurry to leave, but Simon was adamant. "If you don't go now there will be no further piano lessons."

She giggled but sensed he was deadly serious; and so she reluctantly dressed and prepared to leave. But before she did so, she looked Simon straight in the eye and accusingly said, "You failed to use a condom. What if I'm now pregnant?"

Simon returned her unblinking stare and replied, "I don't think you've anything to worry about. I tried to make my wife pregnant for nineteen years but without success. I have a very low sperm count. You've nothing to fear." So saying, he gave her one long, last lingering embrace before leading her to the front door to see her on her way.

As fate would have it, just as he ushered Vicky out of the house, who should be driving along the road but Lizzie Osbourne. Lizzie could hardly believe her eyes when she saw the young girl leaving Simon's house with him waving lovingly to her as she went.

That evening, when she and Rex were together in their sitting-room after putting their children to bed, Lizzie asked Rex, "I bet you don't know what I saw today?"

"Of course I don't, love," replied a whimsical Rex. "Even though we've been married for eternity, I still haven't learned to read your mind. You must tell me."

"Well," said Lizzie ignoring her husband's whimsy, "I was driving past Simon Copeland's house just as his front door opened and who should emerge but a young girl. I guess she was about sixteen or seventeen. She had long chestnut hair and was wearing a very short miniskirt. And there, standing on the doorstep, was Simon waving to her as she walked away. What do you make of that?"

Rex raised his eyebrows. "Perhaps it was a piano student. Music teachers take private piano pupils, you know."

"Maybe," answered Lizzie without any real conviction in her voice. Then, after a moment's thought she said, "Do you think I should tell Sandra what I saw?"

"No," replied Rex. "It would only cause unnecessary distress to the poor girl. And you might be putting an entirely false gloss on an otherwise perfectly normal occurrence. Keep quiet about it."

And so that was how it was left.

Simon, meanwhile, experienced the full gamut of emotions, ranging from otherworldly exaltation to abject and bitter despair. He had relished the passionate lovemaking with Vicky and felt buoyed-up by the physical expression of her love for him, but he feared he was embarking on a path that could only lead to ruin. He realised he had committed adultery with the schoolgirl on the Friday before Easter: Good Friday of all days, when Jesus Christ hung on the cross atoning for the sins of the world.

Simon was unable to have further contact with Vicky during the coming week, and so, as Friday approached once again, he viewed their meeting with both eagerness and apprehension.

Vicky knew only eagerness. She threw herself into his arms as soon as he opened the front door to her. Piano music and clothing were discarded as the two of them reprised their former lovemaking. It was as passionate as before, although Simon noticed Vicky was much more in control on this occasion. Rather than Simon guiding her into the Elysian Fields, she steered him to what pleasured her. Her erotic initiatives only served to excite Simon further. She was a powerhouse of sexual delights, he thought; and there was nothing he could do to resist her.

"You're fantastic," Simon panted at the conclusion of another bout of erotic lovemaking. "I've never known lovemaking like it. You're absolutely wonderful!"

The "piano lesson" occupied a full hour before Simon, yet again, had to remind Vicky of the need to return to her boarding house lest suspicions were aroused.

The following week, the third and final "piano lesson" followed exactly the same course as the previous ones. As the two of them lay panting on the bed, Simon smiled and said, "I hope we don't have a visit from a Royal School of Music examiner to see what progress you're making with your piano playing. I think he would be very censorious of your rate of progress."

"What do I care about the piano, when I have you?" replied the seductive Vicky. "I much prefer you teaching me about the birds and the bees."

"I'm afraid that home tuition will have to cease for a while now the Easter holidays are coming to an end. Our piano lessons will have to resume in the school music room. We may be able to snatch a hurried kiss but anything else will be impossible. But don't worry. I've got a plan for the summer."

Vicky's eyes opened wide in anticipation.

Simon continued: "You said that your parents live in Singapore. How about telling your boarding house-parents you're going to spend the summer holidays in Singapore with your parents whilst telling your parents you'll be spending the summer holidays in this country with one of your school friends? That way we can go away together to somewhere exciting and exotic for the entire summer holidays."

Vicky liked the plan and agreed to instigate Simon's suggestion. She knew it was a conceit to tell her parents she would be spending the long summer holidays with one of her school friends. She no longer had any school friends. The girls with whom she was friendly whilst working on

Meet the Pooters, had all drifted away. She had effectively built an impregnable barrier around herself by her secrecy, so that her friends found her distant and uncommunicative. Vicky herself became introspective. She no longer wanted to chatter with other sixteen-year-old girls. She considered herself infinitely more mature than them. She was now a woman of the world with no time for immature schoolgirls. All of which meant she no longer had friends at school. But then, she reasoned she did not need school friends. She had Simon as her exclusive property and she was happy with that.

The summer term proved a great strain for both Simon and Vicky. Whenever they encountered each another around the school, they had to maintain a strict teacher-pupil relationship. It was only when Vicky came for her Friday end-of-the-day piano lesson in the music room that more intimate moments were possible. But there was always the danger of being discovered; and this placed a great strain upon their relationship.

Vicky also worried about becoming pregnant. Although Simon had assured her he was incapable of fathering a child, she was not so sanguine. And so, unbeknown to her boarding house-parents, she made an appointment to see her GP so she could be prescribed the contraceptive pill. Once this had been achieved, she felt greatly relieved. Somehow or other, the two of them managed to chart a course through the rocky straits that separated them as they eagerly looked forward to the end of term and the time they would spend together.

"Make sure you have your passport with you," Simon instructed Vicky as the end of term approached. "Book a taxi to take you to the airport, but instead of going to the airport, re-direct the taxi to my house. The next day we can drive to the airport together. Instead of boarding a flight to Singapore we'll board a flight to …" at which point he broke off with a teasing laugh.

"Where are we going?" asked an eager Vicky.

"Just you wait and see," replied Simon. "It's a surprise. But I think you'll like it."

"I can't wait," she responded with undisguised passion in her voice.

"Well, we haven't long to wait. It will soon be the end of term."

The last day of the academic year eventually arrived and, after all the farewells and valedictory services for which Simon had to provide orchestral and choral contributions, he and Vicky were free to be together for eight whole weeks.

Waving goodbye to her boarding house-parents, who thought she was flying to Singapore to be with her parents, Vicky climbed into a taxi and instructed the taxi-driver to take her and her suitcase the short distance to Simon's house. Here she greeted her lover and the two of them made up for the sexual abstinence they had been forced to observe throughout the summer term.

That night, after they reposed on their pillows after another passionate outpouring of unbridled sensuality, Vicky turned to Simon and whispered, "Tell me about Sandra."

"What's there to tell?" asked Simon.

"Why did you marry her?" enquired Vicky.
"Because I thought I loved her and she loved me. We shared a great love of music and I thought that would bind us together; but, alas, it didn't."
"Was she anything like me?"
"She was beautiful, just like you."
"And so why did you divorce?"
Simon refrained from telling Vicky he and Sandra were not divorced but merely separated. Almost a year had elapsed since they parted and he had heard nothing from Sandra during that time. He half-expected to hear from her solicitors informing him she was seeking a divorce, but no such communication arrived. He was still married to Sandra, even though they were living completely independent lives. He considered it wiser to let Vicky think they were divorced.
"We somehow grew apart," answered Simon after a moment's thought. "The music went out of our lives. Life became humdrum and ultimately empty. It was best that we separated and went our different ways."
"I'm glad you did," replied Vicky, "otherwise I wouldn't be here now."
Simon agreed: Vicky would not be lying in the very same place previously occupied by Sandra.
Vicky had achieved what she had set out to achieve. She had discovered the facts about her music teacher's personal life; but, somehow, that was now unimportant. She had fallen in love and the feelings she had towards Simon eclipsed everything else. As she lay with her head on the pillow next to his she felt life could never be better.

It was Simon who broke in on her revelry.

"Tell me about your life," he prompted. "I'd like to know everything about you – right from the very beginning."

"There's not much to tell," answered Vicky. "I was a mistake. My parents didn't want children. They lived busy lives and enjoyed socialising and travelling. My arrival got in the way of that. I was a disruption: an inconvenience. I once heard them arguing about me. Each blamed the other for not taking the necessary precautions to prevent my arrival. I was unwanted. And so, as soon as I was old enough to be packed off to a Preparatory School that is exactly what they did. It was the ideal solution for them. Someone else looked after me whilst they continued with their globetrotting and high-flying lives."

"You poor thing!" Simon whispered tenderly in her ear. "They may have starved you of love, but I have oceans of it just for you. You'll never be starved of love again." And with that, the two of them fell asleep in each other's arms.

The following morning they prepared to leave the house, with Simon driving to the airport.

"Have you packed your case with both warm and summer clothes?" Simon teasingly enquired.

"Does that mean we're we going somewhere cool or warm?" countered Vicky.

"Warm, sultry and erotic," was his mischievous reply.

"I can't wait!" exclaimed Vicky.

The two of them gathered up their suitcases; Simon gave one last look around the house to make sure everything was left as it should be; and the two of them carried their suitcases down the path to Simon's parked car. As they did so, Lizzie Osbourne drove past in her car.

Following her first glimpse of the young girl emerging from the Copeland's home, Lizzie had repeatedly driven past the house on the off-chance of seeing something further. Her innate woman's instinct told her things were not as they should be and she was inquisitive to discover the truth. Her suspicions were confirmed when she saw Simon and the young girl emerging from the house carrying suitcases. The girl looked young enough to be Simon's daughter. But Lizzie knew Simon had no daughter. This young girl was his mistress, and the two of them were embarking on a secret tryst together. Her suspicions had been confirmed and her heart went out to Sandra, her work colleague.

Simon and Vicky's journey to the airport was uneventful. It was only as the two of them entered the Departures Hall that Simon revealed their ultimate destination.

"I've booked flights for us to Buenos Aires – the city of good airs. It's one of the most exciting cities in the Americas. I've always wanted to visit it, especially with a beautiful companion like you. We'll have an unforgettable time together there."

Vicky had often wondered where Simon might take her. She had thought of Paris, Vienna or, maybe, even New York. But Buenos Aires had never entered her head. She knew nothing about the city except it was the capital of Argentina.

"This is going to be a summer holiday like no other!" she exclaimed as they negotiated the airport's check-in and security procedures. "You do think of the most exciting things to do!"

Simon smiled at her youthful enthusiasm. He had considered some of the destinations that had occurred to Vicky, but had judged them too risky. There was the possibility they might encounter someone they knew, and then they would be in big trouble. The odds of encountering anyone they knew in Buenos Aires were so slim he thought they would be perfectly safe. The flight took over thirteen-hours; that, he thought, should deter anyone else they knew from travelling there.

It was indeed a long flight, and when the two of them eventually arrived in Buenos Aires, all they wanted to do was get a taxi to their hotel and sleep. Without bothering to unpack their suitcases, they fell into bed and, enfolded in each other's arms, drifted into oblivion: before them stretched six exciting weeks together.

Simon's desire to visit Buenos Aires was fuelled by the city's rich cultural life. He had heard it described as "The Paris of South America". It had over three-hundred theatres, innumerable festivals, an outstanding opera house, symphony orchestra and numerous choral societies. It had museums of history, fine arts, modern arts, decorative arts, popular arts, sacred art, arts and crafts, theatre and popular music. Added to all of this was the vibrancy of Argentinian nightlife. The people were known as night-owls, cultured, talkative, uninhibited and also a little arrogant. All of this was encapsulated in their national dance: the tango. The city was a heady mixture of multicultural diversity. It appealed to him immensely. He believed that here he could shake off the sense of failure that followed the breakup of his marriage to Sandra. Turning his back on the stultifying conventions of England, he could let his hair down and behave in an uninhibited, sensual manner with his lover. Vicky, for her part, was overwhelmed by the sheer novelty of visiting an exotic country with a man who clearly adored her and would do anything for her. She resolved to live life to the full and savour every minute of the coming six weeks.

Their days soon followed a set pattern. After a late breakfast, they would walk hand in hand amidst the eclectic European architecture of the city, stroll in the Botanical Gardens and the myriad landscaped parks and squares and visit places of interest. They peeped inside many of the ornate baroque churches that adorned the city.

"I always feel uncomfortable in churches," declared Vicky. "They're so dark and shadowy. I never know who might be lurking behind one of the pillars."

Simon laughed at her girlish fears.

"Don't you feel uncomfortable in churches?" asked Vicky.

"No: just the opposite. I love the stillness and sense of peace contained within the walls. They're places that have been hallowed by centuries of prayer. They convey a sense of the numinous. The world would be a much poorer place if it didn't have buildings like this."

"Are you religious?" asked Vicky with a combination of genuine amazement and scorn in her voice.

"It depends what you mean by religious," he answered. "I don't go to church, if that's what you mean. But I have a spiritual dimension, as do all people. Perhaps I express it best through music. I've always found music speaks powerfully to my soul. It's the means by which I achieve inner peace and tranquillity."

Then, seeing that Vicky was regarding him in disbelief, he quickly added, "But you're too young to experience such things. Girls of your age want excitement, fun and ..."

"Love," interposed Vicky. "Unrestrained love and passion."

Simon smiled again. "I seem to remember that churches have quite a lot to say about love; although I'm not sure it's quite the same sort of love you're talking about. Perhaps we'd better leave before we become too theological."

Passing hand in hand out of the church, they blinked in the bright sunlight of the world outside and continued on their way.

"Did you know that Buenos Aires is known as 'the city of books'?" asked Simon as they sauntered down yet another street in the old quarter of the city. "It's because of its numerous bookshops and libraries. There's one spectacular bookshop called *El Ateneo Grand Splendid*. It's an enormous bookshop housed in a former theatre. All the theatre seats have been removed and replaced by bookshelves. The whole of the ground floor resembles a library with rows and rows of shelves; and then each of the higher tiers is also fitted with shelving. Even the stage has been fitted with shelving. *The Grand Splendid* has been described as one of the most beautiful bookshops in the world."

Entering this spectacular theatre bookshop, Simon soon became absorbed in the books for sale, especially those with a musical theme. He would gladly have spent the entire day leafing through the thousands of books contained within its walls, but Vicky had the impetuosity of youth and soon tired of looking at books.

"We have to read books at school," she declared with asperity in her voice. "The last thing I want to do is read books on holiday!"

Simon sighed inwardly. He realised a great gulf existed between him and his sixteen-year-old companion. She was exciting and passionate when it came to lovemaking but she was no soulmate. She lived for the moment and knew little of life or the things of real value. Maybe he could teach her and help her become more discerning in her ways; although, somehow, he doubted if that was possible. Maybe he should simply be grateful for the lovemaking and banish all other thoughts from his mind.

Living for six weeks in the city of tango meant the sounds and rhythms of tango music were never far away. After tentatively watching the uninhibited Argentinians posturing and striking extrovert attitudes on the dancefloor, they joined in and, by imitation, quickly developed their own style of tango dancing. They arched their backs and strutted and postured on the dancefloor as if they were native Argentinians. The adrenalin flowed and their laughter sent them into convulsive fits. Tango dancing was liberating. It turned them into extroverts. They preened and pouted in a very South American manner and banished any inhibitions they may have harboured.

There was no shortage of other entertainment for them to experience in the evenings. Simon took Vicky to the *Teatro Colon* to see a performance of the opera *Carmen* by George Bizet. He thought the seductive and sultry Carmen, with her sexy mezzo-soprano voice, would appeal to Vicky, as indeed was the case.

"I think you could sing that role to perfection," he opined with a mischievous glint in his eye. "You have the same seductive and sultry voice as the girl from the cigarette factory. The part could have been purposely written for you."

Vicky gave Simon one of her long, seductive and sultry smiles in return.

It was only when Simon recalled the fate of Carmen's lover Don Jose that a shiver of apprehension crept over him. Was he so besotted with Vicky that his inevitable fate would be disaster and ruin? He quickly banished the thought from his mind.

Vicky's musical interests veered more towards light musicals than grand opera. She pleaded with Simon to take her to a performance of *Evita* by Tim Rice and Andrew Lloyd Webber.

"What better place to see the musical than in the city of Eva Peron?" pleaded Vicky.

Simon was not so sure. He disliked the work. Indeed, he secretly agreed with Bernard Levin who described attending a performance of the work as "one of the most disagreeable evenings I have ever spent in my life, in or out of a theatre." But Vicky was adamant she wanted to see it and so Simon purchased tickets for the show being staged in one of the city's three hundred theatres.

At the conclusion of the musical Vicky was full of praise for the production.

However, a pained Simon asked, "But doesn't it concern you that Rice and Lloyd Webber have glamorised Eva Peron's rise to power, and the megalomania, dictatorship, cruelty and corruption and made it acceptable?"
"I think you're reading too much into it," replied Vicky. "It's a musical that's meant to be enjoyed. You shouldn't concern yourself with the politics. Just enjoy the music."
Simon said nothing. He secretly loathed the music.
Opinions may have differed on many of the cultural and artistic experiences they shared, but the lovemaking that ended each day remained as sensual and passionate as ever. Simon was willing to forgive Vicky her immaturity in other areas in return for her masterful maturity in bed.
As the six weeks in Buenos Aires drew to their conclusion, Simon remarked, after a particularly athletic bout of lovemaking, "If we stayed here for much longer I think we would extinguish all the suggestions in the *Karma Sutra*."
Vicky laughed before adding, "It's been the most wonderful six weeks of my life. Thank you for bringing me to such a wonderful city. I'll never forget the time we shared here."
And with that they drifted to sleep in each other's arms.
The return journey to England had none of the excitement of the outward flight.
They knew there was still two weeks remaining before the commencement of the new school term. It was agreed that Vicky would spend those two weeks with Simon whilst keeping a very low profile, lest anyone saw her.
Whilst Simon and Vicky were away, Lizzie Osbourne underwent agonies of indecision. Her husband, Rex, cautioned her against telling Sandra what she had seen. "It

will only make matters worse and sour their relationship further," he warned. But, working alongside Sandra in the engineering office every day, Lizzie felt she could not keep silent. By hiding what she had seen she felt she was being disloyal to her friend. And so, after much soul-searching, she eventually summoned her courage and spoke to Sandra.
"I know it's none of my business," she began, "and I know you no longer want anything to do with Simon, but you are still married to him and he is still your husband."
Sandra looked into Lizzie's eyes. "What are you trying to tell me?" she enquired.
"I happened to be passing your home a while ago," said Lizzie, "when I saw a young girl coming out of the house. She was carrying something and I thought she might just have had a music lesson with Simon. But there was something about the way in which Simon waved to her as she walked away that didn't seem right."
Sandra stared impassively at Lizzie. "Go on," she said.
"Well, I happened to be passing your house again last week and I saw the same young girl and Simon emerging. They were both carrying suitcases. It looked as if they were heading off somewhere together."
Sandra's face remained inscrutable as Lizzie continued.
"I've driven past your house a number of times since and it seems to be deserted. Simon's car is missing and the house looks empty. I can only think the two of them have gone away together on an extended break."
Sandra bowed her head. There was a tense moment's silence before Sandra spoke.
"How old would you say the girl was?" she asked.

"I would guess she was about sixteen or seventeen."
Sandra nodded, as if this was the answer she was expecting. Then, without commenting on what she had heard, she thanked Lizzie for sharing the information with her. "You're a true friend," she added. "Thank you for being honest with me. I'll have to think about what you've told me before I decide what to do."

For the next day or so, Sandra could think of nothing else apart from the information Lizzie had shared with her. In her mind it seemed like a chilling case of déjà-vu: a music teacher and a young girl student leaving for a holiday together just as she and Simon had done nineteen-years before. Surely history could not repeat itself so cruelly? All those years ago she believed she was embarking upon a lifetime of happiness with her music teacher and, no doubt, the young girl accompanying Simon thought exactly the same. But her journey ended in disaster. She felt she could not simply ignore what was happening now. She had a moral duty to protect the young girl from the heartache and misery she had endured. Simon's penchant for young schoolgirls had to be stopped before more damage was inflicted on unsuspecting and innocent girls. She could not sit idly by and watch another young life destroyed. She knew she had to act.

And so, at the end of each working day, when she left the engineering office, she drove her little Fiat 500 along the road where her marital home was located, keenly observing the house. Every day it looked exactly the same. Simon's car was missing and the house appeared deserted. Sandra even drove past the house on Saturdays and Sundays just to be sure she did not miss anything. Week succeeded week with nothing to reward her surveillance. But Sandra was patient and persistent. She knew that if she persevered she would be rewarded.

She had to wait six weeks before her patience was rewarded. It was only then that Simon's car reappeared on the road and the house displayed signs of habitation. He, and presumably his young lover, was back.

In much the same way as Sandra had seen private detectives in the movies position themselves surreptitiously in the vicinity of the person they were observing, Sandra parked her little Fiat a short distance from the marital home so she could observe all the comings and goings. Every evening after work, she took up her position in the road and waited. She was destined to have many abortive missions. No one appeared to enter or leave the house in the evenings. The lights went on as darkness descended, but it was always Simon who drew the curtains and blotted out any further observation on her part. She began to think her mission was destined for failure. Indeed, she felt she was demeaning herself by acting as an addictive Peeping Tom. But when she felt this way, her thoughts always returned to the young schoolgirl following her fateful footsteps and she banished her doubts and resolved to continue her surveillance.

Sandra efforts were eventually rewarded one Saturday morning. She had parked her car in its usual place, giving her an unrestricted view of the front of the house. The curtains remained closed until 11.00.am. It was Simon who drew them back and within minutes he was opening the front door to leave the house. Standing by his side, wearing just a bathrobe, was a young girl with chestnut hair cascading onto her slender shoulders. Reaching for her mobile phone, Sandra captured the moment on camera. Simon turned and kissed the girl before leaving the house to a cheery wave from the girl. Sandra had the evidence she needed. It confirmed her worst fears. She knew she had to act.

CHAPTER TEN

"Why do I have to remain indoors whilst you go out?" asked a disgruntled Vicky.
Ever since their return from Buenos Aires, Vicky had been in purdah within Simon's house. Simon was adamant she must not be seen otherwise their cover would be blown. He knew that if anyone saw Vicky out and about in the locality they would want to know why she wasn't in Singapore with her parents. They would also want to know where she was staying – and that could only lead to him, with unimaginable consequences. Simon, therefore, attempted to placate the unhappy Vicky.
"I only go out to buy food," he reasoned. "It isn't long now to the beginning of the new term. Please be patient for just a few more days."
"I'm bored trapped within these four walls every day!" she asserted. "It's so boring and tedious after all the excitement and brilliance of Buenos Aires."
"I know darling," consoled Simon. "But the alternative is returning to the boarding house and spending the last days of the school holidays with your house parents. Which of the two would you prefer?"
Vicky gave a resigned sigh before replying, "Being with you, of course."

THE WAGES OF LOVE

They passed their time watching films on television, preparing and cooking meals and discussing plans for the future.

It was whilst they were in the kitchen preparing their evening meal that there was a knock on the front door. They looked at each other in surprise. Simon was not accustomed to having visitors.

"Stay out of sight," he whispered to Vicky. "I'll go and see who it is."

Opening the front door, he saw a man and a woman standing on the doorstep. The man was middle-aged, with neatly-trimmed greying hair and the woman, who was considerably younger than him, had vivid blue eyes. It was her eyes that registered most with Simon. He might easily have mistaken the pair for Jehovah's Witnesses cold-calling in the hope of gaining a new convert, were it not for the fact that the woman with the vivid blue eyes was wearing a police officer's uniform.

"Mr Simon Copeland?" enquired the man.

Simon was too nervous to speak and merely nodded his head.

"I'm Detective Sergeant Addison and this is PC Collins." So saying, the two of them showed Simon their official identification warrants. "May we come in? We'd like to have a word with you."

Simon's mouth went dry. He knew why they wanted to have a word with him and inwardly trembled with fear. He had occasionally wondered where his secret liaison with Vicky would lead, and a police-cell was one such outcome. But he always banished such thoughts as morbid and fatalistic. He believed that, as long as he was careful, all would be well. Provided he maintained absolute secrecy, no harm could befall him. The presence of two police officers on his doorstep told him otherwise. He felt in a daze as he slowly edged backwards to allow the officers to enter. Closing the front door, he ushered them into the sitting-room. On no account must they see Vicky.

Regaining his composure as best he could, Simon asked, "What's the purpose of your visit?"

Rather than answer his question, Detective Sergeant Addison asked, "Are you a teacher at Stoneybrook School?"

"I am," replied a nervous Simon. "I'm Head of Music there."

"And do you know a Miss Victoria Burrows, a student at the school?" continued the police officer.

"She is one of the students," answered Simon.

"Mr Copeland: we have reason to believe you are guilty of an abuse of trust in relation to this pupil and have engaged in sexual activity with her. I am therefore arresting you under Section 16 of the Sexual Offences Act 2003. You do not have to say anything, but anything you do say may be recorded and used in evidence against you. Do you understand?"

Before Simon could answer, the door of the sitting room burst open and Vicky rushed into the room shouting, "No! no! You can't do this! He's done nothing wrong! You can't do this to him!"

PC Collins imperceptibly moved towards Vicky and placed a reassuring arm around her slender shoulders. "Don't worry," she said soothingly. "You've nothing to fear. We'll ensure you're well cared for. I think it would be best if you accompanied us to the police station. We can then make all the necessary arrangements for your wellbeing."

While PC Collins was attending to Vicky, DS Addison placed handcuffs on Simon's wrists.

"Come along, now," ordered the police sergeant. "Is your house safe to leave as it is? Nothing cooking in the kitchen? Good. Then let's be going."

Simon was escorted in handcuffs from his home by the detective-sergeant to a waiting police car whilst PC Collins ushered the sobbing Vicky into a separate police vehicle. It was the last Simon saw of her.

When they reached the police station, Simon was registered into custody by the Duty Sergeant where the charge against him was read out.

"Simon Copeland, you are charged with an abuse of trust under Section 16 of the Sexual Offences Act 2003 in relation to sixteen-year-old Victoria Burrows who was a pupil in your care and have engaged in sexual activity with the said girl."

The Sergeant informed him, "I have to remind you of your legal right to have a solicitor present during interviews. Do you wish to avail yourself of that right?"

"I don't have a solicitor," Simon replied abjectly; to which the Duty Sergeant answered: "I can supply you with a list of solicitors who undertake criminal work if you wish to see it."

"I would," replied Simon, thinking that the more help he had the greater his chances of escaping his impending doom.

Having cast his eyes down the list of solicitors, he chose, quite at random, Stanley Walton, simply because the solicitor's surname reminded him of one of his favourite composers.

"Right," declared the Duty Sergeant. "We'll contact Mr Walton and arrange for him to visit the police station."

This done, Simon was led to one of the cells where his handcuffs were removed. There he was left to contemplate his fate. Food arrived some time later, but Simon was not hungry and the food went uneaten. He lay on the single bed in the cell looking abstractedly at the ceiling until he eventually drifted into sleep. It was not a restful sleep. He imagined himself pursued by demons snapping at his heels and angrily trying to tear him apart. He felt his flesh ripped by their claws with blood trickling down his legs. He frantically struggled to escape their venomous fangs, but no matter how hard he strove, he could not escape. They were intent on destroying him. Their howling filled the air. They were hungry and wild to claim their property, and gather his soul for hell. In horror and dismay he awoke screaming, "O Jesu, help! Pray for me, Mary, pray!"

As consciousness slowly returned, he realised he had uttered words from *Gerontius*. The demons in *The Dream of Gerontius* had become his demons. He was undergoing his own spiritual death and, in his extremity, called out for divine help. He heard Elgar's setting of the words in his mind's ear:

> *I can no more; for now it comes again,*
> *That sense of ruin, which is worse than pain,*

That masterful negation and collapse
Of all that makes me man ...
... And, crueller still,
A fierce and restless fright begins to fill
The mansion of my soul. And, worse and worse,
Some bodily form of ill
Floats on the wind, with many a loathsome curse
Tainting the hallowed air, and laughs, and flaps
Its hideous wings,
And makes me wild with horror and dismay.
O, Jesu, help! Pray for me, Mary, pray!

Hearing the words in the midst of his affliction gave him a strange strength and peace. The experience he was undergoing was not unique. He was not alone. Countless others had trodden their own way of the cross. Now it was his turn to suffer. If only, he wished, he had the faith of Gerontius!

Soon after his meal-tray had been removed, Simon was led from the cells to an interview room in the police station. Sitting on a chair in the corner of the room was a bald-headed man, with a venous nose and half-moon spectacles perched precariously on the end of his nose. Rising from his seat and clutching his briefcase to prevent it from falling to the ground, he introduced himself. "Good afternoon, Mr Copeland. I'm Stanley Walton and I understand you wish me to represent you in respect of the charges brought against you." He spoke with a high-pitched voice and precise enunciation. Someone more unlike the composer William Walton would be difficult to imagine and Simon began ruing his choice of solicitor simply on the basis of an English composer's name. Nevertheless, Mr Walton was now his solicitor and he must make the best of it.

Once Simon and Stanley Walton were alone, Mr Walton took control.

"Are you familiar, Mr Copeland, with the workings of the British judicial system?"

"Not at all," replied Simon.

"In that case let me explain the procedure before we turn to your defence. The police will take you to the Magistrates' Court tomorrow morning where you will be asked to confirm your name and address and whether or not you wish to enter a plea. I would advise against entering a plea until after you've consulted with Counsel. As the charge carries the possibility of a custodial sentence, the magistrates will refer the case to the Crown Court. There will then be a two or three month delay before your case can be heard. But we will not be idle during that time. I will ask for bail on your behalf so you will not have to spend time on remand in prison. I see no reason why bail should be refused. You are not exactly a menace to society or likely to flee the country – or at least, I hope you're not. I would strongly advise against any precipitous action. It will be in your own best interests to observe whatever bail conditions are imposed.

"Before the case comes to the Crown Court, I will instruct a Barrister-at-Law on your behalf. You are at liberty to choose whomsoever you wish to defend you, but, if you would like a recommendation from me, I would suggest Mr Digby Barrington-Jones. He's skilled in these matters and will give you good advice and procure the best outcome. Would you like me to instruct him on your behalf?"

Simon felt he had entered another world. Only a week before, he was as happy as a sand-boy revelling in the delights of South American life and culture. Now he was a captive, trapped within the British judicial system, about which he knew nothing. All he could do in answer to his solicitor's question was to meekly nod his head in agreement.

"Good," declared Mr Walton. "Now, let's go through the details of your relationship with Miss Burrows. I will prepare a brief for onward transmission to Mr Barrington-Jones. Let's begin at the beginning, shall we? When did you first meet Victoria Burrows?"

For the next hour or so, Simon bared his soul to the little solicitor. Mr Walton extracted the pertinent facts and made precise notes on a large foolscap pad.

"It seems so unfair," bewailed Simon, "Vicky is sixteen and has reached the age of consent. There's nothing illegal about a man falling in love with a sixteen-year-old girl and for the two of them expressing their love in a sexual way. But, just because I'm a teacher at her school, I'm branded a criminal. It seems so unfair!"

Mr Walton replaced the top on his pen and sighed. "It must seem that way to you," he answered. "Our parliamentary lawmakers do seem to have been particularly hard on teachers, as opposed to other groups where there is contact with those in the sixteen-to-eighteen age-bracket. But, no doubt, they had their reasons."

"Tell me," enquired Simon looking straight into the eyes of his diminutive legal representative, "What is the maximum sentence I can expect?"

"Five years," replied Mr Walton.

Then, rising from his chair, he said, "I think we had better steel ourselves for your interview with Detective Sergeant Addison."

The two of them were led to a bare room having just a table and three chairs. On the table was recording equipment. Simon was directed to a chair on one side of the table whilst DS Addison and another plain clothes officer took their seats on the other side of the table. Mr Walton occupied a seat in the corner of the room.

DS Addison activated the recording equipment and announced the date and time and the names of the four people present. Then, addressing Simon with an upward note of interrogation in his voice, he stated, "You are Simon Copeland and a teacher at Stoneybridge School?"

Simon nodded.

"Please answer all questions distinctly," retorted the officer. To which Mr Walton interjected, "My client has the right to remain silent if he so wishes, Sergeant Addison, and say 'No Comment' if he so wishes."

The police officer was not pleased with this interjection; but, maintaining an unruffled countenance, he answered, "You are perfectly correct, Mr Walton. But the Court will take into account any attempt to avoid questions and will draw its own conclusions. Shall we continue? Mr Copeland: are you a teacher employed at Stoneybrook School?"

"I am," answered Simon. "As I previously informed you, I am Head of Music."

"How long have you been employed at that school?"

"Nineteen years."

"And during that time you have taught both boys and girls, ranging in age from eleven to eighteen."

"That is correct."

"During those nineteen years, have you provided one-to-one musical tuition for any of the students?"

"Occasionally," replied Simon, even though he knew the only occasion he had done so in earnest was for Vicky.

"What are the names of the students with whom you undertook one-to-one tuition?"

"There have been so many it would be impossible to recall all their names. When one is directing a school production it's necessary to devote time to a large number of individual performers and give them personal tuition to learn their parts."

"Did you undertake one-to-one musical tuition with Victoria Burrows?"

"I did".

"What form did that take?"

"I gave her a number of piano lessons."

"Where did these take place?"

"In the school music room."

"Nowhere else?"

Simon could see where this was going and frantically racked his mind for an answer that would not appear suspicious.

"During the Easter holidays, when the school music room was unavailable, and Vicky was keen to continue her piano lessons, I undertook them at home."

"Do you normally invite students into your home?"

"Not as a general rule."

"Such behaviour leaves you open to accusations of inappropriate conduct with such students."

"I realise now it might not have been a wise thing to do, seeing the perverted interpretation your depraved mind is placing on the lessons."

At this, Mr Walton sprang to life and said, "Mr Copeland: I advise you simply to answer the officer's question rather than seek to provoke him unnecessarily."

"Thank you, Mr Walton," replied Detective Sergeant Addison. "Let us continue. Was anyone else in the house when Miss Burrows received her piano tuition?"

There was just the slightest hint of irony in the last two words of his question.

"No. I live alone."

"How many times did Miss Burrows come to your home for piano lessons?"

"On just three occasions – on the three Fridays of the Easter holidays."

"I see. Did any sexual activity take place on those occasions?"

"I told you. She was there for piano lessons. I'm a music teacher, not a sex therapist."

"Let's move on to the eight-week school summer holidays. Did you see Miss Burrows at all during that time?"

"Yes. I saw her for the duration of the summer holidays. Her parents live abroad and she had nowhere to stay and so, as I had spare rooms in my house, I offered her accommodation, which she was pleased to accept."

"A highly unusual arrangement, I think you would agree, Mr Copeland, for a male teacher and a sixteen-year-old female student to undertake."

"It may seem that way to someone with a perverted mind," countered Simon, only to be reminded of his solicitor's presence by a discreet cough emanating from the corner of the room. "I felt sorry for her. She was unwanted by her parents. She had no close friends, and she was destined to spend eight weeks in an empty boarding house whilst everyone else was enjoying themselves. I took pity on her and extended the hand of friendship."

"Is that why you took her with you on holiday to Buenos Aires?"

"I had a holiday booked there and I asked if she would like to visit the city with me."

"Where did you stay in Buenos Aires?"

"*The Hotel Mercure.*"

"Did you occupy separate rooms?"

"Of course."

"We will, of course, be able to check that out."

"Perhaps you would also like to check out the theatres we visited, the restaurants in which we ate, the festivals we attended, the museums we visited and the hundred and one other cultural delights we experienced."

"That won't be necessary, Mr Copeland. All we are interested in is the sexual activity in which you engaged with

Miss Burrows. Why don't you drop this façade Mr Copeland and admit to the sexual acts that took place between you and Miss Burrows."

"Detective Sergeant Addison," interposed Mr Walton, "You're asking my client to incriminate himself before he has even had the opportunity to discuss with his Counsel the form his defence will take. I must ask you to withdraw that suggestion."

Scowling, the detective officer looked at his wristwatch, and, deciding he would make no further headway, concluded the interview by saying, "You'll appear before the magistrates tomorrow morning charged under Section 16 of the Sexual Offences Act 2003. Is there anything else you wish to add?"

Simon sighed, shook his head and whispered "No."

"Interview terminated at 3.47.pm."

The two police officers rose from their seats as did Mr Walton.

"I wonder if I might have a moment with my client?" enquired the unprepossessing solicitor to the detective sergeant.

"By all means," replied DS Addison. "Perhaps you can persuade him to face up to the truth."

Once the police officers had left, Mr Walton informed Simon, "The police officers will now present their evidence to the Crown Prosecution Service and they will decide whether or not to proceed with the case. I think we must be realistic. The evidence against you is considerable and we should proceed on the assumption you will appear before the Magistrates Court tomorrow. But do not worry. I will be there to secure bail for you."

With a reassuring smile and a shake of the hand, Mr Walton went on his way whilst Simon was led back to the cells.

Simon spent a second restless night in the police cells. Mercifully, he was spared the nightmares of the previous night, but awoke the following morning feeling dishevelled and listless.

His appearance at the Magistrates' Court went just as Mr Walton had outlined. The three magistrates sitting behind the raised bench heard the details of the charge, ascertained Simon's name and address and ordered reporting restrictions to remain in place to protect the identity of the person they referred to as The Victim. The case was then referred to the Crown Court. Mr Walton respectfully requested police bail on behalf of his client. After some discussion, this was duly granted subject to Simon having no contact whatsoever with any student or teacher at Stoneybridge School, observing an exclusion zone of one-mile around the school premises and surrendering his passport.

Mr Walton considered this a favourable outcome and assured Simon of his best endeavours to bring about a successful resolution of the case.

There then followed an anxious three months during which Simon's life existed in limbo. He received a letter from the Chairman of Stoneybridge School Governors suspending him from the teaching staff until the criminal case against him had been heard. But this was merely a formality. Simon was prohibited from going anywhere near the school. He knew that, even if by some miracle he was eventually acquitted, he could never return to Stoneybridge. That chapter in his life had closed. He had no idea what the next chapter would contain.

His thoughts often turned to Vicky. He wondered how she was coping. Did she still love him with all the passion and excitement they shared in Buenos Aires? Or had her love turned to fear at the enormity of the consequences? Was she still bound to him by love or had her mind been poisoned against him by others? Would she look back on the time they spent together as the best time of her life or would she bitterly regret eloping with a married man who was old enough to be her father? There was no way of knowing. The agony of not knowing was even worse than being told the truth. He was desperately unhappy. The only solace he found was in music. He translated the pain in his heart into writing new music – some of it soulful but much of it surprisingly joyous and uplifting. This was his way of combating loneliness and despair. By composing new music, he was able to rise above his troubles and inhabit a world where there were no laws, sentencing or punishments but only beauty, nobility and eternal yearnings.

He learned from Stanley Walton that his case was due to be heard on 4 January at the County Crown Court. His solicitor arranged a video conference with Mr Barrington-Jones in his chambers at the Inner Temple in London; and so, at a pre-arranged time, Simon and Stanley Walton gathered in the latter's Dickensian offices to speak with Mr Barrington-Jones.

Digby Barrington-Jones was a no-nonsense man. He did not waste words. He was nearing retirement and had represented a succession of clients accused of sexual misconduct. There was nothing that shocked him. All emotion had long since been drained from his heart. He was simply there to represent the best interests of the Defendant. It was a job. He sometimes likened his job to that of a taxi-driver. A client came along and asked for his services. He provided them to the best of his ability, received a fee and proceeded to his next fare. His craggy face and white hair witnessed to his longevity as a barrister-at-law.

He stared intently at Simon from the screen before him as if forming a judgement as to his new client's character.

"Good morning, Mr Copeland. Good morning Mr Walton. Thank you for facilitating this video conference call. I see from the brief I've been given by Mr Walton that no plea has been entered in relation to the charge: the charge being an abuse of trust involving sexual activity with a student at the school at which you, Mr Copeland, taught. We need, therefore, to decide how best you should plead when the case comes to the Crown Court. If you plead guilty to the charge of which you are accused, I will do all in my power to mitigate the punishment you receive. I can do that by citing your previous blameless conduct, the enrichment you have brought to the lives of countless young people through music, the enormous emotional strains you were under following the breakup of your marriage and so on. By so doing, I would hope to reduce the maximum sentence of five years imprisonment to, say, two years. That may still seem a long time to serve, but, in effect, you would only serve one year before being released back into the community on licence. Better still, I might be able to secure a suspended sentence for you that would allow you to remain free provided you did not reoffend.

"Alternatively, you could plead Not Guilty. In that case, I would have to show that the Prosecution's principal witness, Miss Victoria Burrows, is a liar, a fantasist, a scheming and devilish individual intent on ruining the career of an otherwise exemplary teacher. I would have to tear her apart in the witness-box, cause her to contradict herself, reduce her to tears no doubt, and generally make her evidence appear so unreliable that the twelve men and women of the jury would feel unable to convict you beyond all reasonable doubt on such shaky evidence. If we follow that course, but fail to convince the jury and they return a verdict of guilty, I regret to say the judge is likely to take a very dim view of our tactics. In all probability he will reprimand us for subjecting a sixteen-year-old schoolgirl to such an emotional mauling and this would be reflected in the subsequent harshness of his sentencing.

"That is the choice before you, Mr Copeland. I cannot advise you how you should plead. I can only present the facts, as I see them, so you can make an informed decision."

Simon knew he had no choice. He could not bear the thought of Vicky being subjected to public humiliation and trauma on his account. In the eyes of the law, he was the one in the wrong and he must accept his punishment.

"I couldn't bear to see you tearing Vicky to shreds," he replied. "She has the rest of her life before her and I wouldn't want to harm her further. I'll plead Guilty and take the consequences."

"If that is your decision," replied the barrister-at-law, "I will do my utmost to secure the judge's mercy and obtain the most lenient sentence possible. Now, unless there is anything else you want to ask me, we'll terminate this conference call and meet next at the Crown Court."

Simon expressed his thanks to the barrister and the conference call terminated.

"I think you've made the right decision," added Mr Walton. "The evidence against you is very strong and it would be cruel to put Miss Burrows through the undoubted trauma of cross-examination. I'm sure Mr Barrington-Jones will use his considerable persuasive powers to obtain a lenient sentence for you."

The days leading up to Simon's appearance at the Crown Court were anxious times for him. He had no friends to whom he could turn. He felt unable to return to his family home and face his aging parents. None of his former colleagues were able to approach him. He was isolated, lonely and not a little afraid. It seemed to him as if he was already serving a self-imposed prison sentence.

He spent a lonely and miserable Christmas with the court case hanging over him. Were it not for the solace he derived from listening to music, playing the piano and composing, he might well have been tempted to end his life. Whenever he entered those dark nights of the soul, it was the memory of the love he once shared with Sandra and, more latterly, with Vicky, that kept him alive. Love was stronger than death. He had experienced love in all its power and transforming beauty. What was there to prevent him experiencing it again at some point in the future when his present troubles were behind him?

Monday 4 January eventually arrived and Simon travelled to The Shire Hall for the quarterly sessions of the Crown Court. He had arranged to meet his solicitor and barrister in the entrance vestibule. After an anxious few minutes, the two of them appeared – Mr Walton in his shabby working-suit and Mr Barrington-Jones in a billowing black gown over a smart chalk-stripe three-piece suit. The barrister sported a pair of white bands protruding from his collar and had a barrister's wig on his head.

After greeting each other, the two legal men engaged in some desultory chatter whilst waiting for their case to be called.

They were to appear before Judge Imogen Ecclestone QC.

"What's she like?" asked a nervous Simon.

"She's usually fair," replied the barrister-at-law. "She will naturally be more biased towards Miss Burrows as a member of her own sex, but we'll seek to play on her maternal instincts and the gentle and caring nature of your relationship with Miss Burrows. We'll appeal to her compassion. In my experience, female judges are more compassionate than their male counterparts."

Once they had taken their place in the courtroom, the usher bade everyone stand for the entrance of the judge.

Imogen Ecclestone was a stately lady in her late fifties. Whatever hair she possessed was hidden beneath her judge's wig. She surveyed the court with a regal sweep of her eyes before inviting everyone, except the Defendant, to be seated. Simon was asked to confirm his name and then the charge against him was read out: "Regina versus Simon Copeland. Mr Copeland you are brought before this court on the following counts: that between Friday 19 April 2019 and Friday 30 August 2019 you engaged in sexual activity with a sixteen-year-old student of Stoneybridge School where you also were a teacher, in contravention of Section 16 of the Sexual Offences Act 2003."

After a moment's pause, Simon was asked, "How do you plead?"

Simon surveyed the courtroom. He caught a glimpse of Sandra sitting impassively in the public gallery with her eyes firmly fixed upon him. To one side of her sat her fidgeting mother, but there was no black-skinned second husband sitting with her. To the other side of Sandra sat her father with his tanned and leathery face exuding undisguised hatred for his son-in-law. There were many others in the gallery whom Simon did not recognize. Maybe Vicky's parents from Singapore were there to comfort and support their daughter and see that justice was meted on the man who had robbed their daughter of her adolescent innocence. All eyes in the court were focussed on him. Taking a deep breath, he quietly whispered, "Guilty."

A ripple of murmuring went around the public gallery before Judge Ecclestone called for order and invited Prosecuting Counsel to speak.

"Ma'am, The Accused who stands before you today occupied a position of trust. He was a teacher and, as such *in loco parentis*, with the students in his care. The parents of such students had every right to expect their sons and daughters would be safe and protected from predatory individuals intent on using their children for their own personal sexual gratification. Alas, in the case of the Accused, this trust was woefully abused. Purposely selecting a young sixteen-year-old girl, who was separated from her parents and lacking friends of her own age, he groomed her for his own predatory ends. He lured her to his home under the guise of giving her piano lessons and there engaged in penetrative sex. To compound the felony, he even failed to protect her from the consequences of his behaviour by eschewing the use of a condom. The schoolgirl had, therefore, to bicycle to various pharmacists in order to purchase morning-after pills. After deliberately deceiving her parents into thinking she was spending the summer holidays with a school-friend in England, the Accused took the young schoolgirl with him to Buenos Aires where he engaged in six weeks of depraved sexual activity. Her parents were unaware of this deception until they received their daughter's GCSE results. Upon informing the school that these results had been sent to the wrong location and should be sent to the friend's address where their daughter was staying, the scope of the deception became apparent. Simultaneously, the Accused's wife, suspecting duplicity on her husband's part, informed the police of her suspicions and the Accused was apprehended at his home in the company of the young schoolgirl. It is not without note, ma'am, that the Accused met his own wife nineteen-years before when he was a teacher at a school where she was a student. History appears to be repeating itself.

"In sentencing the Accused, Ma'am, we would ask that you take into account the psychological harm inflicted upon the young girl and the devastating effect this will have on her subsequent life. Schoolgirl A acknowledges that the Accused gave her a feeling of confidence, but that now she feels embarrassed at how easily she was manipulated. She became isolated from her friends and had to practice deceit, lying and falsehood. She rightly says she was a child whom the Accused ruthlessly manipulated in order to fulfil his own desires. She says the Accused led her to believe he was a divorced man whereas, in fact, he was only separated from his wife. 'He led me to believe,' she says, 'that sex was the only area of life where I excelled'."

Simon could hardly believe what he heard. This was not the Vicky he knew. She had either been brainwashed or else undergone a Damascus Road conversion. In place of the coquettish, seductive, highly-sexed girl he knew, the Court was being presented with a timid, helpless, innocent child in whose mouth butter would not melt. But he was powerless to object. All he could do was shake his head in disbelief and hope his Counsel would correct the record. Meanwhile, the Prosecuting Counsel moved to his peroration.

"Ma'am, in view of the predatory nature of the offence; the secrecy and devious scheming employed by the Accused and the most gross abuse of that sacred trust invested in members of the teaching profession, we call upon you, Ma'am, to register the Court's acute disapproval by subjecting the Accused to the full sentencing severity permitted by law, in order to act as a deterrent to other members of the teaching profession who might be tempted to act in a similar deplorable manner."

With that, the Prosecuting Council flopped into his chair with a self-satisfied look of a job well-done and mopped his brow with an ostentatious red handkerchief.

The lady Judge then asked Mr Digby Barrington-Jones if he had anything to say in mitigation on behalf of his client.

"Yes, ma'am, if I may," said the barrister, as he rose to his feet clutching the lapel of his gown.

"My client is a most unfortunate man. Had he been a church youth-club leader and the sixteen-year-old Schoolgirl A a member of his club, he would not be standing before you today. It would be entirely within the law for the two of them to engage in consensual sexual activity. Had my client been a sports coach - say a netball coach - and sixteen-year-old Schoolgirl A a member of his netball squad, it would be entirely within the law for the two of them to engage in consensual sexual activity, if they so wished. Had my client been the Commanding Officer of a uniformed cadet force and sixteen-year-old Schoolgirl A one of the cadets, it would be entirely within the law for them to participate in consensual sexual activity, if they so wished. The age of consent in this land is sixteen and, provided both parties to a consensual sexual act are over sixteen years of age, the law is not interested in them. Furthermore, if Schoolgirl A had been a pupil at a school just fifty yards down the road from the school where my client taught, and the two of them engaged in consensual sexual activity, there would be no case to answer. It is merely because my client and Schoolgirl A both attended the same school that the full weight of the law has fallen upon him. For reasons best known to our lawmakers, teachers and students at the same school have been singled out for especially harsh treatment. Prior to the passing of the 2003 Sexual Offences Act, innumerable teachers and students fell in love and expressed their love in a physical way through sexual intercourse. Many of them went on to lead full, content and happy lives as husbands and wives. I could parade before the court, if that were deemed helpful, numerous examples of happily married teachers and the sixteen-year-old students who are now in their fifties, sixties and seventies and who met and fell in love in the school classroom. The pursuit of love leads some to lifelong happiness and fulfilment, whereas for my client it has led to the courtroom. The feelings are identical: it is just the outcome that is different.

"Ma'am, you will have noted in the Victim Impact Statement, that Schoolgirl A admits my client never forced her to do anything against her will. It was an entirely consensual relationship motivated by mutual love.

"Ma'am, my client is a sensitive man. He is a richly talented musician who has brought happiness and wonder into the lives of countless young people. He has composed music, some of which achieved commercial success, and has enabled young people to sing and perform in concerts, giving them confidence and enabling them to grow in maturity and self-worth. My client's Headteacher speaks of his undoubted musical talent, hard work and diligent teaching. Of course, all of this is now impossible. His career is at an end. But should he be labelled a criminal? Should he be sent to prison in the company of murderers, terrorists, drug-dealers, rapists and the like? Should the flame of creativity within him be snuffed out by a custodial sentence? Such a thing would be cruel indeed!

"My client, ma'am, is not an evil man. He grew up in a vicarage and was endowed with the values and morality that went with such an upbringing. It was not his fault he endured an isolated childhood, far removed from the company of other boys and girls of his own age; unable to form friendships and learn the arts of courtship and successful interpersonal relationships. The mere fact he is standing before you today is humiliation and punishment enough for him. He is a man of previous blameless conduct who has been labouring under enormous emotional strains due to the breakup of his marriage. We ask, therefore, ma'am, that you look with compassion on a life that has been broken and extend the possibility of forgiveness for his foolishness and allow him to make a new start in life. Rather than incarcerate him behind prison walls, we respectfully ask you to consider a suspended sentence."

With that, the barrister-at-law returned to his chair and sat down.

Ignoring the pleading of Simon's barrister, Judge Ecclestone warned the accused he should expect a custodial sentence and ordered him to be remanded in custody pending reports. She announced sentencing would take place in four weeks' time, or as soon thereafter.

Once Simon was conveyed to the cells to await transportation to prison, his two-man legal team visited him.

"I will maintain contact with you whilst you're on remand," promised Mr Walton.

The three men then went their separate ways: the legal practitioners to freedom and the prisoner to incarceration and despair.

Life on the remand block of Her Majesty's Prison was reckoned to be more relaxed than life on the prison wings, but Simon found the experience degrading and life-sapping. The other offenders, who were either awaiting trial or sentencing, were not the type with whom he would normally consort. When he learned of the crimes some of those on remand were accused he feared for his personal safety. He did however find one kindred spirit in a choirmaster awaiting sentencing for crimes against young boys. Simon had no sympathy for the pederasty crimes the man had committed but recognized a fellow sensitive musician undergoing his own personal purgatory. The two of them spent time together discussing music. In so doing they were able to escape the claustrophobic confines of the prison and inhabit another world where beauty and joy reigned untrammelled by the baser things of life.

During the four weeks prior to his sentencing, Simon was visited by the prison Probation Officer tasked with writing a pre-sentence report about him. He was surprised to discover she was a young woman - and a good-looking one at that. Perhaps it was her attractive appearance and gentle manner that made Simon open his heart to her. She was keen to hear his life-story. She was particularly interested in his early years, growing up in a vicarage with elderly parents and without the company of other children. He answered her questions without dissimulation. He even hoped she might be able to tell him where he had gone wrong and why his pursuit of love had led to prison; but she was tasked with extracting information from him and not providing him with a life-repair kit. At the end of the interview she appeared to have all she required whilst he felt as dejected and empty as ever.

A period of three weeks elapsed before Simon was summoned to re-appear before Judge Ecclestone for sentencing. As he entered the dock, he glanced at the public gallery and noted that Sandra and her father were present once again, but not Sandra's mother. Simon recalled that Sandra had always been much closer to her father than her mother. The other faces in the gallery were unknown to him.

After the formalities were enacted, all eyes focussed on Judge Imogen Ecclestone QC. Removing her spectacles, she addressed the courtroom.

"The crime of sexual activity between a teacher and a student is a most serious one. It destroys the trust parents place in the teaching profession when they commit their children into a teacher's care. The law recognises this and makes provision to protect children from sexual activity by members of the teaching profession. Despite Mr Barrington-Jones' eloquent observations on the dichotomy between adult instructors or leaders of other children's organisations and teachers and students at the same school, we are concerned only with the law. The law specifically prohibits all sexual activity between a teacher and a child at the same school. The inequality between a teacher and a student means it is inappropriate for that relationship to become a sexual one, notwithstanding the ability of the student to consent to sexual acts. The law exists to protect teachers and children from themselves and others. Counsel for the Defendant alludes to the many happy marriages that have resulted from teacher-student liaisons prior to the passing of the 2003 Sexual Offences Act. What he failed to mention is the number of disastrous relationships that also occurred when young and impressionable students realised they had been groomed and exploited by someone in authority over them. The prisoner's own failed marriage would seem to bear witness to this.

"I am satisfied the Defendant's conduct was wholly inappropriate, predatory and involved a significant degree of planning. Furthermore, he presented a false view of his marriage to Schoolgirl A thus encouraging her to respond favourably to his advances.

"It is the purpose of this Court to register society's disapproval of such actions; to reassure parents that their children are safe when they entrust them into the care of a school or college; and to deter any teacher who, in future, might be tempted to act in a similar way. I, therefore, sentence the Defendant to two-year's imprisonment with the stipulation he be banned from all work involving contact with children for the next twenty-years. Reporting restrictions are lifted, but, the name of Schoolgirl A must not be disclosed as she is a minor."

THE WAGES OF LOVE

Having delivered her sentence, Judge Ecclestone placed her glasses in her handbag, rose and left the court.
Simon looked ruefully at his solicitor. It was not the verdict he was expecting. Two years of his life to be spent in prison: it was not a welcome prospect. Even when his solicitor attempted to soften the blow by assuring him he would serve only one year behind bars before being released back into the community on licence, it did nothing to lift the pall of despair that descended upon him. In the eyes of the law he was a criminal and society demanded retribution. He would have to suffer, alone and forlorn. He heard the voice of Gerontius singing in his ears:

> *Take me away, and in the lowest deep*
> *There let me be,*
> *And there in hope the lone night-watches keep,*
> *Told out for me.*

He was led away to his own purgatory: the Reception Block of one of Her Majesty's Prisons, to begin his two-year prison sentence.

CHAPTER ELEVEN

As Simon lay on his back in the prison's hospital bay, he replayed the events of his arrest and trial. The judge branded him a predator. She inferred he had deliberately and systematically gone out of his way to entrap Vicky for his own sexual gratification. He knew this was untrue. He had never deliberately pursued the sixteen-year-old schoolgirl. It was not a case of predator and victim, but rather of two lost souls, deprived of love, that somehow collided in a cosmic explosion. Vicky had been deprived of love all her life and he had opened her eyes to its transforming powers. He had been starved of love following Sandra's departure and needed to experience its life-giving qualities again if he was to survive and function as a creative human being. Both of them desperately needed to be loved, and this need found its realisation in the time they shared together. Simon refused to believe he used his position as a teacher to prey upon an innocent young student.

Then he remembered Vicky's Victim Impact Statement. She claimed she was embarrassed at being so easily manipulated by him. He shook his head in disbelief. If anyone had been manipulated it was him, he thought. She was the one who persuaded him to give her private piano lessons. She was the one who provocatively revealed her cleavage to him. She was the one who flashed her eyes and made coquettish comments that were designed to lead him on. Now, she claimed she was an innocent child who had been manipulated to fulfil his carnal desires. He could only assume she said these things out of fear. He could only suppose she had assumed the attitude of a poor, defenceless child ruthlessly exploited by an older married man in order to shield herself from the condemnation of other students and adults. It was her form of self-defence. She had probably employed such tactics throughout her life to protect herself from hurt and deflect blame onto others. She was more to be pitied than censured. She craved love and feared blame. She had to protect herself even if that meant being economical with the truth.

The more Simon thought of Vicky the more he realised the futility of their relationship. Vicky was beautiful, sexually alluring and vivacious but she was also immature, vapid and jejune. He recalled her preference for *Evita* over *Carmen*; her boredom when visiting the magnificent *El Ateneo Grand Splendid* bookstore; and her complete absence of spirituality when stepping inside the churches of Buenos Aires. She was immature. The intellectual gulf between them was ultimately unbridgeable. She was a child whereas he was an adult. The relationship was destined to fail. If only he had realised that at the beginning, he might not now be incarcerated in Her Majesty's Prison.

He lay on his back in the hospital wing and stared at the ceiling. He realised he had made so many mistakes. But, rather than dwell on his mistakes, he knew he had to look to the future. He needed to make a new start. His life needed a new direction.

Whilst recuperating in the prison's hospital wing, he spent a great deal of time reading the books he had been given on Zelenka. He was able to lose himself in the life and works of the Czech composer. The musical quotations within the text were not merely black dots and squiggles on paper but sounds that resonated in his head. Sometimes he found himself quietly humming the musical examples and smiling -at their originality and Zelenka's remarkable creativity.

It was on one such occasion that he received a visit from the prison chaplain.

"It's good to hear you singing," smiled the little man of God. "It must be a sign you're recovering. What's the book you're reading?"

Simon explained his plans for a musical doctorate studying the music of the Czech baroque composer Jan Dismas Zelenka and the influence the composer had on subsequent composers.

"Splendid!" replied the chaplain. "It's always good to have a goal to work towards, especially in a place like this, where life can be very humdrum and tedious. I know nothing about Mr Zelenka and so I'll wait with interest to read the fruits of your research."

Simon smiled at the chaplain's enthusiasm. The chaplain had shown no previous interest in music and so, the thought of him reading a scholarly dissertation about an

obscure eighteenth-century Czech composer seemed highly unlikely. Nevertheless, Simon welcomed the chaplain's encouragement.
"Now, tell me," continued the chaplain, "how are things going with the forthcoming Carol Service? There are just ten days to go. Do you think you'll be sufficiently recovered to direct proceedings?"
"Undoubtedly," replied Simon. "The members of the choir have largely mastered the notes and it's now just a case of applying the polish."
"I think you've worked wonders shaping such a motley collection of men into a disciplined choir," exuded the chaplain. "I can't wait to hear the results. Are you feeling well enough to lead the Tuesday evening choir practice?"
"Yes," Simon confidently answered. "Making music is the best medicine there is as far as I'm concerned. It will greatly aid my recovery."
"Excellent," beamed the chaplain. "I'll ensure the members of the choir are assembled in the chapel on Tuesday evening."
With a prayer of blessing over the bedbound Simon, the chaplain continued on his pastoral rounds whilst Simon returned to the musical delights of Zelenka.
After three days in the prison's hospital wing, Simon was transferred back to E Wing and given light prison duties to perform.
The members of the choir were most solicitous as to his health when he returned to lead the Tuesday evening rehearsal.

"God be praised!" shouted one of the Caribbean choristers. "Zee choirmaster is back from the dead."

"Alleluia!" shouted the others, as jostling and congratulatory punches were exchanged amongst the inmates.

"Now don't you worry man," reassured Winston in his deep growling voice. "Them bastards that beat you up have flown the nest. The Screws sent them packing. Man, are they lucky! If they'd a-stayed here we would have redesigned their faces so not even their mothers would recognize them. They won't worry you no more, man."

Simon was visibly moved by the loyalty and friendship of his choristers. They might be a motley bunch, but the common desire to make music created a bond between them and turned wildly disparate individuals into caring friends.

"Right," said Simon, adopting a business-like attitude to proceedings, "Let's get down to work. This is the last full rehearsal before the Carol Service, and, although we may be able to squeeze in a last minute run-through on the day, we need to make sure we've got everything firmly in place for Sunday. Let's start with *Mary had a baby*. It always brings a smile to our faces and gets us into fine singing voice. Winston, Reginald and Cecil: give a good lead on the harmonies so as to support the melody. One, two three, four…"

The sixteen men - of various shapes, sizes and races - launched into a spirited and rhythmic version of the Caribbean carol. They turned the bare echoing chapel into a tropical island in the sun, replete with palm trees gently swaying in the breeze above the shack where Mary cradled her new-born baby son. At the end of the carol there was a moment's silence. Simon was loath to break the spell. It was music from the heart that spoke to the heart.

"Very good," Simon eventually declared. Then, with that striving after perfection that is the hallmark of all good musical directors, he added, "But in verse five – *Named him King Jesus* – we could create more of an impact by gradually increasing the volume each time we sing the words. That way, we would create a thrilling crescendo that would bring the piece to a resounding conclusion. Let's try that verse again doing just that and see how it sounds."

Once Simon was satisfied with the Caribbean carol, he turned to Sarsung's solo *Malam Kudus* with the gently supporting choral backing supplied by the other members of the choir. Although the piece had very special memories for him (in its English version) he was able to distance himself as he heard the light tenor voice of Sarsung weaving his magic over the softly changing chords below. The carol sounded so different from Sandra's singing of it that he was able to be objective and focus on the choir's accompaniment.

"Excellent," declared Simon. "There won't be a dry eye in the chapel at the end of that."

"That's because tears of laughter will be rolling down their cheeks," declared the morose Duncan, only to be immediately assailed by all the other members of the choir for his negativity.

"The only thing they's going to laugh at is your bum notes," countered Winston. "What about making Duncan sing it, Simon? Then we can laugh at him."

This was greeted with cheers, catcalls and an explosion of physicality. Seated at the piano, Simon could not help thinking he had never known a choir like the prison choir. There was never any way of telling when beautiful music-making would suddenly erupt into physical and verbal mayhem. Making music in prison was an experience like no other.

The choir practice continued with the specially-composed carol Simon had written, followed by carols from other countries around the world and culminating in the modern Welsh carol *Sir Christemus* with its flashing accompaniment, off-beat *Nowells* and final fortissimo shout. Despite the difficulty the men experienced learning this piece, they now had it firmly under their belts and relished the opportunity to flex their musical muscles and demonstrate their skill. Simon planned to use this number as the final carol in the service. He knew it would bring the house down and prove a memorable end to what he hoped would be a memorable Carol Service.

The two prison officers tasked with being present in the chapel during the choir practice were genuinely impressed with the sounds they heard. As they led the inmates back to the cells, one of them remarked to Simon, "You've worked bloody miracles getting that lot to sing like that." Simon smiled. "It's not me," he replied, "It's all to do with the music. Music brings out the best in people."

"In that case," continued the prison officer, "you'd better use it on all the other lags here."

Back in his cell, Simon ruminated on his conversation with the prison officer. Music did possess transformative powers. He recalled learning in childhood of the shepherd boy David playing his harp to the agitated and psychotic King Saul in order to calm him; Elgar organizing music at the Worcester County Lunatic Asylum to bring peace and comfort to the disturbed inmates; the sound of bugles on the battlefield to rouse spirits and spur combatants to untold feats of courage and valour; Bach's *Goldberg Variations* written to soothe an insomniac and bring sleep to a tortured soul. Yes, music possessed tremendous power to change lives and calm the troubled breast.

The following day, as Simon was undertaking cleaning duties on E Wing, he was called aside by one of the prison officers.

"You've got a visitor," announced the prison officer.

This came as a complete surprise to Simon. He had received only one visitor from the outside world since he was sent to prison, and that was his mother. It had not been a particularly enjoyable meeting and Simon was not keen to repeat it or anything similar.

"Who is it?" enquired the puzzled Simon.

"The Reverend Evans," replied the officer.

Simon knew of no one by that name. Furthermore, he had no desire to meet an unknown clergyman. The only reason clergymen visited people in prison was to rescue their souls from hell and notch up another convert in their heavenly book of good deeds. He recalled the infamous Lord

Longford and his religiously-inspired prison visits. The last thing he wanted was some evangelical Do-gooder attempting to save his soul from hell.

"I don't know anyone of that name," answered Simon "and I've no desire to meet an unknown clergyman."

"Who said it's a clergyman?" retorted the officer. "Didn't look much like a man to me. In fact, she looked very attractive. I wouldn't let the opportunity of spending time with an attractive woman pass me by. She says she's travelled a considerable distance to see you. It would be very rude to say you don't want to see her."

The officer's words only caused Simon's puzzlement to deepen. He knew of no lady vicars; but his curiosity was aroused. If the person was good-looking as the officer claimed, it would be foolish to let a rare opportunity of spending time with an attractive woman pass him by.

"OK. I'll see her," agreed Simon.

The prison officer led Simon to the Visitors' Centre and directed him to a seat on one side of a table. There was an empty seat on the opposite side.

"Sit here and I'll go and get the young lady," announced the officer.

Simon stared at the door that opened into the Visitor Meeting Room wondering what sight would greet him when it opened. So great was his anticipation that it seemed like eternity before the door actually opened to reveal a slender, middle-aged woman, wearing a winter coat and scarf. Her face looked strangely familiar. Simon racked his brains to recall how or when he had previously met her. He noticed that her blue eyes were widely set apart. Her hair was light brown with the first traces of grey at the extremities. As she looked across the room at Simon, she smiled. He was sure he recognized that smile, but was still unable to place the woman as she slowly advanced towards him. It was only when she reached the other side of the table and he was able to look into her eyes that he knew who she was. Her blue eyes were not the blue of the sky but the deep blue of the sea. It could only be one person: Rosie, the girl he last saw thirty-years before; the girl with whom he shared idyllic summer days in the woods and by streams; the girl with the great love of the outdoors; the girl he had so cruelly abandoned on the orders of his father.

"Rosie Evans!" exclaimed Simon in a paean of surprise and delight. "Well, of all people! Fancy seeing you again after all these years! This is a wonderful surprise! I can hardly believe my eyes!"

Rosie smiled at his boyish excitement.

"I'm so pleased you're glad to see me. I thought I might not be welcome. It's a long time since we last met, but I've never forgotten you."

"Nor I you," returned Simon. "You must have thought me a very poor friend to abandon you without a word of explanation. It wasn't my doing. My father found out about our friendship and ordered me to stop seeing you. I don't think he had anything against you personally, but I understand he and your father quarrelled and he didn't want me associating with anyone from your family. It all seems so petty, but I was powerless to do anything about it. I was confined to the house and I had no way of contacting you. I am sorry."

Rosie smiled and gently nodded her head. "I guessed it was something like that," she replied. "My father was a difficult man. He was a staunch atheist; but, rather than keep his atheism to himself, he pursued a one-man crusade to spread his irreligion and gain converts. It invariably resulted in trouble. I came to think he was not as secure in his unbelief as he maintained, and his need to proselytize was really a way of bolstering his insecurities. I've noticed other people behave in a similar way. You'll remember Saul of Tarsus. He was a very militant persecutor of Christians before his conversion. I suspect his militancy was to disguise a deep psychological insecurity that he only confronted after the events on the Damascus Road. Unfortunately, my father never had a Damascus Road experience and remained a militant atheist to the end of his life."

Ignoring the religious illustration, Simon asked, "But what brings you here? How did you know I was here?"

"I met your mother," replied Rosie, "whilst out shopping. She did not recognize me; indeed, I don't think she ever really knew me. But I recognized her. I had often wondered what had become of you. I remember you telling me you wanted to be a composer, and I was curious to know if you'd achieved your ambition. So, I approached her and enquired after you. She was not keen to talk. Indeed, she attempted to walk past me. But I was persistent. I wanted to know what had become of you. It took me a long time to extract the information I wanted. She was clearly deeply embarrassed and ashamed that you were in prison. I did my best to console her. I didn't enquire the reason for your imprisonment because I could tell that would only increase her distress; but I resolved to visit you in the hope we could renew the friendship we shared all those years ago."

"That's very good of you," whispered Simon. "I get very few visitors and I can't tell you how uplifting your visit is." Then, after a pause, he confided, "I almost refused to see you. When I was told a Reverend Evans was here, I never, for one moment, thought of you. How long have you been a priest?"

"Not very long," answered Rosie. "It's been a long and painful journey getting to this point; but I don't want to bore you with my life history."

"You won't bore me," assured Simon. "I'd genuinely like to know how your life has unfolded."

"Very well, then," Rosie replied, "if you really want to hear."

Then, gathering her thoughts, she began, "You'll remember, when we last met, I was enthralled by the natural world. I loved Nature in all its wonder and glory; and so it wasn't surprising that, when it came to choosing a university course, I chose molecular biology. I was fascinated by the micro complexity of living things and the intricate way all living plants and creatures form part of a wondrous web of interconnected matter. I discovered my metier in the biology lab. I also discovered Robbie. He was an undergraduate just like me. We soon discovered we had a lot in common. Our friendship developed and I honestly believed I'd found my soulmate for life. Then, alas, disaster struck. Robbie was a keen rock-climber. He belonged to the university rock climbing group and often went off at weekends on expeditions to Scotland and Snowdonia. It was on one such expedition that something went terribly wrong. Robbie fell three-hundred feet and was killed. I was absolutely devastated. It seemed as if the bottom had dropped out of my life. I became very depressed and withdrawn. Life no longer held any attraction for me. I experienced deep despair. Looking back, it was without doubt, the lowest point in my life.

"My friends did their best to jolly me up. They attempted to divert my attention from the aching grief in my heart. They took me to dances in the hope I'd meet another boy and form a new relationship. But no boy wants to know a depressive girl, and that was what I was. Then, one of my friends invited me to accompany her to church. I was not keen. I'd never been a churchgoer. I suppose something of my father's atheism had rubbed off on me. I couldn't see the point worshipping an unseen being when the natural created world all around provided limitless wonder and cause for adoration. But, somewhat reluctantly, I agreed.

"I can still vividly remember entering the shadowy interior of St Mary's Parish Church. It struck me as very strange. It was certainly unlike any other building I had previously entered. I also found the church service very strange. But the people attending were not strange. They were very kind and gentle. My friend introduced me to some of the others and explained to them about Robbie's tragic death. The others listened with obvious compassion, and their words were gentle and comforting. I felt I was amongst friends.

"I continued attending St Mary's and gradually grew to be more at ease inside the building. I listened attentively to all that was said – especially about the church's *raison d'être*,

Jesus Christ. Of course, I knew the outline of his life and teaching. I had sat through innumerable RE lessons at school. But I'd always seen Him as simply the founder of another world religion, on a par with Mohammad, Gautama, Moses and such like. What struck me at St Mary's was the way in which the members regarded him as a living person, alive and active in the world today. They regarded him, and prayed to him, as if he was their friend. And what a friend! A friend who listened to their doubts and fears; who spoke words of wisdom and encouragement; who provided guidance through the difficulties of life; who was constant, unchanging and infinitely loving. I suppose I was in need of just such a friend at that time.

"Then came my moment of illumination! I remember it vividly. I was listening to a passage being read from the Sermon on the Mount."

Looking over Simon's head, Rosie pulled the words out of the air and quoted them from memory:

> *"Consider the lilies of the field, how they grow; they toil not, neither do they spin: yet I say unto you, that even Solomon in all his glory was not arrayed like one of these. But if God so clothe the grass of the field, which to-day is, and to-morrow is cast into the oven, shall he not much more clothe you, O ye of little faith? Be not therefore anxious, saying, What shall we eat? or, What shall we drink? or, Wherewithal shall we be clothed? For after all these things do the Gentiles seek; for your heavenly Father knoweth that ye have need of all these things. But seek ye first his kingdom, and his righteousness; and all these things shall be added unto you.*

"Perhaps it was the reference to the natural world – the flowers and the grass that I study in the science lab - that opened my eyes. Jesus Christ saw the same things I saw but he saw through them. He found meaning in the natural world. He understood the natural world to be a pointer to Someone who loved us and cared for each and every one of us.

"Little by little I emerged from my shell of depression. Life began to regain some of its former wonder and joy, greatly assisted by the friendship of the other members of St Mary's. The more I opened myself to my New Friend - as I began to call Him - the more I felt myself growing as a person. I realised that, at last, I'd emerged from the darkness and into the bright light of day. It was a wonderful experience!"

Simon, who had been listening attentively as Rosie spoke, and sensing that her words came from the depths of her heart, softly added, "It must have been a wonderful moment of transformation."

Rosie smiled and gently nodded in agreement. "It was the turning point in my life. From then on, I still delighted in molecular biology and the incredible miracle of the natural world, but I came to see it, not as an end in itself, but more as a lens through which to perceive its Creator and its purpose. I came to see that everything had been designed so we could grow as human beings and realise our full potential as children of God. My love of the natural world was a lens through which I came to see the transforming power of God revealed in Jesus Christ. Once I had made that discovery, I felt I had to share it with others. One thing led to another and eventually I was ordained as a non-stipendiary minister. I still work as a biologist, but I'm able to combine my scientific work with my spiritual understanding, and put both of them at the service of others."

As Simon listened to Rosie's journey of faith he marvelled at life's paradoxes. He had been brought up in a religious household but had never, somehow, developed a faith of his own; whereas Rosie, who had been brought up in an atheistic household, had not only discovered a faith of her own but was actively seeking to share it with others. How strange, he thought!

After a brief moment of reflection, Simon said, "I suppose music is my way of glimpsing the transcendent. Whenever I immerse myself in music I find I'm taken out of myself. Ordinary, everyday cares and concerns disappear and I'm transported to another level where my feelings and emotions are magnified and enhanced. When I open myself to music, I glimpse the things of real value and worth – things like love, beauty, heroism, courage, tenderness, joy, compassion."

"You could almost be quoting St Paul's 'Gifts of the Spirit,'" smiled Rosie. "They are all good and life-enhancing. But where do they come from? You can, of course, see them simply as good things in themselves; but I've found they are the lens through which to see my New Friend. I've come to think that unless we discover the giver of these gifts, we will never be fulfilled. We all need to be loved. We were created that way. Unless we experience the limitless love of God in Jesus Christ we will never be happy, contented or at peace with ourselves."

"My attempt to find love has brought me to this place," Simon confessed ruefully. "I sought love and happiness through other people. I thought I'd found perfect love when I met and married Sandra. We shared a great love of music. Music was the umbilical cord that bound us together. But, alas, it was not able to continually renew our love and draw us closer to each other. And then, when I met Vicky, I thought I was being given a second chance. Her love was spontaneous and free. I felt I'd been blessed beyond measure by the absolute trust and life-giving joy she freely gave me. Both Sandra and Vicky were good people; but, alas, they were unable to satisfy my eternal yearning for unconditional love and acceptance."

"Maybe you were pursuing the wrong kind of love?" reflected Rosie. "There is love that is possessive, erotic and sensual: nothing wrong with that, but it's not the love that brings inner peace and fulfilment. I have come to realise that the love of Jesus Christ is a very different sort of love. It's accepting, endlessly forgiving, freely bestowed, constant and wonderfully empowering."

Then, with a sudden peal of laughter, Rosie exclaimed, "Hey! I didn't come here to gain a convert. I came to renew the friendship that was so abruptly broken off thirty-years ago."

"I can't tell you how pleased I am to see you again," beamed Simon. "Do promise you'll come again."

"Of course I will," smiled Rosie, as the prison officer on duty called 'Time Up'. "Wild horses wouldn't keep me away!" And with that, the two of them stood and, separated by the table, shook hands, before Rosie turned and left the Visitor's Room and Simon was led back to his cell.

Simon could not get over his surprise and pleasure at meeting his former childhood friend after an absence of thirty years. He marvelled that she still possessed the openness and acceptance she had as a young girl all those years ago.

As he replayed their conversation in his head, he realised Rosie had not enquired after his crime and the reason he was in prison. She said his mother refused to disclose the reason and so, either she had learned it from some other source, or else she was simply not interested. If it was the latter, she was indeed a remarkable person, thought Simon. Perhaps it was all to do with her "New Friend."

Simon did not have long to dwell on Rosie's visit because the long-awaited Christmas Carol Service was almost upon him. The fresh-faced prison chaplain summoned Simon to his office to discuss the format of the service.

"I know you've been working very hard with your choir on a number of special Christmas carols," began the chaplain, "and I'm greatly looking forward to hearing the results. Even if they do not meet your high expectations, you must realise you have done a laudable job in teaching some very troubled men to work together as a team. You've presented them with a challenge and they've responded with determination. Hopefully, they've learned some musical skills from you; but, even if they haven't, the very opportunity of working together as a group on a common purpose is reward in itself. I want you to understand that -

even if, as I say, the musical results do not meet your extremely high standards."

Simon smiled at the little chaplain's words of encouragement. His scratch choir was certainly unlike any other musical group with which he had ever worked; but the sense of camaraderie that had developed had not been lost on him. Music, he mused, had the ability to calm the savage breast and bring out the best in people.

"Now," continued the chaplain, "I thought we would follow the same pattern as Kings College Cambridge for our Christmas Carol Service. The prison chapel may not be a perpendicular architectural splendour, and your choristers – if you will excuse me saying – may not be innocent little trebles attired in white surplices and ruffs, but the traditional framework of the Nine Carols and Lessons Service should serve us well. I propose recruiting members of the prison staff to read the nine lessons and I suggest we include half-a-dozen familiar carols for the congregation to sing. That then leaves room for the six pieces you've been rehearsing with your choir. How does that sound?"

"That's fine by me," assented Simon. "I just wondered if the choir could have a last-minute rehearsal an hour before the start of the service, just to make sure everyone knows what's happening."

"I'm sure that will be possible," beamed the chaplain. "It is, after all, the season of goodwill and I'm sure I can play upon that sentiment when I speak to the Prison Governor."

The plans had been laid. The music had been rehearsed. All was in readiness for the service on Christmas Eve.

The day before Christmas Eve, a prison officer approached Simon carrying a package. "It looks as if you've got a Christmas present," observed the officer as he handed the package to Simon. Like all in-coming letters and parcels, it had been unwrapped and examined, in conformity with prison regulations. The torn and ripped wrapping paper revealed a book inside. Simon pulled back the wrappings and saw it was a book about the French composer Francis Poulenc. His eyes lit up. He liked what little he knew of Poulenc's music. He knew he would enjoy discovering more about the composer and his music. But who was the book from?

Opening the front cover he found an inscription on the flyleaf: *Christmas 2019 To Simon, with all my love, Rosie* followed by two kisses. A smile spread over Simon's face. Not only had she remembered him at Christmas, she possessed the insight to buy the perfect Christmas gift for him.

"Is it one you've read already?" asked the prison officer.

"Not at all," replied Simon. "In fact, I know very little about the life and music of Poulenc and so I'll greatly enjoy reading it over the Christmas period."

"Each to their own, I guess," responded the dour officer, who could think of nothing more boring than a book about a French classical composer. "Put it in your cell and get on with your work."

*

Christmas Eve dawned just like any other day in Her Majesty's Prisons. The regular routine of ablutions, cell inspections, meals and work followed their usual course.

The sound of clanging metal gates and rattling officers' keys echoed around the galleries as prisoners sought to banish memories of Christmases Past spent with families and loved ones and assume a devil-may-care attitude to the annual celebration of the Birth of Christ.

At 4.00.pm, Simon and his motley choir assembled in the chapel for a final rehearsal before the service. Simon smiled inwardly as he saw how nervous his choristers were. Standing before him were men who thought nothing of pitching into a melee, with fists flying, completely impervious to the harm they might sustain; men who had undertaken audacious robberies requiring nerves of steel; and men who had exuded confidence sufficient to persuade normally sensible and level-headed people to part with their life-savings. These strong, self-assured men were now visibly anxious at the thought of singing before the prison population.

"When we sing this evening, I want you to forget about the other people in the chapel and I want you to sing just for me," instructed Simon. "That's what you've been doing ever since we started rehearsals in September. So, forget about everyone else, and just sing to please me. If you do that, the results will be tremendous."

"Don't worry, man," reassured Winston, adopting an attitude of implacable confidence, "We ain't goin' let you down."

"Of course, you're not," replied a confident Simon. "I just don't want nerves to affect your singing. Forget everyone else. Just sing for me as you've been doing for the past four months. Now, let's start with a warm-up exercise."

Up and down the scale the sixteen singers went in their well-used warm-up singing exercise. There then followed a run-through of the six pieces they were soon to sing - although Simon interrupted each of the pieces before they were halfway through, with a curt, "That's fine: on to the next piece." He did not want the actual performance to be merely a tired repeat of the rehearsal. He wanted to keep something new and fresh in reserve for the actual service. At half-past-four the prison population began to file into the chapel under the watchful eyes of the prison officers. The inmates slowly filled the rows of wooden chairs until the entire chapel was packed with prisoners. Prison Officers stood, with their backs to the walls of the chapel, keeping an eye on those in their charge. Simon accompanied the entrance of the prisoners with the overture to Corelli's *Christmas Oratorio* played on the paino entirely from memory.

When everyone was seated, the chaplain entered in his cassock and surplice and the prisoner officers issued a stern "Quiet now" to the assembled congregation. The chaplain took his place at the front of the chapel and introduced the form the service would take. His announcements over, he launched into the Bidding Prayer:

> *"Beloved in Christ, at this Christmastide, let it be our care and delight to hear again the message of the Angels, and in heart and mind to go even unto Bethlehem, and see this thing which is come to pass, and the Babe lying in a manger. Let us read and mark in Holy Scripture the tale of the loving purposes of God from the first days of our disobedience unto*

the glorious Redemption brought us by this holy Child; and let us make this place glad with our carols of praise.

"But first, let us pray for the needs of his whole world; for peace and goodwill over all the earth; for the mission and unity of the Church for which he died, and especially in this country and within this community.

"And because this of all things would rejoice his heart, let us at this time remember in his name the poor and the helpless, the hungry and the oppressed; the sick and those who mourn; the lonely and the unloved; the aged and the little children; and all those who know not the Lord Jesus, or who love him not, or who by sin have grieved his heart of love.

"Lastly, let us remember before God all those who rejoice with us, but upon another shore and in a greater light, that multitude which no one can number, whose hope was in the Word made flesh, and with whom, in the Lord Jesus, we for evermore are one.

"These prayers and praises let us humbly offer up to the throne of heaven, in the words which Christ himself hath taught us: Our Father...."

And so the service was launched on its way. The barriers of time and space melted away as the men and the handful of female prison officers contained within the walls of the prison chapel were transported back to the stable in Bethlehem along with their memories of childhood, school nativity plays, Christmas dinners, presents and loved ones. A deep calm and hush descended upon the prison population. Tears welled up in the eyes of the more sensitive. Thoughts of severed relationships, lost friends, abandoned children and hurt loved ones invaded the minds of the serried ranks of prisoners as they contemplated the birth of the baby in a stable two thousand years ago. The experience of singing well-known Christmas carols was too much for some prisoners. The carols rekindled times when all was well: life was well-ordered, love and kindness proliferated and worries were unknown. It was a land of lost content that had somehow been lost. Rather than join in the singing, they kept their lips firmly pursed and fought back their tears.

The readings came almost as a moment of light relief. As each of the nine prison officers came to the podium to read, it was possible for the inmates to revert to being emotionally tough once more. The person reading was "one of the screws" – the enemy to be despised.

The first lesson was read by the Director of Education. Normally, the appearance of a woman on stage would produce wolf-whistles and ribald comments, but not when it was the Director of Education. She exerted no sex appeal and her reading of Eve tempting Adam to eat the forbidden fruit in the Garden of Eden simply confirmed most prisoners' view of women like her: they were cruel and uncaring and treated men with contempt.

After the Director of Education had vacated the lectern, it was the turn of the choir to sing its first carol. It was the beautiful and tranquil *Malam Kudus - O Holy Night* – sung by Sarsung with a gentle choral accompaniment provided by the other singers. Sarsung's lyrical tenor voice floated effortlessly on the air, filling the chapel with the peace of that first Christmas night. He poured his heart into his singing and no one could doubt the sincerity of his rendition. It was as if he was giving his own personal Christmas gift to the infant Christ – the gift of his beautiful singing voice.

At the conclusion of the piece, a great roar of approval went up from the congregation followed by prolonged applause. It took the prison officers a considerable time to restore order, but it gave confidence to the members of the choir. Their fellow prisoners appreciated well-performed Christmas music. It augured well for the other pieces they were to sing.

Simon's specially composed Christmas carol received a polite response rather than an enthusiastic one. Perhaps it was because the carol was new and needed to be heard a number of times in order to be appreciated; but Simon was pleased with it and the exemplary way in which his choir performed it. He thought it might well take its place alongside Messiaen's *Quartet for the End of Time* composed in the prison camp at Stalag VIII-A during World War II: two musical compositions from within prison walls.

The Caribbean version of *Mary had a baby* was enthusiastically received. The sheer vitality and emotional energy the Caribbean members of the choir injected into their famous national carol was infectious. Many members of the congregation joined in with their own vocal lines as the carol worked towards its climax. Smiles abounded. Christmas had become a time of happiness and joy.

The biblical readings of the Roman census, the birth in a stable, and the appearance of angels to the shepherds on the hillside brought vividly to life a story Simon had known since he was a child. He had always liked the story, but nothing more. Once Christmas was over, it was forgotten and life continued as before. But, whether it was because of his conversation with Rosie, or whether it was because of the strange circumstances in which he was observing Christmas this year, it assumed a greater interest. He certainly subscribed to the Christmas message of "Peace on earth, goodwill to everyone." He longed for peace. He longed for peace to quieten his conscience and replace the guilt he carried within for the harm he had caused others. Inner peace and goodwill were qualities he most earnestly desired.

The ninth and final lesson was read by the ex-military Prison Governor. He adopted a no-nonsense approach to St John's unfolding of the great mystery of the Incarnation. Few in the chapel may have understood the theology and, from the matter-of-fact way in which the Governor read the passage, it was doubtful if he did, but the cosmic dimension of Christmas was affirmed and all was set for the choir's final carol: *Sir Christemus* by William Mathias. Simon punched out the staccato chords that opened the piece and the sixteen male voices punched out the opening Nowells with the emphases on every other note. The questions and answers in the text were hurled backwards and forwards between the various voices followed by a great "Welcome to all, both more or less, Come near, come near, come near". The announcement of the birth of Christ was punctuated by flashing syncopated phrases played on the piano by Simon. These led to the final outburst of Nowells culminating in a final fortissimo shout of Nowell!

This final shout brought the house down. The chapel erupted in a paean of excitement and joy. It was a fitting conclusion to the prison population's celebration of the birth of Christ.

The chaplain concluded the service with a blessing and thanked everyone who had contributed to "our gift of praise and thanksgiving to the Christ-child". He singled out the pianist and members of the choir. To Simon's astonishment, they received an enthusiastic round of applause from the prison community, including the prison officers.

"That was magnificent!" enthused the chaplain after everyone had left the chapel and just he and Simon remained. "You really do have a great musical gift. You must promise me you will continue to use it, for the greater glory of God, once you're released."

"Some of the greatest composers have done just that," declared Simon. "Perhaps, one day, I will be able to emulate Bach and Elgar and put AMDG on the title page of something I've written."

The chaplain smiled. He had no idea of the works to which Simon referred, but he did know that AMDG stood for *Ad Maiorem Dei Gloriam* – For the greater glory of God.

"That would be tremendous!" he declared. "Let me escort you back to your cell."

Incarcerated in his cell for the next twelve hours, Simon was able to turn his attention to Rosie's Christmas present. He smiled as he opened the book she had given him. He read once again the dedication written on the flyleaf. What a kind soul, she was, he thought! He lingered over the dedication as he recalled their childhood times together. He was amazed and humbled she had remembered him; and even more humbled that she had visited him in prison. That really was an act of exceptional kindness, he thought. And what a life-story she had to tell! He never imagined that the girl who led him to badger's setts and wooded lakes populated by toads, and whom he took underground into a churchyard vault would one day become an ordained priest. Who could predict the course of life?

Comforted by his thoughts of Rosie, he settled down to read the book she had given him. It was an account of the life of Poulenc with a detailed examination of each of his works. There were numerous musical examples that instantly produced music inside Simon's head. He laughed as he hummed Poulenc's early satirical pieces. The composer clearly had a keen sense of humour and was not above mocking and poking fun at musical conventions. His early ballet *Les Biches* of 1923 had no story but was simply the random interaction of a group of mainly young people at a house party on a summer afternoon. The music was witty, full of high spirits and irreverent.

Simon frowned. Why had Rosie given him a book about a humorous and lightweight composer he wondered?

The *Concert Champetre* of 1928 was a bizarre concerto for harpsichord and full symphony orchestra. Any composer worth his salt would know that a harpsichord could never compete with a full symphony orchestra, especially one with a full battery of percussion instruments: they were unequal. Why did Poulenc write such a work? He really was a strange man, thought Simon. But there was no escaping his gift for melody. As Simon scanned the musical extracts, he heard the music in his head. His prison cell became a French salon and he was a guest at a sociable soiree. It was a highly unusual way to spend Christmas Day.

Then, just as Lights Out was shouted along the galleries, Simon came to the turning point in Poulenc's life.

The composer's friend and fellow composer Pierre-Octave Ferroud was decapitated in a horrific car crash. The impact of this sudden and unexpected death was transformational for Poulenc. It made him re-evaluate his entire life. He realised he had frittered away his years in sensual frivolity and he needed to take stock.

Just at that moment the lights went out in his cell and Simon was plunged into darkness. He would have to await another day before he could discover what new direction Poulenc's life took.

*

Simon's own life was about to take a new direction. He had almost completed one year of his sentence. Immediately after Christmas he was summoned to an interview with the Prison Probation Officer.

The Probation Officer was a young woman. Simon warmed to her immediately. But she had no intention of allowing him to use his charm on her.

"I have here the papers relating to your Court case," she informed him in a very business-like manner. "The Court has prohibited you from having any contact with young people under the age of eighteen and you have been barred from ever again teaching in a school."

Sheaving through the papers in her hand she said, "However, your conduct in prison has been adjudged exemplary and full recognition has been given for the contribution you've made to the musical life of the prison. Furthermore, you are not thought to pose a threat to the general public."

Then looking up from her papers she asked, "Where do you intend living when you're released on licence?"

"I had a house before I was sent to prison," Simon replied "but my wife has put it up for sale. Even so, I should receive half the proceeds. That should enable me to purchase a small flat somewhere."

The Probation Officer appeared unimpressed. "You will have to live in a probation hostel until such time as you are able to purchase accommodation of your own. You are also required to attend regular scheduled meetings with your designated probation officer." Then, without pausing, she asked, "How do you intend earning a living?"

"I'm willing to undertake any work I can find. Clearly, I can never work with children, but I should be able to use my musical skills and qualifications with adults. I would dearly like to pursue my own musical compositional work."

The Probation Officer made no comment on this latter point. She merely emphasised the importance of observing the conditions of his licence and the dire consequences of not doing so.

The days following his meeting with the Prison Probation Officer were relieved only by the unexpected reappearance of Rosie at the following week's visiting session.

Simon's face was radiant as he greeted Rosie once more.

"Thank you so much for coming to see me again," he said with obvious warmth and sincerity. "You may not have to do so for much longer. I've nearly completed a year of my sentence and I'm now due to be released into the community on licence. This means, as long as I behave myself for the next twelve months and observe the conditions imposed by the Probation Service, I'll be free to return to normal life once more."

Rosie smiled in unison with Simon. It was good news, but not entirely unexpected. She had undertaken some investigative work of her own after realising that Simon would shortly be allowed out on licence. She guessed that accommodation and employment would pose the greatest difficulties and so she had instigated enquiries accordingly. She informed Simon of a one-bedroomed, fully-furnished flat very near to where she lived that was currently vacant and being offered at a very reasonable rent.

"I realise you have no money at present," continued Rosie, "but I can cover the rent of the flat for the time being and you can reimburse me when you find employment."

Simon's initial reaction was to demur. He did not want to be beholden to Rosie. But she was adamant.

"I know you would do the same for me if our roles were reversed," she laughingly declared.

Simon was genuinely overwhelmed by her generosity.

"I'll pay you back immediately," he asserted, "even if it means working as a bin man."

"You won't have to do that," assured Rosie. "You have much greater talents than that. I've been putting a few irons in the fire on your behalf. You'd be surprised at the number of opportunities there are for those with musical talent. Composing and arranging jingles for television adverts might not be your preferred method of earning a living, but it might well open doors into other areas of television or even the film industry. I have only recently come to realise just how much music there is all around us. Someone must compose and arrange it. Well, why not you? It would keep your hand in whilst you work on your symphonies or great choral masterpieces."

"You don't mean to tell me you actually know people who work in television?" asked an incredulous Simon.

Rosie smiled a knowing smile before adding, "You'd be surprised the number of people an ordained priest gets to know."

Simon shook his head in disbelief.

"So, is it agreed you'll take this flat?" Rosie anxiously enquired.

Simon nodded his head in silent acceptance.

"You're too good for me," whispered Simon.

"Hardly," retorted Rosie. "I want to help you because I believe in you. I've asked the prison authorities to let me know the date of your release so I can collect you and transport you to your new home."

Simon smiled ruefully at Rosie. He needed someone to believe in him and give his life meaning. But all he could say was a gentle, "Thank you."

Then, gathering his thoughts together, he abruptly changed the subject. "I haven't thanked you for the wonderful Christmas present you gave me," enthused Simon. "I've read it from cover to cover and greatly enjoyed it. I knew almost nothing about Poulenc before reading the book. How did you know about him?"

Rosie smiled before admitting, "I knew nothing about him. My musical knowledge is very deficient. But I hope you can rectify that. I may not know very much about music at present, but I do know a number of music teachers. I asked them to recommend a suitable book for you, and they suggested a biography of Poulenc."

"It couldn't have been a better choice," replied Simon. "In many ways his life mirrors mine. He largely wasted the first half of his life in pleasurable entertainment and sensual experiences. I think that's how I've frittered away my life up until now. And then, along comes the great jolt. In Poulenc's case, it was the sudden and tragic death of his dearest friend. In my case, it was being given a two-year prison sentence. Both of us were halted in our tracks. We were both made to re-evaluate our lives. Poulenc still continued to compose, but he turned away from frivolous subjects and explored the great themes of life – the purpose of life and death. And, boy, did he express his feelings powerfully! I've been humming the opening bars of his *Organ Concerto* and I've never heard anything so commanding and affirmative. It's as though all doubts have been banished and a new landscape of exhilaration, beauty and grandeur has been revealed. I don't think I've ever heard anything quite like it before."

Rosie smiled at Simon's new found enthusiasm for the French composer. "You'll have to let me hear it," she added, "so I can experience these new exciting horizons."

"Nothing would give me greater pleasure," replied Simon. "Perhaps we could also seek out a performance of his opera *Dialogues des Carmelites*. It has a very religious theme. I'm sure you would appreciate that. And then there is the *Gloria* for Soprano, Chorus and Orchestra. It sounds tremendous if the brief extracts in the book are anything to go by. There's a whole new world of wonderful music out there just waiting to be discovered!"

Simon's enthusiasm and zest for life was returning.

"But as well as teaching me about music," said Rosie, "I want you to write new music yourself. When we were children, you told me you would capture the beauty and wonder of life in your music. I'm going to hold you to that. I want you to compose music that is even greater than that by Poulenc."

"There's a challenge!" exclaimed Simon. Then after a moment's reflection, he added, "I'd like to do that. I would like to write really great music: something to storm the gates of heaven; something to express the restless quest of my soul for fulfilment and peace. I would like to write something worthy of the letters AMDG on the title page."

The following day Simon learned his release date was to be 4 January.

On the morning of 4 January, Simon was led to the Discharge Room where he was met by the Prison Probation Officer. He was reminded of the conditions of his licence and warned of the severe consequences of breaching those conditions. The Probation Officer then added, "You seem to have made a new friend in the Reverend Rosemary Evans. She has procured a flat for you and says she's working on your behalf to find you employment. You're a lucky man. Don't let her down."

"I won't," affirmed Simon. "Actually, she's not a new friend at all, but a very old one – a true friend. She came to my aid when I most needed help. I will never let her down."

So saying, the gates of the prison swung open and Simon stepped out into the big wide world at the end of his year's imprisonment. There, on the kerbside, waiting to greet him was Rosie. She threw her arms around him and hugged him. A new life awaited him and his joy knew no bounds.

END OF BOOK ONE

LIST OF MUSIC
referred to in the book

Adam, Adolphe
O Holy Night (Malam Kudos) 81, 139, 140, 233, 340

Anon.
Mary had a baby 136

Bach, Johann Sebastian
Goldberg Variations 324

Beethoven, Ludwig van
Fur Elise 259
Missa Solemnis 128
Moonlight Sonata 260

Berlioz, Hector
L'Enfance du Christ 160

Bizet, George
Carmen, 282

Bruckner, Anton
Symphony No 9 243

Chopin, Frederick
Preludes 49

Corelli, Arcangelo
Christmas Oratorio 81, 338

Debussy, Claude
Arabesques 49

Elgar, Edward
Introduction and Allegro for Strings 32
The Dream of Gerontius 292, 316
The Music Makers 207

Gluck, Christoph
Orfeo et Eurydice 135

Grieg, Edvard
Peer Gynt: Death of Ase 227

Handel, George Frederick
Messiah: I know that my Redeemer liveth 105, 159

Liszt, Franz
Six Consolations 243

Lloyd Webber, Andrew
Requiem 207
Evita 282

Mathias, William
Sir Christemus 58, 124, 224, 233,323, 342

Mendelssohn, Felix
Elijah 207
Symphony No 4 "Italian" 32

Messiaen, Oliver
Quartet for the End of Time 341

Poulenc, Francis
Concert Champetre 344
Dialogues des Carmelites 349
Gloria 350

Les Biches 344
Organ Concerto 349
Purcell, Henry
The Fairy Queen 267

Schumann, Robert
Scenes from Childhood 138

Shostakovich, Dimitri
Symphony No 4 134

Smetana, Bedrich
String Quartet "From My Life" 126

Strauss, Richard
Four Last Songs 88

Sullivan, Arthur
Trial by Jury 97, 117

Tchaikovsky, Pytor
Fantasy Overture Romeo and Juliet 74
Symphony No 4 95, 255

Verdi, Giuseppe
Requiem 207

Vivaldi, Antonio
The Four Seasons 199

Wagner, Richard
Tristan and Isolde 107, 142

Walton, William
Belshazzar's Feast 162, 207

Zelenka, Jan Dismas 117, 131, 221, 234, 319

Printed in Great Britain
by Amazon